Praise for *In the Cards*

"Infused with . . . fresh detail. Between the sweetness of the relationship and the summery beach setting, romance fans will find this a warming winter read."

—*Publishers Weekly*

"Fans will love the frank honesty of her characters. [Beck's] scenery is richly detailed and the story engaging."

—*RT Book Reviews*

"[A] realistic and heartwarming story of redemption and love . . . Beck's understanding of interpersonal relationships and her flawless prose make for a believable romance and an entertaining read."

—*Booklist*

Praise for *Worth the Wait*

"[A] poignant and heartwarming story of young love and redemption [that] will literally make your heart ache . . . Jamie Beck has a real talent for making the reader feel the sorrow, regret, and yearning of this young character."

—*Fresh Fiction*

Praise for *Worth the Trouble*

"With strong family ties, loyalty, playful banter, and sexual tension, Beck has crafted a beautiful second-chances story."

—*Publishers Weekly*, Starred Review

Worth *the* Trouble

Also by Jamie Beck

In the Cards

The St. James Novels

Worth the Wait

The Sterling Canyon Novels

Accidentally Hers

Worth *the* Trouble

A St. James Novel

Jamie Beck

This is a work of fiction. Names, characters, organizations, places, events, and incidents are either products of the author's imagination or are used fictitiously.

Published by Montlake Romance, Seattle

www.apub.com

ISBN-13: 9781503954502
ISBN-10: 1503954501

Cover design by Jason Blackburn

Printed in the United States of America

To my dear friend Ramona, one of the best moms I know. Thank you for graciously allowing me to steal aspects of your journey for Cat's story.

Cat's Journal

Mom,

Tomorrow I go to Block Island for David and Vivi's wedding weekend—unescorted, of course. Still, the ceremony should be a memorable affair. The only thing missing will be you.

Who but you would've believed David would marry my best friend? Their love gives me a hopeful feeling, but it also makes me a little lonely.

Hank will be there. Thinking of him makes me feel hopeful and lonely, too. Not that I'll ever admit it aloud.

Chapter One

Cat loosely tied the plastic ribbons of the paper gown she'd been provided—a far cry from the Armani couture she'd worn in yesterday's *Vogue* photo shoot—before sitting on the exam table. The thin paper beneath her crinkled as she leaned back to rest her weight on her elbows.

She glanced at her watch.

Her train to New London, Connecticut, departed Penn Station at eleven thirty. If she missed it, she'd never catch the ferry to Block Island in time for her eldest brother, David's, wedding rehearsal. But despite the inconvenient timing of this particular appointment, she couldn't afford to reschedule it *again*.

She glanced around the stark, impersonal room, wondering about the other women who would pass through it today. Some would arrive, carefree, for regular checkups. An expectant mother might listen to her baby's heartbeat for the first time. Another, like her own mother, might receive news of a fatal breast tumor. How absurd that such a sterile environment served as the setting for pivotal moments in a woman's life.

Cat hoped her own concerns were baseless, but doubt was gnawing at her when the doctor entered the room and proceeded to the small sink to wash her hands. Although Dr. Wexler was neither beautiful nor young, Cat envied her and her confidence, competence, and obvious sense of purpose. Intangible qualities that burned brightly from within, and shone through clear, lively eyes.

"Catalina, what brings you in today?" She glanced over Cat's chart while waiting for an answer.

"Well," Cat began, "I went off the pill ten months ago and, except for a little spotting early on, never got my period. At first I assumed it was because I was under a lot of stress." She tucked a length of hair behind her ear, averting her gaze. "But now it's June, and I'm concerned."

"Any unusual cramping?"

"Not really." She tried reading Dr. Wexler's politely detached expression but, like Cat, the doctor had mastered the art of hiding emotions.

"Disturbed sleep, irritability, or pain during sex?" The assessing tilt of Dr. Wexler's head discomfited Cat, who hated discussing personal issues.

"Well, I haven't had sex since then either, but before that there was nothing remarkable about it. I mean, not in terms of pain." Heat rushed to her cheeks as the innuendo struck. "So, anyway . . . jet lag often messes with my sleep. And I suppose I'm no more irritable than normal." Cat grimaced.

"Was the source of stress extreme?" Dr. Wexler asked, ignoring Cat's lame attempt at levity.

Cat's muscles tensed, like they did every time she thought of her ex, Justin. Throughout their two-year on-and-off relationship, she'd mistaken his jealous, possessive rages for intense love. Sadly it took Vivi getting caught in the crossfire and ending up in the emergency room with a skull fracture for Cat to wise up.

"An ugly split with my ex involving assault charges and unpleasant PR." Her skin became clammy when her doctor's eyebrows shot upward. Fighting the urge to slink beneath the exam table, Cat feigned nonchalance. "But things have settled down."

Settled down because Cat had practically gone into hiding to avoid the paparazzi and men. Of course, hiding from photographers hadn't been a great career move, which now created a new layer of stress. At twenty-eight, she'd already been fighting to sustain her modeling career. Thanks to Justin (or, more accurately, her response to the fallout), her cover-shoot days were probably numbered.

"Sorry for your trouble."

Cat hoped to evade a prolonged discussion about that relationship—a relationship that thrust every one of her faults into the open, where they couldn't be ignored or dismissed. Thankfully, Dr. Wexler patted the stirrups and redirected her interrogation. "Any family history of autoimmune disorders such as hypothyroidism or lupus?"

If Dr. Wexler intended her relaxed tone to calm Cat, it wasn't working. "Not that I know of."

Staring at the ceiling tiles, Cat tried to quiet her mind during the ensuing silence. Thankfully, Dr. Wexler spoke again. "Many women experience amenorrhea when they first go off the pill, although it typically sorts itself out within three months. Stress can substantially affect your cycle. Also, extremely low body fat could cause the disruption. That's fairly common among models and dancers." She stood, peeled off her gloves, and tossed them in the trash.

Cat sat upright and smoothed the wrinkled paper gown, the knot in her chest beginning to loosen.

"Everything looks normal from a physical perspective. While you're here, let's order some blood work." Dr. Wexler sat on her little round stool. "I don't want to jump to conclusions, but something more serious could be causing the disruption."

"Something life threatening?" Cat's mind immediately veered toward her mother's unlucky fate. Her next breaths were strained and tight, as if the small room suddenly lacked enough oxygen.

"Doubtful. But we need to consider all possibilities."

Cat's stomach acid began to churn. Intuitively she'd known something was wrong, but she'd been putting off this appointment in order to forestall bad news. Why had she thought she'd be ready today? "Possibilities such as?"

"Well, thyroid or hormonal imbalances, sexually transmitted diseases, or the less likely candidates: primary ovarian insufficiency and premature menopause."

"Menopause?" The word struck with the force of a punishing slap. "But I'm only twenty-eight."

"Granted, it's uncommon. It affects about one in one thousand women under thirty."

Cat's scattered thoughts collected, latching on to one unfortunate memory. "Didn't my mom enter menopause fairly early?"

Dr. Wexler nodded. "Yes, your mother's history is a factor, but it isn't decisive. Let's draw some blood to check your FSH and estradiol levels, among other things."

A small, thin version of her voice wove its way through the haze that consumed her thoughts. "So I might be infertile?"

For years she'd wrestled feelings of emptiness while forced to project an image of absolute confidence and sensuality. How ironic now to possibly be—quite literally—empty. *Barren.* To confirm that, all this time, her insecurities hadn't been a figment of her imagination. That all along her father's perception had been true. She really, truly was just a pretty face.

Her customary armor of indifference slipped for a second. Anxiety tightened her throat, making it feel like she'd swallowed a golf ball.

"Statistically speaking, your problem is more likely the result of stress and unhealthily low body fat. But ten consecutive months of missed cycles is significant, and unfortunately infertility is an issue with both POI and POF." Dr. Wexler's lips pressed together in a tight line.

"How long until you receive the test results?" Cat's voice sounded distant and tinny in her ears.

"Not too long. In the meantime, try to relax and gain a few pounds." She smiled. "I'm sure many women would love that prescription."

Cat closed her eyes while the doctor completed a few forms, determined to reject the dread winding its way through her mind like a rat in a maze. She had barely begun to fit the splintered shards of her heart back together. How would she manage to fix this latest blow to her soul?

"I'll be in touch soon." Dr. Wexler handed her the forms. With a brief nod, she exited the room. Cat sat, stuck to the table, taunted by the steady ticking of the clock on the wall.

~

By three o'clock, Cat's ferry was cruising across the Long Island Sound toward the Atlantic and Block Island. Staring out the window, she scanned the wide-open sea. If she focused only on its inviting surface, glittery with sunlight, she could almost ignore the realities of its murky darkness, the turbulent churning of sand, the sharks and other creatures lurking beneath its surface waiting to strike without warning.

Absently, she clutched the fabric of her skirt in her fist.

What a cruel joke! Pregnancy—something she'd actively prevented since losing her virginity—might now never be an option. Pressure gathered behind her eyes despite the fact she had no husband, no boyfriend, nor any immediate desire to be a mother.

Enough! Given her lifestyle, stress and low body weight made more sense than menopause, for God's sake. Perhaps this wake-up call meant the time had come to change her life. To parlay her "brand" into some new career—one that allowed her to eat.

A brief smile formed at the thought of enjoying an occasional dessert, but then her mind returned to work.

She certainly wouldn't be the first model turned entrepreneur. The real question was what, exactly, could she do next, given her limited skill set? If she'd finished college or had other work experience to fall back on, perhaps she'd meet this challenge with less reluctance.

Cat heaved a sigh just as her phone rang.

"Are you getting close?" Vivi asked before Cat even said hello, her bright voice instantly lifting Cat's mood.

"I should be there in thirty minutes." Cat scanned the horizon.

"Oh, good!"

"Excited much?" Cat chuckled at her memories of Vivi's blatant devotion to her brother. "How many times did you imagine being Mrs. David St. James? I lost count by tenth grade."

Despite Vivi's abiding love for David, *his* unexpected romantic turnabout last summer had caught Cat and her other brother, Jackson, by surprise.

At first she'd worried things would end badly and destroy her and Vivi's friendship. Thankfully she'd been wrong, and by tomorrow night her dearest friend would be an official member of her family.

"Go ahead and laugh. Meanwhile, look at where my optimism got me." Vivi paused. "Be warned, now that my love life is perfect, I'm free to work on yours."

"No, thanks." Cat noticed a young mother playing peekaboo with her giggling toddler. The little girl must have felt the pull of Cat's attention, because she turned her wide-eyed gaze on Cat. The child's mother quickly diverted her attention with a hug and kiss. Cat's interest remained fixed on the spot where the mother had planted a kiss, while her own fingers came to rest upon her lips.

"Cat?" Vivi's voice came through the phone. "You still there?"

Tamping down the flush of embarrassment from her behavior,

Cat resisted the urge to share her infertility worries. "Yes, I'm here. And I'm still not looking for a matchmaker."

"Oh, it's well past time for a romantic intervention," Vivi insisted. "You haven't been out with anyone since you broke up with Justin."

A shiver danced through Cat's core at the mention of his name, at the time she'd wasted while unaware that her biological clock had been ticking in double time. "I just want to celebrate with you and my brothers this weekend, okay?"

While Cat felt nothing but happiness for Vivi and her brother, their impending marriage did force her to reexamine her own loveless status.

Contrary to popular belief, her career and modest fame *hadn't* helped matters. Sure, professional recognition, monster paychecks, VIP access to clubs and parties, and attention from men—worldly men who'd momentarily made her feel fascinating—had been a rush. But less than a decade later, she had little to show in the way of genuine, lasting relationships.

Like her airbrushed images, nothing had been real.

Modeling *had*, however, fulfilled one important goal: success. Her need to succeed had been nurtured by her dad's favoring her brothers and their accomplishments while reducing hers to her appearance.

He hadn't been cruel. If anything, he'd considered his remarks to be complimentary—he'd just never realized how hollow they were when compared with those he gave her brothers.

Driven by pride and a dash of spite, she'd worked tirelessly until her "pretty face" graced everything from magazine covers to designer-label billboard ads—proving her worth to him, if not to herself. To her chagrin, maybe all she'd really accomplished was living up—or down—to the trivial role he'd assigned to her since middle school.

Perversely, the *hollow* victory now seemed rather apropos.

Once again, Vivi's voice pulled Cat from her stray thoughts. "Hank's coming tomorrow."

Hank Mitchell: the blond-haired, green-eyed carpenter who worked for Jackson's construction company.

"Jackson will enjoy having his wingman around." A little surge of warmth blossomed at the thought of seeing Hank.

Fourteen months ago, she'd spent one unforgettable night flirting with and kissing that soft-spoken man before passing him over to return to Justin. Not her finest decision. Thank God no one kept track, because her list would probably make the Guinness World Records.

"Don't pretend Jackson's the only one who'll be happy to see Hank," Vivi drawled. "Come on, admit it. You're ready to date again."

"No, I'm not." Experience confirmed that men expected Cat to be the sexy woman portrayed in advertisements, not a *real* woman with everyday interests and complaints. Probably just as well. Given her waning career and potential diagnosis, she'd be better off keeping love at the bottom of her to-do list. "Besides, Hank's not the right man for me."

"Exactly what part of Hank doesn't work for you?" Vivi demanded. "His gorgeous face? His integrity? His good heart? Or maybe you object to the tool belt?"

Cat smiled, recalling how Vivi thought Hank's whole "carpenter" thing was scorching hot. Of course, it was. *He* was. But no matter how handsome and nice Hank appeared to be, he was still a man, which meant his main interest in her was physical. The idea of trying once again to live up to her own image to hold his—or any man's—attention filled her with prickling resentment.

"Hank and I live in different worlds." Then again, his low-key lifestyle and attitude held more appeal now than they had before. Too bad it took being burned once too often for her to appreciate a good guy when she met one. "We'll never be a couple. Best you give up on that particular wish."

"Pfffft. Have you forgotten that I watched you two dance around each other on the island last July, each stealing glances at the other yet pretending your secret make-out session at Jackson's party earlier that year never happened? So don't tell me there's not unfinished business there," Vivi said. "The more you protest, the more sure I am."

Cat laughed, unable to envision a more mismatched pair. Hank rooted in sincerity, and her flying around untethered to anything. She could only imagine what he must think of her and her way of life. "You've always had a vivid imagination."

"I guess we'll find out soon enough which one of us is right. See you shortly." Vivi hung up before Cat could respond.

Even if some part of Cat still harbored a little crush on Hank, it didn't matter. She'd chosen to walk away from the chemistry and easy bond they'd discovered that long-ago night at her brother's. She winced, deeply regretting the cowardly way she'd snubbed him afterward to run back to Justin.

Vivi may have hoped Cat and Hank had unfinished business, but if last summer's week on the island proved anything, it was that Hank had had enough self-respect not to chase after Cat. *Danced around each other, my ass.* They'd avoided each other—her from embarrassment, him out of pride.

Surely, in addition to her many other shortcomings, all of Cat's prior behavior made her the absolute last woman Hank would ever consider dating now.

Mom,

You've been in my thoughts all morning, and I'm sure David is wishing you were here to witness this occasion.

I'm now dressed and ready to help Vivi prepare to walk down the aisle. She's so good for David—quite the opposite of Justin's effect on me. You loved me because I'm your daughter. But the fact I chose Justin for so long pretty much proves I don't deserve someone who's good for me, doesn't it?

Too bad, because I saw Hank checking in this morning . . .

Chapter Two

The violinist's sharp note sliced through the air with the crisp breeze that caused Cat to shiver. Huddled near the corner of the seaside veranda, apart from the crowd, she was sipping her champagne cocktail when she felt Hank approach her from behind.

"They look happy." The timbre of his masculine voice held an appealing soft note. Like everything else about him, his voice soothed.

Across the hotel's expansive lawn that dipped toward the ocean, Cat watched David posing for photos with Vivi, her brother's tender feelings evident in every gentle touch and kiss.

"They are." Cat smiled, her gaze fixed on the newlyweds.

"Proof love exists," he said, leaning in close to her ear.

"For some, anyway," she muttered into her champagne flute, trying to ignore the way Hank's body heat warmed her more effectively than a bonfire. Even as she willed herself to resist, her body swayed closer to his.

A faint puff of air brushed her hair when he chuckled. "For those willing to try."

As she turned to meet Hank's provoking gaze, her breath hitched at the memory of his blistering kiss—a memory that reawakened dormant parts of her anatomy.

"You mean those willing to play a game they've little chance of winning?"

"Not shocked *you* consider it a game." He peered into his glass of whiskey, temporarily hiding his green-and-gold-flecked irises. She'd always thought those green eyes reflected his serenity, but tonight their sunny flecks blazed like tiny flames, hinting at a deep well of passion.

"Aren't most things?" she replied, keeping a measured tone to cover even a hint of vulnerability.

A shadow of disappointment crossed Hank's face. "That's pretty jaded, even for you."

She shrugged. Her adult life had been an unending chess match, one in which she'd learned to dodge the threat of checkmate.

Averting her eyes so he couldn't read her thoughts, she glanced over Hank's shoulder and noticed Vivi's alcoholic father—a man who managed to spoil most of Vivi's happy moments—stumble headlong into a cocktail table. "Oh, no. He's going to embarrass her again."

Hank turned toward the commotion. "I'm on it."

Within seconds, he'd gripped Mr. LeBrun's elbow and begun leading him away from the reception. Cat's gaze followed the unlikely pair of men as they trudged across the porch.

Once they vanished from her sight, she looked once more toward the glittering sea. The timelessness of the tides lapping against the shore provided the perfect complement to David and Vivi's abiding love.

Steady. Constant. And while she'd never admit it to Hank, inspiring.

David and Vivi were now making their way up the lawn toward the hotel. At Cat's insistence, Vivi had surrendered to wearing high heels tonight—cute silk ones with a rhinestone strap around the ankle. When those heels sank into the damp ground, she began walking on her toes, making her look like a little fairy flittering about at dusk.

"Hey, Cat," Jackson called from across the porch, where he stood with their father and new stepmother, Janet. "You coming?"

Glancing around, she noticed other wedding guests making

their way toward the sprawling white reception tent in the side yard. The cocktail hour had ended.

"In a second." Her family disappeared down the steps before she stole one final look at the magnificent view.

The ocean calmed her. Somehow its endless horizon connected her spirit to something much bigger than her daily life. Oddly freeing, that feeling of relative insignificance.

Tonight the twinkling hurricane lanterns atop the cocktail tables scattered in the grass enhanced the evening's mingled sense of mystery and possibility.

In Cat's peripheral vision, she caught Hank returning from delivering Vivi's father to his room. He looked gorgeous in his gray pinstriped suit and navy tie, a vast improvement over the worn T-shirts and casual shorts he favored. Seeing him this weekend left a bittersweet taste in her mouth.

If she had chosen Hank over Justin, might her life be different now? Maybe she'd already be pregnant instead of facing the possibility of never conceiving. Quite a sobering and unwelcome thought.

"Still enjoying the view?" He stopped beside her, hands in his pockets, and surveyed the gold-and-peach sunset reflected across the sea.

He'd set her up so beautifully, she couldn't resist teasing him to elicit one of his endearing blushes. After all, she hadn't sworn off flirting. Her eyes grazed the full length of his six-foot-two-inch, drop-dead body before she cocked a single brow. "It's not too shabby."

As she'd intended, streaks of color invaded his cheeks, giving her a little thrill. "More games," he muttered. Head bowed, he stared at his feet before meeting her gaze. "Have a nice evening, Catalina." And then, as if resigned to something she couldn't identify, he simply nodded and walked away.

She continued admiring his backside until he, too, wandered down the steps. A wistful sigh passed through her lips. *Good grief.* Ruthlessly, she shoved aside her attraction.

Straightening her shoulders, she set her empty champagne flute on an obliging tabletop before striding across the now-deserted porch. When she reached the tent, the din of lively chatter and tinkling stemware greeted her.

A broad smile spread across her face as she surveyed the candlelit party with its abundance of artfully strung lights, tuxedos, and music. The cool ocean breeze swept through the party. Table arrangements overflowed with peonies and tendrils of multicolored flowers and ivy, infusing the salty air with a sweet perfume.

Rustling fabric caught her attention before Vivi's arms reached around to squeeze her from behind.

"Having fun?" Vivi toyed with her diamond earrings, made more visible once she'd pinned her wild blond locks up into a French twist and tucked tiny flowers into the mass. "Everyone *loves* my 'something new' earrings. Thank you for the extravagant gift. You spoil me, as always."

"For the sister I've always wanted, there will never be too much spoiling!" Cat stepped back to admire the effect of the diamond studs with Vivi's tea-length gown. Its layered organza skirt flared out from the snugly fitted bodice—the crystal-encrusted sweetheart neckline its only adornment. Flirty, fun, and unexpected, just like her quirky friend. "You look gorgeous. That dress is so perfectly *you*."

Vivi stepped back and fingered Cat's organza wrap and moss-green, silk-satin gown. "I'm glad I let you pick your own. Love the way it drapes off your shoulder and around your waist. So sexy!"

"Thanks," Cat said. She brushed her palm across the fabric, appreciating its sumptuous texture. The material gave a semblance of curve to her bony physique. "The point of this drab color was to keep the spotlight on the bride."

"Oh, please. I never had any delusions about who would be the prettiest woman walking down the aisle today. I think half of David's partners came for the chance to meet his sister, the real-life 'cover girl.'" Vivi grinned and then gave a little wave of her hand. "But I don't care. There's only one man whose attention I want. Fortunately, he will never, ever look at *you* with desire. Our friendship is secure!"

"Always." Cat hugged her friend.

"Even when I meddle in your love life—and Jackson's?"

"I think she prefers us to stay out of it, *muñequita*." David suddenly appeared and handed Vivi a glass of champagne. Like all of the St. James siblings, David had inherited their Hispanic mother's dark hair, eyes, and coloring, and looked even more dashing than usual in his tuxedo. He kissed Vivi's cheek and wrapped his free arm around her waist, fastening her tightly to his side. "That goes for Jackson, too."

Vivi scowled, forcing an exaggerated pout. Staring at her lips, David murmured, "Don't tempt me in the middle of the party." He leaned down and kissed his wife.

"Ahem. Still here." Cat cleared her throat, feeling a tad awkward watching their simmering passion. "Anyway, I'm too busy to deal with any man."

"Not even a really good man?" Vivi asked as she stared across the crowd.

Cat followed Vivi's gaze, which landed squarely on Hank, who was now listening with rapt attention to Vivi's cute schoolteacher friend. Perfect. That woman was probably patient and sweet and genuine . . . and fertile. Apparently Hank wasn't blind to the woman's curvy figure and flirty blond hair, either.

"A really good man deserves an equally good woman. Given how I treated Hank last year, we both know that's not me." She tore her eyes away from him, ignoring the faint pinch in her stomach. She'd chosen flash over substance and paid the price in more ways than one. The possibility of infertility drifted through her thoughts again. Lifting her chin slightly, she said, "Honestly, Vivi, I'm not searching for someone right now."

Especially not a man like Hank, who'd never settle for anything less than total honesty. Cat wouldn't lie, but neither would she spill all her secrets. Rather than give him the long-overdue apology he deserved, she'd rather push him even further away . . . for his own good, of course.

"I hope you don't regret it later," Vivi said with a sigh. "Come on, let's go sit so dinner can be served." She tucked one arm in David's and let her other hand play with the flouncy fabric of her wedding dress.

Cat joined her father and her stepmother at the family table with the bride and groom. A year ago, this seating arrangement wouldn't have been possible. She suspected Vivi deserved credit for the fact that David invited their father despite their tenuous reconciliation. She'd long ago given up wondering about the source of the rift. Neither David nor her father would discuss it with her or Jackson, so for now she settled for being grateful that it might be mending. Someday, though, she'd demand answers.

"You look beautiful, honey." Her dad kissed her cheek.

"Thanks, Dad." Unsatisfied with his standard praise, she attempted a grown-up conversation. "What's new with work?"

He patted her shoulder. "Nothing that would interest you."

Before she could protest, another guest came over to shake his hand. Sighing, she glanced at Janet, who still lingered at the fringe of the family despite being married to their father for nearly a year.

Tonight, however, David remained polite and conversant in her presence—a first. Cat had no doubt he did this for Vivi's sake. Vivi hated conflict, and David hated anything that hurt Vivi.

"Sit next to me, Janet," Cat suggested, hoping to assuage the woman's discomfort.

"Thank you." Her appreciative smile warmed Cat, who'd always had a soft spot for underdogs. "Such a beautiful ceremony. Your father's already dreaming about a grandson. But he'll be even more pleased when you settle down and start a family. I take it you haven't met anyone special lately?"

Attending a wedding alone in her late twenties, Cat had expected questions. Still, love-life questions sucked, especially when she doubted single *men* had to endure the same torture.

"Not even looking." Cat lifted another glass of champagne to her lips. "I'm fine on my own. Better than fine, actually. I prefer my independence." Especially after freeing herself from Justin's control.

Janet politely smiled, but Cat sensed her doubt. Doubt likely planted by her father. Heaven knew he'd always assumed Cat would end up as the wife of someone important rather than *becoming* someone important.

When Jackson arrived, she pulled him onto the seat to her right. David was the responsible one, but Jackson, the middle child, had always been her playmate. Partners in crime since childhood, they'd pranked David and their parents, helped each other break curfew and, as adults, regularly vacationed and socialized together. Since their mother died, he'd become her favorite person in the world.

When he rested an arm along the back of her chair, Cat sensed the sideways glances of the male guests. Being on display to strangers was nothing new but, surrounded by family, she resented the invasive curiosity.

Of course, it bothered her that one particularly handsome blond carpenter paid no attention to her. But the fact that she detected Hank's indifference bothered her most of all.

Puzzling, then, that she couldn't tear her eyes away from him. She watched him pull out a chair for the woman with whom he'd been chatting earlier.

She drained the contents of her water glass, letting one small ice cube flow into her mouth. When Hank's face lit with laughter from something that other woman said, Cat ground the ice cube to bits. *Stop staring!*

As the waiters began serving the first course—a spicy gazpacho soup—her father adjusted his tie, stood up, and tapped his butter knife against the rim of his wineglass. On cue, the guests quieted down.

"I know the best man traditionally toasts the bride and groom, but I've asked Jackson to allow me the honor this evening." His deep voice resonated throughout the tent. Cat's father smiled at the wedding guests before settling a soft gaze on David. "No father has ever been prouder of a son than I have always been of you. You've lived your life with purpose, integrity, and principle, and you've been rewarded with the love of a woman who has always had the rare courage to be herself."

Despite their troubles, David remained their father's golden child, and now Vivi would enjoy some of that favor. Cat couldn't deny any of the things her father said about the couple, but it stung to never be on the receiving end of such high praise.

"Vivi, you've been part of this family since childhood," her father continued. "If David's mother could be here with us tonight, her eyes would be shining to see you two as husband and wife. She predicted it long before anyone other than you thought it possible. On her behalf, I'd like to present you with this gift."

He removed a small ring box from his jacket pocket. Inside sat Cat's mother's simple diamond-and-emerald band. Cat could barely believe two and a half years had passed since her death.

Recollections of her mother's face and voice saturated her consciousness, drowning her in a sea of nostalgia and longing. When the fine hairs on her arms rose, she glanced around the party hoping to catch a glimpse of her mom's loving eyes, but then tucked her chin for being so foolish.

Her father plucked the ring from the box and took Vivi's trembling hand in his own. "I bought this ring for Graciela to commemorate David's birth. She wore it every day until she died. She'd planned to give it to his wife one day, and I'm certain she couldn't be more pleased than to see it find a home on your finger. Welcome to our family, officially this time." He kissed Vivi's hand. She surprised him by springing from her chair and embracing him. Tears streamed down her cheeks, leaving streaks of mascara in their wake.

Cat squirmed with empathy at her undemonstrative father's awkward attempt to hug his sobbing daughter-in-law. She glanced at David as he tried to hide his flushed cheeks and watery eyes. The sight of her stoic brother coming undone formed another lump in her throat.

Like him, Cat shunned overly sentimental spectacles, especially in public. She sucked down another glass of champagne and blinked until the stinging behind her eyes subsided.

Some of the guests seemed to be searching the family table, probably expecting to hear Vivi's dad's father-of-the-bride speech. *Oh, shoot.* The drunkard was passed out in his room.

Cat toyed with the pearl necklace lying on her collarbone, mild perspiration dotting her forehead, as she considered how to spare Vivi discomfort. Before she could formulate a plan, Hank stood at his table with a glass in hand.

Surely all the other women in the room were now taking stock of his perfectly symmetrical features—the horizontal brows, straight nose, square jawline, and sinfully formed lips.

"Unfortunately, Mr. LeBrun wasn't feeling well this evening, so he retired early. Before he left, he told me David had been watching out for Vivi for most of her life, so he knew she was in good hands now, and would be in the future. I'm pretty sure he'd appreciate my sharing his thoughts with all of you, and welcoming David to his family. I've had the privilege to get to know Vivi this past year, and it's fair to say David is a lucky and wise man."

When Hank's clear green eyes lingered on Cat, she tensed with awareness. He paused, as if he wanted to say more, but then he didn't. Instead, he raised his glass. "To David and Vivi."

"To David and Vivi," answered the collective voices of the guests.

Vivi blew Hank a kiss for his chivalry. Once again tonight, Hank's quick thinking had spared Vivi undue embarrassment. In that moment, the appeal of a good guy struck a little too close to Cat's heart, causing her heart rate to soar.

But it would pass.

She'd make sure it would pass.

After the main course, Cat excused herself from the table to find the restroom. She reapplied her plum-colored lipstick, adjusted the strap of her dress, and then drew a deep breath. She hadn't heard from her agent this week to confirm whether her fragrance endorsement contract had been renewed. Cat was bracing for it to go to someone younger, or some up-and-coming actress, which made each day of waiting for news seem an eternity.

A week ago she might not have cared as much. But yesterday's doctor's appointment had awakened her, had sharpened the teeth of apprehension. Having lost control over her own body, she now needed to take charge of something in her life. It may as well be her career.

She leaned closer to the mirror and traced the fine lines around her eyes with her fingertips. The bronzed complexion she'd inherited from her mother now showed the subtlest signs of aging—signs that would accelerate if, in fact, she were menopausal.

As she studied her face, she couldn't help but compare herself to the fresh new talent so eager to replace her. Soon enough they'd shove Cat aside, just as she had others a decade earlier. The fierce competition produced a paranoid mindset, hardening her and making genuine friendship a rare gift. She wouldn't miss that aspect of the industry whenever she did finally call it quits.

Yet, having walked away from college without a second glance, modeling was her sole accomplishment, the only thing she really knew. Who would she become when she was no longer young and beautiful—when she was no longer a cover girl?

Her spine stiffened in response to the pathetic moment of fear and vanity. She smoothed her long, dark hair and straightened her shoulders. *Screw it. Time to go have fun.*

Three of David's colleagues stopped her as she passed by the bar. Their alert, hungry eyes temporarily boosted her ego, so she spent several minutes with them while downing yet another glass of champagne.

Years of runway experience had trained her to recognize their Brunello Cucinelli and Armani suits, Fendi shoes, and Prada cuff links. Cat adored fine things, whether clothing, jewelry, or furniture. Yet it was Hank who, in his off-the-rack attire, made her skin feel tight and tingly whenever he passed by.

Why now, after all this time?

Determined to stop tracking his every move, she excused herself from the other men and retreated to her table, which suddenly seemed a million miles away.

David and Vivi started dancing to Ben Folds's "The Luckiest." Jackson slid his chair closer to Cat while keeping his eyes on the newlyweds.

"I still find this all a little hard to believe, but they're damned happy." He slung his arm around Cat's shoulders. "Good for them."

An undercurrent of melancholy simmered beneath his tone. Naturally, he refused to acknowledge or discuss it. Standard St. James behavior.

"You haven't been traveling as much lately," Jackson said, turning his attention away from the dance floor. "What's up with that?"

Cat lifted a fifth glass of champagne off the tray of a passing waiter and sucked it down. "I've been working closer to home." She feigned a carefree smile to avoid a deeper conversation about her career. "I'm starting to consider some different opportunities."

"Different opportunities. We could all use those, huh?" Jackson's smirk and remark caught her by surprise.

"Really?" She'd envied his autonomy—the utter control he exercised over his destiny—so his tone of dissatisfaction caught her off guard. "What changes would you make?"

But he merely shrugged a shoulder before changing the subject. "Speaking of changes, how's the new condo?"

"It's okay." She sighed when Jackson turned and waited for her to go on about the Lenox Hill unit she'd impulsively purchased in order to move before the restraining order against Justin expired. "Not enough closet space. When I brought you to see it before I made an offer, I'd assumed your home-building expertise would keep me from making a bad purchase. You failed me." She playfully cocked her brow.

He threw back a large swallow of his drink. After setting the tumbler on the table, he covered her hand with his own. "You've got increased security there. That's what matters to me."

Cat nodded, although the anonymous "love" letters, e-mails, and tweets she received from men never spooked her as much as the real-life nightmare she'd experienced with Justin.

Apparently Jackson sensed her discomfort and, once again, swiftly changed the subject with a devil-may-care grin. "Shall we take over the floor and show them how it's done?" He tugged on her hand.

"Sure." She rose from her chair. *Oooh, was the floor crooked?* "But promise you won't dump me for another partner once you get me out there."

"Let's take it one step at a time." He winked and broadened his toothy grin. "You know I don't make promises I can't keep. Besides, Vivi invited some cute friends. Don't deny me the pleasure of making their acquaintance."

She pinched his shoulder and followed him into the crowd, gripping his solid arm for balance. The band was playing an upbeat Bruno Mars song when they first hit the floor.

Her brother danced better than any guy she knew, so within minutes the two of them had taken over the floor. Thumping music pulsed around them, seeping into every nook and cranny of her mind as her hands circled the air above her head. Then Jackson twirled her twice and donned a self-satisfied smirk, which made her giggle.

When the band shifted into a slow song, Jackson held out his hand and pulled Cat in for a hug. He kissed her cheek and murmured, "You ought to be here with someone special, sis. It's time you get on with your life. Don't let that bastard Justin steal your future, too."

"Pot, meet kettle," she said wryly.

"Hey, I go out with plenty of women."

"That's worse than not going at all," she answered. "Ever since Alison, you've gone from being a serial monogamist to bordering on becoming a man-whore."

"Ouch!" Thunderclouds briefly dimmed the light in his golden-brown eyes then scattered when he deflected by grinning. "I'm not that bad. Just keeping things light while I'm building my business so no one gets disappointed. So, let's call a truce before we spoil the night."

"Okay, but only because I love you," she teased.

"Love you, too, sis." He kissed her cheek and dipped her.

It was the first time in months he'd broached the subject of her nonexistent love life, and she was grateful he'd been willing to let it go. She couldn't bring herself to tell him about her potential diagnosis. If her family learned of it, they'd suffocate her with sympathy and reassurance.

Cat abhorred *that* kind of attention.

Feeling slightly light-headed, she rested her chin on Jackson's shoulder and sneaked a peek at David and Vivi, who clung to each other as if they'd been sculpted from a single block of clay. Cat had never known that depth of safety or closeness with any man.

Jackson suddenly pulled away to tap Hank on the shoulder. "Switch partners, pal." Before Cat could object, he continued. "Don't make me slow dance with my own sister like some pathetic loser."

Cat would have smacked him for the insult, but that fifth glass of champagne she'd consumed had slowed her reflexes. The ground pitched, as if she'd tried to stand too soon after jumping off a merry-go-round. She reached out one steadying hand before willing herself to look up at Hank. Habit then took over, yanking her to the safety of cool detachment.

Hank hesitated, but Jackson prodded him further. "Come on, Hank. You aren't afraid of a little competition, are you?"

Before anyone could reply, Jackson swiped the other woman's hand, stealing her from Hank's grasp and into his own arms. He flashed a victorious smirk at Hank before spinning his new partner toward a distant spot on the floor.

The heat creeping up Cat's neck added to her increasing wooziness. Hank's gorgeous, jade-colored eyes bore into hers, making her feel dizzy in a way that had nothing to do with champagne. She hadn't realized she'd been holding her breath until he shrugged his shoulders and held out his hand.

Part of her wanted to turn away, but the naughty part she'd kept locked away for months longed to drag her hands through his honey-colored hair. He had thick, sexy, bedhead kind of hair. She remembered its silky texture from the one time she'd played with it.

He took her hand and gently snaked his arm around her waist, pulling her a little closer while never taking his eyes off her face. A ripple of alarm curled through her thoughts from the way he seemed determined to see through her mask.

She cast her eyes downward, but since Hank still stood an inch taller than her despite her spiky shoes, she then had a close-up view of his lips. She remembered them well, too, especially his full bottom lip.

"Catalina?"

His voice snapped her out of her dreamy daze.

"Hmm?" She dared another look into his eyes then nudged a little closer. He smelled clean and fresh, not overly perfumed like so many men she knew. Suddenly the reasons she'd sworn off men or, more precisely, Hank, vanished. Refraining from brushing her nose against the bristly hairs of the two-day stubble he'd cultivated required every ounce of willpower she possessed.

"You okay?" His honeyed voice seeped through her skin.

"Sure." She smiled uncertainly. "Unless you'd rather be dancing with your new girlfriend."

"My girlfriend?" He tilted his head sideways and narrowed his eyes. "You mean Amy?"

"Is that her name?" Cat fought to conceal the bloom of envy. "Sorry Jackson stole her and stuck you with me."

Hank paused, still staring at her. "I doubt many men would consider themselves 'stuck' with you. I think I can survive a dance or two, but your concern is touching." A faint grin stretched across his face and, in a lightly mocking tone, he added, "I didn't know you cared."

She couldn't be sure whether or not he'd meant to be sarcastic-funny or sarcastic-serious, but she hated feeling off-balance. If she must suffer discomfort, then he should, too. Nuzzling closer to him, she rested her cheek on his shoulder.

Tactical error extraordinaire. The strength in his broad shoulders and solid chest offered bedrock into which she could tunnel for security.

To her horror, she heard herself emit a small hum of pleasure. His body stiffened in response.

She knew she should back off, but it had been months since she'd had a man's arms around her, let alone the arms of a man who knew how to kiss. A man who looked this good in a cheap suit, and who smelled like a little bit of heaven.

Without thinking, she swept her hand along his chest. He caught it with his own before she could bury it inside his jacket. God clearly had no mercy, because the song ended before she could protest.

Hank promptly stepped away, leaving a chill in his wake. Ever the gentleman, he nodded politely. "Thank you. Enjoy the rest of your night."

Without further comment, he abandoned her on the dance floor. She watched him hustle to the bar at the opposite corner of the tent—virtually as far as he could wander without actually leaving the party.

Cat had never handled rejection or humiliation well, and tonight proved to be no exception. Her ears burned as she turned toward her table, but she summoned her catwalk strut and smiled.

Along the way, she chugged another glass of champagne, enduring the bubbles stinging her throat as punishment for her lapse of control. For allowing desire to dominate her behavior yet again.

Would she never learn?

Prior entry continued

Tell me, Mom, what man would want to date a menopausal woman my age? An infertile woman who could become sick from hormone treatments, lose her hair, and suffer hot flashes, dry skin, decreased sex drive, and mood swings? Would any man choose adoption or egg donors rather than simply find a healthy woman who can give him kids? Based on my experience with love, it seems unlikely. Please, God, don't make this my fate.

Chapter Three

After the bartender handed him a seltzer with lime, Hank immediately swallowed half the contents of the glass. The hint of citrus tasted good as it slid down the pipe. Exactly what the doctor ordered to sober him up, which he needed to do pronto. Being even slightly buzzed made him too vulnerable, and he refused to fall for Cat's phony flirtations again. He'd already learned the hard way she had no real interest in him or his relatively humble lifestyle.

Scrubbing his hand over the back of his neck, he tried to rid himself of the yearning she always aroused. Like the moon caught in earth's gravity, he couldn't escape her hold on him. *Hopeless moron.*

It had all started when he'd first seen her pictures in Jackson's office, before they'd ever met. Her dramatic brown eyes had distracted him every time he sat across the desk from his boss. The fact Jackson happened to be her brother should've convinced him to steer clear. But he'd been too much of an infatuated dumbass to heed common sense because, even in those family snapshots, she looked like a fantasy, with her bronzed skin, shiny long hair, and perfectly chiseled face. He suspected he wasn't the only guy in the crew who engaged in a few inappropriate daydreams following any meeting with Jackson.

He'd finally met her a few years after he'd first seen those pictures, when she attended one of Jackson's informal get-togethers at his house in Connecticut. Hank had been too shy and tongue-tied to approach her, but then she'd surprised him by homing in on him early that evening.

"Hi! We've never met. I'm Jackson's sister, Catalina." She'd held out her graceful hand. A jolt of energy had slammed into his body from the brief contact.

"I'm Hank." He'd managed to say two whole words, which had been a feat, considering the thoughts running through his mind at the time.

"So, Hank, what's it like to work for my brother?" She'd placed her hand on his shoulder and leaned in to whisper, "You can tell the truth. Your secret is safe with me." Her warm breath had wrapped around his neck like a sensual caress. Then she'd slowly retreated, staring at his mouth for a heartbeat before meeting his gaze. He'd felt her eyes fondle him like a hot pair of hands, and it had nearly brought him to his knees.

Since he hadn't yet mentioned his job, he figured she'd asked Jackson about him. Her notice had made him feel damned good, too. Throughout the rest of the night, she'd continued touching his arm when she spoke, tossing her hair over her shoulder, and pretty much sticking by his side for the better part of the party.

Of course, then, like now, she'd drunk a little too much alcohol, which explained a lot of her behavior, in retrospect. But at the time, he'd thought he'd hit the jackpot.

Throughout that evening, he'd learned she was a loyal Giants fan, exercised ninety minutes each day but hated every second of it, loved her big-city lifestyle, considered social media a necessary evil, and never backed down from a dare.

Even more appealing were the glimpses of tenderness he witnessed, like the way she idolized her brother. And unlike Jackson's then-girlfriend, Alison, Cat had hastened to cohost his party by cleaning up after careless guests and extending herself to ensure shyer ones were included in conversations. The mix of larger-than-life mannerisms and thoughtful, attentive gestures had dazzled him. He'd never met any girl like her—or at least not the way she'd presented herself that night.

As the hours ticked by, she'd decided to crash at Jackson's rather than deal with the late-night train to the city. Jackson had left Hank and Cat alone at the end of the party in order to take Alison home.

"I should probably head out so you can get some sleep," Hank had said halfheartedly, savoring the touch of her knee on his thigh as they sat side by side on the sofa.

"That's a terrible idea."

"You're not ready for bed?" He'd grinned at her as she twirled a lock of her hair around her finger.

"Well, when you put it that way . . ." She'd playfully raised her eyebrow then leaned forward to toy with the hair at the nape of his neck. "Sure, I'm ready."

It was all the invitation he'd needed. She'd been priming him all night. He'd become powerless to resist her even though it meant fooling around with his boss's sister in the man's house.

The next thing he knew, those plush lips of hers were glued to his. Both of his heads had nearly exploded from the desire coursing through his veins, but he'd restrained every male instinct and taken things slowly.

If she hadn't been Jackson's sister, he would've gone as far as she allowed. But even in his lusty daze, he'd been wise enough not to cross too many lines, although they'd both been partially disrobed by the time Jackson's headlights streamed through the living room windows. Thank God for that brief warning.

He'd still been flying damned near the sun when he left Jackson's house, so he hadn't minded the blue balls. Even now he needed to loosen his tie just from remembering the taste of her mouth and silken skin.

Cat had suggested they get together again soon, so he'd left her three messages throughout the following week. To his disappointment, she'd returned none of his calls. Looking back, he'd been foolish to consider her casual proposal a declaration of real interest. A famous model dating a carpenter? He'd obviously been drugged by those kisses.

On top of that humiliation, he'd spent the next few weeks wondering what Cat had told her brother, and what, if anything, Jackson suspected. When Jackson later mentioned Cat had reunited with the jerk she'd been dating on and off, he'd finally realized she'd been using him as a distraction.

Months later, he'd endured almost an entire week of watching her prance around in bikinis and silky nighties at her family's vacation home right here on Block Island. He'd had to work hard to conceal his alternating feelings of irritation and lust so that no one else, most especially Cat, suspected his enchantment. They'd kept a polite distance with one another—he'd known she was still entangled in the yo-yo relationship with her boyfriend.

Hank wouldn't lie and pretend some part of him hadn't felt avenged when her ex got arrested on assault charges. But for the most part, he'd been extremely upset Cat and Vivi had been in such danger, especially after learning the guy's lawyer succeeded in keeping him out of jail. Cat's decision to date an asshole, when she could have her pick of any number of decent men, boggled his mind.

He'd come to this wedding convinced he would no longer feel this tug in his chest. Things had been going pretty well until Jackson interfered and made off with Amy.

Yeah, things had been going okay until Cat cuddled up against him during their dance. In an instant, he'd started falling back under her spell. Hell, at that point he'd been counting the parquet floor tiles to keep from reacting to her drop-dead bedroom eyes and those wine-colored lips.

Holding her in his arms again had been the most exquisite form of torture. When she'd purred in his ear, his insides had exploded like a Roman candle.

But she'd been drinking champagne all night, and experience told him that dance was merely another "Cat"-and-mouse game. She may think of him as some lowly carpenter to toy with, but he wouldn't be her fool twice.

"Is that scowl for me?" Jackson slapped Hank on the back. "You know I was just having a little fun. I'm not really trying to steal Amy from you."

"I might be pissed if I actually considered you any kind of threat," Hank joked, thankful Jackson had no idea what he'd really been thinking.

"Well, we'll never know because, unlike my brother, I'm not looking for love." Jackson's gaze veered across the crowd to David and Vivi, who were approaching them. "But I'm glad some people find it."

Hank ignored Jackson and stole a glance at Cat, who was sitting beside her father at her table with her chin propped up in her palm. Her unfocused eyes stared into the distance while she mindlessly tapped her pinky finger against her cheek. When he'd first seen her tonight, she looked brittle, like she might snap in two at any time. Curiosity pricked him, but whatever had her preoccupied wasn't his business.

"Hey, you." Vivi tugged at Hank's forearm. "How about dancing with the bride?"

David nodded in agreement, so Hank set his glass down on the bar and led Vivi to the dance floor. Her big smile made him grin. Meeting her last summer had been a breath of fresh air. She might be a pip-squeak of a girl, but the size of her heart more than made up for her tiny stature.

"Thank you for dealing with my dad." Vivi's gaze drifted to the floor. Her suddenly somber expression kicked his heart. No bride should have to worry about anything on her wedding day, especially Vivi. "I didn't realize he had so much to drink so early."

"Forget about it and enjoy the night," he said, raising her chin with his fingers. "Nothing but good memories, okay? Besides, I have to eat some crow. Seems you were right about David after all. He never once looked at Laney the way he looks at you, and now here we are dancing at your wedding."

As the words left his mouth, he wondered if he could remove the foot he'd just stuffed in there when mentioning David's ex-girlfriend. Fortunately, Vivi seemed unaffected by his blunder.

"You should always trust my instincts." She grinned. "Speaking of which, I saw you and Cat dancing. Does that mean the frost has thawed?"

Hank hadn't thought his and Cat's indifferent behavior last summer had been particularly noteworthy, but apparently he hadn't been as nonchalant as he'd hoped. Had Cat told Vivi anything about their past? Annoyed with himself for giving a damn, he spun Vivi away and back again. "Your friend Amy seems like a nice girl. What's her story?"

Vivi frowned before she wiped the expression from her face. "Well, Amy is a good friend and a thoughtful person. A lot like you, actually." She then pinned him with her saucer-eyed stare. "She's great, Hank. But wouldn't you rather be with someone who challenges you, who pushes and surprises you . . . who excites you? Because I know someone who might do all that and more."

Vivi glanced over to where Cat was sitting.

"Why do newlyweds always try to play matchmaker?" Hank asked before playfully dipping her as the song ended. He kissed her cheek, cutting the conversation short. "Congratulations, Mrs. St. James. I'm really happy for you."

He led Vivi back to her husband, but she promptly stole Jackson for a dance. Hank had never warmed to David, who still struck him as a bit aloof. However, they'd spent a little time together whenever David had visited Jackson throughout the past year.

"Thanks for dealing with Vivi's father, Hank. I'm sure you prevented a disaster tonight." David sipped his drink. "We owe you."

"Don't mention it."

David glanced toward the crowd and said, "Jackson seems more scattered than normal. Everything okay at work?"

"It's been busy." Hank watched Jackson and Vivi rather than meet David's eyes.

Due to the financial strain caused by his mother's illness and his baby sister's college tuition, he shouldn't complain about the extra hours and extra pay. But Hank knew enough about David to recognize his indirect way of checking up on his younger brother.

Hank wasn't without concerns for his friend, either. "We're struggling to keep up with all the deadlines he's promising to meet. It's been stressful."

"Have you discussed it with him?" David's brows gathered.

"Once." Hank folded his arms across his chest, chuckling. "The brief discussion ended with a reminder of who's the boss."

"His behavior has me concerned. Of course, anytime I bring it up, he throws my own mistakes in my face and tells me to butt out." David stared across the room at Jackson and muttered, "Shutting others out is an unfortunate family trait."

Hank already knew this much about Jackson, and suspected it about Cat.

"How's Vivi handle that?" Hank braced himself for David's response, but David merely looked into his glass and grinned.

"I don't have to hide from Vivi."

Hank could've sworn he saw David smile. He stifled a chuckle at his private conclusion that no one could hide much from Vivi, even if they tried.

"Jackson will sort himself out." Hopefully the fallout wouldn't be disastrous, but Hank didn't want to come between the brothers. "Excuse me, I need to step out for a second."

With a brief nod, he left the tent to steal a few minutes of peace and quiet.

Inside the men's room, two lawyers from David's firm were literally engaged in a pissing contest. Their loud voices suggested they were already half plastered.

"She's smoking hot," said a man who looked to be in his late twenties. "Too bad she's David's sister."

"Yeah, he could block your bid to make partner if you mess with her. Lucky for me, I'm already a partner." The slightly older, paunchy man flashed a victorious grin. "Guess nothing is standing in my way."

"You've got no chance of scoring with a girl like her." The slick-haired younger lawyer zipped his fly. "In fact, I'll bet you five hundred bucks you can't close the deal." He stepped away from the urinal.

Hank's jaw clenched, but he kept a cool head.

"You cocky son of a bitch," replied the older man. "You're on. In fact, double or nothing I close the deal before you."

His competition barked a laugh while glancing at the giant gold Rolex on his wrist. "The reception ends in an hour." He stuck out his hand to his friend. "May the best man win."

"The best man . . ." The other man cracked up. "A wedding pun?"

Assholes.

"I sure hope this bet is a lousy joke," Hank interjected. "You two aren't actually planning to take advantage of David's sister at his wedding, right?"

"Who the hell are you?" the younger one demanded.

"A friend of the family." Hank leveled him with a cold look.

"Of course we're joking," said the older man. He shot his pal a "shut the fuck up" look while slapping Hank on the shoulder. "No harm, no foul." He dragged the other punk toward the door. But before the arrogant young prick left, Hank heard him mouthing off.

"That guy should mind his own fucking business. She can decide for herself who she wants to screw."

The vein in Hank's temple was throbbing by the time the two idiots left the bathroom. His first instinct was to tell Jackson, but he doubted Vivi would appreciate a brawl in the middle of her reception.

He considered warning Cat, but in her condition she might also cause a scene. She wasn't his girlfriend or even his friend. It shouldn't matter to him whether or not she hooked up with someone tonight, or any other night. So why was he scouring his hands in the sink as if they were covered with a flesh-eating bacteria?

Hank went back to the reception, wishing to return to the pleasant evening he'd been enjoying before his brief dance with Cat. Now he had to figure out how to protect her without ruining the whole damned party.

He passed by the scumbag lawyers, who'd already coaxed Cat into joining them at their table for a drink. His eyes met hers. She looked resigned—dammit, she looked sad—which made no sense. She turned away from him and continued her conversation with the jerks.

Hank dug the tips of his fingernails into his palms but kept walking. He couldn't rush in like some B-movie cowboy. He needed a plan.

Back at his table, Amy and other guests were chatting about summer vacation plans. He sat and politely listened while keeping one eye on Cat. Her laughter appeared exaggerated—unlike the girl he'd first met last year—but he couldn't guess at the reason for her charade.

"How about you, Hank?" Amy asked. "Are you going anywhere exciting?"

He hadn't been away since last summer's trip here with Jackson's siblings, which he'd only been able to take because the accommodations had been free. This overnight stay had tapped out his disposable income for a while.

Even if money weren't in short supply, his mother's rapidly deteriorating condition handcuffed him to his home. Hell, this thirty-six-hour excursion had already required multiple check-ins with her caretakers.

"Nah. Summer is my busiest time at work." With a wry grin, he huffed. "I rarely get away."

"Kind of the opposite of my teaching schedule," Amy conceded, looking at him from beneath wispy blond bangs. "Maybe you could plan a winter trip to an island and start the New Year off right."

"Not a bad idea," Hank said. Hell, if he could actually find the money and time to go away for the holiday, he wouldn't mind some female company. But he had a better chance of winning the Powerball than taking a vacation this Christmas.

Hank compared Amy's warm smile and feminine voice with Cat's edgier vibe. Vivi's advice floated through his mind, goading him, so he shook his head to rid himself of the thoughts. He rested his chin on top of his fist, listening with half an ear to the discussion around him. All the while he kept watching Cat and those lawyers.

Now they had her doing shots. He couldn't decide which was more repulsive, the bet itself, or the depths to which those assholes were willing to sink to win. All he did know was that he'd make sure neither succeeded.

"David's sister sure seems to capture everyone's attention," Amy said, pulling him from his preoccupation. "Is she as nice as she is beautiful?"

Hank's gaze snapped back to Amy while scrambling for a suitable reply. "She's not easy to know."

"Ah," Amy sighed. "Beautiful and a challenge. Few men can resist the lure of that particular conquest."

Few men indeed.

As the party started to die down, David and Vivi began making the rounds to say goodnight to their guests before they departed for the St. James family home situated a few miles up the road. Jackson had mentioned how the rest of the family had opted to stay at the hotel to give the newlyweds privacy.

"It seems the party's over." Amy looked at him expectantly.

If he weren't concerned for Cat's welfare, he'd probably ask her to join him at the bar for another drink.

"It's winding down," he agreed.

"Guess I'll be heading to my room," she hinted. "How about you?"

The invitation in her voice tempted him. It had been a while since he'd been with a woman, and he was sitting on six tons of pent-up sexual tension tonight. He glanced around the room.

Jackson was MIA, and David and Vivi weren't paying attention to Cat. If Hank left, she'd be easy pickings for those bastards who were hell-bent on winning a bet. Well, on winning a bet and living out every guy's fantasy. Not that either of those guys needed the thousand bucks anyway.

He didn't owe Cat rescuing, but if she got hurt, it would wreck the wedding memories for Vivi and the rest of the family.

Who are you kidding? He didn't want her to be hurt, and he didn't want to think of her in bed with one of those jerks tonight, either.

"Think I'll check in with Jackson and see what he's planning to do. Cigars will probably be involved." He grinned and took a long pull from his beer while trying to ignore the stab of guilt her disappointed expression caused.

"Oh, okay," she said. "See you in the morning?"

"Sure thing," he replied. "Sweet dreams."

Damn. What in the hell was he doing? He should be spending his time getting to know a nice girl. Someone grounded, who wanted the simple life he did—one filled with kids and holidays, bikes and baseball games, and a partner to curl up with at night. Instead, he was babysitting a complicated woman who'd already brushed him off once and whose jet-setting life seemed anything but normal.

His fingers drummed against the tabletop. Minutes later, Cat staggered away from the dickhead gamblers.

Lucky break.

Hank leapt from his seat, trailing her at a distance. He lingered around the ladies' room entrance until she stumbled back through its door into the hallway. She tripped on the hem of her gown, but he caught her before she hit the floor.

"Oh," she said over a tipsy giggle. "Clumsy me!"

He released her arm once she stood fully, but then she raised one leg to start to take off her shoes, and landed flat on her ass. Whatever shots she drank with those men had launched her right to wasted.

Crimson flooded her cheeks as she looked up at him from beneath her thick lashes. For the first time since he'd met her, she appeared vulnerable and uncertain. His heart rammed against his ribs at the sight, and irritation quickly surrendered to a sudden, fierce wave of protectiveness.

"I think it's time you went to your room." He reached down and pulled her to her feet, keeping one arm around her waist for support. "Come on."

"Is the party over?" Her warm breath swept below his ear and across his neck, teasing the fine hairs of his nape. With each encounter he became more convinced she was some kind of test of his willpower. That or a cruel joke God was playing on him.

"It is for you." He began walking her toward the stairwell. Along the way, they came across Amy and another woman talking in the lobby. Amy glanced over, the beginning of a smile forming, but then caught sight of Cat on his arm.

Feeling like a jerk, he started to say, "This isn't what it looks like," at the exact time Cat mumbled, "Uh-oh."

Cat continued to stagger, even with his support. Then she stopped suddenly. Her eyes drifted from Amy to Hank. With her moist lips pressed against his ear, she whispered, "Can't blame her for wanting you. You look sexy in a suit."

Ignoring Cat when she was attached to his side and coaxing tingles all over his skin was a challenge he suddenly realized he might lose. He didn't even need to close his eyes to picture her naked body wrapped around his, their arms and limbs entwined in an erotic dance. *Steady.*

"Stop talking and keep walking." He propped her up. "What room are you in?"

She beamed at him. "Hmm?"

He clenched his jaw, fighting mounting temptation. "What room, Cat?"

"Two Seventeen." After struggling to assist her up the first flight of steps, he lifted her into his arms to carry her the rest of the way. She sighed and laid her head on his shoulder. Her spicy perfume invaded his nostrils, fighting for control of his brain.

At her door, she fumbled inside her purse for the room key. He put her down, prepared to turn and run, but she wobbled again and burst into another fit of giggles while unlocking her door.

There is no God. Heaving a sigh while rubbing his hands over his face, he then picked her up and carried her over the threshold.

"Here comes the bride," she giddily sang out.

Her husky laughter and twinkling eyes affected him like a shot of tequila. The more time he spent alone with her, the more trouble he invited. He strode through the room and deposited her onto the bed, determined to conquer this unholy addiction.

"Hang on." He went directly to the minibar, retrieved a bottle of water, and cracked open the lid. "Do you have any aspirin?" he asked as he turned back to face her. Then he nearly spilled the water all over himself.

In those few seconds, she'd managed to unzip her gown and partially disrobe. Somehow she'd gotten tangled up while slinking out of the contraption of a dress. He couldn't tear his eyes away from her strapless, sheer lace bra, which revealed a hint of her dark nipples as they strained against the see-through fabric.

Cat didn't have big breasts, but they were big enough, and perky. His mind went blank, although he was vaguely aware of the fact his trousers began to feel two sizes too small.

"Don't just stand there." She grimaced while wrestling with the gown. "Help me out of this."

Her command wasn't meant as a come-on, but the corners of his mouth quirked upward. He replaced the lid on the bottle and set it on the nightstand next to a leather journal with a ribbon tied around it.

Cat kept a diary? Now that surprised him . . . a lot. Damn, would he *love* to read it and finally discover what really went on behind those eyes of hers.

"Lie back and I'll grab the bottom," he ordered, unable to conceal the unexpected rasp in his voice. She lifted her hips as he tugged at the dress and, a few seconds later, she was lying on the bed in nothing but her racy, sheer underwear and high heels.

Mother of God, his mouth went dry.

He couldn't show her less respect than he'd demand another man give his sisters. He couldn't. Focusing on that thought, he merely removed her shoes and then pulled back the covers.

"Scoot under here." He thrust the water bottle at her once she crawled into bed. "Drink it, Cat. I don't envy the headache you'll have tomorrow."

She kept her eyes locked on his while she guzzled the drink. The enticing stare down lasted for what felt like minutes while he battled his conflicting desires and morals. Somehow his morals prevailed.

She set the bottle on the nightstand and nestled down into the bed with a smile playing on her lips.

"Good night, Catalina. Sleep well." He turned to go.

"Wait!" She shifted her weight up onto her elbow. Thick falls of hair cascaded over her shoulders as she patted the edge of the bed. "Come back."

He crossed his arms and faced her. "Why?"

"Please," she said, sitting up in bed.

The blankets now bunched around her waist. That familiar longing rushed back once again, tempting him beyond bearing. He could give in, crawl beside her to take what she offered. Use her the same way she would use him. But he'd never been *that* guy, and it'd be a cold day in hell before he'd allow Cat to turn him into one.

Hank inhaled slowly then sat at the edge of the mattress while rubbing his hands back and forth across the tops of his thighs.

"Thanks for helping me," she said.

Her expression reminded him of the way his sisters used to look when suffering through one of his lectures. He stopped himself from touching her. "You're welcome."

Her uncertain smile twisted him up inside as she reached one hand up and fingered the ends of his hair. "Kiss me goodnight."

All the blood drained from his head and raced to his crotch. The relentless throbbing between his legs urged him to comply despite his better judgment. *Just a kiss.*

As if watching himself in a dream, he saw his fingers caress her cheek. She raised her chin and parted her lips, and he pressed his mouth against hers. He gave over to the moment, to taste her once more, to slip his tongue inside her mouth and tangle with hers. The faint taste of champagne and honey overwhelmed his senses as he grazed her lower lip with his teeth.

Time slowed. Every part of his body came alive. She bulldozed her fingers through his hair while moaning, engulfing him in desire.

"Like I remember," she whispered against his skin. He'd been teetering on the verge of making a gigantic mistake, until her words summoned bitter reminders of the last time he fell for her games. Abruptly, he grabbed her wrists and pushed back.

"Hank!" She fell back into her pillow. "Stay."

"No." He had to get out of her room before hell finished freezing over. "Good night."

Rising from the mattress, he reached over and turned off the lamp. His gaze lingered on her diary again, but he retreated from the bed.

"You're mad about before," she muttered, half asleep already. "But trust me, I did you a huge favor."

He froze in his tracks. Glancing over his shoulder, his breathing slowed as he absorbed her words and the glimpse of self-doubt she hid from the cameras. As apologies go, it wasn't much. Would she have admitted it if she were sober? Did she really believe what she'd said? Did it even matter anymore?

Her gentle snore ended his musing. He crept from her room. Standing in the hall with his palm pressed against her closed door, he waited a minute longer before shoving his hand in his pocket and heading down the hall.

Mom,

I'm a mess. A drunk-and-awake-at-two-a.m. mess. How'd I get to my room? And why does my butt hurt? Did I fall? I hope no one snapped a picture. Glad you won't be here to deal with the aftermath of whatever degrading candid photos end up on Twitter and Instagram. Then again, you were always the best at talking me off the ledge in a crisis.

I still miss you so much.

Chapter Four

An intermittent buzzing sound penetrated Cat's brain from a distance. With each passing second, it grew louder and more insistent. *Stop drilling my head!* She pulled a pillow over her ears, only to become disoriented by the starched scent of the unfamiliar bed linens.

Opening her eyes, she squinted in the sunlight flooding through the window. Turning toward the awful alarm clock, she reached over and swatted it with her open palm three times before finding the Off button. *Thank God!* She collapsed back into the bed and rubbed her sore hand.

Her tongue felt like someone had Scotch taped it to the roof of her mouth, and tasted even worse. Despite the silenced alarm, the throbbing in her head continued drumming an echo of that offending beat.

She stared at the ceiling, praying for a miraculous recovery from her hangover before the postwedding brunch.

After several brutal minutes, she sat up. That was when she noticed her dress on the chair, and that she'd slept in her bra and panties. She slid her hands over her face and combed her fingers through her hair.

Cringing, she searched her memory to recall how she'd ended up in this condition. Another quick survey of the room revealed an empty water bottle on the nightstand. Her shoes sat neatly placed under the chair where her dress was draped.

She cocked one brow, doubting she'd done that herself.

Hazy moments began to surface: Hank lifting her off the floor, the smell of his skin, him tugging off her dress, a kiss, him leaving. Within seconds those memories sharpened, and with each new detail, her embarrassment became more profound.

How many people, other than Hank, had noticed her drunken behavior? She itched to write down her feelings, but then another horrifying thought caused panic. Had Hank read her journal? Cripes, it was sitting there for the world to see, and the strap was untied.

She hastily scanned her most recent entries—humbling fears scribbled on paper.

She shut her eyes, forcing herself to shrink the ball of alarm lodged in her heart. She'd barely stifled those thoughts when troubling new ones sprang forth.

Now she'd have to face Hank over breakfast and pretend like nothing unusual had happened last night. Like he didn't know all of her secrets. Like he wasn't feeling sorry for her.

Pressing both heels of her hands to her temples, she squeezed her eyes closed once more. She rubbed her thumb between her eyebrows to smooth out the creases before blowing out a long breath. After jotting down a brief new entry to clear her mind, she tied up the journal and set it aside.

Her muscles ached. It had been a long, long time since she'd gotten drunk to chase away restlessness. Now shame swam through her veins for having been unable to handle all the love at her brother's wedding.

Fortunately by tomorrow she'd be back to other matters, like her career. As for last night, hopefully the hot water of a long shower would wash away her humiliation.

Nope.

Although clean, she still felt like hell. Sighing, she reverted to her typical response—dressing to kill. Riffling through the numerous outfits she'd packed for the long weekend, she chose a sophisticated, blood-orange Robert Rodriguez sleeveless shift minidress and nude-tone, high-heeled sandals.

She brushed her hair into a low, side-swept ponytail, applied a minimal amount of makeup, popped two Advil, and went to breakfast on the veranda.

Seagulls squawked and flew close to the shoreline, with a few braver ones landing on the nearby railing. The view from the Spring House—a 163-year-old historic landmark—was pretty, if not as magnificent as the one from their family vacation home on the Mohegan Bluffs. Admittedly, the magical quality dusk had lent last night no longer crackled in the air. Beneath a brilliant sun this morning, there were no shadows or soft lighting to hide the defects of the sun-bleached wood, dry patches of grass, or the debris along the shoreline.

Jackson had already claimed a table, so she joined him. She noticed David and Vivi were standing at another table, speaking with some of his colleagues. The slick black hair of one guy triggered an unpleasant memory of drinking shots. She swallowed the resulting wave of nausea and sipped some water to break up the acid in her stomach.

"Where's Dad?" she asked Jackson.

"He and Janet took an early ferry." He scratched his neck. Cat noticed his puffy eyelids and the deep creases in his face. "Apparently they had someplace to be this afternoon."

"What time are we leaving?"

"I left my car on the mainland, so we can take any ferry. I'd like to leave in an hour or so." Jackson emptied a packet of sugar into his coffee. "I'll drive you to Stamford so you can catch an express train to Grand Central."

"Sounds great, thanks." The festivities had drained her. She needed to return to her private haven and plan her next move. Plus, her elderly neighbor, Esther Morganstein, relied on Cat to grocery shop for her every Sunday afternoon. They'd formed a tradition of having tea when she delivered the food. Esther eagerly anticipated their weekly visit because her own family now lived in Texas, and Cat enjoyed the plucky old woman's company.

"You look a little rough." Jackson leaned over and tipped up her chin to study her eyes. "Bloodshot! Did you get to your room okay last night? You never said goodnight."

"I'm fine." She waved her hand dismissively, biting back a retort about looking in the mirror. "If you're so concerned, maybe you should pay a little more attention to your baby sister before the fact, not after."

"Well, I got distracted." He winked devilishly. "Actually, I feel a little shitty myself. Hank and I were smoking stogies out here when Amy and her friend Denise joined us for a few late-night drinks. After that, my memory's a bit fuzzy."

"Nothing more to tell?" So Hank had doubled back to hook up with Amy. She nibbled at her lip, dying for more details.

"Nah. I left them all when I finished my cigar." Jackson gulped down some coffee then smiled slyly as he looked toward the hotel doorway. "But maybe Hank has something to confess."

Cat followed his gaze to see Hank and Amy coming outside together. Was it a coincidence, or had they arrived together? She couldn't be sure, but it looked like Hank momentarily blanched upon seeing her. Another wave of nausea gurgled.

"Over here!" Jackson waved his cohort over to their table.

Cat steeled herself, unsure of how to react. The knot in her stomach wasn't helping, nor was the fact that Hank pulled out another frickin' chair for Amy. *Great.*

"Good morning." Hank nodded at Cat before sitting beside Amy. He met her gaze, which she prayed meant he hadn't read her journal. Surely he'd be too uncomfortable to look her in the eye if he had.

"For some more than others," Cat muttered. Wistfully she once again wondered if, in another place and time, she could have had a relationship with Hank.

When Amy leaned nearer to him, pride urged Cat to retreat and regroup. Jealousy was never attractive, and she'd be damned if she let anyone see it affect her, especially when she didn't understand where it was coming from. "I'm going to make myself a plate. Can I bring anything back for the table?"

Thankfully, everyone declined. She stood and sashayed toward the buffet table inside, thankful years of walking runways ensured her departure would look graceful and sexy even when her legs felt a bit wobbly. Amy might have been able to boast an amazing set of "girlfriends," but Cat had great-looking, mile-high legs, and she wasn't shy about using whatever assets she had at her disposal.

The aroma of bacon and sausage made her gag. No big loss considering bacon hadn't been part of her diet for a decade. Given how many liquid calories she'd consumed last night, she should refrain.

She surveyed the fruits and yogurt, but then Dr. Wexler's weight-gain prescription tempted her to consider the basket full of warm muffins. *Oh, screw it.* She needed something heavy to absorb the remnants of alcohol in her system. Without allowing time for hesitation, she snatched a chocolate chip muffin from the basket and took a bite.

"Once again you're the most glamorous woman in the room," chirped a familiar voice.

Startled, Cat turned to find Vivi standing at her shoulder.

"Please speak softly." Cat rubbed her temple, grimacing. "I'm nursing a big headache."

"I thought you seemed a little drunk last night. Trying to deflect attention from your hangover with this attention-grabbing outfit?" Vivi tilted her head sideways. Suddenly she glanced toward the porch and back at Cat, her expression knowing. "Or is it something more interesting? Is Hank the reason for this sexy getup?"

Cat couldn't hide her surprise. She cast a quick glance toward the veranda.

"Spill, Cat. Did something more happen between you two last night?" Vivi bit her lip and, with a hopeful glint in her eyes, squeezed Cat's arm. "Hank probably feels comfortable with Amy, but she's not right for him. Want me to run interference?" Vivi's eyes radiated girlish conspiracy.

"I know you believe in love and destiny, V, but don't go looking for it for me." When Vivi failed to appear dissuaded, Cat added, "And don't expect me to find it with Hank. You make me regret ever telling you about that old kiss."

Vivi shrugged off the comment and threw her arm around Cat's waist. "It's okay. I know you don't mean to be surly to me the morning after my wedding. Now that we're actually family, I'll cut you extra slack." Vivi dropped the subject of Hank and eyed Cat's plate. "You really don't know a thing about how to make the most of a buffet, Cat. Pathetic, that's what your plate is. Pathetic." She smiled and elbowed Cat aside. "I'll show you how it's done."

Cat barked a genuine laugh, which felt great. "I'll see you back at the table."

When Cat returned to her seat, Amy's radar practically reached across the table and touched her.

"So, Cat, Vivi says you two have been friends since eighth grade. This marriage is really a family affair, isn't it?" Amy sipped her tea. "And your father's speech and gift were so touching. I can't wait to tell all of our friends back at work. Everyone's thrilled for her, although we worry she'll be looking for a job on the Upper East Side soon."

Cat habitually managed her own awkward feelings by donning a mask of quiet confidence. Apparently Amy managed hers by becoming chatty.

"I doubt she's planning to switch schools. She's pretty loyal." Cat forced a pleasant smile while speaking with the attractive girl who'd caught Hank's eye this weekend. "Astoria's only a thirty-minute commute from David's."

"I hope you're right." Amy then smiled a genuine, warm smile.

Cat wanted to hate her, but couldn't. It wasn't Amy's fault Cat had tossed Hank aside. Cat had many flaws, but blaming others for her own problems wasn't one of them.

Although life looked challenging today, Cat didn't need Hank or anyone else to help her turn things around. She alone would figure out how to make the best of her situation—whatever it turned out to be—and move on. It was simply a matter of discipline.

That and time.

She cast a sideways glance at Hank, who appeared stiffer than normal as he spoke with Jackson. Cat suddenly needed to know what he'd done after rejecting her last night.

"So, what fun did I miss with my early departure? Jackson tells me there was a private 'after-hours' party out here."

Amy's cheeks turned pink and she darted a quick glance at Hank, which made Cat settle for saying, "Hmm, that good? Sorry I missed it."

Thankfully, David and Vivi arrived at the table, rescuing her from the awkward conversation. But then Cat noticed Vivi sizing up Hank, Amy, and her, and had second thoughts about being saved.

"Good morning, all." Vivi practically sang her words as she set a heaping plate of waffles, bacon, fruit, and muffins in front of her seat. "Everyone feeling well this morning?"

"You eat more than any man I've ever known, yet you never get any bigger." Jackson chuckled. "You're a freak of nature, V."

"So I'm told." She grinned and then bit a chunk off her muffin.

David leaned close to her, wrapping a protective arm around her shoulder, and whispered, "You're perfect," into Vivi's ear before he kissed her temple.

"Oh, boy. Is this how it's going to be from now on?" Jackson leaned forward, resting his elbows on the table, and shot a disappointed look at David. He glanced down and shook his head. "Can't we joke around like always without you getting all sappy? Seriously!"

"I didn't stop your teasing," David said.

"No, but you're worried she'll be hurt by a joke she's heard from me a million times before." Jackson winked at Vivi before spearing David with a withering stare. "Cut it out, man."

David held his hands up in surrender, then brushed his hand along Vivi's thigh and sat back. He scrutinized Cat with the intensity she'd come to expect from and love about her oldest brother. "You don't look like yourself this morning."

"Gee, thanks." Enough already with being told how shitty she looked today. "I'm pretty sure I'm not the only one who had a few too many drinks last night." Cat cast a quick glance at Jackson, who frowned and crossed his arms in front of his chest. David stared at Jackson for an extra second, then returned his attention to Cat.

"I noticed Marc and Eric sniffing around you all evening," he continued. "Were they giving you trouble?"

Everyone's eyes settled on her. Hank, in particular, seemed to be studying her reaction.

"No. I drank too much, but I'm fine." She defiantly widened her eyes when David challenged her with a look of absolute disbelief. "Quit staring at me! Eat your breakfast."

Fortunately they obeyed. The conversation turned to David and Vivi's honeymoon plans, which involved a twelve-day trip to Italy and Spain. Cat's attention to the details waned thanks to her preoccupation with Hank.

David and Vivi departed to make their rounds with the other guests.

"Cat, can you be ready in twenty minutes?" Jackson asked.

"Pretty much." Cat forced another chunk of muffin down her

throat, hoping it would absorb the remnants of alcohol in her system. "I just have to throw some things in my bags."

"Okay. I'm going up to pack. Meet you in the lobby?"

Cat nodded.

"Amy, it's been nice to meet you. Hank, see you tomorrow." Jackson picked the last piece of bacon off his plate and ate it in two bites before he disappeared.

Well, this is awkward. Cat almost ducked out, too, but then a compulsion to speak privately with Hank swamped her. She couldn't leave without knowing whether he'd peeked at her journal. *Now or never.*

"Hank, may I speak with you for a minute . . . alone?"

His eyes flashed. For a second he looked dangerous, like a bear caught in a trap. "Sure."

"Thanks." Cat rose from her chair with as much poise as she could muster. "Sorry, Amy. I need five minutes."

Hank stood and followed Cat into the lobby.

"What's up?" He shoved his hands in his pockets, calling her attention to his jeans. His untucked shirt hid the waistband, but she could tell they hung low on his narrow hips. Despite wishing for a better view, she dragged her eyes up to meet his before he caught her staring.

Cat absently hugged herself then crossed her arms in full defense mode. "I'd like to know what happened last night."

Hank's chin withdrew. "Nothing."

"Really? 'Cause I woke up in my underwear, and I remember you kissing me."

Hank sighed and raked one hand through his hair before meeting her gaze. "I took you to your room to keep you out of trouble. You asked for a kiss goodnight. Rather than argue, I kissed you and left. That's it, Cat. No need to worry."

Sounded reasonable, but she sensed something more had happened. "Did you read my diary?"

His brows rose to his hairline. "No, I didn't invade your privacy while you were passed out, Cat. But that sure confirms what you think of me."

"I can tell you're hiding something, so I'm left to wonder." She peered at him more closely and poked him in the chest with her index finger. "Why did you think I was in trouble? As I recall, I was having fun."

"Fun? Fun!" A fiery shade of scarlet stained Hank's neck. His sea-glass-colored eyes turned as charcoal as thunderclouds as he spoke. "So being the subject of a bet between two assholes over who would get you in bed first is fun?"

"You're crazy." Outrage chased away the remnants of her headache. "We weren't betting anything."

"*You* weren't *in* on the bet." His hands left his hips and flew through the air in emphasis. "Those jerks made the bet in the men's room then, minutes later, had you doing shots. Rather than cause a scene in the middle of the reception, I waited for the chance to get you away from them."

He folded his expressive, powerful arms in front of his chest. Cat was still processing his remarks when he quipped, "You're welcome, by the way."

Earlier that morning, Cat had thought she couldn't feel more disgraced. Apparently, she'd been wrong.

Her eyes began to sting, but she'd be damned if she'd let anyone see her cry. She stared at the ceiling and blinked back tears.

Hank's eyes narrowed. "What now?"

She cast her eyes to the floor, debating her response. Marshaling whatever reserves of pride that remained, she coolly met his gaze.

"I've been highly paid to be used as a sex object to sell things. Guess I can't complain when men objectify me now, can I?" Cat enveloped her waist with her arms, in a protective cocoon. "I've made my bed, so to speak."

"Is that what you think?" Hank grabbed her bicep and stuck his face so close to hers their noses nearly touched. The tension in his hand traveled to her core as he rasped, "Do you really think you deserve abuse because companies use your image to sell stuff?"

Obviously she must, otherwise she would never have put up with Justin for so long.

"My choices have consequences, and this is one of them." *And probably not the last or worst of them, either.* "Ever since my first magazine cover, I've been swarmed by men, but they've all been users, phonies, or jerks."

He abruptly released her and stepped backward.

"I *know* that's not true." Hank's compassion faded, and his face turned to granite. "Maybe it's just that you're only attracted to the assholes."

"What?" Cat replayed their last few remarks in her head and realized why he'd suddenly become offended. "Oh, wait. I didn't mean you, Hank."

"You know what, it doesn't matter. Go pack, Cat. Jackson will be waiting." Hank turned to leave. "I'm going to finish my breakfast."

"With Amy?"

Hank halted and faced her. "If she's still there, then yes."

"Is she the reason you didn't stay with me last night?" Cat held her breath, having surprised herself with the reckless question.

His gaze drifted down the hallway while he formed a response.

"No," he said. Unexpected optimism sprouted in Cat, until he looked at her through narrowed eyes and spoke again. "You're the reason why I didn't stay."

"What's that mean?" She frowned, nearly reaching for his arm.

"Figure it out," Hank muttered before ambling away without glancing back.

Mom,

I rejected Hank last year; he rejected me last night. We're even now, right? Don't think I can't see you shaking your head at me for keeping score. I hope last night is the last of my embarrassing behavior where that man is concerned. What is it about him that makes me so irrational?

Whatever happens next, I must hold my head high, like Dad always expects. He's so unlike you in that way. You never thought twice about showing every emotion. How freeing that must be.

Chapter Five

Hank rubbed both hands over his face as he strode outside. Every single time he interacted with Cat, she pushed all his buttons—good and bad—leaving him revved up and confused.

Jackson was normal. David thought clearly. What the hell happened to make Cat such a hot mess? And dammit, how could he both love and hate his own mixed-up response to her particular kind of crazy?

Even now he nearly turned around and ran back to her despite the fact he knew she'd probably spin on her heel and stalk off. He shook off his frustration and joined Amy, who remained seated, sipping her coffee.

Unlike Cat, Amy welcomed him with an unguarded smile. Last night he'd been glad to prove he hadn't simply blown her off in favor of another woman. Better yet, Amy hadn't pestered him with annoying questions about what had happened between him and Cat. They'd simply enjoyed another hour of mild flirting before calling it a night, at which point Hank had walked her to her room and kissed her goodnight.

Easygoing, friendly Amy didn't play games. But she also didn't make his heart pound in his chest, get him tongue-tied, or inspire dirty fantasies. Kissing her, while certainly pleasant, wouldn't remain burned on his brain for months or years. Precisely why he hadn't accepted her invitation into her room.

Maybe he was as screwed up as Cat, who couldn't seem to make up her mind between flirting with him and pushing him away. But unlike Cat, he didn't intend to live his life at the mercy of his own insanity.

Instinct argued that Cat's distant, sometimes biting, behavior was a protective façade—for what purpose, he had no idea. Yet, in a war between instinct and experience, he'd be an idiot to dismiss her past rejection.

"My ferry leaves soon," Amy said. "I've got to finish packing now."

"Okay." Tossing his napkin on the table, he stood and pulled her chair out for her. "It's been nice meeting you."

"Maybe we can see each other back in New York or Connecticut?" she asked with hope.

"Maybe." *Say yes*, Hank thought right before he shot her down. "Unfortunately, I don't have much free time. That's not an excuse, just the truth."

"Well, if you find the time, you've got my number." Her sweet smile failed to entice him, which perturbed him to no end.

"Thanks, Amy." He kissed her cheek. "Drive safely."

As she walked away, he sat down to finish his meal and savor a second cup of black coffee. Sunlight spilled throughout the veranda, warming his shoulders and easing the tension in his body. He stretched out his long legs and took another bite of a bagel and lox. Unlike the other guests, he wasn't in a rush to end his minivacation.

Out of nowhere, Vivi appeared.

"I swear I'd forget my head if it weren't stuck on my body!" She grabbed the purse hanging on the chair she'd vacated earlier. "Why are you sitting here alone?"

"Not finished eating."

Vivi's eyes darted around the porch before she pulled a chair up beside him. "I saw Amy in the lobby. Did you two make plans to see each other again?"

"You're relentless, woman." Hank smiled and shook his head.

"Among other things." Vivi pushed some of her perpetually tangled hair behind her shoulder and stared straight at him. Her clear, violet eyes scanned his face. "Promise me this, Hank. Don't make the right choice for all the wrong reasons."

What the hell did that mean? His face must've broadcast his confusion, because Vivi rolled her eyes.

"Don't settle, Hank. Don't you dare settle for a love lacking in passion. It's not fair to you or anyone else." She nodded decisively before squeezing his hand and waltzing away. He chuckled because she looked like a kid who thought she just shared a big secret.

Of course passion mattered, but in the long run, maybe loyalty, consideration, and kindness mattered more. Life was tough. Passion, while exciting, didn't always burn so brightly in the face of real obstacles.

Hank cringed as an image of Cat's earlier crestfallen expression popped into his mind. He probably shouldn't have stormed off and left her in the hallway. If he were smarter, he'd take advantage of those moments when her armor cracked—pry it open and get the answers he wanted.

But ultimately he'd prefer to learn her secrets because she wanted to share them, not because he stole them. Too bad the likelihood of her opening up to him, or anyone, seemed about equal to the chances of him ever walking on the moon.

He took another swig of coffee to wash down his last bite of bagel. Its bitter taste matched his altered mood. Waiters scurried about, clearing tables and waiting on vacationers. He noticed the other men his age—husbands and fathers who appeared relaxed and carefree.

Hank tried to imagine himself with a kid on his knee, a smile from a wife, an abundance of cash, then snickered and washed away his envy with more coffee.

His life had been derailed when his father died from a massive heart attack shortly before Hank's high school graduation. With four younger sisters who needed his support, Hank had scrapped his college plans and taken a construction job to help his mother raise the girls and keep their home.

He didn't resent his situation, but sometimes he wished for the freedom to pursue his own dreams—personal and professional. To finally quit working construction and set up a custom furniture design shop, get married, have kids. Maybe one day he'd even return to this island to vacation with a family of his own.

For now, he'd content himself with his sisters and his young nephew.

Having finished his breakfast, Hank reluctantly stood to leave. On his way back to his room, he bumped into Jackson and Cat, who were waiting in the lobby for their taxi to the harbor.

Cat appeared fully recovered from her momentary lapse of self-confidence. A pleasant buzz surged through Hank, irking him. How could he be hot for her even when she pissed him off?

"Hey, buddy." Jackson shoved his phone in his back pocket. "Meet me at the Caine's house tomorrow at seven, okay?"

Hank tore his eyes from Cat's outrageously short skirt—as if anyone needed further inducement to appreciate her incredible legs. "Seven o'clock. Got it." He noticed three designer suitcases at Cat's feet. A lot of luggage for a two-night trip. He covered his mouth, stifling a smart-ass remark.

She scowled.

"You never know what mood you'll be in, or if the weather will change." Cat squared her shoulders while crossing her arms in front of her chest.

Was she so defensive with all men, or did she reserve this behavior solely for him?

"You don't owe me any explanation," he replied casually, taunting her with a lazy smile.

"Come on, Cat. Cab's here." Jackson waved good-bye to Hank, pulling his luggage behind him on his way out the door. Cat hefted her small bag up over her shoulder, looking like she might topple over on those heels as she bent over to deal with the other bags.

"Need a hand?" Hank watched Cat hesitate. He'd never met a woman so determined to refuse help.

She looked surprised. "Sure, that would be nice."

Hank hoisted the largest piece of luggage up off the floor. "What's in here? Anvils?"

"There's a reason for the wheels, Hank." She lifted the retractable handle of her carry-on-size bag and headed toward the door, casting a seductive glance over her shoulder. "Guess you'll have to 'figure it out.'" After hurling his earlier words back in his face, she then strutted outside.

He followed her, trying but failing to keep from gawking at the hypnotic sway of her hips. She was a witch—a sexy, dangerous witch. And apparently some twisted part of him relished being the victim of her particular black magic.

~

Four hours later, Hank pulled his beat-up Ford F-250 pickup into the driveway of the small Dutch colonial home he shared with his mother and youngest sister, Jenny, in Norwalk, Connecticut. He sat in the driver's seat, stealing an extra minute of peace before going inside to deal with whatever the latest problems were. The car door squeaked open just as Jenny blew through the back door of their house and ran over to his pickup.

"You're finally home." She looped her golden hair through a ponytail band, still looking like a kid even though she'd recently turned twenty. Their eleven-year age difference sometimes made him feel ancient. "I'm exhausted, but I still need to study for an exam."

Hank regarded her pursuit of an accounting degree with a mix of pride and envy. Thanks to his sacrifices, all of his sisters would earn degrees. The other three had already graduated and were now employed as a nurse, a teacher, and an office manager, respectively.

Raising four sisters taught him that he'd be a good father. Caring for an infant had to be easier than managing four teenage girls. A baby wouldn't hog the bathroom or yell at him because some *other* man did this or that. And hopefully he'd have a few sons so the women in his life wouldn't perpetually outnumber him.

"May I please have the keys so I can go to the library?" Jenny asked.

"Hold on, where's Meghan?" He slammed the back door of his truck closed after retrieving his luggage. Throwing his free arm around Jenny's shoulders, he kissed the top of her head. "I thought she was staying with you this weekend to help take care of Mom?"

Jenny walked with him back inside the house, where her backpack sat packed and ready by the door.

"Meg bolted around eleven. I fed Mom lunch and got her settled into bed." Jenny grimaced. "She seemed agitated while you were away, but she never asked for you by name or anything."

His mother had been diagnosed with early-onset Alzheimer's seven years ago, at the age of fifty-two. Now in the late stages of the disease, communication had become a real struggle when she felt like talking—which wasn't often these days.

Hank gently tugged on Jenny's ponytail. "I'd have come home a little earlier if I'd known Meg had planned to bug out before lunch."

"It's okay." Jenny offered a bright smile. "How was Block Island?"

"Gorgeous." Hank smiled as he tossed his bag on the kitchen table, privately replaying the highlights from the wedding, which included Cat's late-night kiss and confession. "It was good to get away."

Jenny cast her eyes downward. "You must be sick of taking care of Mom and me, huh?"

"No." He frowned. Sure, he'd given up a lot for his family, but he'd also taken pride in being dependable, needed, and well loved. "I'd do it all over again if given the choice."

"Maybe it's time to consider other options for Mom, like a nursing home," Jenny said while rubbing one wrist with her hand.

Given her young age, Jenny hardly recalled the brave, beautiful woman who'd raised her kids with a firm hand and loving heart.

His mother had set high expectations for their behavior, and her frankness had made it easy for him to understand what she wanted, and what he needed to do to make it happen. Yet even with a lifetime of memories, each month it became harder to remember his mother as she used to be rather than as she was now.

"I can't put Mom in a home full of strangers. Besides, I just finished paying off the mortgage on this house. Not interested in swapping that debt with one to a nursing home. We've hired Helen to help out. Between the two of us and our sisters, we can manage the rest."

"I'm not bailing on you, Hank. But I see how sad you get when you watch her."

"Don't worry." Guess he hadn't been hiding the ache as well as he'd thought. "I'm tougher than I look."

"Sure you are." She hugged him. He savored the warm moment before pulling back.

"Hang on." He strolled through the living room toward the master bedroom. His hand hesitated on the doorknob, which, like all the doorknobs in the house, was covered with a childproof safety cover—one of many precautions meant to keep his mom from wandering and hurting herself. Quietly, he pried the door open, praying he'd find her asleep.

Through the dim light he saw the rented hospital bed. His mother's frail form looked almost childlike as she lay on top of the quilt she'd sewn decades earlier.

Living with her while watching her mind and body slowly

wither away broke his heart. It sucked to lose her in pieces—much more unbearable than his father's heart attack. At least she appeared to be sleeping now, which meant he'd have a few quiet hours to himself. He closed the door and returned to the kitchen and Jenny.

He clipped the handheld receiver of the video baby-monitor system to his belt.

"You headed to your shop to finish that table you're building?" Jenny asked.

"Yep." He opened the screen door and stepped outside. Jenny picked up her backpack and followed him.

A sense of calm washed through his body as he crossed the yard and unlocked the door to the detached garage, which he'd converted into a private wood shop years ago. He'd purchased a used table saw and band saw on Craigslist, and slowly added various incannel gouges, chisels, and hand planes to his collection of hand tools.

At his day job he installed cabinetry and built-in units in people's kitchens, closets, and family rooms. But in this space he dreamed. Here his artistic creations jumped off the page and sprang to life. *This* work fed his soul.

Today he planned to finish the accent table he'd designed for David and Vivi's wedding gift.

"What do you think?" he asked while deciding it needed a final coat of penetrating resin.

"I like how the three curved legs of the pedestal base gather at both ends. Not too feminine or masculine." Jenny tipped her head sideways. "Perfect size for a lamp, too."

Hank passionately enjoyed every aspect of the furniture design and building process. Even measuring each cut to one-tenth of a millimeter tolerance wasn't a nuisance. Whenever he had a little extra money, he'd purchase rosewood and other rare woods to incorporate into his projects.

"Thanks." He smiled, pleased by her approval.

"So, not to rush you or anything, but can I have your keys now, please?"

Hank tossed her the keys and followed her out to the driveway.

She trotted to the truck with her backpack banging against her thigh. "I won't be home for dinner. See you around eight o'clock."

Jenny looked as ridiculous sitting behind the wheel of his gigantic pickup today as she had when he'd taught her to drive, but he knew she'd be safe in the old tank. He waved good-bye and returned to his shop.

Grabbing steel wool, he gently smoothed out the rough patches created by the prior application of resin. Once he'd finished, he wiped the entire piece clean with a tack cloth. Using a clean brush, he applied another liberal coat of resin, working slowly and deliberately in small sections then gradually wiping off the excess with a clean cloth. Occasionally he checked on his mother via the monitor.

During this quiet time, his mind wandered. He recalled images of Cat in her hotel room, flirting with him in her underwear, testing his self-discipline. Was it possible she regretted blowing him off last year? Had she, like him, wasted more than one night since then wondering what might've happened if she'd given him a chance?

But then reality crashed into his daydreams like a wrecking ball. He couldn't picture her being happy with burgers and beer in his backyard any more than he could see himself hobnobbing with the rich and famous. Frankly, that part of her life didn't appeal to him much. Perhaps she *had* done him a favor, but he might've preferred a chance to find out on his own.

He stepped back to double-check the application and admire his work. After wiping his hands, he shut off the lights, and locked the doors.

For the time being, his dream of going into business for himself would remain just that—a dream.

Hank washed his hands in the kitchen sink before collapsing on the sofa to watch the Yankees game. He'd dozed off until his mother tottered through the room with her walker. She stopped and stared at the television, blinking in confusion.

The light from the television screen backlit her thin silhouette, so feeble a whisper could blow her over. Hank rarely noticed the changes in her physical appearance on a day-to-day basis. However, being away, even for thirty-six hours, called attention to those differences.

Although only in her late fifties, she looked at least seventy. Her cheeks hung from her slack jaw. Green eyes that once danced with laughter and flashed with ire now seemed vacant and lost. Her platinum blond hair had thinned and morphed into a silvery-white color.

In a few short years, she'd utterly changed. Even her skin tone had grayed, probably as a result of her daily medication.

He spoke in hushed tones to avoid startling her.

"Hey, Mom. I'm home." Hank rose from the sofa, hands outstretched and open, and calmly approached her. "Come sit."

She looked suspicious, but took his hand, allowing him to lead her to the couch. Once he settled her, he sat on the coffee table and clasped her hand in his.

"Are you hungry?" He continued speaking softly. "Can I fix you something to eat?"

"Rick?" she asked.

Rick was his father's name—a man who'd been dead for nearly thirteen years. The misnomer stung, even though Hank knew she had no idea what she was saying.

He couldn't help it. Not being recognized by his own mother knocked him off balance each and every time. She'd been the person who'd loved him the most throughout his life. How could she not know him anymore?

"He's not here, Mom." He held her gaze but could tell she wasn't computing. "Let me make you a cup of tea, okay? You wait right here."

Hank hustled to the kitchen and microwaved two cups of decaffeinated Earl Grey. While it cooled, he set Spotify to Fleetwood Mac—her old favorite—and hummed along to the tune of "Dreams" while adding sugar and cream to the teacups. Returning to the living room, he seated himself on the coffee table once more and handed her a cup.

His mother held it with one hand, sniffing it before sticking her pointer finger into her beverage. She pulled it out and sucked on it then repeated the gesture. Hank stopped her third attempt and then lifted his cup to his lips and drank, modeling the motion twice before she mimicked him.

While she drank, he shared the events of his weekend. He talked about Vivi and David, described the red-roofed hotel's cupola and its ocean views, and told her about the pretty girls.

She listened out of habit more than anything else. Hank couldn't be sure how much she understood, or if she even recognized him as her son at any point during the conversation. He merely hoped talking to her as if things were normal helped keep her a little bit connected.

As he sat with his own thoughts about the weekend, he laughed to himself. Time spent considering a relationship with Amy, Cat, or any woman, was a pointless waste of energy. He had neither the free time nor the money to date anyone, least of all someone like Cat. He didn't even have any privacy.

Between his mother and Jenny, it would be years before he'd enjoy his first real taste of freedom.

His mother's choked cough snapped him from his musings. He looked away, swallowing the lump in his throat from shame for even daydreaming about the small measure of relief he'd experience at the expense of his mother's life.

Hell.

Mom,

Menopausal at twenty-eight. Even you had a few more years before it struck, not to mention three kids.

I keep telling myself it could be worse—it isn't fatal. But it feels like a fatal flaw. Hiding all of my imperfections is tiring, but what choice do I have? Image is everything in my business.

Without my image, I'm no one at all.

Chapter Six

Cat removed her earphones, tossed the mail on the kitchen counter, and poured herself a tall glass of water. God, she hated running, especially on a muggy summer morning in the city. Unfortunately, at her age, she had to work twice as hard if she intended to compete.

Of course, after her recent reproductive endocrinology appointment confirming her premature ovarian failure, she resented keeping her so-called "perfect body" fit.

Absent significant intervention, donor eggs, and extremely good luck, her taut abs would never distend in pregnancy—her skin would not be riddled with stretch marks.

Don't dwell.

She'd allowed herself a full day of crying about her unhappy fate: increased risk of osteoporosis and heart disease; potential for hair and tooth loss; the decisions to be made regarding the pros and cons of hormone therapy; not to mention the hot flashes, dryness, and other symptoms she'd probably experience sooner than later.

Of course, she still needed time to grieve the pregnancy she'd never experience, and the kids she'd never bear. Time to let go of *that* expectation of motherhood. Time to investigate and understand the other options like adoption and surrogacy. Only then would she be able to share this diagnosis with her family and handle whatever rejection she might confront from men. Until then, she'd cope.

And until she could think about it *and* cope at the same time, she'd shove it aside.

Flopping onto a counter stool, she guzzled her drink while sorting through bills, junk mail, and magazines. Any distraction would do. While flipping through *Elle*, she studied what would likely be her last Estée Lauder ad.

She rubbed her index finger over the crease in her forehead to rub out the frown lines just as her phone rang. Her agent's number appeared on the screen. Maybe Lauder offered her another contract after all.

"Hey Elise, please tell me you have good news."

"Unfortunately, no. Lauder went with Kendall Jenner." After a brief pause, she continued. "As we've discussed, the landscape for models is changing. You still have your couture work to keep you busy for a while, but you might need to start thinking in new directions before you age out of the print game."

Twenty-eight and considered old. Of course, her body was aging out early, too. The soon-to-come symptoms wouldn't help, either. After all, thinning hair, dry skin, and perspiration never photograph well.

"Do you have any suggestions?" Cat sucked down more water.

"Well, given Kendall's recent coup, perhaps you should consider reality TV. Our agency's been contacted about casting a host for a new fashion contest show. Or what about participating in the *Bachelorette* franchise? That show would probably pay well for a celebrity bachelorette."

"Oh, no!" Cat's career needed a life vest, but the absolute loss of privacy, not to mention the editing hatchet jobs she'd seen, made reality TV a nonstarter. The risks of them discovering and publicizing her medical condition were not worth any amount of fame or fortune. And a part of Cat—a new, growing part—wanted out of the limelight. Wanted a life and reputation built on something other than her beauty.

"Television would really bump your profile and relevance. A brief stint could help you secure another cosmetics deal or other TV guest appearances."

"That merely delays the inevitable." She decided to simply lead Elise in new directions without giving her the reasons. Swamped with a sense of urgency, she said, "I think it's time to consider something lasting and stable, something new and challenging. I'm tired of always chasing contracts."

"What about a licensing deal?"

Huh. That could be interesting. "How does that work?"

"Well, there still is some chasing involved, but you'd typically get a lump-sum payment up front, plus annual domestic and international royalties off the affiliated products."

"Sounds intriguing. I'd need to give some thought to what products interest me."

"Clothing and cosmetics would be natural fits. You'd have a built-in fan base to sell to."

"Too common. And I'd still be competing against all the other models, actresses, and reality celebrities hawking those types of products." Products that didn't capture her interest—the thought of continuing to promote beauty as a virtue tasted sour. "I'd rather do something completely unexpected and different, like Kathy Ireland's furniture empire."

"She started with socks."

Cat scowled. Socks didn't sound appealing. "Be that as it may, I'd want to partner with something unique, upscale, and not easy to copy. That way there's less competition right out of the gate."

Elise chuckled. "God love you, Cat. You always shoot for the moon."

"You'll never get there if you don't even try." Cat shrugged, as if Elise could see her. "Maybe something along the lines of lifestyle or travel products."

"Really? It's important that you don't dilute your brand or take on something too risky. The *worst* thing you could do is affiliate with something that fails. If that happens, then your name and image lose credibility and value in the marketplace."

"I'm nothing if not discerning." Her agent's lack of faith in her decision-making ability reinforced all her self-doubts. Not that she'd let it show. Just like her father's dismissiveness had pushed her to succeed before, her agent's lack of faith made Cat vow to reach the moon, at least metaphorically.

If she couldn't make babies, she'd damn well find another way to leave a legacy. And proving everyone wrong would only make the win that much better.

"Let me do some digging," Elise said. "I'll see who's looking for talent."

"Okay, talk to you soon." Cat set down the phone, determined to come up with some of her own ideas, too.

Feeling a bit optimistic about new possibilities, she flung the *Elle* magazine aside and continued sifting through her remaining mail.

She frowned upon discovering a handwritten, ivory-colored envelope with no return address. It looked similar to one she'd received here last month, except the postmark came from SoHo instead of Chelsea.

Biting her lip, she tore it open and scanned the notecard, which featured neatly handwritten block print.

Catalina,

Not a day goes by that I don't dream of you. For now, I'll settle for endless fantasies, but someday you'll realize I'm the only one for you.

While not exactly threatening, the letter disturbed her nonetheless. Being propositioned via Twitter and Instagram, and occasionally accosted at restaurants, seemed relatively innocuous. But this nameless, faceless, eerily personal contact caused concern.

Her first instinct was to suspect Justin. Then again, the wording didn't sound like him, and she doubted he'd settle for such a passive approach. If he were going to break the restraining order, he'd just show up to prove no one could control him.

But if not Justin, then who? She'd bought her condominium via a straw party for privacy. Maybe it was Justin. He had the money and contacts to find her.

She reread the note, searching for clues. The handwriting revealed nothing, but the expensive card stock indicated the person had money and taste . . . like Justin. She sniffed the page, but it held no discernible scent.

Prior experience with creepy fans proved the police wouldn't do anything absent a real threat. No use bothering the cops. Love letters weren't threats. And suspecting Justin was a far cry from offering proof.

Sighing, she placed the letter and envelope in a desk drawer on top of the one she'd received last month. For some reason, she'd decided to keep them as evidence. Evidence of what, she wasn't quite sure.

Her phone rang, pulling her thoughts away from her unsettling admirer. She smiled when Vivi's photo appeared on the screen.

"Welcome home, Vivi. How was your honeymoon?"

"Utterly amazing." Vivi's sigh spoke volumes.

"When did you get back?"

"Yesterday afternoon, but I'm so totally mixed up time wise."

"I'm well acquainted with jet lag." Not so much lately, but still. "So, tell me all about it. Wait—skip the intimate details. I don't want to hear about my brother's sex life." Cat heard Vivi's gentle laugh through the phone.

"Can you come over?" Vivi asked. "David ran to the office to get a jump on things before Monday, so I'm alone and bored."

"Give me thirty minutes to shower and dress."

"Perfect."

When Cat finished drying off, she wrapped her plush towel around her body, trod to her closet, and scowled. Despite her best efforts, she still hadn't managed to organize all of her clothing and accessories. She'd stacked boxes of out-of-season clothes and shoes in the spare room. Even so, pieces of her wardrobe practically fell on top of her whenever she opened any closet door.

She thumbed through her summer tops. Not knowing where her day might lead, she selected a turquoise, tie-dyed Donna Karan scarf top and paired it with white linen shorts. Vivi and David lived two blocks away on East 76th, so she opted for high-heeled, white sandals. If they decided to go elsewhere, they'd have to take a cab.

~

An hour later, Cat sat at David and Vivi's kitchen bar finishing her diet soda while viewing the last batch of honeymoon photos on Vivi's laptop.

"I'm not kidding, V, your photography keeps getting better. Some of these pictures are incredible." Cat stared at the red roofs of Florence a moment longer.

"I'm no Peter Lik," Vivi said.

"You always undersell your talent. Seriously! You should considering starting a photography business on the side, or at least during the summer." Cat slid the laptop away and turned to Vivi. "How about portraits? People pay big bucks for portrait photography, especially new parents. And then there's endless head shot work around Manhattan."

"Maybe someday." Vivi shrugged. "Right now I'm happy with my hobby. I'm too busy during the school year to take on extra work, and I'd rather spend my free time with David."

Cat lifted a single brow. "Sometimes I still find it bizarre you and he actually ended up together. But it's all worked out better than I ever imagined."

"It's better than *I* imagined too, which is really unbelievable!" Vivi laughed and shut the laptop. "So what about you? Ready to start dating again?"

"Not at all, so *stop*!" Cat considered sharing her diagnosis now that the wedding was behind Vivi. But her friend still basked in the afterglow of her honeymoon. Cat's news could wait another week . . . or longer.

"Why not?" Vivi took a giant bite of her chocolate-filled croissant, completely ignoring Cat's request.

"You mean aside from my terrible taste in men?" Cat winced at how she'd overlooked the warning signs with Justin—at what accepting his verbal abuse for so long said about her self-esteem. "I've got a demanding career."

"Now *you* stop." Vivi eyed the remaining pastries. "You're not the only woman in the world who's fallen for a bad guy. Justin was good-looking, and he pursued you all around the world. I can see how that possessiveness might've swept you away at first. But it's been nearly a year since it ended. Don't give up on love, or pretend you can't have both a career and love. That's just silly."

"Let's be brutally honest, V. I'm not good at relationships." Cat tilted her head. She'd become cynical with age. In her world, most people only looked out for themselves. Somewhere along the way, it seemed smarter to accept and live by those rules. "Outside of my family, you're the longest relationship in my life. Sometimes I wonder how you put up with me."

"What are you talking about . . . *how I put up with you?*"

"Come on, I'm not warm like you. I can be prickly and aloof." Cat puzzled at Vivi's incredulous expression. Perhaps her friend clung to the Cat of yesteryear without noticing the way she'd hardened. "Admit it. I'm spoiled."

"You're not spoiled." Vivi twisted her lips. "Well, you're a little spoiled, but you aren't self-centered. You stood by me for years when others bullied me. You offered me friendship and a place to call home. You've shared your secrets with me since childhood—I know you don't trust easily, so I'm honored to have earned it, Cat.

"And you're generous to a fault. Don't think I don't notice how overboard you go on birthdays, Christmas, and any other occasion you can invent."

"You always give everyone the benefit of the doubt, but I'll take what I can get." Cat let out a short breath and grinned. Choosing Vivi as a friend was one of the best decisions Cat had ever made, and thankfully the feeling was mutual. "Still, I really do suck at relationships, especially with men."

"You're being ridiculous." Vivi scrunched her features.

"Am not. Before Justin, every guy I dated was more interested in my VIP passes than in getting to know me. It's degrading, actually. And pointless. In my current situation, I'm better off alone." Then, worried she'd accidentally revealed too much, she wiped her expression clean. Fortunately, Vivi missed the subtle gaffe.

"That's sad." Vivi stared through Cat, contemplating. "I get why you're aloof in public, but maybe you should stop hiding your true feelings all the time. No man can love you if he doesn't know who you are. That's your only problem with relationships. Just let someone in, like you did with me."

Cat didn't like being psychoanalyzed, especially when the words had teeth. She twisted her hair in her fingers as she considered Vivi's advice.

Of course, Hank had accused her of only liking assholes. Maybe he was right. Or maybe assholes were safe because, deep down, she knew they'd never look too far beneath the surface and discover all her faults.

And now, in light of her new circumstances, a superficial relationship might be all she should seek. She couldn't be rejected or overly disappointed if there were no expectations from the get-go.

Yet her thoughts had continually drifted to Hank ever since Block Island. Being near him again had stirred up longing and unwelcome what-ifs. So frustrating, but those momentary butterflies were addictive.

Might the Boy Scout consider a casual fling? Now *that* would be tempting.

She rubbed her stomach, which had begun to churn. "Well, you let me know when my white knight arrives, and maybe I'll give it a whirl."

Cat noticed the gleam in Vivi's eyes as she glanced at her watch for the third time in twenty minutes.

"Why do you keep looking at your watch?" Cat leaned forward as if her physical invasion would force Vivi to fess up. "Are you going somewhere, or expecting David?"

"Oh. No." Vivi's guilty expression set off alarms. "I, um, I'm still a little confused by the time, I guess."

"You're the worst liar." Cat shook her head and tamped down niggling ill ease. "You're up to something. Spill it."

"Don't get all fussy. I'm expecting a delivery." Vivi's enigmatic smile only heightened Cat's nervous anticipation. "Relax! Tell me, are you all settled in the new condo?"

"As much as I can be. I need to rent some storage space." Cat mentally contrasted Vivi and David's sleek, contemporary condo with her cozy, prewar unit. "Honestly, I can't believe Jackson didn't notice the closets when we walked through the unit. Worse yet, I didn't even notice."

"First of all, guys don't think about closet space. Secondly, no woman has a wardrobe like yours. You couldn't really expect Jackson to take it into consideration." Vivi's wide eyes made Cat chuckle. "Plus, he was desperate to get you out of your old place before the restraining order expired."

"Well, that's why I moved."

She frowned. "It still bugs me how Justin's lawyer got him off with a slap on the wrist. I know he didn't set out to hurt you. Still, no jail time and only an eleven-month order of protection?"

Cat contemplated the letters she'd received recently. "Hopefully Justin's moved on by now."

"Why the face?" Vivi's eyes narrowed.

Cat tapped her fingers on the counter, debating whether to share her concerns. "I've received two anonymous letters in recent weeks. Someone has spotted me going in and out of the building, or maybe gone to the trouble of finding me."

"Do you think they're from Justin?" Vivi's eyes filled with concern.

"I'm not sure. It'd be a violation of the protection order. Plus, I can't imagine him sending *anonymous* letters. But the last one said I'll soon realize we're meant to be. Kinda like I already know the person, which points to Justin." Cat shrugged. "Who knows for sure?"

"Are the notes threatening?"

"Not really. They're more like love letters." Cat wrinkled her nose. "No threats, but still a little creepy."

"Maybe David's firm can investigate."

"I haven't told David or Jackson. They worry so much, and I feel pretty safe in my place. I'm concerned but not panicked. *They'll* panic. If it's Justin, he's probably enjoying toying with me. I could see him getting off on making me afraid. I don't want to give him, or anyone, that power. If I go running to the cops or David or whatnot, he wins. Besides, I can't *prove* anything."

Vivi nibbled her lower lip. "You know I've kept all your confidences, but this one feels wrong, Cat."

"If I get one more letter, I'll take action, okay?" Cat tapped her fingers on the counter. "For now, no one has threatened or approached me, and I haven't noticed anyone lurking around."

"I still don't like it." Vivi shrugged her shoulder. "But I suppose it's your decision to make."

A knock at the door spared Cat further debate. Vivi's eyes suddenly lit up with mischievous glee as she crossed the living room. Cat instantly suspected the much-anticipated delivery wasn't innocuous. She smoothed her hair and braced for whatever was coming next.

Although she'd prepared for a surprise, the last person she expected to see was Hank. His mere presence lit the room with sexual energy. Her stomach turned over as if she'd crested the tallest peak of a roller coaster.

Hank stood at the threshold holding an end table with a white ribbon tied around one leg of its pedestal base. His deer-in-the-headlights expression proved he was as shocked and discomforted to see Cat as she was to see him.

"Sorry. Didn't mean to interrupt anything." He eyed Vivi. "You didn't mention having plans this morning."

"Oh my gosh!" Vivi ignored his remark as she held the door open and waved him inside. Hank entered haltingly and set down his gift in front of her. She bent over to inspect the table. "When you told me you made us a table, I never imagined something so gorgeous. Did you really build it from scratch?"

He nodded a greeting in Cat's direction before returning his attention to Vivi wearing a proud smile. Meanwhile, Vivi quickly untied the ribbon and smoothed her hand across the tabletop.

"What is this wood?" she asked.

"Oregon walnut."

The rounded corners of the tabletop lent a hint of feminine appeal. Natural knots marred the tabletop's edges. The streamlined design should also appeal to David, who wouldn't like something whimsical or fussy. It was perfect.

Upscale, unique, not easy to copy—*exactly* the kind of thing Cat would like to promote. What fortuitous timing. She glanced heavenward, as if her mom might appear at any second, having somehow orchestrated this with Vivi.

"Oh, Hank. It's exquisite!" Vivi beamed at him before flinging her tiny body against his impressive chest and hugging him. Unbidden envy shot through Cat when Hank closed his arms around her friend. "I love it."

"Thanks, Vivi." Blood rushed to Hank's neck and ears before he eased out of their embrace. Cat smiled at the involuntary sign of his shyness. Like Vivi, he couldn't hide his feelings well, which made him seem more trustworthy than most. A rare find, that. "I hope David likes it, too."

"He will, but it's going on my side of the bed." While Vivi continued to admire Hank's work, Cat hopped off the kitchen stool to take a closer look.

Vivi hadn't exaggerated. *Exquisite* aptly described his craftsmanship. Cat had heard Jackson boast about Hank's carpentry skills, but she'd assumed he'd been referring to interior finish work and kitchen cabinetry installations. She hadn't realized his talent extended to fine furniture.

While Vivi offered Hank a cold beverage, Cat studied the table closely, her mind racing with possibilities. But as she trailed her fingertips along its surfaces, her thoughts strayed from business. She pictured his hands caressing the wood. Envisioned him bent over, shaving, buffing, and staining each piece.

In her fantasy, he was shirtless, of course—his muscles bunching as he worked, his skin damp with perspiration, his expression keenly focused. The sensual imagery sent her body temperature soaring, as if he were attending to her body with that same attention. Embarrassed by the direction of her thoughts, she shook her head to dispel them.

"It's beautiful, Hank," she finally said on a soft breath. His green-gold eyes gazed at her with the intensity she'd been envisioning moments ago, making her heart kick inside her chest. Powerful lust produced mild throbbing throughout some important and long-ignored parts of her body. She cleared her throat and refocused on the furniture. "When do you have time to do this?"

He shrugged one shoulder. "At night and on weekends."

"Does Jackson know?" she asked, curious about whether or not Hank seriously pursued this talent. "Have his clients requested custom-built furniture?"

"Jackson's not interested in my hobby." He cast his eyes downward for a moment. "Besides, we're so busy lately it took me nearly eight weeks to build this small table. I don't have time to build furniture for his clients."

"Well, I'll treasure it." Vivi handed Hank a cold soda.

Once again Cat noticed Hank's cheeks flush. She adored the boyish charm of his cute reaction. He couldn't be faking it. Regardless, she shouldn't pursue her growing curiosity. *Oh, just confess already. It's more than mere curiosity, and it's for more than his talent.*

"Thanks. I'm glad you like it." He glanced around the apartment. "Sorry I missed David."

"He had to work." Vivi waved her hand. "He'll be sorry to have missed seeing you, too."

Hank popped the tab on his soda and took a swig. "Well, I don't want to interrupt your visit, so I'll head on out."

"Wait a second. You only just arrived. Stay and catch your breath." Vivi's eyes shone as she looked to Cat. "Actually, Hank, you might be able to help us solve a problem."

Cat held her breath. She had no idea what cockamamy scheme Vivi had just devised, but clearly it involved pushing Cat and Hank together.

Hank looked equally suspicious as his eyes flitted back and forth between Vivi and Cat. "What problem?"

"Well," Vivi began, placing one hand on her hip while animating her speech with the other. "Cat's new condo doesn't have enough closet space. Since Jackson's not around, maybe you could take a look and come up with some suggestions? With all the remodeling work you do, I'm sure you've come across this situation before. It's only two blocks away. Fifteen minutes of your time, tops." She finished her plea with a sweet-as-can-be smile.

Cat nearly choked, but she maintained an unruffled demeanor. Hank's thoughts appeared to be racing while he scratched the back of his neck. She hoped to catch a peek of his abs when the hemline of his shirt rose up in tandem with his arm, but he dropped his hand too quickly.

Vivi had relied upon his polite manners to trap him, the wily little sprite. Cat *should* be annoyed by her interference, not grateful. Yet, her body tingled in anticipation of spending a little time alone with Hank.

Her gaze flickered back to the end table, seeing the possibilities it embodied. For a moment she flirted with the idea of testing his interest in some kind of joint venture with his furniture and her name, but then dismissed it, assuming he'd probably laugh at her idea.

"Sure, I'll take a look." He glanced at Cat. "But I can't make any promises about finding a solution."

"Great! I'm sure you two will figure things out." Vivi grinned. She patted Hank's shoulders then feigned a yawn with wide-stretched arms. "Sorry. Jet lag. I think I need a nap. You two feel free to take off anytime."

"Guess that's our cue." Cat retrieved her purse from the kitchen island.

"Thanks again for the gorgeous table. I absolutely love it." Vivi lifted up onto her toes and still barely reached Hank's cheek. She gave him a quick kiss. "See you soon."

As Hank started out the door, Vivi ensnared Cat in a tight hug. "Thanks for visiting," she said loudly, then whispered, "Be your true self, Cat. Have faith!"

Cat rolled her eyes but hugged her matchmaking friend, who remained blissfully unaware of Hank's tempered disdain for Cat. If she hoped to tempt him, she had her work cut out for her.

She shivered at the memory of how he'd spurned her proposition after the wedding reception. Frankly, he'd been the only man ever to walk away from her when she'd been half naked and in bed.

His rejection had unsettled her. She wanted his affection despite knowing she'd done nothing to deserve it.

Until she knew precisely what she wanted from him, she'd need to tread lightly.

She followed Hank to the elevator in silence, enjoying the view. The doors closed, trapping them together in the confined space. With the exception of a few stolen glimpses of Hank, she kept her eyes on the lit floor numbers overhead while fighting the urge to fidget.

Although she didn't know him particularly well, she could tell he didn't trust her, and he wasn't someone to be ordered around—especially not by her. Whichever proposition she made—business or pleasure—would require a seduction of one kind or another.

Of course, one kind would be a lot more fun than the other. Then she remembered the vow she'd made, the commitment to forging a new career.

Cat would be proud to associate her name with such extraordinary work. Of course, the limitations of a handcraft business were an issue, but she needed a challenge to take her mind off her sorrow.

First she'd need to assess his interest. Did she dare?

"Well, this is awkward," she muttered. "You don't have to come over just because Vivi strong-armed you."

He folded his arms across his chest, his presence gobbling up the limited space. A hot flash that had nothing to do with Cat's defective hormones heated her skin. "Do you really need help, or did she make that up?"

"No, I do have a space issue." Cat's heightened appreciation of his masculine build, his gorgeous mouth, thickened the air, making it hard to breathe. "But it's not your problem. I'm the idiot who bought the place without thinking it through."

"I'll come take a look." He glanced at his watch. "I have some time."

"Oh, do you have plans later?" Her blood cooled when she remembered Vivi's work friend lived in the city. "Are you seeing Amy this afternoon?"

"Amy?" His brows furrowed in confusion then arched. "Vivi's friend?"

Cat nodded, fighting to sustain an air of indifference.

One corner of Hank's mouth curled upward.

He can see right through me.

He cocked his head to the left as he spoke softly. "I have plans, but not with Amy."

His evasive reply piqued Cat's curiosity, but she resisted pressuring him further. Maybe because the shallow dimple in his left cheek distracted her. But more likely because he seemed to read her too easily.

If she planned to get involved in a business relationship with Hank, she had to rid herself of these schoolgirl feelings, or learn to manage them better. When she'd said she needed a new challenge, she hadn't imagined this being one of them.

Five excruciatingly awkward minutes later, they entered her building and nearly ran into Esther, who was struggling out of the mail room with the aid of her walker.

"Hi, Esther!" Cat waved. "Need help?"

"Cat, dear. Don't you look lovely!" Esther's New York accent inflected her warble. Her posture straightened a bit when she caught sight of Hank. Flashing a grin too coy for a woman her age—a grin that added several creases to her wrinkled face—she asked, "Who's this handsome young man?"

"Oh, this is Hank." Cat stepped aside. "Hank, this is Esther Morganstein, my neighbor and friend."

"Pleased to meet you, ma'am." Hank shook her hand and used the opportunity to relieve her of her mail. "Let me carry these for you."

"Thank you." Esther smiled. Cat could've sworn Esther purred. As the threesome gradually made their way toward the elevator, Esther turned to Hank. "You look like a nice young man. Be sure to treat my Cat with respect."

"Of course—" Hank began, but Cat interrupted him.

"Esther, Hank and I aren't dating. He works for my brother. He's just here to help me sort out my storage problems."

"Oh, honey, I told you the solution. You have too many things. Get rid of half and you'll still have too much." Esther's fragile chuckle made Hank grin. Cat had to admit he looked damned handsome wearing a grin. Esther pointed a bony finger at Hank. "You'll see. Too many things!"

"I'm sure yours is the easiest and most practical solution, Mrs. Morganstein." Hank cocked his head, eyes twinkling, as he continued. "But she likes having lots of options. One never knows what the weather will be like, or what kind of mood she might be in from minute to minute."

Cat dipped her chin and narrowed her eyes, remembering having uttered that exact rationale to defend the many suitcases she'd brought to Block Island.

"Hmph. I think you're secretly jealous of my fashion sense." She let her eyes deliberately graze the length of him. As usual, he wore a fitted, collarless, cotton T-shirt that hugged each sinewy muscle in his chest and shoulders. Low-slung cargo shorts showed off his trim waist and narrow hips. His orange-and-tan Merrell sandals were practical, if unattractive. They say clothes make the man, but in his case, it simply wasn't true. Not that she'd let him know it. "Clearly, you need pointers, Hank," she said with a grin.

"Touché," he replied, while winking at Esther. Cat noticed his comfortable familiarity with the old lady. He seemed relaxed and at ease in a situation most men might find awkward at best.

They followed Esther to her door, where Hank handed her the mail.

"Don't forget to call me with your grocery list, Esther," Cat reminded her. "I'll be by tomorrow around two o'clock."

"Thank you, dear." Esther turned to Hank with a flirtatious look in her eyes. "I hope this isn't the last time I'll be seeing you." Esther waved her bony hand at Cat's shocked expression. "Well, I'm old, but I'm not blind!"

Hank chuckled aloud as Esther closed her door. Looking at him standing there—a green-eyed, golden-haired hunk of testosterone—Cat couldn't blame Esther for her reaction. Cat wasn't blind, either.

Mom,

It's strange to consider how much David and Vivi's lives (and mine) have changed in just two weeks. They're married, embarking on a sparkly new life together—maybe considering starting a family. Then there's me, facing a childless future and fading career.

When I've felt blue, I've relived parts of the wedding weekend—the flowers, Vivi's constant smile, David's tender glances, Dad's toast, and Hank playing my hero (if somewhat reluctantly). I'm grateful he whisked me away from those jerks, and that he refused to take advantage of my drunkenness (although maybe I could have forgiven him for taking a little advantage, if you know what I mean).

The world needs more men like Hank, doesn't it?

Chapter Seven

Traces of pink stained Cat's cheeks as she snatched her keys from her purse. Before Hank could read much into her blush or ask about her relationship with Esther, he spotted the number of dead bolts on her door and frowned. This upscale neighborhood shouldn't have a serious crime problem, so why all the locks?

When the last one clicked open, Cat looked over her shoulder and smiled. "Home."

The way she'd said it while grinning at him made it seem like they'd arrived at *their* home. *Another freakin' fantasy.*

Even so, he couldn't wait to get inside, having imagined her home many times since they'd met—brightly colored fabrics, stark modern lines, mirrors, and a few frilly accents. When he stepped inside, he immediately saw nothing he'd expected was true.

Brazilian cherry wood flooring lent warmth to the understated, homey space. The painted beige walls were offset with creamy-white trim. Interior French doors added an airy touch despite the small size of the rooms, so unlike the McMansions he'd become accustomed to building.

Her furniture was transitional but not modern, upholstered in neutral silks and suede, with dark, glossy wood accents. It was tasteful, elegant, and relaxing. Not at all what he'd pictured, but so much better.

He smiled at the thought of her here, then frowned at how vivid his daydreams would be after having seen her private space, which held the intoxicating aroma of her spicy perfume mixed with something earthy, like cedar. He scrubbed his hands over his face.

"What's wrong?" Cat stared at him with her head cocked to one side.

"Nothing." He rested his hands on his hips while willing his arousal into submission. "It's pretty, Cat. Suits you."

"Thanks. I fell for its cozy charm." She pressed her lips together and, magically, he felt it between his legs. "It blinded me to its major shortcoming. Come on, I'll show you the problem."

His thoughts raced in all directions as they approached her bedroom. For reasons still unclear to him—especially after being jilted—his body responded to hers like with no other woman on the planet. His caveman instinct to toss her on her bed and take her might be difficult to hide.

Thankfully, they stopped in the spare bedroom first.

"See the piled-up boxes of stuff I can't put away?" She strode across the room to the small closet. When she glanced at him, he noticed a calculating look in her eyes, but couldn't imagine why. Probably just more games for her own amusement. "This closet stores my formal wear."

She opened the door to reveal a space jam-packed with glittering, silky gowns. Gowns that had hugged her body the way he might've liked to, he thought as a shiver traced down his spine. His eyes widened as he processed the fact that the overstuffed closet contained only her formal wear.

Cat held up her pointer finger. "No judgments, please. I know—I have a problem. Hazard of my job, I guess."

He raised his hands in surrender. "No judgments." The price tags shocked him, but maybe she got some of the stuff for free, like movie stars. *Quit analyzing her and focus.* Scanning the small room, he asked, "So what other closet space do you have?"

She tipped her head toward the door. "This way."

He followed her into her bedroom. It was lovely, and that wasn't a word Hank used—ever. A needlepoint carpet covered a good portion of the floor. Her sleigh bed, constructed of a bird's-eye maple and draped in a creamy satin duvet, dominated the room. Three pale-pink-and-green velvet decorative pillows added a splash of color. Feminine yet sophisticated.

Hank bit back a groan as he envisioned her lying amidst the bedding, her long, dark hair fanned out—or tangled around his fingers. The clarity of his vision fed the desire already coursing through his body. Despite his better judgment, apparently Cat St. James would always be his weakness.

Closing his eyes as if he could block out the image, he forced himself to turn away and survey the rest of the room. The only other furniture included a small nightstand and a narrow dresser with a mirror, both of which matched the sleigh bed.

Above her bed hung a sizable charcoal sketch of the figure of a woman with a "V" scrawled in its bottom right corner. He guessed Vivi drew it. Cat's sentimentality—one of the traits he'd fallen for that first night—reinforced his love-hate relationship with the many ways she caught him off guard.

His silence must've drawn her attention.

"You've awfully quiet." She tilted her head and narrowed her eyes. "What are you thinking?"

"It's not what I expected." *I want you so much.*

"How so?" Cat crossed her arms as if preparing to be insulted. He could be misreading her, but he didn't think so. The contrast between her invincible persona and her peculiar moments of self-doubt intrigued him.

"Well, based on what little I know of you—your clothes, your 'image'—I expected something more colorful, maybe even a little wild." He noticed her frown. "I like this much better. It's peaceful. A sanctuary, I guess."

This time her crimson lips broke open to reveal her perfect smile. Making her smile that broadly satisfied him beyond belief. "It *is* a sanctuary. This is where I relax."

"I'm glad." He shoved his hands in his pockets to keep himself from reaching for her. Her spellbinding gaze rendered him speechless. When his chest tightened a little, he had to cough so he could speak. "How about you show me the closet?"

She groaned and pointed to the set of bifold doors. "Stand back," she warned before opening them.

Good God, her stuff consumed every square inch of space. Miraculously, nothing tumbled onto their heads. Hank clamped his hand across his mouth to keep from laughing. Once he collected himself, he studied the closet, then turned to mull over the wall with the single window.

"I know." Cat slumped her shoulders. "It's hopeless."

"Not if you're willing to give up the floor space running along this wall." Hank pointed at the window.

"What do you mean?"

"Well, you could build two armoire-style built-in units on either side of the window, and even put a storage drawer beneath the window."

"Hmmm . . ." She crossed the room to stand next to him and stare at the wall, trying to picture what he'd described.

Her perfume instantly danced across his nerves like fingers on a fret board, making his body resonate like guitar strings. Feeding his insatiable hunger for her. He needed to get out of her apartment soon or he might forget about why she was all wrong for him.

"But that would look generic." She turned to him, the scheming look back in her eyes. "I love what you made for Vivi. Could what you're describing be handcrafted as a single piece of furniture?"

"Possibly." He intentionally placed distance between them to escape temptation. Refocusing on the task at hand, he eyed the length of the wall, which he guessed to be roughly fourteen feet long. "It'd be massive, though, and you couldn't take it elsewhere unless your new place had this same wall configuration and measurements."

He noticed her dark brown eyes narrow in thought, so he continued with his description. "Either way, you'd have lots of extra hanging or shelf space, and the bench seat could house shoe shelves or drawers. It would also free up the old closet for your out-of-season stuff, especially if you install an organization system."

"That's true!" Her hand gripped his forearm, immediately heightening his awareness of her again. She looked around the room as if trying to envision what he'd described, utterly unaware of the effect of her touch on his skin. Wide-eyed and smiling, she asked, "Could you really build it for me?"

No way.

"Cat, I can't do this work for you." Even if he wanted to—and parts of him sure did—he didn't have the time. "I thought you needed help with *ideas*."

"But this could be perfect for both of us." She released his arm, leaving him stripped of her touch. "Once it's finished, I could show it off, introduce you to wealthy friends. To the world! We could turn this hobby of yours into a career."

He didn't want to think about how she'd homed in on his dreams, because he couldn't afford to start a risky new venture at this point in his life. Not while his family still depended on him and his income, and definitely *not* with a woman who'd proven so fickle since they'd first met.

He forced himself to shake his head. "Can't."

"Why not?"

"For starters, I've got a full-time job with Jackson. Secondly, you live an hour's drive from me in good traffic conditions. I need to stick closer to home." He withheld the details of his mother's health to avoid seeing pity reflected in her eyes.

"Jackson would give you time off if I asked him."

"Don't be so sure about that, Cat. We're seriously short-staffed now, and he's made promises we can't possibly keep. He needs me on-site unless he plans to irritate his clients. Besides, I'm getting lots of overtime working for him. I need the extra money."

She stepped back and glanced away, twirling her hair around a finger. "Are those the real reasons, or are you making excuses because you don't like me much?"

The accusation and raw emotion stunned him, knocking him off balance. An hour ago he'd have guessed his opinion of her meant nothing. And dammit, how'd she come to a conclusion so far off the mark? Distrust, yes, but not dislike.

"I don't dislike you, Cat, so get that out of your head." Her doubtful expression slipped behind his defenses, but he wasn't about to stand there and profess his wild desire. "Trust me, those are my real reasons."

Her chin dipped low. "Fine."

Her rapid descent from delight to dejection landed a punch to his gut. "I'll draw some plans for you, okay? Someone else can do the actual work. How's that for a compromise?"

His phone rang before she could respond. Recognizing Jenny's ringtone, he answered the call. "Sorry, give me a second." He turned away from Cat. "Hey, Jenny. What's up?"

"Hank, Mom's really restless and agitated. No one can handle her like you. Will you be home soon?"

"I'm in the city. It'll be at least an hour, maybe a bit more."

"Try to hurry. She keeps pointing out the window. Is it safe for me to take her to sit in the backyard?"

"Sure. Put on some music, too. I'll get there as soon as I can."

Hank hung up and slipped his phone back into his pocket.

"Sorry." He noticed Cat watching him with interest, but she didn't ask about the call. He tried not to speculate about her thoughts, which were as unpredictable as mountain weather. Reaching across his chest, he rubbed a knot out of his left shoulder. "So, do you want me to draw up some plans?"

"Yes, thanks." Cat tilted her head, provocatively raising a single brow. She approached him and touched his shoulder. The single touch sparked a pleasant prickling down the length of his arm, making him almost willing to sell his soul to keep her hands on his body. "A good massage will get rid of that tension."

"I wouldn't know." He crossed his arms again, this time to keep himself from wrapping them around her. "Never been pampered."

"Well," she began, "you've missed out on one of life's great pleasures."

"I'll survive. Anyway, I've got to get going. If you want me to draw up a plan, I need a tape measure." He reached into his pocket for a pad and pencil, but came up empty. "And a pencil and some paper, too."

When she returned with the items, he began taking notes. Within minutes, his mind formed a myriad of thoughts about potential design details. They had to be perfect because she'd be reminded of him each time she looked at them. That recognition altered his breathing.

Whatever he created would live here in her bedroom—a place he'd have enjoyed spending time in, too, under other circumstances. Now he envied the damned furniture. Hell, if this woman didn't make him lose his mind.

"It'd be helpful if you'd send me an inventory of all your stuff." He chuckled when her eyes widened with surprise. "It'll help me plan the interior better. Otherwise, I'll be guessing at what you need most—shelves, rods, drawers, and so on. The more accurate you are in the beginning, the more satisfied you'll be in the end."

"I like to be satisfied." She purred her words, which affected him exactly as he suspected she intended. Maybe someday he'd figure out why she enjoyed teasing him, but he didn't have time this afternoon.

"I'll bet you do, Cat," he uttered. It was all he could muster. Thirty minutes of sensory overload had scrambled his brain. "Here's my e-mail address. I'll do my best to get something turned around quickly. Maybe Jackson knows someone who can do the work."

"Don't worry." Cat shuttered her expression. "I'll call him."

"All right," he said. Her odd tone caught his attention, but he didn't comment. "I've got to go."

She led him back to her front door and unbolted all the locks. "Mustn't keep Jenny waiting."

If he didn't know better, he'd say she sounded jealous. But Cat had never expressed any interest in him unless she'd been drinking. Clearly spending too much time alone with her made him delusional.

"Bye." He hurried down the hallway and jogged to his car.

Halfway into his drive home, Jackson called.

"Hey, buddy. What's up?"

"I just hung up with Cat." Jackson's clipped tone surprised Hank.

"Oh? Do you know anyone who can help her out?"

"Yeah. You."

"Me?" *Hell no.* He didn't need to add self-torment to his already complicated life. "Not me, Jackson. You know I'm too busy."

"I know it's inconvenient, but I need you to do this for me."

"Why?" Hank flashed back to the odd tone in Cat's voice when she'd mentioned calling Jackson. A hot streak of irritation rushed through him like a runaway train. Not that he should be surprised that she was used to getting her way. "I'll design it, but someone else can build it."

"It can't be anyone else," Jackson said. "She doesn't trust strangers in her house."

Hank recalled all the locks on her doors. "Why not?"

"Privacy. Weirdo fans and the paparazzi have become more aggressive in recent years. The idea of inviting a strange man into her apartment for weeks is a risk she won't take. He could snoop around, sell pictures, or worse. But she trusts you."

"Shit, Jackson. Thanks for the guilt trip." He sensed the futility of his protest. No doubt it would suck to live under a microscope. The explanation tempered his anger, but Hank still had his own problems. "What I am supposed to do about our deadlines and my mother? A custom armoire unit will take some time, and the city isn't a quick trip."

"Can Helen work longer hours with your mother?"

"You know I'm already struggling to pay her fees."

"How long will Cat's project take to complete?"

"You mean once it's designed?" Hank mentally walked through the steps needed to build the unit. "I don't know. If I'm working full-time on it, four weeks, maybe less depending on what I can rough cut before I head down there."

A short silence ensued.

"Cat will pay you two-and-a-half times your rate to do the work." Jackson's triumphant tone annoyed Hank. "Problem solved."

Hank bristled at the bald manipulation. Rich people always figured money solved everything. Apparently Cat and Jackson didn't consider Hank's feelings to be significant. Of course, Jackson knew nothing of Hank's fucked-up personal feelings for Cat.

"What about your other jobs, Jackson? You're going to piss off your clients by pulling me off-site for a few weeks, and you're going to fall behind."

"I'll figure something out. It's just temporary, so I'll press forward with tile work and other things in your absence. Besides, you've been pushing me to hire an additional finish carpenter, anyway." In the face of Jackson's remarks, Hank couldn't think of another good excuse. "So, are we agreed?"

"Doesn't sound like I've got a choice, boss," Hank spat.

"What's the problem? You'll have extra income for your mom's care, and extra bank in your pocket."

"You're right." Hank swore under his breath. "Still, I don't like being manipulated by Cat or you . . . or anyone."

"Manipulating you?" Jackson whistled. "Hell, man. I'm your friend asking for a favor, and one that's well worth your while."

"Sorry. No offense intended." He wasn't angry with Jackson. In fact, Jackson was as much a victim of Cat's tactics as Hank. "You just surprised me. Let me talk to Helen and Jenny to see what kind of schedule we can work out. I'll call you later."

Hank sped along I-95, his mind traveling at the same pace as his truck. He resented being hoodwinked by Cat, but what he hated most was the tiny part of him rejoicing in having his options snatched away.

Despite the logic of her case for insisting he do the work, her alternating flirtation and antagonism created doubts about the reasons she wanted him, and *only* him, to take the job.

Who knew, maybe it would be worth exploring something personal now that Justin was out of the picture? One thing was certain—this particular project would change his life. Problem was, he couldn't decide whether it would make it better or worse.

Mom,

Don't be disappointed in me, but I've decided not to share my condition with anyone. Nobody can fix the situation, so what's the point of talking about it?

Better to focus on my career. And on that note, I can't allow Hank *lust to steer me off course.*

Chapter Eight

To: henrytmitchell@gmail.com
From: catalinastjames@gmail.com
Re: Closet Inventory

Hank:

I'm convinced you asked for this inventory to embarrass me. Congratulations, you've succeeded. In any case, here's my list (includes clothing for all seasons/occasions):

62 pairs of shoes
18 pairs of boots
167 blouses (hangers)
29 jackets/blazers
49 pairs of slacks (hangers)
16 pairs of jeans (can be folded)
28 pairs of shorts (16 are linen or silk blend/prefer hangers)
48 sweaters (can be folded)
37 dresses (not full-length)
24 gowns
36 purses
26 belts
8 yoga pants/shorts

10 exercise tops
21 swimsuits

I've excluded personal items like jewelry, lingerie, etc., which have a home in my dresser or safe.

Looking forward to seeing the plans. Thank you for agreeing to build this for me.

Best,
Cat

~

Cat's finger hovered over the Send button. She reread her draft for the fourth time, envisioning Hank's eyes bulging upon receipt. No doubt he'd judge it—and her—as wasteful and indulgent. But as a model, her image mattered.

With gossip sites waiting to mock celebrities at any opportunity, Cat couldn't be too careful about her appearance. What set her apart from other, younger models was her good taste off camera. Of course, she loved her designer clothing and accessories, too. Honestly, what woman didn't—Vivi excluded?

Sadly, her outrageous wardrobe would reaffirm Hank's opinion of her as a spoiled princess—an impression she wanted to overcome because, despite everything, she cared about his good opinion.

She squeezed her eyes shut and hit Send. When she opened her eyes, she couldn't believe the screen hadn't detonated. Sighing, she closed her laptop and went to Esther's to deliver the groceries she'd picked up earlier that morning.

Esther greeted her with a smile, exuding warmth that always improved Cat's mood. She ambled to the woman's kitchen—one that hadn't been updated in twenty-seven years—to unpack the three bags of food.

"Thank you, dear." Esther shuffled toward her purse without the aid of her walker. "What do I owe you?"

"Forty dollars," Cat lied, substantially discounting the cost. No one could replace Cat's mother, but Esther's affection and wisdom provided a quasi-maternal relationship she craved. A friendship well worth the weekly stipend she extended.

"You must be a whiz with coupons." Esther held out the cash. "Thank you."

"You're welcome." Cat tucked the bills in her back pocket. "So, what kind of tea are we testing this afternoon?"

"Oriental Beauty, a fancy oolong tea." Esther gestured toward the teapot.

The delicious floral and peach aromas wafted into the air as Cat poured them each a cup. She then followed Esther into the living room and sank onto a tufted, pale-blue velvet chair.

A busy Aubusson carpet covered the parquet flooring in the living and dining rooms. Ornate, gilded mirrors and picture frames hung on the original plaster walls and matched the antique furnishings. The area basically looked like a botanical garden tinged with gold, and smelled like baby powder. Although Cat preferred sleek design and an absence of clutter, Esther's fussy apartment reminded her of her grandmother's home, where she and Jackson built living room forts with sheets and pillows, and snuck into the attic to pore over her old records and magazines.

Esther had already set out a bowl of mixed berries and a plate of shortbread cookies, one of which Cat dipped into her tea. Not as tasty as the cinnamon-spiced cocoa and churros she and her mother used to share, but they inspired a similar sense of peace and well-being.

"Did that handsome Hank solve your closet problems?" Esther's rheumy blue eyes glittered to life.

"You were quite the flirt. Gives a new meaning to the term 'cougar,'" Cat teased. "But yes, he's going to design and build a custom armoire unit in my bedroom. I'm pretty excited."

"I'd be excited if he were spending time in my bedroom, too."

Cat choked, spitting out a bit of her tea. "Esther, you're naughty!"

"What woman isn't a little naughty now and then?" Her distant smile hinted at a fond memory. "I've always appreciated fine-looking men. Your Hank is a looker, and he's kind. A keeper."

"First of all, he's not my Hank. Secondly, he is nice. Maybe too nice, actually."

"Only foolish women think there's such a thing as a man who's too nice. You've never struck me as foolish, Cat. My husband wasn't nearly as handsome as Hank, but his thoughtfulness kept us married for over fifty years." Esther sipped her tea to soothe her scratchy voice. "So why isn't he yours? Does he already have a girlfriend, or is your brother opposed?"

"I doubt Jackson would care." Cat put her cup down and sighed. "As for Hank's love life, I don't know if he's dating anyone. At David's wedding, he spent time with a girl named Amy. But the other day I heard him talking on the phone to someone named Jenny. In any case, he's no longer interested in me."

"No longer?" Esther smiled. "So there's a story. What happened?"

"A cougar *and* a gossip? Shame on you, Esther," Cat teased, sighing to cover her grin. "I first met Hank last spring at Jackson's house. He was so . . . I don't know, easy to talk to. We flirted all night, but when he called later, I kind of blew him off to get back together with Justin. I'm ashamed of my rudeness, but at the time, I honestly believed Justin and I belonged together. As you know, he turned out to be terrible. Anyway, I burned my bridges with Hank. Since then, he's politely distant, which is better than I deserve."

"Sounds like you have regrets." Esther's perceptive eyes focused on Cat.

Cat sank deeper into her chair. "I doubt dating Hank would've worked out. He should be with someone sweeter and less cynical than me. It's moot, anyway."

"Why?"

Esther's kindly gaze tempted Cat to share her medical condition, but she bit back the words. "Because Hank's not interested in handing out second chances. Besides, I'm more concerned with reinventing my career than pining after a man." *Liar.*

"Nonsense. Careers won't bring the same happiness as love. And a willing heart can always give second chances." Esther waved an arthritic finger at Cat. "You just convince him you're worth it."

"Then I'm doomed, because I can't even convince myself."

Hank might have been a simple man, but he had a dangerous way of looking at her—of seeing more than she wanted to share. Even if she could deal with that kind of scrutiny, her infertility required him to make a significant sacrifice he probably wouldn't otherwise choose. Friendship would be the smartest, most honest relationship she could build with him.

Esther clucked. "Well, if I were you, I'd try before Amy or Jenny gets a firm hold of him."

~

Cat whisked along the Merritt Parkway the following week in the yellow convertible Volkswagen she'd rented for the day. She could've taken the train to Connecticut, but the sunny summer day summoned a need to speed, with the wind in her hair, beneath a canopy of leafy tree limbs.

Her off-key voice was belting the tune on the radio when she turned into the gravel parking area at Jackson's office in Wilton. Years ago he'd purchased an antique colonial situated on nearly two level acres, and converted the old barn on the property into an office from which he ran a lean, highly profitable operation.

Its pastoral setting—a stark contrast to the chaotic city—relaxed her. Having grown up in Wilton, the sights and sounds of the area automatically transported her back to the days when she and Vivi had followed Jackson and David around: Vivi out of adoration for David, and Cat out of interest in their friends. The memories—the *fun* of it all—made her smile.

Surveying the barn, Cat considered what Jackson had built for himself in a short time frame. Although not blessed with David's genius IQ, his hard work and big personality were being well rewarded in the residential construction industry.

If he could succeed in business without David's intellect, then maybe she could, too. Admittedly, she'd been unable to abandon the idea of promoting Hank's furniture despite his apparent disinterest. Handcrafted furniture—no other model represented anything that unique. It appealed to her desire for distinction, and her high standards for quality. And the timing—seeing it right after talking to Elise about the future—couldn't be mere coincidence.

Surely Hank could be persuaded to see the benefits of a partnership. His current obligations posed problems, but all problems had solutions. If she could solve Hank's, maybe she could convince him to reconsider her idea.

At the moment, however, she'd settle for seeing the armoire designs. A twinge of guilt pinched her conscience, but she brushed it aside. Hank seemed concerned about money, so the high commission for this work should make him a little glad for her scheming.

Striding toward the barn, she noticed Hank's mammoth pickup truck parked beside her brother's Jeep. Her stomach fluttered.

Once inside, she stumbled midstride as she heard heated voices coming from Jackson's office. She tiptoed closer to his office door, which was cracked open.

"I need you to finish the moldings in the Caine's kitchen, Hank," Jackson demanded.

"I thought you hired Doug to pick up the slack." Hank sounded exasperated. "I can't be everywhere at the same time."

"Doug's not as good as you. You know the Caines are nitpicky."

"When the hell do you think I can squeeze that in? I'm already stretched too thin, and you roped me into working at Cat's, too. I *told* you this would happen."

Cat winced at the bite in Hank's voice. Apparently she'd overestimated his enthusiasm for the extra income. She crept closer and hid behind the open door.

"Come on, man. We're only talking about several hours." Jackson's chair squeaked as if he'd leaned backward. "Take an evening or two and finish it."

"You know I can't work evenings without a lot of hassle. Plus I'm exhausted with the pace we're keeping. You're taking on too many commitments."

"Don't tell me how to run my business." Jackson's control over his temper slipped. Cat frowned, hating being a source of their conflict.

"As your employee, I'm telling you you're asking too much." Hank's tone softened. "As your friend, I'm concerned. You drink all night, and then run around all day like a crazy man. You look worn out. You're curt with the crew. Something's got to give."

"Yet look at which one of us is whining." The chair squeaked again. "Seems you're the one who can't handle the pace or remember how to have fun anymore. Maybe *I* should be the one raising concerns."

"Go to hell, Jackson. You know what's going on in my life. Back off before we both say things we regret."

The mounting tension seared Cat's stomach like a double shot of Jägermeister. She needed to shut them down before things got out of hand, although Hank's vague reference to problems in his life piqued her curiosity.

"Yoo-hoo, it's me!" she called out, masking her uneasiness with a smile as she swung Jackson's door wide open.

Both men snapped their heads in her direction. Jackson's forehead furrowed in confusion, while Hank rose from his chair. Another snug T-shirt hugged the muscles of his chest and sun-kissed arms. She caught herself before letting her gaze linger, then focused on her brother so Hank wouldn't glimpse her sudden, naked desire.

"Sis, what're you doing here?" Jackson asked.

"Meeting Hank about my armoire, then joining *you* for dinner." She tilted her head sideways in response to Jackson's sudden sheepish expression. "You forgot?"

Jackson let loose a long exhale before looking up. "Sorry. I didn't write it down, and now I've made other plans." He grimaced while stretching his arms out in front of him and drumming his palms on the desk's surface. "Wanna tag along?"

Cat noticed Hank's disgusted headshake before he cast his eyes to the ground. She wanted to support her brother, but perhaps Hank's accusations were valid.

"I'll pass on being the third wheel," she replied.

Jackson sat back and linked his hands behind his head. "If you want me to cancel my other plans, I will."

She knew he would—and probably should—but she declined. "No, thanks. I'll borrow Hank for a while, then maybe stop by Dad's before I go home."

"I feel bad, sis." Jackson's gaze swung from her to Hank and back, then he smiled as if struck with a fantastic idea. "Hey, why don't you two grab dinner together while you talk? My treat."

Hank looked cornered, so Cat let him off the hook. "That's okay. I'm sure Hank has better things to do than babysit me."

"Trust me, the guy could use a night out." Jackson threw Hank a playful smile. "I'm sorry I lost my temper. Let me apologize by treating you both to dinner. Go anywhere. Charge it to my card." He slid his platinum Amex across his desk.

Cat didn't know how to respond without making things worse. She held her breath, glancing at Hank, seeking some kind of cue. *Say yes.*

His eyes remained trained on Jackson. He gripped his waist before glancing at her and over to Jackson. "Keep your damned card. I'll pay for my own meal, thanks." Then he nodded toward the door. "Come on, Cat, I've got your drawings laid out on the conference table."

"Are you two okay?" she asked quietly once they entered the hallway.

"It's best if you stay out of the cross fire," Hank mumbled.

"But I'm responsible." She fidgeted with her hair. "I manipulated Jackson into pressuring you. Don't blame him. He's just being a good brother."

Hank made no reply as they walked into the conference room. He halted at the edge of the table and turned to her. "I figured as much, but I understand your reasons. And this isn't the first or last disagreement he and I have had. Don't worry, though. We always get it all done without bloodshed."

His gracious attitude only increased her guilty conscience, but she kept quiet while he sorted through his hand-drawn sketches.

A carpenter *and* an artist—what could be hotter? A sudden surge of desire produced a gentle ache in her core. The constant twinges of awareness he generated were addictively delicious, but dangerous.

"This is what I've worked out." He presented two separate drawings: one for the three-piece armoire unit, and one for the conversion of the existing closet. "I know you preferred a stand-alone armoire, but this wall unit maximizes storage. I can make the front look like custom furniture, but this is the only way to create enough storage for *all* your stuff." When he grinned at her, her insides melted.

"You needed lots of hanging space, so I've dedicated this entire unit to hanging rods, with the exception of some shelving at the top for out-of-season things."

Hank kept describing the details, but she'd become too mesmerized by his enthusiasm—and watching his lips move—to hear the rest of his explanation.

"It's wonderful." Cat scrutinized the detailed drawings more closely to discover how carefully he'd considered her needs. "What about the exterior?" She pointed at another pile of drawings on the corner of the table. "Can I see your vision for that?"

"I kept the basic design simple with a slight curve to the bench seat unit beneath the window. You could go a few different ways." He spread out the various sketches for her to view. "We could build the front frame and doors from bird's-eye maple to match your existing furniture. Or you might prefer a basic maple, or something richer, like cherry. Either way, we could insert some kind of mottled glass or mirrors in the face of the doors to add more light in the space. Mirrors would be practical, too."

Hank stared at her as if watching for her approval. His plans exceeded her expectations, and she'd never been a slouch when it came to setting high expectations. When she rose up on her toes to kiss his cheek in appreciation, he immediately flushed. His reaction to her touch made her entire body tingle. She burned for him to hold her, kiss her, take her—anything to relieve her sexual frustration.

"I'm speechless, Hank. It's beautiful and practical." She reluctantly withdrew and studied the drawings more closely. "I like this best." She pushed her favorite image, one with narrow, full-length mirrors, toward him.

"Okay."

She liked his boyish grin almost as much as she liked the fact she put it there.

He collected all the drawings and rolled them together before sitting in front of the computer. "I bookmarked a few pages of wood samples from nearby suppliers. The maple in your bed had heavy eye, but in a unit of this size, it might get too busy."

Cat leaned over Hank's shoulder as he opened the laptop and clicked through various images from the different vendors. Suddenly, concentrating on anything other than his musky scent became an impossible task.

The heat radiating from his skin warmed her cheek, but he seemed unaffected by her presence as he toggled through various websites. Yet as she brushed against him to take a closer look at the screen, his quick intake of air proved—thankfully—that he, too, felt an electric attraction.

"It's a little overwhelming." She kept her cheek within inches of his. "Which would you choose?"

Hank kept staring at the screen. If only he'd turn toward her, their lips would practically touch. Even as Cat scolded herself for her own immaturity, she longed for him to share her desire.

"This one would be beautiful," he finally said, his voice huskier than earlier.

Jackson popped his head through the conference room door, causing Cat to straighten up.

"I'm off." He smiled at Cat and then slid his gaze to Hank. "Sure I can't convince you to take me up on my offer?"

"No need, brother," Cat interjected. "I'm taking Hank to dinner as a thank-you for his thoughtful work, and for graciously agreeing to do it for me."

She *wanted* to thank him. But more importantly, his magnificent designs reaffirmed her intention to press for a business partnership. Hank clearly loved the work, and she desperately needed a new direction in her life. A challenging goal, but more importantly, a unique one. Something that stood out, something special and unlike the products models typically licensed.

She needed Hank to make it happen. To give her a chance to walk away from modeling before she was shoved out. And, she admitted to only herself, to give her something other than a child to nurture.

Surely he must want autonomy, too. This idea would be a win-win.

"Like I always say, he's the best I've got." Jackson flashed Hank a contrite look. "Forget about the Caines. I'll supervise Doug more closely over there."

"Thanks." Hank calmly stood his ground.

In the past, she'd misjudged Hank's lack of machismo and unassuming way as weakness. But ever since the wedding, she was coming to see that Hank wasn't a pushover, not by a long shot.

Goose bumps fanned out over her skin in response to her newfound perspective, and the conference room suddenly felt like a sauna. If Hank agreed to her proposition, she'd need to suppress her longing for some kind of personal relationship. All the better, since getting intimately involved with him would mess with her head, or worse, her heart.

"Lock up, okay?" Jackson slapped his hand against the door frame twice before leaving.

Cat faced Hank once they were alone. "So, will you join me for dinner?"

"You're already overpaying me for this project, Cat." He sank back into his chair and stretched out his legs while studying her. "You don't need to humor me with a dinner."

"I'm not," she said, hedging. Her plans would take finesse, not a steamroller. "I'm too hungry to wait until I get back to the city, and I hate to eat alone. My brother did blow me off, as you saw."

He smiled. "I suspect you don't get snubbed too often."

"You Connecticut boys seem to be making a habit of it lately." She wondered if he'd pick up on the reference to his behavior on Block Island. Although grateful he didn't take advantage of her that night, part of her burned for his touch.

He stared at her, clearly considering his options. Finally he gestured toward his dirty work boots and clothes. "I need to shower first."

"Is that an invitation?" Cat lifted a single brow and waited for his reaction to the flirtatious remark, enjoying the buzz she got from teasing him.

His face filled with color before he crossed his arms in front of his chest and narrowed his gaze. Sweet warmth flowed through her veins like melted caramel. Then she remembered that, as much as she loved the flirtation, she'd have to quit it if they became partners.

"Why do you get such a kick out of taunting me?" he finally asked.

"I like the way you blush." She grinned, waiting for the appearance of the dimple on his left cheek. "Keeps you honest, and reminds me of Vivi. Neither of you hides your emotions well."

"Unlike you?" His green eyes shimmered.

"Unlike me." Her reserved mask suddenly tightened like a plastic bag, depriving her of oxygen.

"You should know something, Cat." He stood up and leaned in close, placing his palm against the conference table so his chest grazed her arm. A heady combination of testosterone and anticipation made her dizzy. "You don't hide your emotions as well as you think."

Their eyes locked for a moment, the golden flecks in his green irises blazing. To break the spell, she forced a sigh. "Now you have X-ray vision?"

"Like Superman. So you should know you're not always cloaked in lead." He dropped his gaze to her lips. "But you do surprise me now and then."

She opened her mouth to speak, then hesitated, afraid to reveal more. "So, shall I follow you home? Let's take my car to dinner since I doubt I can climb into your truck in these heels."

Hank's reaction to the sight of her four-inch-high Jimmy Choos reminded her of a *Scream* mask. She'd have scoffed, but she was too busy praying he'd accept her proposal.

Silence stretched between them while he appeared to be wrestling with the decision. Finally he tugged at his earlobe. "Fine. Follow me and think about where you want to eat."

Fifteen minutes later, Cat parked along the curb in front of a cute, beige Dutch colonial set upon an immaculately manicured, emerald-green lawn. The window boxes contained a variety of flowers and ivy. Neatly pruned boxwoods and rosebushes filled the flower beds.

Black shutters flanked each window, and the brick-red roof provided a nice contrast to the tableau. The 1950s television show scene lacked only the white picket fence. Yet it had a feminine quality she couldn't quite align with Hank, who was 100 percent male.

Hank stood beside his truck waiting for her. As she walked along the driveway, a petite blond woman jogged toward him from behind the house.

"You're late, Hank," she said. "Now *I'm* going to be late."

"Late for what?" He wrapped his arm around her shoulder and kissed the top of her head.

"Class!" She scowled until she noticed Cat halt in front of them.

Cat's mind blanked. Who was *this* pretty woman? Blond like Amy, but younger.

"Oh, hell. It's Thursday." He ran his hand through his hair. "I totally forgot, Jenny."

Jenny. Cat cleared her throat before extending her hand. If Hank had been messing around with Amy behind Jenny's back, then he wasn't the man she believed him to be. It shouldn't be a surprise, considering her lousy instincts, but her heart still deflated like a tire crossing a spike strip. "Hi, I'm Cat."

"I'm Jen." She tilted her head and narrowed her eyes. "You look familiar. Have we met?"

"No, we haven't." Cat smiled—a fortunate reflex of her career—despite her blackening mood.

"Cat is Jackson's sister. You've probably seen her in a magazine. She models clothes and stuff." Hank's nonchalant tone suggested her relative fame didn't impress him much. A novel—and welcome—experience with a man. "Cat, this is my baby sister, Jenny."

Sister. Vaguely she recalled Vivi having mentioned something last summer about Hank raising his sisters. Cat hadn't realized he still had one at home. A wave of relief crashed over her that she hadn't misjudged him.

Hank tossed Jenny his keys. "I assume Helen's gone. Is Meg available tonight?"

Jenny's eyes widened. "Are you two going out, like, on a date?"

"Not a date," Hank replied too quickly. "It's a work thing. I'm building her some furniture."

"Oh." Jenny's shoulders drooped. "Well, I have no idea if Meg is free. Give her a buzz. I've got to run. Nice to meet you, Cat."

"You, too." Cat waved as Jenny bounded into the driver's seat and backed Hank's truck out of the driveway.

"Who are Helen and Meg?" Cat smirked. "Part of a harem?"

"Hardly." Hank's expression turned somber. "Helen's a caregiver who helps with my mom. Meg's the only other one of my four sisters who lives nearby." Hank sighed. "If she's not available, I can't go out tonight."

"Why not?"

"Can't leave my mom alone." Hank rubbed his hand along his jaw as he walked toward the house. "She's got late-stage Alzheimer's."

"Oh," Cat replied, only beginning to comprehend the enormous responsibility Hank shouldered. How had she not noticed this strength sooner? "I'm really sorry, Hank. That must be hard."

"You have no idea." Then he opened the back door and waved her inside.

Mom,

If I complained to you about the fact that any admiration I've received from modeling has been distant, superficial, and based on a false perception of who I am, you'd probably wag your finger and remind me that I helped create that perception. And you'd be right.

Well, now I'd like to be admired for something real before I die. How's that for a bucket list?

Chapter Nine

Hank sensed Cat's hesitation, knowing she'd stepped into more than she'd bargained for with her simple dinner invitation. He still wasn't sure why he'd said yes.

Ever since her drunken confession on Block Island, thoughts of her messed with his head with growing frequency. The attention-seeking teasing she'd turned into an art form hypnotized him, convincing some part of his brain that she might actually be interested.

"Give me a second to track down Meg." He dialed his sister while watching Cat's eyes scan the kitchen and living room. Unlike her condo, his humble home contained nothing elegant or expensive, yet he'd worked hard for every scrap. He tried to read her thoughts, but her picture-perfect face offered no hints.

"Hey, Hank." Meg sounded harried. "What's up?"

"Can you come watch Mom tonight?"

"Sorry. I'm covering a shift until eleven."

"All right." He sighed, rubbing his forehead, frustrated. "Talk to you later."

"Maybe next time." Meg's earnest tone didn't soften the blow.

"Sure. See you this weekend." He stuffed his phone in his back pocket.

"Did you make this, too?" Cat pointed at the dining room buffet, which he'd built from mahogany and quarter-sawn sycamore. The streamlined design included a bowed profile, tapered legs, and a band of incised carving above the drawers. Although he rarely used a high-gloss lacquer, he'd opted for it on that piece. "It's really interesting."

Cat's slender fingers traced the carving instead of touching other things in the house—like him. When she glanced up, her smile shot to his heart . . . and other places. "I love the light and dark woods, and the high sheen."

"Thanks." Yanking his thoughts from the gutter, he recollected Cat's furnishings and wasn't surprised she liked the shiny topcoat. "I built it about five years ago."

"You built the dining and coffee tables, too, right?"

"How can you tell?" Most people didn't notice, let alone take an interest.

"They have a similar appeal—visually strong, yet airy, too. Clean lines," she began, then shrugged. "At least, that's what I see."

Her admiration brightened the room and his spirits. "You've got an eye for detail."

"Must be from years of studying photographs and clothing design." She then smiled broadly, lifting a framed photograph of his two-year-old nephew. "Is this you when you were young?"

"No, that's my nephew, Eddie. He does look like me, though. See?" Hank pointed at another photograph—one of him and his mother when he was three or four.

"That's uncanny." Cat set Eddie's photo down, her expression more sedate. "Do you like being an uncle?"

"Love it. Meg brings him by when she stops in to check on our mom. It's pretty cool to see family traits come out in this whole new little person. I suspect, with David and Vivi's recent marriage, you'll be an aunt soon enough." Hank chuckled to himself. "Maybe they'll get lucky and have a girl who looks like you."

Cat's halfhearted nod surprised Hank. She sighed. "Sounds like you're looking forward to fatherhood yourself."

"Some day. Boys, hopefully, to even out the odds around here."

Cat clasped her hands together, her faraway gaze momentarily taking her elsewhere. With her gaze averted, she quietly said, "You'll make a great dad." Her body language screamed "end of discussion." Didn't she like kids? Not that it should make any difference to him.

Then she snapped back to the present. "Why don't you go shower so we can eat."

"About that. I can't go out tonight. Meg's working at the hospital—she's a nurse."

"Oh." She bit her lip and looked up at him through the thick lashes of her bewitching eyes. "We could order pizza."

"You eat pizza?" The shock jerked him from his lusty haze. He'd never seen her plate filled with much more than lettuce and fruit.

"Hardly ever," she admitted. "I need a good excuse to binge on junk food. Being blown off by my brother and your getting stuck here gives me two good excuses, right?"

My God, when she grinned, he revved up like a Porsche running at full throttle. Would his longing ever subside?

"You're the boss," he answered.

A beat of silence settled between them while she appeared to weigh her next words.

"You don't like that about me, do you?" Her hurt tone singed his lungs like polyurethane fumes.

"That's the second time you've accused me of not liking you, or not liking something about you." He gripped his hips and tilted his head. "What've I ever done to give you that impression?"

"The cold shoulder last summer and at the wedding spring to mind." Cat glanced toward the candlesticks on the buffet, avoiding eye contact. Her obvious struggle to be open reminded him of David's remark about the unfortunate St. James family trait. "The way you clam up around me, like you're biding your time until you can escape."

"If anything, we had a mutual cold-shoulder thing happening last summer, which is understandable considering how you blew me off after we first met." Taking a page from Vivi's playbook, he waited for Cat to meet his gaze before continuing. "As for the wedding, you can't honestly accuse me of not caring when I went out of my way to keep you from getting hurt."

Although Hank stood three feet away from Cat, the heat they generated fused them together with some kind of invisible glue. He noticed her pulse throbbing at the base of her neck, her breath falling shallow. Only her troubled expression stopped him from kissing her.

She swallowed hard before replying. "What did you mean that morning when you said I was the reason you left my room?"

Any sense of victory he might've felt about his remark making her think these past several weeks vanished at the sight of her suffering.

Having this conversation hadn't been something he'd planned. However, his mom had always taught him an honest question deserved an honest answer.

"You like to play games and wield the upper hand." He stepped a little closer. "I don't have room in my life for games, Cat. I'm a man, not a puppet."

Cat's eyes widened and her mouth formed an *O*. Before she replied, his mother staggered into the living room with the walker, wearing her pajamas over her other clothes.

"Hey, Mom. Where are you going?"

"Rick?" His mother scowled at him. She drew back while jabbing her finger in Cat's direction. "Who?"

Her brittle voice stopped him in his tracks. Helen had mentioned his mother's more frequent angry outbursts. Of course they'd flare up now, in front of Cat.

"It's me, Mom. Hank." He held his hands up slowly and backed up. "What do you need?"

His mother clutched the fabric above her chest, still pointing at Cat. "Fssht!"

"Mom," Hank began, ignoring her inarticulate last word, then Cat interrupted.

"Mrs. Mitchell, I'm Hank's friend, Catalina." She spoke in even, calm tones. Her smile didn't falter, nor did she reveal any discomfort. "I'm so pleased to meet you."

Still, his mother's eyes narrowed into a confused scowl. "Why . . . you?" She tangled one hand into her hair and shuffled toward the kitchen. In a softer voice, she mumbled something he didn't understand.

Hank winced, avoiding Cat's gaze as he followed his mother, but Cat called to him.

"Hank, I hear something," she said. "Sounds like water."

He strained to listen while keeping an eye on his mother. The faint rush of water from an open faucet hissed from the master bedroom. "Can you check her bathroom? I'd rather not leave you alone with her to go check myself."

Cat nodded before crossing the living room and disappearing into the master bedroom. Her unruffled response to the circumstances surprised Hank, proving how little he really knew about her—things he wanted to discover.

His mother reached the kitchen, stopping at the table. She stared blankly at the refrigerator and released the fabric she'd been groping, which was now smudged with toothpaste. Her hands fell to her sides while he waited quietly.

"Mom," he whispered, his heart wrung out like a tattered dishrag. "It's me, Hank." He wet some paper towels with warm water and began wiping her hands to remove the toothpaste. "Are you hungry?"

She turned as if startled to see him and picked at her clothes, shivering.

"You're cold? Let's go change these pajamas and get you warmed up."

Like a child, she pushed her walker beside him as he led her back to her bedroom. Somewhere along the way she slipped into a trance. Once he helped her back into bed, he removed the pajamas and let her lie there in her housedress rather than risk upsetting her again. After pulling the covers up, he kissed her head.

He pinched the bridge of his nose before going to her bathroom. Cat was kneeling on the vanity—shoes tossed aside—cleaning toothpaste off the mirror with a washcloth.

She'd thrown a towel on the floor to sop up a puddle that had somehow ended up down there. Glamour girl didn't even seem put out, perched up on the sink. Silently, he grabbed another washcloth and worked alongside her to clean up the mess.

Dammit. After witnessing this little episode she'd surely bolt back to her fun, easy life. When they finished, he took the rag from her hand, picked up the soaked towel, and turned off the light. Cat quietly trailed behind him to the living room.

"I'm sorry." He threw the towels aside. "Not sure what to say except thanks for helping."

"Don't apologize, Hank. I shouldn't have just barged in on you tonight." She groped her ponytail while the look in her eyes grew distant. "I remember watching my mother wither away, but cancer never robbed her of her memory. At least she always knew who I was. I can't imagine losing that connection. I'm so sorry."

Cat's dewy eyes and compassion didn't feel anything like pity, and for that he was grateful.

"It pretty much sucks," he admitted.

Cat stepped forward and squeezed his hand in comfort.

He squeezed back, wishing he could tug her closer. "You probably want to get going now."

He smiled, hoping he didn't look disappointed as he prepared for her polite good-bye. She cocked her head, biting her lip.

"Actually, I'm starving. If you don't mind company, let's still order pizza." She withdrew her hands and tucked her thumbs inside her pockets. "Maybe you could even show me where you build furniture."

Another curveball.

She wanted to stay. Hope reached inside his chest and pumped his heart.

"Okay. Pepperoni and mushroom sound good?"

An hour later they'd finished an entire extra-large pizza. To be fair, he'd eaten ninety percent of it while she'd eaten a salad and one slice.

Now she sat with one leg tucked up under her butt and her elbows on the table. Seeing her so relaxed reminded him of how she'd behaved at Jackson's last year—the version of Cat St. James he liked best. He couldn't help but wonder if anyone other than her family, Vivi, and now him, ever had the privilege of seeing her this way.

She set her chin in her palm. "Tell me how you got involved in carpentry."

"When I was eleven, my Uncle Joe had me help him build a garden bench. After that, I worked alongside him each summer." Hank had loved those hot summer days spent woodworking while listening to classic rock, each year taking on more responsibility and more complex projects. "The last piece we built together was a desk for my aunt. It's weird to look back now and realize those skills I learned from him ended up supporting my family. And the closeness I had with my uncle softened the blow of losing my dad so young. Life can be funny that way—you never know which little decisions today will make a big difference tomorrow."

"Funny or scary, depending on your perspective." Cat leaned forward, apparently rapt. "Do you and your uncle still build things together?"

"No. He moved to Florida eight years ago, but we're still close."

"Sounds nice." She tucked her hair behind her ear. Her graceful manner made even such common gestures appear sophisticated—an unwelcome reminder of how she'd never truly fit in his mundane life. "Can I see your workshop?"

"Sure." He tossed their paper plates in the trash, hooked the video monitor to his belt, and opened the back door. "Follow me."

Anticipating her reaction to his private world chased away the sense of calm he typically experienced crossing the lawn.

Although the evening sky still shone with lilac-and-rose-tinted light, he flicked on the overhead lights in the garage. "This is it. It's not much, but—"

"This is where the magic happens," she said on a breath. Her eyes scrutinized every detail as she spun on her heel. She meandered around the small studio, touching various tools and wood planks without speaking. Moments later, she asked, "This is who you are, isn't it? This is what you love, what you want to do with your life."

"Maybe one day." He dug the toe of his right shoe into the ground and noticed he was still wearing his work boots. *Aw, hell.* In all the chaos, he'd forgotten to shower.

"Why wait?" She turned toward him wearing an enthusiastic smile. "Why not start now? Like I mentioned before, I could use my connections to help."

"You make it sound easy, but it doesn't work that way."

"What way does it work?"

"It's a slow process. A highly efficient builder might max out at around eighteen pieces per year. I can't afford all the equipment I'd need to work at that pace, and this space is too small."

"So we rent space, we buy equipment." Her unconcerned grin reminded him of Jackson, who also had no aversion to risk. Of course, unlike Hank, neither of them supported dependents. "What else?"

He chuckled until he realized she was dead serious. "Cat, what exactly are you proposing?"

She stilled, looking uncharacteristically shy for a minute. "How about a partnership, fifty-fifty? You're the talent, and I'll handle the branding and sales."

"When?" He chuckled. "In between photo shoots?"

She squared her shoulders—friendly rapport retreating behind the façade. Clearly his joke had insulted her. "You know, a lot of companies would pay *me* for my name and social reach."

"Probably, but I don't have a furniture company, so there's nothing to promote." When she didn't appear dissuaded, he pointed toward the house. "I need a steady paycheck as long as my mom's alive and Jenny's still in college."

"You've supported your family for so long. It's remarkable, actually." She casually crossed her arms and cocked her head to the left. "Don't you think that, after everything you sacrificed for them, they'd welcome the chance to return the favor?"

"It's not that simple."

"No, but nothing's impossible. Especially not when you have help. Don't you want the chance to pursue your own dreams?"

"I have a lot of dreams, Cat. Not just this one." He crossed his arms to show he was equally resolved to his position as she was to hers. "Believe me, the choices I've made have given me more than I've lost."

Her dubious expression coupled with silence forced him to defend his remark.

"My family loves and respects me thanks to the 'sacrifices' I've made. When my mom dies, I'll be at peace because of the way I've cared for her. All of it—everything I've done—has proven I'm a man who can be counted on, who doesn't walk away when things are hard. That means something to me." He looked around his shop. "I do love building furniture. But even if I had my own business and a brand worth bragging about, it wouldn't give me those other things. Trust me, I'm okay with my choices."

Cat stared at him, whether in admiration or utter bewilderment he wasn't quite sure. "Fine."

Living with five women had taught him that *fine* pretty much meant the opposite. "Why does it even matter to you, Cat? You're a hotshot model with plenty of money, so why fuss around with a little furniture shop?"

She fingered a chisel and worried her lower lip. "When I was young, my dad always bragged about David's IQ and Jackson's athleticism. He even acknowledged Vivi's artistic talent, but apparently all I had to offer was this," she swept her hand from head to toe.

Her sheepish expression kicked him in the gut, but he refrained from interrupting her. Cat St. James had chosen to confide in *him.* His heart thumped at the realization.

"When I was 'discovered,' I grabbed the opportunity to prove I could be as successful as my brothers, even if my only asset was my face. But after the initial thrill of it all, I've never gotten any real satisfaction from modeling." She sighed before continuing.

"Don't get me wrong, I'm appreciative of my career, and it's important to me. Still, I regret dropping out of college, especially now, when I'm on the downside of the industry. I want—need—a chance to reinvent myself. To discover whether there's more to me than the way I look. I assumed you'd jump at the chance to be your own boss, and figured we could help each other fulfill these needs." Cat glanced up, her expression chagrined. "You probably think I'm a whiny brat complaining about my life when, compared to yours, it's so easy."

"Quit thinking for me, Cat. You're never right." He searched her face, but she kept her gaze averted. Why couldn't she see he found *this* woman—soft, honest, thoughtful—far more appealing than the aloof "cover girl"? He stepped closer, yearning to comfort her. "You don't sound whiny. Wistful, maybe."

The heavy pulsing of his heart charged the atmosphere in the garage. As if drawn to him by the invisible thread of his need, Cat drifted within inches of his body.

"You said earlier that all I do is play games." She met his gaze, her wide eyes filled with resolve. "Well, I'm serious about this business idea, Hank. My gut is telling me this could be a great change for both of us. Before you say no, could you at least give it some thought?"

"When I accused you of playing games, I meant the personal kind. And frankly, I'm more interested in that kind of relationship than a business one." Holy shit, he said that out loud. He watched her chew on the inside of her cheek.

"Although it may not seem like it," she said, "I've always been attracted to you."

Heart in his throat now, Hank clasped her hand and stepped even closer. "Is that a yes?"

A dark shadow clouded her features. Then, as if in reflex, she regained her composure. "I'm not looking for a relationship."

"Why not?" He wondered about her ex. "Are you . . . do you miss Justin despite what happened?"

"God, no." She scowled. "I'm over him, and I hope he's over me."

"Is there a reason to think he's not?"

She hesitated long enough to rouse his suspicion. "Not exactly."

"What's that mean?"

"I'd rather not talk about it, actually." She looked away.

Instinct urged him to push, but he respected her privacy. "Okay, but you'd go to Jackson or David if he bothered you, right?"

"He won't bother me," she stated, sounding like she was trying to convince herself as much as him.

He let it go in order to steer the conversation back to the possibility of *them*. "So if there's no another guy, what's the problem? Don't you trust me?"

Her eyes grew misty, but maybe they were reacting to the dusty environment. "It's not that, Hank." She blinked twice. "I'm grateful that you're willing to overlook our past, and I'm flattered by your attention, but you don't really *know* me. I'm not who people think I am, and anyway, I think we should keep things platonic if there's any chance we could be business partners."

When he didn't answer, she chuckled. "Ah, so that's off the table, too. Don't worry. I didn't really think you'd go for it. You don't need me to do this someday. Still, I had to try."

He grabbed her hand. "Listen, Cat. No matter what your dad or anyone else thinks, I can see there's more to you than that gorgeous face. No one succeeds at your level without grit, determination, and smarts. You'll make a great business partner for someone. The timing just isn't right for me."

She looked on the verge of jumping into his arms. If his truck hadn't roared into the driveway, he would've scooped her up and carried her off right then and there.

"I should go," Cat said, her body still close to his.

"Hold on." Hank reached for her cheek, but Jenny burst into the garage.

"Oh, sorry!" Embarrassed, she turned away. "Saw the light and figured Hank was out here working."

Cat and Hank stepped apart, the moment lost. He'd grown used to the utter lack of privacy, although it irked him tonight. "It's fine, Jenny."

"I didn't mean to interrupt." Jenny swirled around and grimaced. "Don't mind me."

"I really should leave." Cat smiled at Jenny. "Long drive."

"See you inside," Hank said to Jenny before he refocused his attention on Cat. "I'll walk you to your car."

They all filed out of the garage, and Jenny headed toward the house.

Cat fell in step beside Hank. Together they meandered down the driveway in silence.

Uncertainty, and lots of other emotions, weighed on him. She liked him but didn't want a *relationship*. If he proposed something more casual, would she go for it? He'd never been one for flings, but given her mercurial nature, maybe it would work better that way. No matter how much he wanted to resist her, she was an itch he needed to scratch.

Cat unlocked the car with her remote, so Hank stepped ahead and opened the door for her. Before sliding into the seat, she turned and touched his arm. He liked her touch—wanted more. He covered her hand with his, enjoying the stirring sensations rippling up his forearm.

Her face brightened unexpectedly. "When will you be starting on my armoires?"

"I think I'll come on Monday. Need to pick up the wood and do some rough cutting this weekend. Once I start, I'll still need to spend a few hours out here now and then to oversee Jackson's projects."

"He relies on you that much?"

Hank nodded.

"Jackson values loyalty." She looked down the street and then at him. "One last thought before I go. You might be an amazing finish carpenter, but in that profession you're still replaceable, right? There are hundreds, maybe thousands, of carpenters in Connecticut that Jackson could hire. On the other hand, your exceptional talent for furniture design—that's not replaceable. It's a gift you shouldn't squander."

Is that what he'd been doing—squandering his talent?

He didn't like that perception one bit, but like a drop of poison in a body of water, it seeped throughout his mind.

Maybe for Cat, throwing a little money and effort to test the waters wasn't a big deal, but Hank didn't have that luxury. Failure could be catastrophic to his family's future. Then again, her proposal was a once-in-a-lifetime offer. Could it work?

"You're determined to tempt me, aren't you?" And oh, did she ever.

"How am I doing?"

Pretty well, considering he hadn't shot it down completely, at least not in his own mind.

"Tell you what, I'll give your idea some more thought." He glanced back at his house briefly, trying to envision a different life.

"You will?" She lit up. "Consider yourself warned, Hank. Next time you see me, you won't know what hit you."

He almost laughed, because he already felt that way whenever he saw her. A mixture of hope and doubt brewed in his stomach.

Mom,

I think you'd really like Hank. He's open, like you. Even with a life full of adversity, he isn't hardened or resentful. He's forgiving, earnest, reliable, fair . . .

He deserves good things now—big and small—and I'm going to make sure he gets them.

Chapter Ten

Despite Hank's protests yesterday afternoon, he caught up with Jackson on-site at the Caine's house. Jackson had been a great boss and friend for years, and Hank knew his friend needed his help. Or perhaps he just had a guilty conscience because he'd spent all night considering Cat's crazy idea.

While discussing the installation of the final touches in the kitchen, he noticed dark circles beneath Jackson's eyes. "Jackson, you look like shit. You need some sleep."

"I'm fine." Jackson rubbed his right hand over one side of his face. "You're one to talk, anyway. When's the last time you got enough sleep?"

"That's different. I'm on call twenty-four seven, but at least when I do sleep, I'm sober." He rested his hands on his hips and kept his gaze on Jackson.

"Don't start again." Jackson raised his hand to stop Hank's lecture. "You never complained when you were hanging out as my wingman. Now I can't remember the last time we went out for a beer."

"It's been a while," Hank admitted. "But I'm not interested in drinking or chasing skirt. My mom's health has been in a free fall the past six months. It's getting more risky to leave Jenny in charge."

"Sorry, buddy. The situation with your mom sucks, but all the more reason you need a woman to help take the edge off." Jackson flashed a devilish smile. "Come on. Come out with me this weekend."

"I've got plans this weekend." Hank tilted his head. "Have to start working on your sister's project."

"I wish I hadn't needed that favor, but I worry about her. You get that—right—you've got sisters. Still, thanks for helping. I owe you big time."

"Don't worry, it's fine." When he recalled how Cat had looked at him in his garage, he couldn't stop a grin from forming. "More than fine."

That last comment slipped out before Hank remembered Jackson wasn't just a friend, he was also Cat's brother.

"Oh?" Jackson's newly alert eyes bored into Hank's. "Are you interested in my sister?"

"Is that really a surprise?" Hank's neck grew hot.

"You'd think after David fell for Vivi, nothing could surprise me. Seems I was wrong." Jackson rubbed his chin, offering no particular encouragement.

"You think I'm not good enough for her?" If Jackson objected, it would crush him.

"Hell, Hank, you're the best guy I know. She couldn't do better." Jackson crossed his arms in front of his chest and sighed. "That, however, might be the problem. How can I put this? Her past boyfriends all took as long as she does to get dressed, and spent a lot of money jetting her to exciting places—you know, assholes like Justin."

"Maybe she's learned her lesson."

"Maybe, but are you two compatible? Her life's full of pseudo-friends and parties, and all that Instagram and Twitter bullshit. I can't picture her hanging out with you in Norwalk every weekend."

"You're talking about her like she's shallow."

"No, she's not shallow. She's got a big heart, even though she hides it from most people." Jackson rubbed the back of his neck. "Fuck it. What the hell do I know? If she's interested, then take her at her word."

"I never said *she* was interested." Hank's muscles tightened in defense of the onslaught of unwelcome, if well-intentioned, advice.

Jackson grinned. "Oh boy, I've been down this road with friends before—many times. Shit, Hank, something tells me you're heading for trouble." Jackson chuckled. "I've got no advice for you, either. She's my sister and I love her to death, but she's no cakewalk. Cat's like a hedgehog, you need to handle her the right way or she's damn prickly."

"Doesn't matter. Chances are nothing will come of it anyway."

"Stranger things have happened. Look at David." Jackson slapped Hank's shoulder. "Let's get out of here. I've got places to be."

~

When Hank finally arrived at Cat's on Monday after a hellish commute to Manhattan, he double-parked to quickly unload his truck, leaving Cat's doorman to guard his supplies while he went to find parking. Once he returned, he loaded the tools and planks of wood onto a dolly, which he rolled into the service elevator. He parked the squeaky cart at her door and knocked.

No answer. He knocked again and listened for footsteps. Still no answer.

What the hell? He checked his watch. Eight o'clock. She'd known he was coming today.

Behind him, Esther opened her door. "When I heard someone in the hall, I looked through my peephole. What a nice surprise to find you outside my door."

"Good morning, Mrs. Morganstein." He smiled at her blatant perusal of his person. "You wouldn't happen to know where Catalina is, would you?"

"She usually runs in the morning, but I'm sure she'll be right back if she knows you're coming. She's very excited for you to begin."

"Desperate for storage space."

"Oh, I don't think that's the only reason she's in a good mood lately." Esther winked.

Another matchmaker in the mix. Could everyone be conspiring?

Before he could respond, Cat strode off the elevator, humming whatever song was playing on her iPhone.

Short, black spandex shorts and a neon-pink jog bra barely covered her body. A thick white headband kept her hair off her face. The rest of her silky hair was pulled high into a ponytail.

She saw them and waved cheerily, oblivious to his frustration and, admittedly, fascination. Her skin gleamed with sweat and he could see the muscles in her legs and abs contract as she moved toward him.

Hot damn. Temptation weighed heavily.

"Good morning!" She smiled as she pulled the earbuds from her ears. "I didn't realize you'd be here this early. Hi, Esther. Do you need something?"

"No, dear. I'm just keeping this handsome young man company. I'll leave you to it, now." She smiled and closed the door.

"She wants you baaad!" Cat giggled while unlocking the various dead bolts. Hank couldn't stop staring at her tight ass. "Come on in."

"Thanks." Hank followed behind her, pulling the dolly into her entry and then closing the door. He focused on the task at hand in order to avoid slamming her against the wall and peeling off those wet clothes. "I'll be getting here early each day, so we should work something out if you won't be here to let me in."

"Okay. Maybe I should get you a key?" She looked at the pile of wood and clasped her hands together, oblivious to the fact she had him hot and bothered without even trying. "I can't wait for you to get started."

Hank pulled the dolly toward her bedroom, which she'd emptied in preparation for his arrival.

"I'll cover the vents to cut down on sawdust traveling throughout the condo."

"Okay, thanks. Now I really need to shower." She winked at him and strode into the master bathroom, closing the door behind her.

Hank stared at the door, imagining her stripping out of those skimpy clothes, wishing he actually did have the X-ray vision she'd teased him about last week.

What would she do if he slipped into the shower and helped her wash those hard-to-reach places? Hell, he'd just managed to give himself one of his bigger hard-ons. Shaking his head in frustration, he unloaded the dolly and took it back down to the lobby.

When he returned, he nearly bumped into her as she came out of her room wearing nothing more than a towel. The sight and scent of her nearly naked body almost knocked him flat on his ass.

"You're blushing, Hank." Cat stood still, her long hair hanging heavy and wet down her back.

Either his imagination was working overtime, or she was planning to get him so turned on he'd agree to anything, including her business proposal. He didn't know which made him more irritated, her plan or the fact that it could work.

"As I'm sure you intended." Two could play her game. Her goal might have been only business, but his was personal. He brushed his finger along the length of her arm until she trembled. "You're shivering," he whispered in her ear, lingering there for a moment without saying more. Then he pulled back. "Go get dressed and let me get to work."

She stared at his mouth before disappearing into the guest room. Hank smiled and then shackled his strong urge to chase her down and toss her on the bed. Mutual lust was a weak substitute for what he really wanted, and what he wanted was probably as far-fetched as her business plans.

Deep down he couldn't shake the feeling he'd only get close enough to get his heart ripped out.

Get to work.

~

By noon, Cat had popped in at least four times to check on him. She'd offered him something to eat or drink, asked if it was too hot or too cold for him, and even commented on his musical taste.

Her minidress covered no more than the damned towel, and she made sure to come close and bend and twist right near his body. Each interruption cost him at least ten minutes in daydreams before he could refocus. So it didn't surprise him at all when she came through the door again.

"Lunch break?" She leaned against the doorjamb.

"Already?" Hank surveyed how little he'd accomplished that morning.

"Come on." Her knee swung side to side while she spoke. "I have some surprises for you."

More mouthwatering than an icy beer on a sweltering day.

"Okay, I'll take a quick break." Hank set his hand plane down and grabbed his lunch bag.

"You won't need that. I have something better." She summoned him with her pointer finger and wicked grin. "Follow me."

Like a lemming, he trailed after her, trying and failing to tamp down his anticipation of her next ploy. A tangy aroma wafted down the hallway as he drew nearer to the kitchen. Barbeque? Cat stood by a kitchen chair and gestured toward the pile of ribs in the center of the table. "Voilà!"

"My favorite," he uttered with surprise then looked at her. "How'd you know?"

"You mentioned it last summer."

"Did I?" And she remembered? That had to mean something. He noticed coleslaw, corn bread, and a cold beer on the table. "Cat, this is really thoughtful. I didn't know you cooked."

"I don't cook!" She laughed. "But I'm a real whiz with takeout. Now sit."

She went to the sink and returned to the table with a glass of water.

"Guess you're not going to help me eat this Fred Flintstone–size portion of ribs?" He plucked a few off the pile and put them on his plate.

"I'm meeting Vivi for a late lunch, but trust me, passing on those ribs is not a sacrifice." She shook her head and drank her water. "Now, if your favorite food were chocolate mousse cake, then I'd be tempted."

"Duly noted." He wasted no time digging into lunch. As he licked his fingers, he asked, "Why all this, Cat?"

"Because you're always taking care of others." She dipped her forefinger into a dollop of extra barbeque sauce and tasted it with a slow lick. *Oh, yeah.* He wanted some of that. He eyed the barbeque sauce and quickly thought up a few creative uses. She dipped her finger in the sauce again. "I thought you should know how it feels to have someone look after you."

Dazed, he had to drag his gaze away from the finger in her mouth and take an extra few seconds to process her response. "It feels really good."

His remark earned him a gigantic smile, which flipped his heart over a time or two. Hell and damnation, Jackson was right. He was in trouble.

He ate quickly so he could get back to work.

"This was a real treat. Thanks. But honestly, don't put yourself out on my account." He tossed the bones in the garbage and rinsed his plate. "I should get back to work."

"Hold on. I have one more thing to show you. Can you sit for five more minutes?"

He did as he was asked while she pulled a sheet of paper from her fancy purse. She laid it in front of him and asked, "What do you think of this name?"

A walnut-brown rectangle read: "Mitchell/St. James, handcrafted fine furnishings," written in a modern, golden-yellow font.

He stared at her, unsure how to respond.

She eyed the paper again. "Once you promised to consider this, I got a burst of creative energy. All weekend I kept thinking of a name to convey upscale, unique furniture while also taking advantage of whatever cache my 'name brand' lends. But it didn't seem right to focus solely on my name because *you're* the designer. Then it hit me . . . our names work nicely together, and as the talent, you get top billing."

Her excited smile wormed its way inside his chest. The slightest encouragement from him had prompted that joy and confidence. How could he snatch it away now?

"They sure do." Seeing their names blended together brought to life a bunch of other unrealistic fantasies.

"That's not all. Once this brand becomes very chichi, we could expand to mass manufacturing knockoffs. We could call that line 'CT Chic' to capitalize on the whole New England thing people love. At that point, the revenue potential would grow significantly."

"Wow. You're jumping way ahead." Her contagious enthusiasm hooked him a little, but hers were huge dreams, and none of them addressed the risks. "There are still a whole lot of questions to answer before this idea gets off the ground."

She withdrew the paper and shot him a disappointed scowl before smacking him with a sarcastic, "No kidding."

"I'm not belittling you, but these ideas sound expensive. And I'm only one guy. There's a limit to what I can produce, which I can't imagine can actually support you, me, and my family."

"All of that can be worked out. Maybe I just take enough to cover my costs in the beginning or something, or offer internships to apprentices or whatever to help you work. Meanwhile, I could start to spread the word among my close friends, with the goal of growing a wealthy clientele—maybe even approach some upscale boutique inns and retail clients who want a specialty display table or armoires or something." Cat looked triumphant. "We'd keep prices high by being selective at first. Create buzz and mystique, then once we'd established a reputation and an amazing portfolio, *then* we'd launch the affordable furniture line."

"You don't lack ambition." He chuckled before turning sober. "Your confidence is contagious, but the devil is in the details. Can I do this without risking my family's stability? They count on my paycheck, and I sure don't have any money to invest. If I were on my own, I'd be all-in in a heartbeat. But I don't see how this works for me right now."

Cat leaned forward, undaunted. "In just ten years, Kathy Ireland expanded her brand from a line of socks to a multiline empire that grosses two billion in sales annually. If she can do *that*, surely *we* can build this idea into a business that generates enough income to comfortably support us both."

"She's clearly the exception, though, not the rule." Hank rubbed his jaw. "Didn't you hear me tell you I've got about a twenty-item cap on what I can build in a year?"

Her smart-ass expression—similar to a look his sister Meg often shot him—warned him he was about to be corrected.

"I read a series of in-depth articles about two guys who did exactly what I'm proposing. Something Chang . . . Hellman. Hellman-Chang. One guy handled marketing; the other started building tables after work and on weekends. In just a couple of years, they've got an eight-thousand-square-foot facility and other artisans to help them churn out handmade furniture for small hotels and stuff." She sank back in her chair. "Besides, you *said* you'd keep an open mind."

"An open mind doesn't mean I'll close my eyes to the risks. Maybe you can't appreciate that because you've only got yourself to worry about. Actually, have you even thought about how your brother will feel if I walk out on him to join forces with you?"

"Jackson will be pissed for a while, but he'll replace you and life will go on. Trust me, our dad made sure we all understood the way of the world. I can't tell you how often he repeated 'no one owes you anything. You've got to work for what you want and *make* it happen.' So, I promise, Jackson will understand and forgive us both for chasing our dreams."

When Hank didn't respond immediately, she continued. "Unless this isn't your dream? Maybe I misread you?"

"No, you didn't."

"So what's the problem? I'd think you'd be more excited. Don't *you* believe in your work? Or are you afraid to fail?"

"I can't *afford* to fail because it would hurt the people I love."

She pressed her lips together, clearly disturbed.

"You mustn't have meant anything you said about me in your garage, because if you did, then you wouldn't be convinced we'd fail." The hurt in her eyes about killed him. She stood abruptly and set her glass in the sink, ready to bolt from the kitchen. "You probably thought you were being nice, but I wish you would've just been honest, like everyone else who thinks I can't do anything other than pose for the camera."

He clutched her arm to stop her. "That's not what I think. All I'm saying is we're in completely different situations and this huge undertaking has tons of complications and risks."

Like every time they touched, a shock of energy zipped through his limbs. She must've been struck, too, because her breath caught.

Collecting herself, she issued a challenge. "Maybe you should stop thinking about the risks and focus on the opportunities."

She dragged her gaze from his mouth to his eyes and held it there, linking him in her intensifying energy.

Before it ebbed, he hauled her closer to deliver his own dare. "I could say the same thing to you about relationships, Cat."

Her pupils dilated, and she tried to shrink from his grasp. *Not this time.* Cupping the back of her neck, he bent down to nibble on her bottom lip before drawing her into a soft kiss.

He deepened the kiss to stoke the flames of whatever might be developing between them, savoring the thrum reverberating throughout his body, the thud of her heartbeat against her chest, the urgent mewl in her throat as their tongues intensified their probing exploration.

Cradling her face with his hands, he pressed himself against her until he pinned her against the counter. She moaned into his mouth, but then pushed him away.

"Hank, stop. I told you, I'm not looking to date."

That kiss only made him more determined to have her, even if that meant resorting to a fling.

"I'll tell you what." He crossed his arms across his chest. "I'll seriously consider your business proposal on two conditions."

She gripped the counter behind her. "Which are?"

"First, do more homework while I'm busy working on your closets. I have to reduce the risk to my mom and Jenny in order to move forward *now*."

"Done." She nodded.

"Second, give this," he said, gesturing between them, "some kind of shot."

Her shoulders sagged. "Why won't you believe me when I tell you I don't want a relationship?"

"A casual fling works for me." Hank shrugged, calling her bluff. "It's not like I've got time for a serious commitment, Cat. You've seen all the demands in my life, which will only get worse if we actually start Mitchell/St. James."

Her eyes widened and she hesitated. "Wouldn't it be a bad idea to be in business *and* bed together?"

"A second ago you told me to quit focusing on the risks. Did you mean it, or were you just trying to get your way?"

She glanced out the small kitchen window, hands on her hips. "Let me think about it. Right now I need to catch up with Vivi."

"You got it." Hank strode across the kitchen. "I'll be in your bedroom if you need me."

Mom,

I need your advice, because I don't know what to do. Last night I dreamed about Hank dressed in the suit he wore at the wedding. He was standing on the Spring House lawn, near the sea, his hands on his hips, the wind tousling his hair. He glanced over his shoulder and saw me—really saw me—but then I woke up in a cold sweat.

Chapter Eleven

Cat waved at Vivi, who waited beneath the burgundy awning of Candle 79. "Am I late?"

If so, she blamed Hank for putting her in a stupor with his enticing suggestion and that wicked-hot kiss. She needed to get a hold of herself before her preoccupation with him ruined the pleasant get-together she'd planned with Vivi.

"Nope." Vivi opened the restaurant door. "I'm early."

A waiter seated them at a two-top table in front of the wall of wood-framed glass doors that offered a street view. When Vivi scanned the menu, the creases in her forehead became more pronounced with each available selection.

"All vegetarian?" She peered over the top of her menu. "The portions better be huge, or I'm going to need to stop for pizza on my way home."

"The food is awesome, V. I promise you won't leave hungry." Then again, Vivi's bottomless pit of a stomach did prefer quantity to quality.

"You eat salad without dressing. Sorry, but I don't give your opinion about food much *weight*." Vivi stared at the menu another minute before setting it down. She rested her chin atop her clasped hands and tossed Cat a sly smile. "So, how's your armoire project coming along?"

"Hank started construction today." A brief flashback of their kiss shot another blast of heat to Cat's cheeks.

"Ah ha!" Vivi's eyes widened with excitement. "Something happened. Tell me!"

Much as Cat could fool most people with a pretense of indifference, she'd rarely managed to fool Vivi. No use trying to do so today.

"I don't suppose you'd take no for an answer." Cat feigned boredom, enjoying building Vivi's anticipation to the point of explosion.

Vivi leaned across the table. "Oh, this must be good. And you're right, I won't stop asking until you spill it."

"I propositioned Hank," Cat began, only to be interrupted by Vivi's gasp and excited clapping. "Not a sexual proposition, a *business* one."

Vivi's smile collapsed into a confused frown. "That was *not* the goal of my grand plan, Cat."

Cat coyly swirled her wineglass in the air. "I keep warning you not to play matchmaker."

Vivi's disheartened sigh practically blew out the candle on the table. "So what's this business proposal?"

After Cat explained her general idea, she waited to be peppered with well-intentioned questions designed to point out all its flaws.

"Actually, that's an awesome idea." Vivi smiled while picking at the edamame. "He's gifted, you're savvy and sophisticated. A perfect union of talents. In fact, I'll be your first customer. I'd love a custom dining table."

Cat chuckled, realizing she should've expected the unexpected from Vivi. Her friend's enthusiasm temporarily buoyed her own until she remember Hank's less-than-committed outlook.

"Well, I didn't say Hank agreed." She absently pressed her fingers to her lips, remembering their kiss.

Vivi's bright smile inverted to another deep scowl. "What's the problem?"

"Where to start? His financial obligations to his family, loyalty to Jackson, our lack of business experience and industry knowledge . . ." As she recited the long list of obstacles, she wrinkled her nose. Maybe he had a tiny point.

Cat could see the wheels turning inside Vivi's head before her friend set her elbows on the table and narrowed her eyes in determination. "Surely there are solutions. So the real question is how will you change his mind?"

Vivi could always make Cat laugh, even when she didn't mean to. "Well, he's entertaining the idea, but he's also asked me to consider a more personal relationship."

Vivi's tiny body shook as she drummed her feet on the floor in exultation. "I knew it! I *knew* you two had unfinished business. This is exactly the push you need. See? I'm glad I sent him to your apartment that day." She made a show of patting herself on the back. "You can thank me with chocolate or cheesecake."

"Don't go getting your hopes up. *If* I agree, the most I'd consider would be a very casual, no-strings kind of thing. I know you don't believe me, V, but I'm not looking for love."

The waiter interrupted them to take their lunch order. After he left, Vivi began her inquisition. "Are you attracted to Hank?"

"Who isn't attracted to Hank?"

"Don't dodge. What I'm asking is, are *you* interested in a personal relationship with him?"

"It's crossed my mind." A hundred times or more, but that confession could be omitted.

"For how long?" Vivi thrust her pointer finger toward Cat. "Be honest!"

"I suppose since your wedding, when he saved me from making a big mistake—which I don't wish to discuss." Cat's quelling glance caused Vivi to fall still. "I've gotten to know him better—his history, his family, his strength. He makes me feel like maybe he wouldn't be disappointed that I'm nothing like the sex symbol splashed all over the magazines. Like maybe being myself would be good enough."

"Being myself is exactly how I've always been with David. He appreciates me and all my quirks." Vivi's eyes sparkled with happy tears. "So, then, why limit yourself to a casual fling?"

"I doubt *any* fling is a good idea if we go into business together. It will only add complications. My life doesn't need more complications." She debated telling Vivi about her condition. Finally speaking about it with someone would be one step toward better accepting reality. She shifted in her chair, twitchy from her secret.

"Lots of couples run businesses together, so that excuse doesn't fly." Vivi huffed before sipping her iced tea. "Has Justin completely soured you on relationships?"

"No. It's not about Justin." Cat swallowed a gulp of wine to settle her nerves. She set the glass on the table and tapped her fingers in emphasis. "This is about me being realistic. Trust me, my future's better served if I focus on work."

Vivi clasped Cat's hand. "Five years from now, which will be more meaningful, your career or a life and family with a man you love?"

"Not everyone can be like you and David. And who says I could love Hank, or he could love me?" She withdrew her hand from Vivi's grasp, her mind replaying the family element of Vivi's question. "But if I *could* love him, it would be kinder to turn him down."

"You're not making any sense." Vivi pulled a lemon face.

Cat hesitated. Revealing her news in public was a gamble, but it would ensure the conversation didn't drag on endlessly. *Do it.* "I want to tell you something, but I don't want your pity."

"When have I ever pitied you?" Vivi asked. "And why do you sound so ominous? Does David know whatever this is you're about to tell me?"

"No. No one knows. I'm not even sure I should tell you, actually, and I know I'm not ready to tell my family."

"More secrets?" She sat forward, eyes alert. "Did you get more of those darn letters?"

"It's got nothing to do with that." Cat frowned at the reminder of that troublesome topic. It had been a few weeks since the last letter, which meant it was only a few weeks longer until Justin's restraining order expired. Coincidence? Cat stifled a shiver and returned to the subject at hand. "Promise you won't make a scene or tell David?"

"I'm sure I'll regret this, but yes, I promise." Vivi chewed her lip. "But this is my last secret from David. I love you, but he's my husband. Things are different now."

"Fair enough." She'd known Vivi's love for David would eventually eclipse their friendship, as it should. Cat drew a long breath and exhaled slowly. "Remember how I'd been complaining about skipping all those periods after I went off the pill, but I still felt all PMS-y?"

"Because of the stress surrounding the fallout of Justin's criminal case."

"I wish it were something that minor." She mindlessly refolded the napkin on her lap, buying time. "Unfortunately, it's not, and there's no cure."

"No cure? Are you sick?" Vivi's eyes immediately filled with tears. "Is it serious . . . is it cancer?"

"No, I don't have cancer." Cat smiled wryly. "I'll be hounding you for years to come."

"Oh, thank God." Vivi pressed her fingers to her temples. "What, then?"

"Basically, it's early menopause." Cat took another breath, feeling surprisingly calm despite sharing her secret. "Given my family history with breast cancer, I was a little leery of the hormone replacement therapy, but at the specialist's urging, I decided to take it and vitamin D, and will have to watch out for heart disease and put up with hot flashes and skin changes and all that stuff about twenty-five years ahead of schedule. The kicker, of course, is my chances of getting pregnant are pretty much zero."

Vivi closed her eyes and inhaled slowly. Tears threatened to form behind Cat's eyes, but she blinked them into submission.

Vivi opened her eyes, placed her hands in her lap, and looked solemnly at Cat. "But not entirely zero? Could you freeze eggs and do IVF later?"

"The recommended course would be to use a donor egg. It's complicated and overwhelming to think about. Pointless, really, considering I'm not even in love and planning a family."

"Premature, maybe, but not pointless," Vivi began cautiously. "This diagnosis doesn't mean you can't have kids, Cat. There are plenty of ways to build a family. And science is always making advances. Why not preserve all your options?"

"No, V. I've had time to think about it from every angle. I might feel differently if I were in a serious relationship. But I'm alone, and I don't want to chase pipe dreams. That's a recipe for ongoing heartbreak. It hurts less to simply accept this future."

"You've known for a while?" Vivi cried. "Why didn't you tell me sooner?"

"I wanted to celebrate your wedding without you feeling sorry for me or feeling guilty about being happy." Vivi's helpless expression triggered another wave of tears. Cat dabbed at her eyes. "Please, Vivi. Not everyone needs marriage and kids to be happy. But now you see why someone as family oriented as Hank isn't the guy for me."

"Hank doesn't strike me as a guy who'd leave a woman he loved because she couldn't have children."

"Well, we'll never find out. After the lifetime he's spent sacrificing for others, I'm sure not going to be the one to ask him to give up something so fundamental." Cat toyed with her fork. "Honestly, I can't imagine asking *any* man to do that. I'd feel like I robbed him of something sacred, and I'd always wonder if he regretted it."

"I don't know what to say to that, except I disagree. A man who loves you will feel blessed to be with you, not robbed of anything. Many, *many* women face this situation, and most of them find good men and have happy families. Don't be a martyr or avoid the chance of love out of fear." Vivi reached both hands across the table and grabbed Cat's.

"I bet most other women in my shoes were probably in serious relationships before they discovered they couldn't have kids. That's different from knowing in advance. Now I'll have to decide when to spring the news on a new boyfriend—right away, after the first 'I love yous,' when a ring is offered?" Cat sighed, weary from riding the tides of emotion. "A no-strings policy suits my St. James nature. It gives me all the benefits of a relationship while avoiding any awkwardness and disappointment."

Cat withdrew, intending her tone to shut down the discussion in the hopes her churning stomach would settle. It had been difficult enough to share her diagnosis, let alone having to defend her feelings or, God forbid, consider sharing them with others. This was *her* pain. Regardless of what other people said or thought, Cat sure as hell had the right to her own feelings about *her* situation. About *her loss.* She alone would fashion a life around it.

Vivi, however, ignored the warning and issued one of her own.

"I doubt you can avoid heartache by isolating yourself." She shot Cat an arch look. "And by the way, your plan leaves out the most important benefit of any relationship—love."

Cat welcomed the interruption of the delivery of their lunches. Vivi scrutinized her quinoa concoction with a skeptical eye while Cat stabbed at her vegetables.

Love. *Ha! Can't miss something I never had.* On the other hand, she might as well engage in a fun fling with Hank. It was risky, but that kiss was pretty convincing. Surely if they set ground rules, sex wouldn't hurt their business relationship. As for all the rest of it, there'd be plenty of time to worry about that later.

Reassured by her own conclusion, she looked at Vivi and changed the subject. "Speaking of love, what's up with you and my dear brother?"

~

Hank walked into the Caine's entry at seven in the morning, chugging the rest of the coffee in his thermos.

"You need to recut that, Doug." Hank pointed at the two sections of crown molding. "They aren't perfectly aligned."

"No one but you would notice." With a huff, Doug crossed his arms. "The home owners aren't going to climb up on ladders or pull out measuring tapes over a millimeter."

Hank shook his head. Doug, who looked to be in his early twenties, was a bit too lazy for Hank's taste. Jackson had impulsively hired two extra crewmen, then stuck Hank with honing Doug's work to meet his standards.

"Look, your job is to make it damned near perfect. They might not know why something doesn't look quite right, but if you get a little sloppy here and there, the overall effect will be visible. Besides, Jackson will inspect and notice. If you want to keep this job and build a reliable reputation, take more pride in your work product."

"Shit, Hank. You sound like my dad." Doug shook his head in disgust and picked up the moldings. "Why are you here, anyway? I thought you were working on some 'special project' for Jackson's sister. How'd you pull that lucky gig? Bet there are some fringe benefits to working at her place."

"How 'bout you concentrate on your job instead of worrying about mine. I don't have time to deal with bullshit rumors." Hank continued his inspection of the woodwork in the entry. "I also don't have time to micromanage you."

"Who asked you to?" Doug spat. "I'm good at my job."

"You've got promise, but consider losing the attitude." Hank rested his hands on his hips. "Jackson's fair and can be a hell of a generous employer, but he's exacting. Besides, this crew is a team, so don't screw over your teammates by trying to cut corners. In the end, everyone will lose."

"Fine." Doug rolled his eyes before lowering his safety glasses and turning his back on Hank. "I'll refit the damned moldings."

"Good." Hank turned and walked out the front door.

The summer sun pounded on his shoulders as he crossed the lawn to the driveway. Before he reached his truck, Jackson pulled up. His sunglasses couldn't hide the deep lines carved around his eyes and mouth, which revealed a high level of exhaustion, and probably a hangover to boot.

"Hey, Jackson. Didn't expect to see you here this early."

"Doug and Ray need a big push. We've got to finish this job and move forward at the Hudson's house," Jackson said as he slammed his door shut. "With you rotating out of the team for a few weeks, it's going to be a little rough."

Hank shrugged. How many times could he say "I warned you" without sounding like an ass? "I'll finish Cat's work as quickly as possible."

"Oh, I doubt that." Jackson flashed a teasing smile. "I haven't forgotten about your crush on my baby sister. I'm a guy, too, you know, so it's a safe bet all the 'distractions' will make you less efficient than normal. Don't pretend you'll be dying to race back here to Doug and me."

Jackson chuckled at his own joke.

Eager to change the subject before Jackson discovered exactly how much Hank hoped to be distracted by Cat, he glanced back toward the house. "Speaking of Doug, I already talked with him about the entry, so don't go in there with guns blazing. He won't respond well to your 'shout first, ask questions later' method. It's going to take a few go-rounds, but I'll up his game."

Jackson nodded thoughtfully. "How about Ray? Is he almost finished rewiring the overhead lighting in the kitchen? He's behind by at least two days. I don't know what the hell is going on."

"Well, your schedule is aggressive." Hank sighed. "It's getting a little better, but these guys are new to these projects."

"You're too soft, Hank." Jackson scratched his head. "They need to do their jobs. No excuses."

Jackson's attitude certainly did mirror the St. James mantra Cat had mentioned. Their dad had ensured his kids would be independent and successful, but at what personal cost? Somehow Vivi had broken through David's defenses, but it had taken her more than a dozen years. Who would work that hard and wait that long for Jackson, or Cat? Because as much as she fascinated him, Hank couldn't imagine spending years butting his head against a brick wall if it never showed signs of cracking.

"Where are you heading?" Jackson asked when he realized Hank had moved to his truck.

"Your sister's place." Hank tossed the thermos through the open window, onto the passenger seat.

"Damn. I should've listened to you." Jackson spit in the grass and shook his head. "She's always talking me into things that come back to bite me."

Hank grinned, no longer minding Cat's manipulative streak. "That's what sisters do, Jackson."

"All kidding aside, wrap things up down there as fast as possible. You're my best employee, Hank. I can't survive too long without you." Jackson slapped Hank's shoulder before wandering inside, unaware his compliment heaped a boatload of guilt on Hank's shoulders for even considering Cat's crazy business idea.

If he did green-light her plans, it would put Jackson in a hell of a spot. He shuddered at the thought of how much further Jackson might sink if handed that news.

Mom,

Maybe I'm being foolish, but I woke up feeling hopeful. It's not the idealized life you would've wanted for me, but I can be happy in a business partnership and breezy affair with a sexy, talented man. That's more than many enjoy. So I choose to be grateful rather than wistful.

And now I can keep my secret, because a casual affair doesn't obligate me to tell Hank the truth.

Chapter Twelve

As soon as Cat answered her door, Hank noticed her fidgety hands and caffeinated gaze.

"Sorry I'm late." He stepped inside. "Stopped by one of Jackson's projects before coming down."

"That's fine." A tentative smile spread across her face.

"Mind if I grab some bottled water?"

She gestured toward the kitchen and then followed closely behind him, practically skipping. He unscrewed the cap and took a swig, squinting at her. "What's up? You're a bundle of energy today."

Clasping her hands in front of her body, she swayed side to side. "I've been considering your conditions."

"Have you?" His body flushed with prickly heat. He set the bottle on the counter. "Are you about to dazzle me with facts and figures already?"

"No."

Deep disappointment pierced his heart, like a pin to a balloon. Foolishly, he'd dared to hope she'd agree—that like him, she'd been overcome with longing. "Well, it's probably for the best. Maybe in a few years the timing will be better for this business idea."

"Oh, you misunderstand." She wet her lips and stepped closer. "I'm accepting your terms, but I'm not nearly done researching. I am, however, prepared to 'dazzle you' with that second condition."

"You are?"

"I am."

He blinked in disbelief, even as his heart galloped in anticipation. "But what if we can't agree about the business risks? Maybe we should wait . . ."

Absolutely *not* what he wanted, yet he had to make sure she was ready to take this step.

"I don't want to wait." She boldly met his stunned gaze.

His feet wouldn't move. In fact, his whole system seemed to be shutting down from shock.

"Hank?" She tilted her head, peering curiously at his frozen body. "Please don't tell me you've changed your mind. I really can't start my day with a serving of humiliation."

Without speaking, he reached for her face with both hands and then claimed her mouth with his own. Her hands caressed his shoulders before her fingers threaded into his hair. Every inch of his skin tingled in response to her touch.

The room around them fell away as he became absorbed by the citrusy taste of her mouth. Euphoria spread through him like helium, lifting his heart, making him weightless.

This woman he fiercely desired wanted him, too. This moment—the truth of it—seemed as beautiful yet fragile as porcelain. Something his calloused hands could easily break if mishandled. But the scent of her hair and soft skin beneath his fingers made him anything but careful.

A groan rumbled in his chest. Without breaking contact, he kissed her harder, his tongue engaged in heated dance with hers, his arms squeezing her tighter against his body. He acted on pure instinct, couldn't think, didn't really know what he was touching, but needed to feel every gorgeous inch of her body.

"Cat," he growled as he tore his mouth away and dragged it down the length of her neck. Appreciative little noises coming from deep in her throat heightened his arousal. He slid his hands down to her waist and then cupped her bottom, tugging her against his raging erection. "I want you so much. *So* much."

She inched her leg up his, wrapping it around his thigh. "No one's stopping you."

He hoisted her onto the counter raining unapologetic, hungry kisses on her mouth and neck. His hands grasped her knees and skimmed beneath her skimpy dress, making him dizzy with anticipation. She thrust her hips forward, seeking his touch, lighting him on fire. He couldn't hear anything but the rush of thunder in his ears, pierced only occasionally by her soft moans.

Suddenly he realized where they were. "Wait, not here." He lifted her, despite her protest.

"Here's fine," she said before she suckled his neck and sank her hands into his hair.

He set her on the floor. "You can be bossy everywhere except with this." He yanked her against his firm body. "When it comes to this, I'm in charge."

He lifted her into his arms and carried her to the spare bedroom. After laying her on the bed, he crawled on top of her, holding her gaze. For too long he'd imagined this moment, and now it was here. He wouldn't rush. He'd savor every single second.

She writhed beneath him, as if seeking relief from her own pent-up desire. He was so stiff it hurt.

Closing his eyes, he kissed her. Warm, pliant kisses. Silky tongues wrestling. Hands combing through loose hair. Hot, heavy breath brushing against his neck. A waterfall of sensation submerging all conscious thought.

Tumbling back to earth, he broke their kiss and nuzzled the sensitive part of her neck below her ear.

She ran her hands along his back and over his hips, urging him into the cradle of her legs. Tugging at his shirt, she explored his heated skin, leaving tracks of gooseflesh wherever she touched. Surges of pleasure and sweet relief pumped through his lungs and limbs.

He reached up and tore off his shirt then brought his free hand down on her collarbone and traced down her ribs until his hand filled with her breast. She arched her back to meet his touch. He feathered his thumb back and forth over her nipple. Despite the layer of clothing, it hardened under his touch. His erection jumped in response to her reaction. *I'm on fire.*

He kissed her swollen lips again and slowly unbuttoned the front of her dress. As he peeled it back, his breath caught at the sight of another set of sexy underwear. A bra and matching panties—sheer netting with lemon-yellow embroidery, trimmed with lime-green silk ribbon—barely covered her.

"Your underwear is amazing." He clamped his mouth over the thin fabric covering her breast and sucked until she squirmed. "If I didn't know it must be expensive, I'd rip it off with my teeth."

"I can buy more." She pressed his head back to her chest. "Shred it."

Sorely tempted, he refrained and simply used his hands to pull her panties down her long, lean legs. Barely able to contain his excitement, he worked his hands back up her legs while his mouth took equal care of her other breast. Frustrated by the ribbons, he stripped away the fancy bra and let his eyes roam her naked body, which she'd stretched out before him.

She propped up onto her elbows and cocked a brow. "We have a bit of disparity here." She stared at his shorts and back up to his eyes. "Your turn to strip."

"Vying for control?" He reached for his zipper but halted, awaiting her answer.

"Sorry, habit." She smiled and lay back.

He grinned and disrobed quickly, eager to be skin to skin.

"Oh," she whispered, her sexual haze turning up the heat in the room as she studied every inch of him.

He traced her cheekbones and jaw then down along her waist before sweeping his palm across her abdomen and lowering it to the juncture between her legs.

Sinking his fingers into her hot center, he used the palm of his hand to stimulate the sensitive nub until she rocked her hips to match the rhythm of his movements.

"Hank," she panted.

He continued stroking her, kissing her sumptuous mouth, nipping at her lip before dipping his head back to feast on her nipples. Determined to make this the best experience she'd ever had with any man, he focused entirely on her satisfaction. He lost track of time and space until her hands clamped around his shaft and he nearly exploded.

"Now, Hank. Please," she begged, lifting her hips.

"You don't have to beg." He tore himself away to search for the condom in his wallet. Ripping it open with his teeth, he quickly fastened it in place.

He pinioned her hands above her head and kissed her long and hard, lowering his body onto hers again, letting friction from the contact warm them both. She wriggled and moaned beneath him until he couldn't wait another minute. Guiding himself to her entrance, he thrust inside the tight, hot space.

"Catalina," he rasped. Her muscles gripped him hard. *Feels so damned good.* "I've imagined this for so long."

He wanted to go slow, to take care not to hurt her, but the urgency of his desire overwhelmed him. Everything tightened as he moved inside her—deep, slow thrusts.

"Yes, Hank," she groaned. "Don't stop."

He opened his eyes and took in her features. She lay beneath him, bathed in sweat, lips parted, eyelids heavy with pleasure. "So beautiful."

He kissed her.

Be mine—his last coherent thought before his control slipped and his hips took over.

Tension and desire played tug-of-war, escalating every sensation until Cat screamed his name and clawed his back, sending him exploding over the edge, fully inside her, hands clamped around her ass as he let himself come down.

Absolutely spent, he rolled over, bringing her with him while his hands rubbed her back. He kissed the top of her head and inhaled her perfume and the scent of their lovemaking.

Perfect. She was perfect.

He was doomed.

Cat's head rested against his chest. She seemed relaxed, sated, and content. For several minutes, he closed his eyes and traced his fingers along her shoulder blade, down the curve of her spine, over her hip and back again. Then reality crashed down as he realized where he was—at work. Jackson's remark about distractions zipped through his head. *Shit.*

"Cat," he said softly.

"Hmm," she purred without lifting her head off his chest.

"I'd love to stay like this all day, but I should probably get back to your closet." When she lifted her head to protest, he said, "Sorry. I've never done this before . . . at work, I mean." He kissed the tip of her nose.

She chuckled. "Actually, I'm surprised none of Jackson's female clients ever hit on you."

"I didn't say that," he teased. "I just never took the bait."

"So I've got a place of distinction?" she asked lightly.

He lifted her chin with his finger. "That and more." He searched her eyes, looking for affirmation. "I know this is no strings, but it's still special to me."

He noticed a mix of emotions, and maybe a little doubt, in her eyes.

"You promised you could keep things light and it wouldn't affect our ability to work together." She tugged at the duvet. "We're two friends enjoying an attraction, right? *Not* falling in love."

"Well, then, I'll try to rein in my charm." He grinned playfully. "But don't be shocked when you fall hard. I'm a lovable guy."

He nibbled on her lip and kissed her once more before getting up to dispose of the condom.

She rolled onto her side, watching him cross the room. "Nice view."

"Mine's better." He winked and disappeared into the bathroom. When he returned, she was sitting in the middle of the bed, pulling her pretty underwear back over her body.

He sat near her and crooked a finger at the edge of her bra. "How many more of these things do you have, and when can I see more?"

"Many sets," she said as she brushed a bit of hair off his forehead. "And we'll see about when. First, we've both got lots of work to do."

"True." He kissed her, then pulled away with a sigh. "I really do have to keep things moving along."

"Yes, you do." She pulled her dress back over her head and buttoned it. Her expression turned mischievous. "But I'm the boss again, right? I mean you are, in fact, working for me."

"Yeah," he replied cautiously.

"So if I say you can take ten more minutes . . ." She crawled toward him, pushed him back against the mattress, and kissed along his jaw.

"Back to vying for control? You're in for a battle." Her mouth felt so good he might just let her win. But not today. He rolled over, pinning her to the mattress before stealing a final kiss and then easing away. "Now let me go."

He could have sworn he heard her whisper, "Even if it hurts."

~

Cat rode the elevator up fifty-one floors to David's office, still flush with the afterglow of her morning with Hank. She'd missed sex this past year, but after being with Hank, she now realized she'd been missing out on amazing sex her whole life.

Somehow he'd known exactly how and where to touch and kiss her, when to be gentle or a little rough, when to give in and let go. Everything about the encounter had connected on levels she'd never even known existed. All this time she'd thought he'd need protection from her, but now she feared she'd miscalculated. Her heart might be more at risk than his.

The elevator dinged before its doors opened, which drew her from her thoughts. After checking in with the receptionist, she took a seat in the law firm's lobby. The space had a retro vibe, with marble floors, wood-paneled walls, and midcentury modern–influenced furnishings. Copies of the *Wall Street Journal*, *The Economist*, and other business magazines covered its enormous coffee table.

She stacked a few magazines to the side to get a better look at the table itself, and then her gaze wandered to the other furnishings. Maybe office reception areas were another potential market for some of Hank's work. And perhaps they should focus on tables first and then diversify?

The soft click of shoes against the hard floor caught Cat's attention. Upon seeing David crossing to greet her, she stood and kissed him hello.

"You've got me curious about the reason behind this formal appointment. Vivi pretended she knew nothing, but I suspect she still keeps your secrets." He nodded down the hall. "Shall we begin?"

"Absolutely." She projected confidence, although her stomach lurched a bit in anticipation of David's reaction to her plans. It never mattered much that her face was more recognizable than his would ever be, or that none of her six hundred thousand Twitter followers had any idea who he was—David would always be the family superstar, even in her eyes.

The plate-glass window in his office offered expansive views of hundreds of buildings on the Manhattan skyline. His desk—large and perfectly neat—looked imposing, as did he in his gray Canali suit.

On the credenza behind him, she noticed a picture from his and Vivi's wedding beside an old group photograph of her, Vivi, Jackson, and David. That homey touch helped settle her nerves a bit as she took a seat in the black leather chair opposite his desk.

"The most logical conclusion is that you have a contract problem your agent can't resolve." Her brother studied her with his typical intensity mingled with overprotectiveness. "Or is this about Justin's soon-to-expire restraining order?"

"I'm a bit worried about the fact that Justin can contact me in a couple of weeks, but I'm equally determined to get past my fear. I'm sick of giving him so much power." She was, too. "But I'm not here about Justin or a contract problem. I came to discuss what steps I'd need to take to set up a new company."

She set her purse on the edge of his desk and braced for his questions.

"You want to start your own business?" His skeptical gaze didn't shock her.

"Yes. I need to plan my next career move before I'm too old to compete for print campaigns. My agent suggested I look into licensing my name, and it got me thinking."

David nodded. "Makes sense. So are you considering associating with an up-and-coming clothing designer or skin-care line? Because I'd presume they'd already be incorporated, and you might only need to negotiate a license agreement."

"No. I'm not interested in pimping beauty products or pasting my name on some other person's venture. I want to be involved in all aspects of the business."

David sat forward and steepled his fingers. She recognized his pensive expression from years of practice. His mind was quickly assessing a variety of scenarios and beginning to create questions. He would wait until he had all the information before offering any opinions or advice—something she both loved and hated about David.

He retrieved a yellow notepad from his desk and took out a pen. "Start from the beginning. What's your plan?"

Drawing a deep breath, Cat launched into her idea about working with Hank, explaining her vision of splitting the products into two lines. When she finished, she crossed her legs to keep her knee from bouncing.

"I see. And how do you plan to finance this venture—loans, investors?"

"I have money."

He narrowed his gaze. "I know you have money, but surely you don't intend to invest a substantial portion of your personal wealth on a risky start-up. Do you even have any idea of the costs associated with something of this scale?"

"Not yet. That's why I'm here talking to you. I want you to help outline what I need to research in order to make this all work."

David tossed his pen on the paper. "Cat, I'm not an expert in the furniture industry."

"But you work with a zillion corporations, doing all their legal work. You know about business law and financing, so you must know the basics. Aren't you the super genius of the family?" She huffed. "If you can't or won't help, then I'll find someone else who will."

David pressed two fingers to his temple. "I don't want to crush your dreams, but I think you're being impulsive and getting in over your head."

"Oh? So, unlike you, I'm not smart enough to learn? Unlike Jackson, I can't work hard enough to succeed. I should simply resign myself to dressing up for the camera?" She intended her sharp tone to cover any trace of self-doubt. *Trace? Ha!* More like piles.

"I didn't mean it like that, Cat. But you can't deny your impetuous history. I'm not convinced you've really thought this through. And speaking of Jackson, how will he react when you steal Hank from his crew? His erratic behavior is concerning enough without you throwing another monkey wrench into his situation."

"Jackson doesn't own Hank. If Hank wants to quit, that's his right." Cat shot out of her chair and grabbed her purse. Pride urged her to fight, to cling to Hank's faith in her abilities, to refuse to allow David to get in her head.

"Where are you going?" David stood, too.

"Apparently you're not interested in helping me. You don't have to believe in me, but I won't sit here while you try to convince me to give up." She looked at the ground, shaking her head. "Honestly, if this is how you treat all your clients, I can't believe you made partner so young."

"Sit down, Cat." David sat and gestured toward the chair. "I'm sorry. Let's start again."

Cat paused before taking her seat again.

"Before I get to the details you're looking for, tell me why this is so imperative. It seems hasty, your newfound entrepreneurial interest. I'd assumed that, once you'd moved into your new place, you'd start living your life again. Instead you've been avoiding social engagements and sticking closer to home than usual. Vivi's been concerned, too. Is it possible that you're pursuing this idea as a way of avoiding thinking about Justin, or dating, or whatever?"

She knew her brother well enough to know he didn't mean to insult her. Sincere concern must be behind his bluntness. However, she hadn't yet told her family about her diagnosis, and she wasn't about to discuss it with David here and now.

That would only convince him that she'd latched on to this business idea to avoid the pain of dealing with her new reality. Maybe it had started that way, but now she had several reasons—including genuine interest—to pursue this venture.

"Please stop bringing up Justin. Part of the reason I can't get beyond what happened is because everyone's always bringing it up. And besides, I've already told you, my agent's advising me to explore career alternatives. After seeing the table Hank built for you and Vivi, as well as his other work, I got excited."

David leaned forward. "Why do I feel like you're withholding something?"

Because you're too freakin' perceptive? Regardless, David didn't need to know about her diagnosis to do his job. Covering, she said, "You've got a suspicious nature?"

"Fine, don't tell me, but don't think you've pulled something over on me, either." He quirked a brief smile. "If Hank's going to be your partner, why isn't he here? I'm sure he's knowledgeable about certain facts I need in order to best advise you."

Cat wrinkled her nose. "Well, he's not fully onboard yet. Like you, he thinks we've got a lot of homework to do before he can quit Jackson's payroll. His mom's very ill. She and his youngest sister depend on his support, which is why I need to find a way to minimize the risks."

"Sis, without Hank's enthusiastic buy-in, it sounds like you're setting yourself up for a major disappointment." His gaze softened with his tone. "I don't want to see you hurt."

"Which brings us back to why I'm here. I need to get the information together to prove this is something he and I can do together. So please humor me for the next forty minutes. I swear I'll consider all your advice and won't do anything rash or stupid."

David sighed and picked up his pen. "Let's discuss the pros and cons of different entity structures, then we can explore various sources of financing that might be available, and perhaps we can even do a little digging into some industry-specific issues before my next appointment. But I cannot, in good conscience, advise you to move forward with any of this until you've done the due diligence to understand as much about this industry as possible before you making any commitments."

"That's all I'm asking." Cat frowned. "Well, that and to keep quiet about this until Hank does agree. I don't want to stir up trouble between him and Jackson."

David cast her an incredulous look. "I think we both know that can't be avoided if you move forward with these plans."

"One step at a time, David." She scooted her chair closer to the desk, determined to prove to her brother and everyone else that she could succeed. At that moment she realized nothing had ever been so important.

Mom,

This week I've caught myself fantasizing about having a normal, healthy relationship. Imagine that! Seems that Justin hasn't completely destroyed my faith in all men after all. Of course, that scares the pants off me, so I've been avoiding Hank. I wish I'd never gone to the doctor. If I didn't know about my condition, I could be free to be with Hank—honestly and without guilt.

But wishes and fairy tales are for little girls, not aging, barren ones like me.

Chapter Thirteen

Hank had been counting: minutes, hours, and now days since he'd made love with Cat. Just the memory of touching her—of being touched—set off a series of shivers. Yet in the six days since they'd first gotten together, she'd been keeping herself exceedingly busy. Unavailable, in fact. She'd whet his appetite, then spent the rest of the week running around Manhattan on "appointments."

She'd pass him in her apartment, compliment his progress on her armoire, then toss him a smile and dash out the door. Making a serious dent in her project had been the only upside to her absence. Too bad the progress he most wanted to make had nothing to do with construction.

This morning he'd met with Jackson in Wilton until eleven, which left him only a few hours to work at Cat's in the afternoon. All week he'd run ragged, back and forth to Manhattan, juggling his work and his family. When he'd finally get home, he'd find Jenny at her wit's end, incapable of dealing with his mom's increasingly difficult behavior.

He needed a break, but first he hoped to squeeze in an early dinner and more with Cat. Of course, he suspected she had some big-city plans of her own. His grand plan to woo her into a real relationship had stalled out before it even got started.

He knocked before unlocking Cat's front door, then entered her apartment with his key.

"Hi!" Cat greeted him with a kiss—on the damn cheek—and then gestured toward another woman. "Hank, this is Melissa."

"Melissa, nice to meet you." He shook her hand. Apparently Cat had already made other plans for her afternoon, as he'd guessed. Plans that didn't include him. "Sorry to interrupt you ladies. I'll head to the bedroom and get out of your hair."

"Not so fast!" Cat grasped his forearm. "I've actually brought Melissa here as a surprise for you."

"Huh?" A couple of crazy scenarios raced through his mind, none of which made any sense.

"She's my absolute favorite masseuse, but today she's all yours. Follow her back to the guest room and prepare for the best ninety minutes of your life."

Melissa grinned while Cat beamed, so he hated to douse them both with a dose of reality. "Cat, in case you forgot, I've got a schedule to keep."

"No one's going to die if my project takes an extra day or two. This is a little treat for you. A bit of the pampering you never allow yourself."

"I promise I won't bite." Melissa joked, apparently noticing his discomfort.

He scratched his head. "Melissa, I don't want you to have wasted your time by coming, so how about Cat takes the appointment and I get to work?"

"Good grief, Hank. I really want you to do this. Or, more honestly, I want to do this *for* you. Please." Cat set her hands on her hips, clearly growing agitated with his reluctance.

"Guess I don't have a choice." He raised his hands in surrender. "Lead the way, Melissa."

As he followed her down the hall, he glanced over his shoulder at Cat. With a self-satisfied wave, she said, "I'm going to visit Esther. See you later."

In the guest room, a scented candle burned on the nightstand.

The lights were off and shades drawn, so only the bit of daylight coming through the sides of the blinds lit the room. Although he'd much rather get an unprofessional massage from Cat than an official one from Melissa, he kept his trap shut.

His little temptress kept him guessing, as always. But he couldn't deny the way her thoughtful gesture wrapped around his heart like one of his nephew's full-body hugs. Just as loving, too, even if she wouldn't ever admit to it.

"I'll step outside while you undress. Then lie facedown on the table." Melissa turned to go, but then said, "Feel free to pull that sheet over yourself and I'll rearrange it once I come back in."

Ninety minutes later, Melissa left him alone after mentioning that Cat had said he could use her shower before he got dressed. Neither his body nor his muscles had ever been so relaxed. In fact, he doubted he could lift his limbs, and didn't even want to try. The lavender aroma, the quietude, the absence of tightness in his neck and shoulders—Cat had been right. Ninety minutes of bliss.

After indulging another few moments of utter contentedness, he forced himself to slide off the table, pick up his clothes, and duck into the guest bathroom. By the time he'd cleaned up and dressed, Melissa and her heavenly table were gone.

He meandered down the hall to the living room to thank Cat for her thoughtful, generous gift. He found her arranging flowers amid several lit candles. Her smile worked over his heart like Melissa's hands had worked over his body.

"Was I right?" The told-you-so expression on her face made him chuckle.

"Yeah, you were." He glanced around, wondering if this little intimate setting was meant for him, or if she had other plans. A small plate of chocolate-chip-and-walnut cookies sat on the table. "You baked?"

"God, no. Esther did. Eat them all . . . please."

He took two because they looked like something straight out of a cookbook. Tasted even better. "Thanks for the massage, Cat. You were right; it was awesome. Not sure how I'll get anything done now that my arms feel like overcooked spaghetti."

"Never fear. There's work to do that doesn't involve saws or sandpaper."

"Oh?"

She poured beer into a chilled glass, handed it to him, then pointed at the sofa. "Sit, please."

At least she tempered her high-handedness with good manners. The more he got to know her, the more he realized her bossiness grew out of enthusiasm rather than a genuine need for control.

She lifted a notebook from her bag and took a seat beside him. If he tackled her on the sofa, could he seduce her into submission?

"I've done a bunch of research and have some ideas of how we can give this business a try without breaking the bank or putting you at too much risk." She smiled, unaware of his self-restraint. "Ready to listen?"

He nearly spit out his beer as her plans became more transparent. Flashing a smile of admiration, he shook his head in defeat. "Oh, you're good. Got me all buttered up so I'm too relaxed to object, didn't you?"

"Not at all!" She slapped his thigh. "I've been thinking about that massage since I first mentioned it weeks ago. One has nothing to do with the other. Besides, you've already promised to hear me out if I agreed to your conditions, which I have."

He nodded in silence, although he'd wanted to revisit that second condition again. Now, even.

"After talking with David, I think forming a limited liability company would be best because it gives us the protection of a corporation with the tax advantages of a partnership. If we set it up fifty-fifty, I'll put up the initial capital, and you contribute sweat equity. Both of our financial risk is basically limited to what we put in. Does that sound fair?"

He nodded, surprised to learn she'd sought David's opinion. Heck, he hadn't even given real thought to how he'd tell his family, or Jackson. It seemed premature at this point, but apparently Cat didn't agree. "Will David talk to Jackson about this before we make a decision?"

"No. Client confidentiality and all that stuff. And he'd never stir up trouble, especially when we haven't committed to anything." Her gaze turned sober. "But we will soon."

Hank scratched the back of his head, uncomfortable thinking about leaving Jackson with a lesser-trained crew than he'd really need. Plus, starting a business meant he'd be spending even less time at home, which put Jenny under more pressure. Would that affect her schoolwork?

The cookies that had tasted so good going down now settled like stones in his gut.

"Anyway, I also found a flexible, inexpensive solution to the space and equipment problems. There are co-op spaces where you rent a small work area and share a common equipment room. It's a perfect way to get started without having to rent a big facility or invest in a bunch of equipment. There are a few in Brooklyn, but I did find one up in Connecticut, not too far from Norwalk."

He sat forward, suddenly curious. "How much?"

"Reasonable rates, and available for short-term leasing. So, for example we could start with a three-month lease and see how it works out."

For the first time since she'd come up with this whole idea, it didn't seem completely impossible.

"Go on." He chugged more of his beer, his body now strung

with cautious enthusiasm and a healthy dose of admiration for the courageous, headstrong woman to his right.

She smiled and flipped the page. "There are a couple of traditional ways to get noticed, like submitting designs in competitions for awards, and attending design trade shows. There's a big furniture expo in Chicago in a few weeks. I know it's totally last minute, but I might be able to press a personal contact to squeeze us into a small exhibit room. I can set up a website on WordPress for practically nothing, and Vivi volunteered to shoot photos for free. Naturally, I'd use my social media platforms to drive traffic to our site."

"I doubt the horny guys who follow you are interested in buying fine furniture." He chuckled when her mouth fell open.

"I have a lot of female followers. And aside from them and my personal network of celebrity friends, I'm thinking we could target boutique retail owners, maybe small offices with nice reception rooms, and so on. We could open with a line of tables: end tables, coffee tables, dining tables. You could design two of each that we'd showcase. Perhaps we could do privately commissioned pieces in time, too. An informal survey of a few friends revealed one who spent twenty-six grand on a custom-built dining table, and hers doesn't look anywhere near as unique as yours."

Hell, he'd been so busy working to make ends meet, he'd never taken the time to investigate the kind of money he might be able to make building furniture. Then again, without Cat's reach, he wouldn't have personal access to super-rich folks, either.

It struck him then. Here he sat, next to his fantasy woman, who'd taken it upon herself to make his dreams come true. Even if it never happened, he was grateful for her enthusiasm. She'd reminded him that his life could be more than a string of obligations. That maybe duties and dreams didn't have to be mutually exclusive.

It'd been close to fourteen years since he'd felt that way. If it ended up being the only thing he took away from this relationship, it would be enough. Well, maybe not, but it would be something he'd always appreciate.

"I'm impressed, Cat. This is a lot of information in a short time. Still, I'm not loving you footing the bill. Also, you didn't mention anything about income. Then there's Jackson. I hate to leave him high and dry."

"If we start slow, you can keep working for Jackson and build stuff at night and on weekends. As far as money goes, we can charge fifty-percent deposits to help generate a little up-front income."

"Working at night might be a problem. I've got my mom to deal with, and Jenny takes night classes. Apparently my mom's been more irritable since I started working here and spending less time at home."

Cat set her notebook aside and sighed. "You're incredibly committed to your family. But don't you deserve something of your own, too?"

"I do. But, unlike my mom, I've got time later. She's had a tough life. Widowed very young, and started losing her memory not long afterward. I don't want her to feel like she's lost me, too."

Cat nodded thoughtfully, possibly considering his feelings, or maybe thinking of her own mother.

"If I were a mother, I'm pretty sure I wouldn't want to hold my children back from living their own lives. I think you're missing the most important lesson of her situation. Life is short. None of us can count on getting a chance 'someday,' so we need to seize each opportunity in the moment. That said, I'm done begging. If you aren't willing to make any compromises, then I'll find something else to sink my teeth into."

He set down his empty glass, shamefaced. "You're right. I'm sorry. Guess I'm so stuck in my life, I can't see a way out, even when it's being handed to me on a platter."

"Does that mean you're willing to try?"

He drew a deep breath, his stomach knotted, whether with excitement or panic he didn't know. "Let's try. At least your plan lets me give Jackson time to find a replacement without me giving up a paycheck too soon. Jenny graduates in six months, so that will be one less expense I have in the not-too-distant future."

Cat threw her arms around Hank. "I'm so excited!"

Him, too—but from the hug at least as much as from the business. He'd been craving the feel of her body pressed against his again all week—he didn't want to let go.

"Thank you for believing in me, Hank. This chance to prove that I'm capable of more than looking pretty means everything to me. Absolutely *everything*."

Hank brushed her hair behind her ear. "You don't need this business to prove that to me or anyone else."

"I do. I need it to prove it to myself." Her cheeks flushed at the admission, but then she appeared to shake off her temporary embarrassment. "The first thing we need to do is get Vivi out to your house to take some promotional pictures for a website and a brochure. I can coordinate with Helen so you don't need to take time from all your other work. I promise, I'll make sure you're glad we did this, Hank."

"I'm already glad, Cat." He slid his hand up her thigh, unable to refrain.

Cat laid her hand on Hank's to stop its progression up her leg. "One last surprise."

~

He'd expressed a fondness for her lingerie, so she'd purposely worn an especially sweet pair in case they had cause to celebrate. She stood up and slowly unbuttoned her dress, then let it fall to her ankles.

Hank catapulted off the sofa and fingered the fine white lace bra before his mouth slanted over hers and stole her breath. She surrendered to his passionate assault, collapsing against him as her knees softened like warm butter.

"God almighty," he murmured, breaking the kiss. He trailed his fingertips along her jawline, neck, and collarbone. "You're like a dream, Cat."

It is a dream, she thought while praying she wouldn't wake up too soon. She wished it could remain light and playful indefinitely yet knew that would be impossible.

His thumb circled the hollow notch at the base of her throat. Closing her eyes, she craned her neck, and when his hot mouth latched on to that spot, her breath audibly hitched. Somehow Hank's kisses were more intimate than Justin's, or any man's. That fact thrilled and frightened her, but she wouldn't give them up—not yet.

"Hank," she said hoarsely, groping at the hem of his T-shirt, angry with the fabric for denying her skin contact.

His hands slid up her waist and cupped her breasts. His gentle ministrations continued until her nipples ached with want.

"Please," she moaned, gripping his shoulders. He made her body hum like a tuning fork, and she loved it.

"Patience." His lips curled against her neck. When she uttered a protest, he swept her into his arms and carried her down the hall. "You're not the only one with an agenda today."

Before she could question him, he set her on the bed.

Swept up by passion, she reached for his shorts, but he stilled her hands.

"My turn to take charge, Catalina." He straddled her on his knees and pushed her wrists above her head, pinning her against the mattress before kissing her. Her skin prickled with heat wherever his touch or mouth grazed her body.

A throbbing ache down low caused her to arch her back. When he released her hands to remove his shirt, she grasped his thighs. His heavy breathing made her wet and needy. She bucked her hips, seeking relief.

Responding with a shower of deliberate, hot kisses to her neck and breasts, he then pushed her hands above her head. "Stay."

He dragged his mouth along the slopes of her waist, working his way south until his head rested between her thighs. His thumbs flicked her nipples while his tongue circled her most private parts. Squirming with pleasure, a frustrated moan escaped her lips. "Hank, please."

Within minutes he brought her to shattering spasms. When her body quieted, he flashed his lopsided grin. He rose up on his knees to unzip his shorts and ease a condom over his rampant erection. "My turn."

"Thank God." She raked her hands through his blond locks. Everything about him aroused her, starting with the hair on his head. Something about Hank set her spirit loose in a way she'd never experienced with any other man.

He entered her swiftly, greedily thrusting deep inside her, igniting a fire even their sweat-soaked bodies couldn't douse. After an exalted groan, he tempered his pace and reverently uttered, "Catalina."

In that moment, when he seemed lost, she was found.

His mouth joined hers. His hips drove into her in a frenzied pace until they came together with a blissful shout.

Hank collapsed, breathing heavily against the nape of her neck. She relished the weight of his sculpted body pressing her into the mattress. Her hands roamed his shoulders and back, memorizing each line and sinew. Moments later, he kissed her temple, then rolled over, cradling her body against his.

He molded her to his body. His steady heartbeat droned like a metronome, lulling her into a sense of lazy security. Too soon, he spoke.

"Hate to do this—and I mean hate—but I've got to head home." He hooked his finger under her jaw, lifting her face to his. "I promised Jenny she could go out tonight."

"Five more minutes." She snuggled against his chest. "Maybe ten."

"Okay, ten." He gently brushed his fingers along her back and kissed her temple. "Any chance you might want to renegotiate this no-strings business?"

I wish I could. The thought echoed in her chest, causing an ache. Yet if she let him closer, it would only hurt more when it ended. "Let's not ruin a perfectly good celebration by getting serious, Hank."

He didn't respond other than to hold her a little tighter while keeping his gaze on the ceiling. After a moment, he said, "You know, you just gave me some good advice about seizing opportunities when they come. Of course, maybe you don't view me and my lifestyle as an opportunity."

"It's about me, Hank. Not you. I'm not good at relationships. I . . . I'm just not the kind of woman who can make you happy for the long haul."

"Why don't I get to decide that for myself?"

Of course he'd say that, because from his perspective things looked perfect. But she knew nothing in life was ever as perfect as it seemed—least of all her.

After a lengthy internal debate, she confessed the minimum she could while warning him not to get too attached. "Because I'm not willing to open up just to be left devastated when you discover what I already know."

Hank tucked his finger under her chin and raised her face to meet his gaze. "You've obviously got some doubts, maybe even secrets. I'm not demanding full disclosure and wedding bells, Cat, but I'm not a fan of the sex-buddies thing, either. Can't we have a normal dating experience? You set the pace."

Logic told her this was too good to last. Yes, logic dictated she keep things light and remain focused on their business plans so she didn't end up heartbroken. But then again, Cat had never been all that well acquainted with logic.

"One day at a time?" Or perhaps one hundred . . .

"Baby steps." He chuckled and kissed her forehead.

She snuggled back against his chest, closing her eyes, praying for forgiveness because, despite everything she knew about herself and her secrets, she heard herself saying, "I can do that."

Mom,

I'm in trouble. Big trouble.

I like Hank. Really like him. Like, think-about-him-way-too-often kind of liking him. He's genuine and kind and honest, which is why I doubt he could ever really like the real me.

But it feels so good when he smiles at me, I can't walk away.

See? Trouble!

Chapter Fourteen

Hank had insisted he be the one to share their plans with Jackson, mostly to spare Cat the brunt of her brother's anger. A year ago he wouldn't have been as concerned, but Jackson's recent bouts of impatience and moodiness made Hank wary.

His truck tires kicked up dust plumes when he drove across the gravel leading up to Jackson's office. That grinding sound had greeted him hundreds of times since the first day he'd parked in front of this old barn. God, back then he'd been so eager to begin a new job.

Jackson had always been generous with all his employees, but particularly with Hank. Whether their shared experience of caring for sick mothers or their obsession with perfection in their work forged a kinship, he couldn't say.

What he could recall were Friday-afternoon Coronas on the patio, road trips to Vermont to pick up reclaimed hardwood, daily bets on the number of change orders they'd receive from the client from hell, crazy Mrs. Holloway.

Yet this past year, his friend had become cynical, driving, and unfocused.

Jackson needed Hank's help now more than ever, which heaped a whole lot of guilt about leaving on Hank's shoulders. This would be the first time he ever walked away from someone who depended on him, and Hank couldn't shake off the doubts clinging to him like ivy strangling a tree trunk.

Sighing, he stepped out of his truck and meandered inside, hoping to catch his friend in a good mood.

"Hey, buddy." Jackson yanked an old printer toner cartridge out of the machine. "Give me a sec."

"Take your time." Hank glanced around the office, projecting now toward his future.

How would he weather the ups and downs faced by small businesses? Would the pressure change him the way it seemed to be changing Jackson? Would it change Cat?

"Thirsty?" Jackson withdrew two beers from the refrigerator, tossed the caps in the trash, and handed one to Hank.

"Guess so." Hank raised the bottle at Jackson before taking a swig, then noticed a few empties in the trash can. "Drinking on the job?"

"After hours, when wrapping up paperwork." Jackson's eyes, which didn't quite meet Hank's, told a different story. Almost in defiance, he drew a long pull from the bottle. "So what's up? Is Doug still giving you a hard time?"

"No." Heightened awareness of Jackson's drinking worsened the pit in Hank's stomach. For an instant he reconsidered his plans, wondering if perhaps he and Cat could wait until Jackson's new crew was better trained and his friend more stable. But Hank had made a promise to her—one he intended to keep. "I've got some news that will probably surprise you. It's going to put you in a tough spot, but I hope you'll wish me well."

"Oh?" Jackson's eyes twinkled with mischief. "Does this 'news' have anything to do with my sister?"

Had Cat already told?

"Yeah, actually." Hank's body flushed when an image of her naked body glimmered before his eyes, a memory he didn't want Jackson to suspect.

"So she agreed to go out with you?" Jackson waved his hand in the air. "I already told you that'd be great news. Not like you need my permission, anyway."

"Well, that's not exactly what's happening." Hank frowned at how he'd bungled the opening of this little talk. *Just come clean.* "She and I are going into business together."

Jackson's brows scaled his forehead. "What?"

"Cat fell in love with my furniture designs and proposed a partnership. I design and build, she brands and sells." Hank scowled at Jackson's dismayed chuckle. "It's not a joke."

"Sorry." Jackson composed himself. "No doubt you build beautiful furniture, but Cat doesn't know the first thing about that business—or any business, for that matter. How'd she convince herself and you that she'd be a good partner?"

"You don't give her enough credit."

"Oh? So she came to you with a business proposal. Backed up her ideas with data about target markets, competition, fixed costs? Her pro forma projections look reasonable?"

Maybe Cat hadn't quite fleshed out that much detail, but she'd presented a reasonable-sounding approach. "She did research and devised a plan that allows us to ease in without taking a huge risk."

"Ease in? Right there's a problem. You can't 'ease in' to a business and expect to succeed. You've got to go all-in, twenty-four seven." Jackson shook his head, disgusted. "All due respect, wouldn't I be the better partner? I've started and run a successful small business, I have built-in clients, and we've worked well together for several years."

"And in all that time, you've never once expressed any interest in my furniture, or proposed this kind of arrangement. Plus, based on our history, it might be hard for you to view me as a partner instead of an employee."

"As if I ever treated you like some 'employee.'" Jackson shoved off the desktop, resentment brewing in his eyes. "I see what's going on. I'm losing my top guy because Cat's restless, and you're so hot for her, you'll do anything she asks just to make her happy."

"First of all, that's damn insulting to both your sister and me." Hank glared at Jackson. "Maybe you think Cat's flighty, but I think she's as capable as you or David, and she's obviously got a lot of drive and determination to have achieved such success on her own."

"You don't have to sell me on her strengths. I know she's a hard worker and enthusiastic, and she can charm the pants off anyone when she wants her way. But please tell me some part of you questions her plan? Having a recognizable face and name doesn't automatically translate to sales, especially in a business unrelated to her fan base. Cat's got street smarts, but she didn't finish college, she's got *no* business experience—not even a summer internship—to draw from, and she's as stubborn as me. Trust me, she's going to end up getting you both in over your heads."

"I believe in her, Jackson. More to the point, I believe in myself. This is a chance for me to finally do something *I* want for a change. Something I'd only fantasized about until recently. Don't I deserve that shot? Haven't I earned it?"

Jackson held Hank's defiant gaze for a full minute before he let out a long sigh. "Of course you have."

"Besides, you've admitted in the past that you didn't know everything when you started this business. You took a risk and worked hard because it mattered to you. Well, Cat and I can do that, too."

The two of them stood there, arms crossed, in silence. Hank could tell Jackson's mind was reeling, but he had no idea what his friend would say or do next.

Jackson gulped his beer and tossed it in the trash. It landed with a clank. "So when are you bailing on me? Do I at least get two weeks notice to find a replacement?"

"Actually, I was hoping to keep working for you nearly full-time for a few months, until Cat and I are established and have a pipeline of projects."

"Wait a sec. You want to keep working for me *and* try to start your own business?" Once again, Jackson's expression grew incredulous. "I'm saying these things out loud and yet you don't react in a way that indicates you hear how batshit crazy you are to think you can manage a full-time job, a start-up, *and* all your family shit, Hank."

When Jackson put it so bluntly, it did sound unreasonable, if not flat-out preposterous, but Hank had committed himself now, so he couldn't back down.

"It's basically what I'm doing now by working at Cat's while still working for you. And it gives me a chance to continue training Doug and whoever you hire to replace me while allowing me to maintain a steady income for my family's sake."

Jackson planted his hands on his hips and shook his head. He crossed to the other side of his desk, blankly staring at a stack of paperwork before knocking his knuckles against the desktop twice.

"Tell my sister, next time she asks for a favor, the answer is no. Some gratitude she's shown after I agreed to get you to do those damn closets. Honestly, I'm a little hurt by her plotting all this without any warning or discussion. And you—you're supposed to be my good friend, but you also cut me out. Guess it just proves my theory. Can't trust *anyone*." Jackson narrowed his eyes. "Six weeks, Hank. That's it, then you're on your own. If I'm going to lose you, I need to hire someone soon, and I can't afford to keep both of you on the payroll indefinitely. And if this really is your dream, I'm doing you a favor by cutting you off. No safety net. You need to live and breathe the business. That's the only way you two are going to succeed."

Six weeks?

He'd overestimated his value to Jackson, because he hadn't foreseen being cut loose so easily. Was Jackson simply striking back out of anger, or was this his way of calling Hank's bluff?

Only six weeks of steady income. Without it, how would he pay the bills, Jenny's tuition, Helen's hourly wage?

"Good luck, Hank." Jackson grabbed two more beers and handed one to Hank. "You deserve your shot, I guess. I hate the way you two went about it, but for your sake, I hope it works out."

No turning back now.

As Hank watched Jackson drain his bottle in one continuous guzzle, a chill consumed him.

~

"I guess this makes it all official." Hank finished reviewing the last organizational document.

"Once we sign on the dotted line." Smiling, she glanced at her watch. "Esther's going to stop by to be a witness. Later today I can set up company accounts and deposit start-up money."

"I wish I could help with that."

"You're contributing all the talent. Without you, there's no business, so stop feeling bad. After Vivi and I get the pictures we need, I'll get the website up and running and start chatting on my social media. I'll also get a brochure made. Did you check out the co-op space? I'm ready to send a check if you're all set."

"I ran out on Sunday and took a look. They've got some great equipment. Seems pretty relaxed and friendly."

"So we'll sign a short-term lease and send a check." Cat added another item to her to-do list. "By the way, I was able to pull a few strings and nab a little showroom space at that international furniture expo in Chicago next month, which could give us exposure to fifty thousand design professionals. We can take the table you built for Vivi and some of your other pieces to showcase your talent. It's a gamble to rush like this, but another opportunity of this scale won't come around until next year."

Hank settled his hand on her thigh and rubbed his thumb back and forth. "If I haven't said it before, thanks. I know I've been reluctant, but I'm grateful for this opportunity. I hope I don't let you down."

"You won't. Let everyone doubt us. We can't fail. You're too talented, and I'm too determined. We're in this together now." Of course, she'd never tackled anything so far from her limited area of expertise.

She might not have utter faith in love, but she did have faith in him. And his faith in her gave her confidence.

"I did some prototype drawings." When he handed her the drawings, he brushed his fingers against hers, which made her consider tossing aside work and dragging him to bed. "But before we barrel ahead, I want to talk more about your idea of churning out a few products over and over . . . I've got issues."

Before he could continue, her phone rang.

"Hold that thought." She looked at the screen and then at Hank. "It's my agent. Need to take it."

Hank nodded and sat back.

"Hey, Elise. What's up?"

"I think I've found a great licensing opportunity for you. It's not clothing or beauty products, but it works nicely with your reputation for elegance and good taste. Are you familiar with Elena Bautista's jewelry? She works mostly with eighteen- and twenty-four-carat gold and semiprecious stones. Very contemporary, feminine style—akin to Marco Bicego's work. I think it's a perfect fit, and she was more than a little excited about designing a line under your name."

"Oh? That does sound interesting, but I'm not sure it's right for me." Cat grimaced, having not yet informed Elise about her plans with Hank.

"I know you wanted to be in on the nuts and bolts, but while the company will still be hers, she is willing to give you some input in the creative aspect of the line. She's offering five hundred thousand up front, and a six-percent royalty on sales for two years, with an option to renew."

"Five hundred thousand up front?" That lump-sum payment would further feather her nest egg and give her an injection of cash to devote to Mitchell/St. James. Could she do both? Cat noticed Hank lean forward, observing her, so she turned slightly away. "Based on her average sales, what would I make annually, and what other obligations would I have?"

"She recently signed a distribution agreement with Neiman Marcus. I don't have all the sales data yet, so I can't ballpark a number, but there would be an exclusivity clause attached to this deal."

"Exclusivity meaning I couldn't promote other jewelry?"

"No, total exclusivity. You couldn't attach your name to any other product during the term of this contract."

"That won't work." She cast a furtive glance at Hank. "Can it be negotiated?"

"I don't know, but why doesn't it work? You'd still be able to model because the clothing lines aren't in your name. Is there some other product you're interested in branding?"

Drawing a deep breath, she fessed up. "My own, actually. I'm planning to partner with a furniture designer to start a new business, Mitchell/St. James."

Elise's silence stretched out forever, and the weight of Hank's stare grew heavier. Finally a frosty voice came through the line. "I wish you would've informed me of this before I wasted my time investigating licensing deals for you, Cat."

"I'm sorry. I didn't realize you were speaking with anyone. I would've thought we'd have discussed any possibility beforehand." Cat sighed, wishing Hank weren't able to hear every word of her end of the conversation. "Is there any chance that exclusivity can be pared back?"

"I don't know, but it doesn't sound like you'll have time to commit to this project, uphold your prior commitments to Armani, and start a new business, anyway."

"The Armani contract isn't overly demanding." Cat then asked, "Are you sure there's no chance she'll consider carving out an exception to that clause?"

"I doubt it. Exclusivity is fairly standard in these license agreements. Are *you* sure you want to pass up this kind of money for something so risky? If your venture fails, the value of your name, for branding purposes, will plummet. That means less money on the table next time, assuming I can even secure you another deal down the road."

Cat's living room walls appeared to be closing in. Perspiration broke out across her chest.

A clear-cut test of her readiness to walk away from a sure bet and risk her reputation on a business and man she'd only begun to know. A man with so many other obligations pulling at him. A partnership that could hit a rocky road when their personal relationship cooled.

She faced Hank, his lush green eyes watching her and waiting. How could she turn her back on him after building up his hopes? After standing up to David? After letting Hank quit his job?

People had always underestimated her; Hank believed in her. He was giving her the chance to prove herself as much as she was giving him the chance to live his dream. He'd put his own family's security at risk for her, so she should do the same for him.

Her mother's heavily accented English drifted through her mind. *Stick to your guns, hija preciosa.*

"I'm sorry, Elise. If you can't negotiate an exception, I have to pass."

"I hope you don't regret this. Should I also assume you'll no longer have time for modeling, either? Perhaps we should reconsider our relationship once your Armani contract concludes."

"I can still take on occasional modeling work, but if you're no longer interested in representing me, then I'll respect that decision." Cat felt Hank squirming beside her on the sofa.

Elise sighed through the phone. "Let's talk after you return from Milan next month."

"Fine." Cat tossed her phone aside and drew a deep breath. When she turned toward Hank, he was staring at her as if she had two heads.

"Tell me you didn't just walk away from half a million dollars and more, Cat."

"I didn't have a choice. It was this," she pointed at his drawings, "or the other."

Hank sprang off the sofa and paced in a tight circle. "Half a million dollars? I can't even imagine having that kind of offer, let alone turning it down."

If he kept forcing her to think about it, she might get a little sick, too.

"Hank, that was a two-year deal. We're building something that will last decades. Something in which I have a vote, too. And we're going to make money."

"I told you before, maxed out I might be able to build eighteen or twenty quality pieces of furniture per year. A great year would gross maybe two-fifty. For me, grossing sixty is about break-even with what I make with Jackson, so I might even be ahead of the game depending on our expenses, but it's a huge step down for you." He stabbed his fingers through his hair.

When he put it that way, it didn't sound like she'd made a good decision. But her mortgage was minimal, she had money, and they had time to grow the business. Short-term sacrifice for a long-term gain. For something real and meaningful, for something that would be hers.

"So the first year will be lean, but then we'll hire help, or take on interns at a really low cost who can help beef up production." And then, whether to convince him or herself, she added, "Don't forget, the endgame is mass-producing knockoffs. That's when volume and real money will come."

"I'm worried you're going to resent me if this all doesn't turn out like you plan. What if it never becomes more than a small, distinguished business? Can you be happy without all of this?" He gestured around her posh apartment.

"First of all, I'm not going to resent you for an idea *I* pushed you to consider. Please don't let concerns about our personal relationship interfere with making business decisions. Let's agree—right now—that the two are separate, and promise not to let one affect the other."

"Is that possible?" He pinned her with his direct gaze.

"I think so. We both have a lot at stake, so the business needs to remain the priority, at least until we're on some solid footing." She licked her lips, feeling antsy under the weight of his scrutiny. "Wouldn't you agree?"

"So you're already backing away from our personal relationship?"

"I agreed to try dating, but I've always been honest about my hesitation to get involved in a serious relationship." She clasped his hand. "Given the stakes of this venture, if push comes to shove, the business interests should come before personal ones."

Hank looked torn and, honestly, disappointed. "Seeing as you've just walked away from a ton of money, and are also putting up all the money for our company, I'd be a jerk to disagree, wouldn't I?"

"One thing you could never be is a jerk." She smiled at him, hoping to ease his tension.

He scrubbed his hands over his face, clearly concerned. "I'm not used to being in this spot, and I don't like it."

"What spot?"

"Getting a lot more than I'm giving."

"I'm not *giving* you anything. Who has to build all this stuff?"

Hank stared at her, then nodded. "I still feel lousy that you've walked away from a sure thing."

"Don't feel lousy. Just be committed. We've got to put everything into this launch. I know the business will grow slowly, but let's step out with our best foot forward. Our trade-show debut should be flawless despite the rushed circumstances. I'm betting my reputation on it, so promise me it's your top priority, too."

Hank's silence only made every other noise in the apartment sound louder, sharper. He clasped her hand. "When I make a promise I keep it. You want flawless, you got it. I promise, you can always depend on me, Cat."

"I never really doubted it. So once Esther arrives, we'll finalize the organizational papers." She lifted his sketches off the table and started shuffling through them. "Before we were interrupted, you wanted to discuss some concerns about these?"

Without warning, she saw desire flicker in his eyes, hunger crowding out all other thoughts.

"First, let's celebrate." He held his hand out. When she took it, he yanked her off the sofa and up against his body and kissed her.

She allowed herself three, maybe five, seconds of pure pleasure before planting her hands against his chest. "Hank, let's stay focused. We've still got a lot to lock down, and Esther's going to be here in a bit."

He looked at her like she'd slapped him across the cheek, but then stepped back, hands held up. "I see."

"Please don't look at me like that. We've just agreed to keep the business the priority."

She felt his retreat as much as she saw the coolness descend between them. Apparently her idea of separating business and personal relationships would be a huge challenge.

"Yes, we did. Speaking of which, I need to finish your closets. Guess I'll get back to work, then, partner. Call me when Esther arrives." He turned away from her and disappeared around the corner, whatever issues he had wanted to discuss apparently forgotten.

Mom,

You always warned me that the bigger my secrets, the lonelier my life would be. I admit, until recently I didn't really believe you. Now I've never felt lonelier despite spending so much time with a wonderful guy who seems to really like me more than "the model."

It's getting harder to keep my infertility a secret. If I were as good a person as him, I'd end things now or tell him the truth so he could understand why he should move on. But something always stops me.

I wish I could talk to you.

Chapter Fifteen

When Cat and Vivi pulled up to the curb in front of Hank's home, they discovered him shirtless and mowing the lawn. Glistening skin stretched across muscled, broad shoulders. Slick rivulets of sweat streamed down his tapered waist and disappeared beneath the waistband of low-slung gym shorts.

From behind, he was sex-on-a-stick hot. Then he switched directions to mow another strip of grass, treating Cat to a spectacular view of his washboard abs and the little indents near his hips. Seeing him half naked and sweaty intensified the desire twining through her limbs.

She saw his determined face and noticed the shadows under his eyes. Anxiety and exhaustion had replaced his customary soft grin and half dimple.

Jackson's stunt last week had thrown Hank, and increased the pressure on Cat, too. Her brother's typical cooling-off period extended several days, so she'd left him alone to brood rather than get into an argument. Her guilty conscience didn't exactly motivate her to pick up the phone, either. For now, she focused on working fast so Hank didn't need to dip into his savings.

She'd begged, borrowed, and stolen to secure that last-minute spot in Chicago. Not ideal, but at least they could showcase his talent and drum up interest on an international stage. At a bare minimum, her presence should garner *some* curiosity. Once people met Hank and saw his work, they'd surely fall in love with both.

Vivi's photographs would lend a professional touch to their brochures, which must be ordered immediately if they were to have them ready for the show.

"This is the cutest house *ever*!" Vivi's hands landed across her heart. "What a perfect little family home."

"He grew up here." Cat smiled thinking of the sweetness of Hank's attachment to his home. Probably the same house where he'd prefer to raise his own children someday. Heaviness settled around her heart, because odds were his wife would be some other woman.

An image of that cute teacher, Amy, flickered in Cat's mind, shooting a searing streak of jealousy straight to her toes. Scowling, Cat helped Vivi unload her photography equipment from the rental car while trying to shove the unpleasant thoughts aside.

Hank cut the mower's engine when he saw them.

"Need a hand?" He jogged across the yard.

"No. We're good." Cat whipped out her camera-ready smile before he noticed her mood. "Just need to get started so Vivi can finish before David shows up to whisk her off to Block Island for the weekend."

"Nice." Hank kissed Vivi's cheek hello before doing the same to Cat. Just the brush of his lips against her cheek sent a shower of tingles to her stomach. She caught Vivi watching them and, for a moment, wondered if maybe her friend was right. Maybe she should lay herself bare. The fact that her entire body instantly went numb at the mere idea told her she wasn't ready. Hank gestured toward the door. "Helen's inside. My mom should be resting for a while, so hopefully you can finish up without disturbing her."

"This is so exciting, Hank. You know I'm going to be your first customer. I want a dining table—a really enormous one for entertaining."

Hank chuckled. "That's the criteria? Big?"

"Enormous!" She grinned. "Design it however you like. I trust you completely."

As did Cat.

"Thanks. You two might as well get started so you're done before David arrives." Hank led them inside and, after introducing them to Helen, said, "I'm going to finish up the yard, then run and pick up Jenny from her class. Good luck." He waved and disappeared through the front door.

Once Vivi had taken dozens of shots of the coffee table and sideboard, she and Cat staged the dining table. They'd adjusted its position and the lighting, added flowers, and were moving the chairs out of the way when Helen wheeled Hank's mother from her bedroom.

Mrs. Mitchell's jaw hung open beneath eyes whose gaze exposed fear and confusion. Cat scanned the space—cluttered by the tripod, the strobe light, strangers, and displaced chairs—and guessed the chaos would further agitate the poor woman.

"Da!" Mrs. Mitchell's garbled attempt to speak squeezed Cat's heart.

Vivi quickly moved the cables out of the way.

"What? What?" The sharp edge of Mrs. Mitchell's warbled voice indicated a bit of distress. Helen helped situate her on the sofa, but she began pointing at the strobe light and at Cat and Vivi.

"Should we stop?" Vivi asked Cat.

Cat and Hank *needed* these shots for the brochure, and they had no time for delays. "We only need *one* good shot of this table." Cat looked at Helen for approval. Helen nodded, suggesting they could take a few more minutes. "Let's hurry."

Vivi adjusted the lights and snapped a few pictures, quietly directing Cat to move this or that. Cat kept glancing at Mrs. Mitchell, whose hazy gaze no longer appeared upset. As soon as they'd finished, they dismantled the photography equipment.

When they began moving the furniture back into place, Mrs. Mitchell flailed her arms and barked unintelligible words. At that very moment, a woman Cat presumed to be Meg walked into the house with Hank's nephew, Eddie.

"What's going on?" She shot a harsh glance at Cat and Vivi before kneeling at her mother's feet and stroking her arm. "Hey, Mom. It's me, Meggy. I brought Eddie." Meg pushed the toddler in front of her mother, which settled Mrs. Mitchell. In fact, Cat thought she saw the older woman's mouth curl into something resembling a grin. "Kiss Grandma hello, Eddie."

Vivi continued packing up her equipment while Cat stood, frozen, watching Meg and her son, aka mini-Hank.

Every detail of their interaction stood out: the casual affection of Meg's pat on Eddie's little bum, the way she brushed a curl of his hair from his forehead, the similarity of their eyes and jaws. The mother-son bond, so pure and trusting, planted a lonely ache in Cat's chest, the roots of which coiled around her lungs until she could barely breathe.

Meg's stern glance over her shoulder broke the spell. The woman clearly resented Cat and Vivi's presence.

As Meg stood, Cat caught *her* resemblance to Hank, too. Strong genetics, just like Cat and her siblings.

Meg's sharp voice asked, "What's going on here?"

Cat extended her hand. "Hi, Meg. I'm Hank's business partner, Cat. This is my friend, Vivi. We were taking a few pictures of his work for our website and marketing brochure. Hank should be back any minute."

Meg acknowledged Vivi with a brief nod and reluctantly shook Cat's hand. "You're Jackson's sister . . . the model."

Her mildly derisive tone surprised Cat.

"Yes."

"I have no idea what business you're talking about—" Meg began.

Hank hadn't told his family? Cat could scarcely believe it. Why would he keep it a secret, especially when he had always been so aware of its effect on his mother and Jenny? She suppressed the queasy gurgle brewing in her gut.

"Rick?" Mrs. Mitchell called out, the creases in her face broadcasting anxiety as her glazed eyes scanned the room.

"He's not here, Mom." Meg focused on Cat again even as Eddie trotted to her and wrapped himself around her leg. "Since my brother's not here to supervise, I'm going to ask you two to shut down for the day. Your work is upsetting my mother."

"Of course. We were just wrapping up." Cat flashed an apologetic smile that failed to melt Meg's icy demeanor. "Your son is beautiful. He looks so much like you, and Hank."

"Thanks." Meg's tone softened at the compliment. "He's a joy and a handful at the same time."

A handful Cat envied—a novel sensation considering she had never been particularly fixated on kids until she learned she couldn't have any.

"Cat, I'll take these things out to the car." Vivi smiled in an attempt to ease the tension in the room. "I'll wait outside for David while you finish up in here."

Traitor.

"I'm sorry we disturbed your mom." Cat moved another chair back under the table. "We thought we'd be in and out before she woke up."

"Mm hmm." Meg lifted one of the dining chairs, miraculously able to maneuver around her son, who never left her side. Eddie warily stared at Cat, unaware of how the sight of him wrung her heart. "Why don't you go with your friend and leave the house to me?"

"Let me help and we'll have it finished in no time." Cat smiled, but her attempt to befriend Meg failed.

Meg set the chair by the table. "Really, Cat, Helen and I have got it covered. It's fine. Please just go."

Unaccustomed to being summarily dismissed, Cat couldn't stop herself from asking, "I'm sorry, but have I somehow offended you?"

"Aside from turning the house upside down and upsetting my mother?" Meg finally hoisted an insistent Eddie onto her hip.

Perhaps Cat should've backed away quietly, but Meg's excessively rude tone made her defensive. This was *Hank's* home, and *he'd* permitted the photo shoot. No one had meant to harm Mrs. Mitchell. "I'm very sorry about that. But I promise, you happened to walk in at the worst possible moment. Your mom came out of her room only five minutes before you arrived. Helen thought we could get one or two last shots without causing problems."

"Fine. But you might as well be on your way since you've gotten whatever you came for. It's Friday night, surely you have plans."

"Actually, your brother and I had planned to discuss business tonight, among other things. He's expecting me to be here when he gets back." Meg's presumption to kick Hank's company out of his own house rankled her. Understandably, the woman wanted to protect her mother, but Cat sensed more to Meg's cool attitude. "Would you prefer I wait in the kitchen, or is there an office where I can sit without disturbing you all?"

Sighing, Meg deposited Eddie in the corner of the living room and opened a drawer full of toys. Once she'd gotten him settled with blocks, she returned to the dining area.

"The first time Hank met you he'd been excited. Hopeful. Hank hasn't had much to be hopeful about in years, so we were all thrilled. Then you dropped him for someone else. Now you're here and getting involved in some kind of business together. That worries me." Meg locked eyes with Cat. "He hasn't mentioned it, which tells me he's uncertain about it and *you*, too. So now I'm wondering what kind of shape he'll be in when you disappoint him this time around."

Meg's pointed accusations struck hard, nearly knocking the breath from Cat. Fortunately, her self-assured persona could be summoned precisely to deal with this kind of situation.

"You certainly don't beat around the bush." A defensive tone wouldn't help, and on some level Cat understood—applauded, even—Meg's protectiveness. "I've apologized to Hank about last year. Then, when I saw all of his beautiful furniture, I suggested we could work together to sell it. Frankly, I think he's excited to get out of construction."

"He quit his job?" Meg's wide eyes and high-pitched voice made Cat wary.

Cat chose to frame the situation in its most positive light. "He's still working for Jackson now, but we already have one order for a dining table, so soon enough he'll be spending all of his time doing what he loves. I'd think that would please you, considering everything he's done for all of you."

Meg absorbed the subtle censure and then tilted her head, her eyes quickly studying Cat from head to toe. "You've already got a successful career, so why get involved in such a small business?"

"I can't model forever. I wanted a new challenge, and I admire your brother's talent. He's due a lucky break, and I can help him and his work get the recognition they deserve."

"So there's nothing more personal between you two?" Meg relaxed her stance.

"I'm not sure that's your business, but Hank and I are very honest with each other." As the words passed through her lips, she realized the lie. She hadn't been completely honest, but she didn't feel obligated to share her infertility yet. "We're taking *everything* one step at a time. No promises or expectations."

"I don't know what kind of men and relationships you're used to, but Hank's not a player. He never was. So I'll ask you nicely, once. Please don't lead him on and break his heart."

"I'm not leading him on." At least on that score she could hold her head high. She'd been honest about her reservations regarding a relationship. All she'd promised him was to take things one day at a time. "We're on the same page."

"I seriously doubt that, but I hope I'm wrong."

Cat rubbed her thumb over the creases between her eyebrows. Before she could form a response, Hank and Jenny walked in with David and Vivi.

Eddie jumped up and ran straight at Hank. In one fluid movement, Hank scooped up his nephew, twirled him upside down, and cradled him in his arms, tickling him. Eddie squealed with delight, and Hank looked just as happy.

Cat's heart squeezed, like paper crumpled in someone's fist. The bond between Hank and Eddie made obvious what she'd suspected all these weeks. She could hand him this business opportunity, pamper him with gifts, maybe even risk exposing herself completely to give him everything she had—body and soul. But even if that made him happy, none of it would give him a son or daughter who shared his eyes, his gentle attitude, his bloodline.

Grief chafed like sand inside a shoe.

"Rick?" Mrs. Mitchell's eyes fixed on her son.

Hank set Eddie back on solid ground, graced his mom with a beautiful smile, and kissed her head. "It's me, Hank. I'm right here."

Mrs. Mitchell's entire body relaxed in Hank's presence. Could that mean, on some subconscious level, she *did* still recognize him? Was that why Hank insisted on keeping her close?

Hank glanced at Meg and Cat, then frowned. "Is everything okay?"

"It will be now that you're home," Meg said with affection before shooting him a shrewd look. "I'll start dinner. Can't wait to hear all about your new business venture."

Hank's guilty expression appeared to satisfy Meg before she

turned on her heel and strode from the room with Eddie following close behind.

"How'd it go?" Hank asked Cat.

Before she responded, David interrupted. "Excuse us. We popped in to say good-bye, but need to hit the road now so we don't miss the ferry."

Vivi added, "I'll e-mail you the photos as soon as possible."

"Thanks, Vivi," Cat and Hank replied in unison, while Cat avoided David's assessing gaze.

After her brother and friend departed, she looked at Hank. "I think we got what we needed, although your mom got upset at the very end. I'm sorry."

"Not your fault. I should've stuck around and asked Jenny to find another way home."

Yes, he should have. He'd promised to make this business his priority, and yet he hadn't even mentioned it to his family. "Why haven't you told them all about our plans?"

Hank glanced at Helen, Jenny, his mother, then back at Cat. "Come out back to the garage for a minute."

"Fine." She followed behind him, eager to leave the house.

Once they'd secured a little privacy, he placed his hands on her arms. "You look a little shaken. I'm guessing Meg bit your head off?"

"Something like that." Cat stared at him, narrowing her eyes. "So, 'fess up. Why have you been keeping the truth from your family?"

Hank scrubbed his hands over his face. "With all the stress around here, I thought it would be better not to worry them too soon. I hoped, if we got an early order, then the fact I'd only be working for Jackson for a couple more weeks wouldn't seem so risky. If Vivi's serious about that table, that should help soften the blow."

"So you're not having doubts, or thinking of backing out?"

"No, Cat. I made you a promise. I'm all-in."

Cat heaved a sigh to relieve the tension coiled in her gut. "I wish Jackson weren't punishing you by kicking you off the payroll so soon."

Hank shook his head. "It's not a punishment. He's a little pissed at us, but in his own way, he's trying to help."

Maybe, but Cat knew her brother well enough to know how strongly he valued loyalty. If Jackson had a weak spot, it was his inability to handle slights or betrayals, so she couldn't help but wonder how long he'd view her and Hank as disloyal.

"You're still going to stick around, right? Meg's a good cook, and she'll leave after dinner. Jenny will probably go out. My mom will sleep." He reached for her hands. "I know your priorities, but that doesn't mean we can't enjoy a little privacy later. If you're nice, I'll give you a private tour of my room."

Tempting as he was, Cat eased out of his arms.

"That last part sounds nice, but it'd be a mistake to force myself on Meg tonight. Besides, I think it's time I go see Jackson. He and I haven't spoken since you dropped our bombshell. Looks like we'll both be facing off with siblings tonight."

~

The pungent odor of garlic filled Hank's nostrils when he walked into the kitchen, rousing a growl from his stomach. Meg, Jenny, and his mother were already seated at the table, with Eddie practically falling out of his booster seat.

"Grab a plate," Meg said.

"Smells good, thanks." Hank approached his mother's wheelchair and kissed her head before sitting between her and Eddie.

His mother's expression remained passive, staring vacantly at her untouched meal. He shook his head, trying to hide from his sisters his increasing concern over her lack of appetite. After sticking a straw in a can of Ensure, he raised it to her mouth.

Within minutes, she'd spilled her drink down the front of her shirt just as Eddie spilled sauce on his own. Jenny hung her head at the sound of his special toddler wail.

Meg nodded toward their mom. "You help her; I'll deal with Eddie."

Guess it'd be another lukewarm dinner. Sighing, Hank dabbed the soaked cotton of his mother's shirt with his napkin and then wheeled her into her bedroom to help her change.

"No!" She batted his hands. "No."

"Mom, let's get this on first." He calmly helped her into a clean shirt, despite her swatting his hands. "Do you want to rest in here?"

"Want home."

"I know." He knew she meant she wanted to go back to a time when the house and family were familiar. When things made sense and life had been easier and filled with laughter. Hell, he wanted to "go home," too.

Hank helped her into bed and locked the wheelchair wheels after parking it next to her. "I'll check on you in a bit."

She stared at him from the bed, unperceiving. Each day she drifted further from reach, he thought wearily. *I'm so damned tired.* He squeezed his hand over his eyes to stop the stinging.

When he returned to the kitchen, Jenny and Meg fell suspiciously quiet. Hank sat to finish his dinner while they loaded the dishwasher.

"Thanks for cooking, Meg." He speared a meatball. "This is good."

"You're welcome. Maybe now we can talk a bit about this new business you're starting with the model." Meg wrinkled her nose.

"She has a name. It's Catalina." He set his fork down and leaned forward. "Why the face?"

Meg cast a quick glance at Jenny then inhaled before answering.

"Imagine my surprise to find her here, moving things around, and announcing a new business that you never bothered to mention."

"I didn't want to worry you two before things were more settled." He spent five minutes filling them in on Cat's proposal and the upcoming trade show. "Whatever your opinion, 'the model' is offering me a chance to own my own business doing what I love."

"I'll bet the business isn't the only thing she's offering." Meg raised her eyebrows.

"What's with the attitude? And if you think I'm going to talk about my personal life with you now, think again."

Meg ignored his reprimand and shot back, "After the way she flaked out on you last year, how can you trust her with anything, let alone your livelihood? This has disaster written all over it, for you and our family. Mom's already been more agitated with you out of the house for longer stretches these past weeks." Meg folded the dish towel, shaking her head. "Honestly, I never thought I'd see *you*, of *all* guys, let your little head control your big one."

"Meg!" Jenny gasped, wide-eyed. "Gross!"

For Eddie's sake, Hank repressed the urge to toss the kitchen table on its side. With utter control, he set his silverware down, wiped his mouth, and then spoke to Meg in a deadly calm tone. "For the first time in forever, I've got something more in my life than working to take care of everyone else. Some*one* who is helping me with *my* dreams. Someone who goes out of her way to do thoughtful things for me, and who hasn't asked for a single thing in return other than for me to take advantage of the opportunity she's tossed in my lap. I'd think, after *everything* I've done for all of you, you'd cheer me on, not set out to destroy my happiness."

"I'm *trying* to keep you from getting hurt." Meg sat, arms crossed. "Do you honestly think this *flirtation* will last? And how long until she wants to flee the workshop and paperwork to return to life in the spotlight? You and I both know you're not the type to traipse around Manhattan at fancy restaurants and clubs, let alone make the income to keep someone like her satisfied for long."

Jenny buried her face in her hands, ill equipped to deal with the conflict between her much-older siblings.

Hank shoved his plate away. "Jenny, take Eddie in the living room, please."

Jenny's gaze darted from Hank to Meg before she lifted Eddie off the booster and left the room. The second she disappeared, Hank tore into Meg.

"You know, maybe I'd have more fun and money if I hadn't given up everything I ever wanted so you all could go to college, pick a career, fall in love, start a family. Deb and Anne barely stuck around for five minutes once they graduated, neatly getting away from all this stuff by living up there in Boston. Jenny's almost got her degree. Meanwhile, I haven't done a damned thing for myself since I left high school. When do I get a turn to have a life?"

"Don't act like I never help you and Jenny."

"A couple hours a week and two hundred bucks a month, Meg."

"Hey, I work full-time, and have a mortgage and other expenses."

"So do I!" Hank's hand slapped against the table before he lowered his voice. "I work ten- and twelve-hour days. I've practically raised Jenny by myself. I've paid off this house even though *I* don't own it. I've helped each of you with your tuition, and I'm carrying the bulk of expense for Mom's care. Meanwhile, I'm up several times a night with Mom and haven't been on a real date in six months!"

"I didn't know you carried all this resentment."

"I don't resent you, but I thought, at the very least, you appreciated all my sacrifices. Yet here you are, sabotaging me with your doubts and suspicions." He stood and dropped his plate in the sink.

Adrenaline pumped through his veins. Sensing himself being too close to shouting things that couldn't be unsaid, he stormed toward the back door.

"Hank, wait!" Meg's voice followed him as he strode outside and into his workshop, slamming the door behind him.

Much as he hated to admit it, Meg's remarks weren't the sole source of his fury. After all, his gamble did put Jenny and his mom at some risk. If this venture failed, like Jackson seemed certain it would, he'd be out of work. He hammered his fist against a table. The thought of starting over with another contractor depressed the shit out of him.

And whatever *he* felt for Cat didn't turn their fledgling relationship into something more serious. Not yet, anyway. And given her hesitancy, maybe not ever.

Meg was right. He was probably headed for a fall on both fronts. Doubt spread like wildfire, causing him to sweat. Glancing at his watch, he called Cat, hoping she could douse the flames.

No answer. Hopefully Jackson wasn't going to chew her out too much.

Hank stood in his studio, remembering when she'd been there with him the first time, of how she'd surprised him by exposing some of her insecurities.

A lot had changed between them since that night, most of it good. Still, her priority remained their business relationship, not their personal one.

He slipped the phone in his pocket, shut off the light, and dragged himself back to the house, where Jenny and Meg were waiting.

Whatever romantic dreams he harbored about Cat, this here was his reality.

His sisters and mother loved him. They depended on him. And they would be in his life forever. At this point, he couldn't say any of those things about Cat, which made it damn hard to blame Meg for her concerns.

When he reentered the kitchen, he raised his hand to stop his sisters from speaking. "I'm sorry I lost my temper. I know you're worried, and I know I'm taking some risks." He spread his arms open for a hug, wrapping his arms around them and resting his cheek on Jenny's head. "I love you guys and I don't regret anything I've done."

"We appreciate everything you do, Hank," Jenny choked out. "I swear we do."

"I know."

Eddie trotted over and raised his arms. "Up!"

Hank's chest warmed every time the little guy grinned at him, so he bent over and raised Eddie up onto his shoulders. He then forced himself to meet Meg's eyes. "We're okay, right?"

"I'm sorry if I hurt you." Meg sighed. "You're right. We've left all the heavy lifting to you, probably because you've made it look easy and never complained. But I know better than anyone how hard it is to care for the chronically ill." She reached up to take Eddie off his shoulders. "I'll speak with Anne and Deb about pitching in more, both financially and physically. They ought to get their butts back here more often anyway."

"Thanks. Every bit of help will make a difference." Yet he couldn't shake the premonition that things were probably only going to get worse.

Mom,

Another anonymous "love note" arrived. Same paper, same block print, different post office. I called the police this time, but as I suspected, there isn't much they can do without a real threat or proof that it's Justin. The potential downside of questioning him (inciting him, negative publicity, giving him the satisfaction of knowing I'm bothered) outweighs any chance that he'd actually confess.

Without a confession or other proof, I can't get the restraining order extended, so I asked them not to approach Justin yet. I think it's smartest to ignore him. If he really wants me back, he'll be on his best behavior, right? Not to mention the fact that he might not be the one sending the notes.

Maybe the fact that you're watching over me is what makes me feel safe?

Chapter Sixteen

Instead of using the ten-minute drive to prepare for a confrontation with Jackson, Cat spent it rehashing her conversation with Meg, whose disapproval clung to her like a silk shirt on a muggy day. Between that and Hank's reluctance to tell his family about their venture, she wasn't in the best frame of mind to deal with her brother.

Sitting in her car, she stared at his house and thought through her position. Sure, she'd poached Hank from his crew, and yes, she knew how much Jackson relied on Hank. But like she'd told David, Jackson didn't *own* Hank. And he didn't have the right to scold her for starting a business he'd never considered, let alone pursued.

Bolstered by her private pep talk, she marched up the front walkway. Glancing around, she noticed his overgrown shrubs and small patches of rotted wood and peeling paint on the clapboard home. Frowning, she knocked on his front door. From inside, she heard him call out "coming" as he shuffled to the entry.

When the door swung open, his surprise quickly faded into a familiar smirk. "Didn't expect to see you tonight, Judas."

"Ha-ha." She reverted to an old diffusion technique by patting his cheek and kissing him hello. That's when she smelled the whiskey. "Hard liquor?"

"Don't start." He crossed his arms. "I'm not up for a lecture, Cat. If that's why you came, then turn around and go home."

"No lectures. I came to talk." When she entered his house, her stomach dropped.

The faint stench of cigar smoke permeated the stale air. A half-empty bottle of Glenfiddich sat on the coffee table amid a dirty dish, empty Chinese food cartons, and a handful of Snickers wrappers.

"What's with the mess?" Other areas of the house in her sight line revealed the same marked difference from his usual tidiness.

"It's Friday. I'm a guy and I wasn't expecting company." He collected the trash and dirty dish from the coffee table. She followed him into the kitchen, only to discover additional dishes piled in the sink, and papers and mail scattered across the countertops.

Quietly she collected the discarded, torn envelopes. When she opened the garbage bin, she glimpsed two empty whiskey bottles at the bottom of the trash can.

She slid the garbage drawer closed. He *was* drinking too much, just as David and Hank had suspected. She refrained from lecturing in favor of poking around for an explanation. "What's a ladies' man like you doing home alone on a Friday night anyway?"

"I'm done with dating for a while." He didn't glance up from the sink.

"That I can understand." Only two months earlier, Cat had felt exactly the same way. Since then she'd let Hank into her life, and now everything was changing.

"Hmph. Seems to me you're doing just fine. Thanks for taking my wingman. Especially after I convinced him to do your project in the first place." Jackson placed the last dish in the dishwasher before drying his hands. "Sure hope you know what the hell you're doing, or you're going to screw up his life six ways to Sunday, Cat. Can you handle that responsibility and pressure?"

Apparently not very well, she admitted to herself.

"He wouldn't have as much pressure if you hadn't only given us six weeks to get things up and running."

The corners of Jackson's eyes crinkled above a smile. "You think I should keep him on my payroll and continue to fund his health insurance even though he's essentially given me notice that he's quitting?"

"What would it hurt? You always say he's your best employee, that you depend on him."

"Hank works harder than two guys, but I've already hired Doug and Ray this summer, and now need to hire a replacement for Hank. I can't have three new people on the payroll *and* keep Hank employed indefinitely. Not good business."

"No one said indefinitely, but six weeks seems a little harsh for someone you consider a friend." Cat rested her hands on her hips.

"Says the one with no experience managing employees or the expenses of running a business. Talk to me a year from now, then we'll see how your perspective has changed. That is, if you're still *in* business."

"You're so sure I'm going to fail, but I didn't know anything about modeling when I started, either, and look what I accomplished." She narrowed her eyes. "I can't wait to prove you and David wrong."

Jackson raised his hands. "I hope to hell you do prove me wrong. You think I'd be happy for you to lose money and Hank's whole family to suffer? Hell, one of the reasons I'm cutting Hank off is to make sure you dig in and give one-hundred-fifty percent. Trust me, anything less won't cut it."

"So you're not holding a grudge?" Cat tilted her head, and Jackson grabbed her in a mock headlock like he did when they were young.

"Oh, I'm holding a little grudge." He kissed her forehead before releasing her. "Don't worry, it'll pass before Christmas. But tell me this, what's really going on between you two aside from this business stuff? Norwalk's a long way from Park Avenue. And Hank isn't exactly your 'type.'"

"Sometimes a change is good for the soul, Jackson."

"Amen," he mumbled as he meandered to the living room sofa, where he plopped himself down and picked up the remote. "I could use a change."

"How so?" Cat sank into the leather chair, hoping to exploit the opening he'd provided.

"Never mind." He waved her off and poured another tumbler of scotch. "Want some?"

"No, thanks." She bit her tongue to keep from commenting on the booze. "Tell me, what do you mean when you say you need a change?"

"Nothing, just talking." He stared at the television screen while scrolling through the channels. She watched him chug half the contents of his glass in a matter of seconds.

"Maybe you should slow up, Jackson."

He held up his pointer finger. "Stop."

"Fine," she said on a sigh. After all, lots of people drink on Friday night. At least Jackson wouldn't be driving.

While the television blared, Cat's mind wandered back to Hank. Contrary to her plan, she'd grown attached. Vivi's advice threaded through her conscience like the weeds sprouting through the cracks in Jackson's front walk. *"And by the way, your plan leaves out the most important benefit of any relationship—love."*

At twenty-eight, Cat knew little to nothing of real love. She'd thought Justin loved her, but he'd merely considered her a trophy. Before him, all she had to show for her efforts was a string of past lovers who'd become disenchanted when she'd fallen short of the sex appeal and femininity of her image. And now infertility—the antithesis of that image—would also require Hank to be open to adoption or egg donors, or maybe give up children altogether.

If only she weren't infertile, if only she and Hank weren't starting a business, if only, if only, if only . . .

Commitment required honesty. Honesty required Cat to open up, be vulnerable, and risk rejection—three things she'd never done well.

The clink of a glass caught her attention as Jackson poured himself another drink.

Maybe her brother didn't want her help with his problems, but she needed his help with hers. "Jackson, I need to talk to you about something serious. Something personal."

"I keep warning you, I'm not up for a lecture." He turned off the TV and tossed the remote aside.

"No, this is about me." *Oh, God. Am I really going to do this?* She swallowed hard, but her mouth remained dry.

Jackson's forehead wrinkled with concern. Sitting forward, he shoved aside his drink and rested his elbows on his knees. "Talk to me."

And there he was, the brother she could depend upon. Focused, caring, willing to listen. A lifetime of love between them—childhood secrets, inside jokes, the security of unconditional love. She couldn't imagine life without him or David, which only underscored the fact she might never create a family of her own.

Family. Hers hadn't really recovered from her mom's death. Her dad and Janet orbited the family now rather than being the center of it, as her parents had been. Vivi's love literally saved David from being completely isolated. She also provided a bridge between him and the family, yet his and their dad's secret kept David circling the periphery. Meanwhile, Cat and Jackson remained stuck, unable to ask for help, yet failing to find happiness.

Something had to change, because it would break her heart to see Jackson continue to flounder, and, to her own surprise, she knew the solitary life she'd all but accepted as fate was too empty an existence.

As close as she considered herself and Jackson, it had been years since they'd truly confided in each other. Left with only their father's guidance to go by, they'd somehow retreated further within themselves. That had to end, and she needed to find the courage to take the first step.

Heart in her throat, she swallowed again, hoping to loosen the tightness and get the words out without falling apart. Heat crept up her entire body, making her clammy. She dabbed her hand at her forehead and licked her lips.

"Jesus, Cat, you're scaring me. What's wrong?"

Before looking him in the eye, she blurted, "My doctor diagnosed me with premature ovarian failure, which basically means premature menopause. Even with all kinds of intervention, I'm probably never getting pregnant."

A confused scowl seized his face. "Wait, how'd this even come up?"

After she'd walked him through the details leading to the diagnoses and ongoing health risks, he scooted to the edge of the couch. "You've known for almost two months?" Jackson clasped Cat's hand. "Why didn't you tell me sooner?"

"Shock, at first. You know I never really fantasized about a happily-ever-after featuring me as a stay-at-home mom, but the finality of this knocked me off balance." Her nose began to tingle, but she pressed on. "I needed time to absorb it. It's taken me this long to be ready to share it with anyone in our family. I only recently told Vivi."

"Not Dad?" Jackson asked, still rubbing her hand and forearm.

"No. If I never get married, maybe he never needs to know." Cat felt her face crumpling. Her father had always assumed she'd be some kind of trophy wife and mother, so this news would disappoint him on several levels. The mild panic incited by imagining his reaction caused her voice to break. "I can't tell him. He'll force me to visit every specialist on the planet, despite getting the same answer over and over. You know he was never very good at consoling any of us anyway—that was Mom's job."

"Come here." Jackson pulled her beside him on the sofa. She sank into the cradle of his bear hug and let her tears fall. "Infertility is a profitable business, Cat. They're always looking for answers. Never say never. You're still young."

"My follicles aren't producing eggs. I have to accept facts, not cling to fantasies."

The harsh truth caused tears to clog her throat. Telling Vivi had been much easier than sharing this news with her brother.

Jackson squeezed her harder, as if he thought his strength could somehow alter the situation. His big hand brushed against her hair and then he kissed her head. Hearing him sniffle made her cry harder.

"I can't stand to see you hurting, sis." He gently set his fingers beneath her chin and tipped her face up until she met his gaze. His cognac-colored eyes affected her just like a glass of his beloved whiskey, searing yet soothing. He'd always had the most beautiful eyes in the family. Flecked with so much gold, they glowed warmer and richer than even their mother's. Mesmerizing eyes that carried you away from your troubles, at least until you noticed them starting to glisten with tears. "Listen up. I can't imagine what you feel, and I'm not telling you what to do or preaching or anything, but if you want to be a mother, there are other options. Adoption, donors, whatever . . . this condition doesn't mean you can't ever be a mom. And you've got a lot of love locked up in that heart. I know you'd be a good mother, like Mom."

Memories of her mother's smile, her accent, her humming in the kitchen while cooking paella curled around her heart like a warm hug. Then again, despite Jackson's compliment, Cat had never been warm and open like their mom.

And despite his good intentions, none of the parenting alternatives he'd recited diminished her sorrow. Whether it made her shallow or petty, she couldn't deny a primitive longing to see Jackson's smile, David's smarts, or her mom's flair in her own offspring.

Confused, painful thoughts swirled with self-loathing, inciting a crying jag. She clung to Jackson's chest, burying her face against his shirt. He held her in silence until her crying quieted to hiccups.

Her head ached from the emotional outburst, but she mined through the rubble to recover the courage to ask the scariest question of all with a raw voice.

"Is it fair to ask a man to give up biological kids for me?" She peered up at him.

"More fair than stealing one from him." Jackson's expression turned grim and distant, as if brushing aside a painful memory.

"What's that mean?" Cat felt his body turn as rigid as granite, so she eased away.

"Never mind. I'm probably not the best guy for this conversation. Besides, you shouldn't worry about it until you meet a guy you think you could love." He cocked his head suddenly. "Unless . . . is Hank that guy?"

Maybe.

"*Hypothetically*, when would be the right time to share this information? Not too soon, or he'll think I'm already planning our future. But if I wait until we start talking about the future, is that fair?" She looked in her brother's eyes. "You're a guy. When would you want to be told?"

Jackson's eyes widened as he rubbed his chest.

"I don't know." Once more she detected a pained expression crossing his face. His joints made popping sounds as he stretched his arms and cracked his knuckles. "You know I've always wanted a big family. If I learned about it *after* I fell in love, I'd be sad, but it wouldn't be a deal breaker. I mean, at the end of the day, no one knows what the future holds anyway, and I'd be happy raising any kids with a woman I loved.

"But if she purposely withheld the information from me until I proposed or something, maybe I'd feel a little betrayed. I can't say. The heart and the mind don't always go together when it comes to these things." He squeezed Cat. "Maybe the right time is whenever you and your 'hypothetical boyfriend' have a conversation about the relationship becoming exclusive." Jackson ran his hand through his hair, looking lost. "Shit, I don't know. I suck at this kind of thing. You should talk to David."

"No, you don't suck. And I will tell David this week." She squeezed his hand and stared into space. "I guess there's no right answer."

"Sis, I'd never let you end up with some guy who doesn't love you as much as I do, which means he'll love you enough that this won't be an issue. Count on that, okay?" Jackson sighed. "I'm sorry you didn't feel like you could come to me sooner. I'm not sure if I'm angry or impressed that you've hidden this so well for so long. But it's not healthy."

"Aren't secrets the St. James way?" Now she saw another chance to get him to confide in her. "I don't hear you confessing your sins to me."

"You got me there." He shut down her attempt to unearth the root of his trouble with a sheepish grin. He then glanced at the bottle on the table. "Maybe we both need another drink."

"No. Even *I* know there aren't any answers at the bottom of that bottle."

"Maybe not, but it sure helps pass the time."

"Jackson," she started.

He glared at her with one brow cocked, so she bit her tongue.

"Fine, but I can't sit here and watch you drink that whole bottle, so I'll get going." She stood up and whipped her hair behind her shoulder. "Thanks for listening. Please don't share this with anyone."

"Of course not." He stood and hugged her. "It's your secret to tell."

~

When Jackson had warned Hank that Cat was no cakewalk, he'd sure as shit been right. Trouble with a capital *T*.

Throughout the week following the photo shoot, she'd run hot and cold. One minute she'd hammer him with dozens of questions pertaining to the business, the next she'd surprise him by tossing aside her spreadsheets and whisking him into the shower or guest bedroom. Admittedly, those moments were more than pleasant. Yet all the while, a thick emotional wall remained between them—one he couldn't bust open.

Sighing in frustration, Hank shut off his engine. Looking at his home, he prayed his mother would have a peaceful night because he really needed the rest.

Hank walked through his front door at nine o'clock to find Meg asleep on the sofa with Eddie tucked against her side. Ever since their argument, she'd offered to watch their mom one of the nights when Jenny had class so they didn't have to pay Helen extra. Looking at his exhausted sister and her son on the sofa filled him with guilt. He'd always been more comfortable doing favors than receiving them.

He knelt beside the couch. "Shhh. Just me."

Despite his attempt to be gentle, Meg woke with a start.

Hank carefully slid his arms around Eddie and hoisted him against his chest while Meg stretched and became fully alert.

"Jenny's not home yet?" Hank swayed side to side with Eddie in his arms.

"She mentioned something about a study group tonight after class."

Hank rested his cheek against Eddie's head, loving the feel and scent of the sleepy child. "How was Mom?"

"Nothing different from what you're used to, but I think we need to have a serious talk about the future."

"What about it?"

Meg glanced at Eddie. "We can talk about it later."

"Let's talk now. He's dead asleep." Hank settled himself on the sofa. He brushed his big palm across Eddie's back as the child snuggled against his chest. "God, I love this little guy. You're so lucky."

"One day you'll get your chance."

"Hopefully." At the rate Hank was going, it didn't seem like it would happen anytime soon. "Now, what's up?"

Meg combed her fingers through her hair to push it off her face. "I think it's time to make alternative arrangements for Mom's care. I know you're loath to send her elsewhere, but this situation can't continue. Her faculties have declined sharply, even since the weekend I stayed here when you went to the wedding. This isn't a safe environment for her anymore, or a healthy one for you and Jenny."

"All due respect, Meg, I've been dealing with this for a long time. I think I know what I can handle."

"It's past nine. You'll be keeping this crazy schedule while getting your business off the ground, and you can't expect Jenny to handle Mom alone. It was hard for me with Eddie here, too, but at least I'm a nurse and used to dealing with sick, elderly people." She hugged her knees to her chest. "If we all pool our resources, we can afford a nearby facility for Mom and you'd finally have some freedom."

"That's too high of a price, and I'm not only talking about the expense." When Eddie shifted, Hank stilled for a second, then spoke in hushed tones. "I'm doing okay. Don't hold my recent outburst against me, or use it to come in here and change everything."

"Just because you think you can handle it doesn't mean it's what's best. And, all due respect, I'm a nurse. I think I have a better take on Mom's condition and needs than you."

Pow! She'd pulled the nurse card on him and it stung. Closing his eyes, he inhaled slowly, counting to ten. He didn't need a nursing degree to tell him how bad the situation had become.

He knew his Mom rarely recognized him. He knew she was in diapers, couldn't remember how to shower or dress, and ate things like toothpaste and glue when she found them. He knew it was a pain in the ass to live with baby-safety locks on doors and drawers, to hide sharp objects, to give up a normal social life to babysit his sick mom.

But what Meg, Jenny, and no one else seemed to get was that Hank couldn't live with himself if he passed those problems over to strangers. Strangers who wouldn't genuinely care whether his mom was comfortable or afraid. Strangers she'd never recognize, not even for a millisecond.

"I won't put Mom in a home. I can't do it. I'd never sleep peacefully worrying about how confused and alone she'd be in completely unfamiliar surroundings with unfamiliar faces."

"Hank, we're unfamiliar to her ninety percent of the time."

"That still leaves ten percent of the time when she has a flash of recognition. I've seen it, Meg. Those few moments now and then bring her a little serenity. And maybe she hasn't retained every little memory of this house—like cleaning up the glitter after a visit from the tooth fairy, or soup and pizza Friday nights, or Monopoly marathons—but it's familiar to her. It's her safe place. I can't take it away. I won't. If it's too hard for you to come here and help, then I won't complain. But I'm not moving her out of her home."

Meg buried her head in her hands. "You make me feel like a bad daughter, and that's not fair."

Hank laid Eddie on the sofa and then hugged Meg. "I'm not trying to make you feel guilty. I'm only telling you what I won't do, even if I'm a little crazy."

Meg eased away. "Do you think any of this is good for Jenny? She worries about messing up, about what she'd do if Mom got hurt on her watch, and she worries about you, too. And more of the burden will fall on her as you become invested in this new business. You're so busy thinking about how *you* feel, I doubt you've had an honest conversation with Jenny about *her* concerns. Yes, Mom may struggle with the change at first, but at least she'd be physically safe. Isn't that most important consideration?"

Hank's muscles twisted and tightened in defense from her accusations. He rubbed his hands against his thighs, feeling like a failure despite all he'd sacrificed. Throwing back his shoulders, he turned to Meg.

"I hear you. I'll think about it. But as long as I'm able to care for Mom, that's probably what I'll choose to do."

She threw her hands heavenward. "You're more stubborn than Dad on his worst day."

He grinned at the remark, knowing it wasn't a compliment. "Maybe."

Sighing through a smile, she hugged him. "This conversation isn't over, but I'll drop it for now. I'm going home to get some sleep. Good luck."

Hank carried Eddie to the car for Meg before going back inside. His phone buzzed in his pocket, so he checked the incoming text.

Site is live. Check it out then call me ASAP.

He typed the URL and landed on their webpage. The home page featured a great shot of his dining table with tabs to other pages that discussed their mission, their background, and the upcoming trade show.

It looked sophisticated and professional. The portfolio page featured the side table he'd built for Vivi, his coffee table, the sideboard from his dining room, and sketches he'd drawn with several other designs. He liked his new designs, but still wanted to reconsider her plan to create "lines" rather than concentrate on client-commissioned pieces. He just hadn't found time to really think it through or discuss it with her in his zeal to finish her closets before the trade show. But time was running out. He needed to tell her before they went any further.

He'd make sure to raise it when he saw her tomorrow.

Still, seeing his pieces online allowed him to view them objectively. A burst of pride shot through him. Cat may not be giving him everything he wanted from her, but she'd helped change the direction of his life, and he couldn't deny getting caught up in the thrill.

Vivi had snapped some photos of him and Cat, one of which Cat put on the site. He stared at it—at her—wishing he could find the key to unlocking the door to her heart.

It was getting harder to settle for glimpses of her feelings, for the fits and starts of her affection that were always followed with her nearly frantic need to retreat.

The extent of damage other men, including her own dad, had done to her self-esteem couldn't be underestimated. But when would she finally see that he was different from them? That the woman he liked best was the one he saw beneath her physical beauty?

He dialed her. "Looks great, Cat."

"Learning WordPress isn't a major accomplishment, but I think I did a pretty good job, right? And as soon as I posted it on my Facebook and Twitter pages, they blew up. Go search hashtag Mitchell-StJames."

Hank took a second to pull up her Twitter page and began browsing the comments. Within a minute, he scowled. "Who the hell is SecretAdmirer and why is he calling you 'love'?"

"That's what you're focused on? Not the comments about the furniture?"

"It's a little disturbing, Cat. Don't you think?"

After a brief silence, she replied, "Look, I get a lot of flirtatious love notes from harmless fans. All models do. But I admit, SecretAdmirer makes me a little uncomfortable because the wording is similar to the letters I've been receiving this summer."

"What letters?" She'd been receiving random love letters?

"Short notes. They never threaten me or anything, but they're . . . possessive." She paused before adding, "I think they may be from Justin."

Hearing that man's name injected liquid heat into Hank's veins, but he kept his cool. "Why him instead of someone else?"

"Because he was possessive. And because I don't know who else would take the time to find me after I went to some trouble to cover my tracks when I bought the condo."

Hank cursed, his body temperature soaring even higher at the idea that Justin, or any man, was watching her, stalking her, scaring her. "What do the cops say?"

"Oh, please. They didn't even put Justin in jail the first time, and without proof that he sent the letters, they can't do anything about nonthreatening mail. And there's no way to get a restraining order against an anonymous author."

Dammit, he didn't like being powerless to help. "At least Justin's forced to keep his distance."

"Not anymore. The restraining order expired today."

Both of his hands balled into fists. "I don't like any of this, not one bit."

"Then don't think about it. Honestly, I'm okay. My building's very secure, and I'm always aware of my surroundings. No one's going to catch me off guard." He heard her sigh. "How about you focus on all the compliments about your work. And by the way, you don't see me getting worked up by all the women making sexual overtures to you. It's mostly playful chatter."

Hank scanned more tweets and felt flush with embarrassment. "I don't like being part of this virtual world."

Once again Cat fell silent for a few seconds. "Unfortunately, it's part of my life. If you want a personal relationship with me, you're going to have to get comfortable with it. Can you do that?"

Hank had never once stopped to consider how his life might be invaded by her relative fame. How had he been so naïve? And could he ever be comfortable with random men constantly hitting on her, whether online, in public, or apparently by sending private love notes?

"Guess I'm gonna have to adjust." Overwhelmed by exhaustion and a fair amount of distress, he yawned. "Listen, I need to catch some z's. I'm planning on finishing up at your place in the morning."

"My publicist helped me get an interview with someone from *Town & Country* magazine tomorrow at eight, so I won't be here when you arrive. If we can get in front of its audience, we'll reach over half a million wealthy, middle-aged home owners. Just the type who can afford handcrafted furniture."

"That's great, Cat. But I guess I might miss you altogether then, because once I hang the doors and add the hardware, I'll be coming back to Connecticut to work with Jackson's new hire." Hank refrained from mentioning his lingering regret about how they'd handled things with Jackson, or his concerns about whether or not Jackson's present emotional state would cause problems with his new crew.

"Training your replacement must be weird. Is Jackson treating you okay?"

"Pretty much. Our friendship will survive my leaving. At least, I hope so. Right now he's focused on making sure he and I get the new guy up to speed. He makes wisecracks about my new job, but it's mostly good-natured."

"Don't let him make you feel bad about leaving, Hank. It's business, not personal."

"I don't know that he can separate the two like you can." Shit, did he say that out loud?

A beat of hesitation passed before Cat spoke, her voice subdued. "I warned you that I'm not good at relationships. If you're not happy, then you should move on. But you did promise we could take it slow, and that we'd concentrate on the company in the short term."

"You're right." He was about to reassure her that he didn't want to move on, but he heard a noise coming from his mother's room. "Hey, my mom's stirring. I'll talk to you tomorrow."

He jogged to his mother's room and found her on her knees reaching under the nightstand for her sippy cup.

"I got it, Mom."

He settled her back in bed before refilling the cup with fresh water. "Here you go. What else do you need?"

Out of nowhere, she touched his face, eyes alert. "Good boy." For a millisecond, she appeared to recognize him.

"Right here, Mom," he answered, with tears in his eyes. He felt foolish crying in a dark room, but the rare moment of recall overwhelmed him.

Then, like fog in sunlight, the moment vanished and a glaze engulfed her eyes. He tucked her under the covers and closed the door behind him when he left.

The once-in-a-blue-moon memory made it impossible to seriously consider Meg's warnings or Jenny's concerns. For more than a dozen years, he'd taken care of his work and his family. There'd be some readjustment thanks to his new schedule, but he'd handle it without dropping any balls.

Mom,

I've been thinking about my discussion with Jackson and the way Hank adores his nephew. Hank promised I could tell my secrets only when I was ready. But will I ever be ready for him to look at me as anything less than a whole woman? Maybe that sounds silly, but that's how I feel. Did you feel that way, too?

Should I tell him everything and see what happens?

Please send me a sign. I want to believe he could accept me—the real, unvarnished me.

But I don't want his pity.

Chapter Seventeen

Cat turned the corner and continued walking toward her building, frowning. The woman who interviewed her must've seen Hank's photo on their website, because she'd asked a lot of questions about Hank's personal life that seemed wholly unrelated to the business or the furniture. Cat replayed the interview in her head as she strode up the block, thinking about what she could or should have said.

"Catalina."

That stringent voice had haunted her nightmares since last fall. She froze, eyes glued to the pavement, mind blank. Chills rushed through her limbs, tightening her muscles.

"These are for you." Justin thrust a bouquet of flowers under her nose.

Her peripheral vision blurred; passing cars drove by in slow motion. Her arms stiffened at her sides, unmoving, as if caught in a hunter's gun sight.

"Catalina, take the flowers." He wiggled them again.

"Justin." She briefly closed her eyes before raising her gaze to meet his. "What are you doing here?"

"The restraining order terminated yesterday. I've paid for my mistake, learned from it. Now I want a second chance. You know I never meant to hurt you or Vivi." He reached for her hand to force them around the flowers, but she withdrew. "Come on, Cat. Please take the flowers."

Cat straightened her shoulders and cast a furtive glance toward her building. The thirty yards between her and the front door may as well have been a mile. Alone with Justin—the very last place she wanted to be. The memory of Vivi lying in a pool of her own blood flashed through Cat's mind.

Stay calm. Be smart. You're safe in public, but you are in public! *Don't draw unwanted attention.*

"Thank you, Justin." She offered a weak smile. "Unfortunately, I'm not interested in a reunion. I'm sorry."

He blocked her when she tried stepping to his left, then he grasped her arm.

"Why not?" His grip tightened in concert with the muscles in his jaw. "You and I have something special."

"Whatever we shared is in the past, Justin." *Fighting only makes him worse.* "Please let me go."

"How can I when I'm always thinking of you?" A flicker of agony dimmed his eyes. "You were the best thing in my life. Please, Cat. Give me another chance. I love you. I swear I'll never hurt you. Come on, you know I'm the only one for you."

I'm the only one for you. Cat's eyes widened in recognition of the phrase she'd read in big block print. "You sent those anonymous love notes, didn't you?"

He hesitated before confessing. "Yes. Being cut off from you was killing me. I had to remind you of what we have." He still held her arm, tugging her closer, eyes pleading yet determined. "I know you feel it, too, even if you're still afraid. I promise I've changed. Forgive me so we can start over."

"I'm sorry, Justin. I don't feel anything." Cat shrugged her arm, but couldn't break free. The memory of the media frenzy surrounding their breakup flashed through her mind, urging her not to cause a scene. The last thing she needed was ugly new headlines surfacing days before the trade show. She had to diffuse him carefully. "It's over. If you really care about me, please let me go."

Her heart jumped as he yanked her against his body. The flicker of anger hardening his eyes, the tight grip on her arm, the sound of his heavy breath near her ear, all caused her to go limp. Justin rested his cheek against her head to inhale the scent of her hair. When he shivered, she nearly threw up.

"It's not over, Cat." His voice quaked with repressed fury, and then he whispered in her ear like a lover, "It'll never be over."

Unable to find her voice, which was as paralyzed by fear as her body, Cat closed her eyes.

"Hey!" Hank's voice cut through Cat's panic. Out of nowhere he'd arrived and now glared at Justin. "Is everything all right here?"

"Just a lovers' spat. Nothing to worry about." Justin didn't spare Hank a glance. "Cat, tell him."

"Justin, no—" she began, but Hank interrupted.

"I think it's time you let her go." Hank didn't reach for Justin, but rather appeared to be assessing the situation to determine the safest way to save her, just as he'd done at David's reception.

"Oh, do you?" Justin smirked, now turning his attention to Hank. "And why should I care what you think?"

"I'm not as easy to bully as a woman half your size, you son of a bitch." The vein in Hank's temple pulsed and Cat notice a streak of red traveling up his neck. "Step away now so no one gets hurt."

Justin's expression turned incredulous and mocking. "Who the hell is this clown, Cat?"

She met his gaze. "My partner."

Wrong move.

Justin snapped his head toward Hank. His eyes narrowed as he studied Hank's clothes and face. In her peripheral vision Cat noticed a few passersby slowing their pace, taking notice of them. She ducked her head, hoping to avoid recognition.

"You're the guy on the website. The carpenter?" Justin turned from Hank and looked at Cat. She winced as Justin gripped her bicep harder. "And you? Getting your kicks with the blue-collar class these days?"

Jealousy had caused him to lower his guard and turn his back on Hank for a moment. In a rush of movement, Hank twisted Justin's arm behind his back. The roses fell, lying splayed on the sidewalk, as Hank brought Justin to his knees.

Justin released Cat in order to break his fall. He shoved his elbow back toward Hank's torso, but Hank twisted to miss the blow. In the midst of the struggle, Hank's fist connected with Justin's right eye.

Hank leaned over Justin, waiting.

Justin rolled onto his back and spat at Hank, missing him by an inch. "I'm going to sue you for assault, you bastard. Nobody sucker punches me and gets away with it."

Oh perfect, her ex and Hank sharing a jail cell. She could see the headlines now. All she wanted was to get the hell off the street without involving cops or lawsuits.

"If you sue Hank, I'll notify the police about the letters you sent, Justin." Cat kept her eyes on Justin. "Breaching the restraining order *and* assaulting me in broad daylight will land you in jail this time. Or you could finally move on and let this, and me, go. Your choice."

Hank bent over Justin, reaching under his arm and lifting him to his feet. "Time to apologize and say good-bye."

Justin shrugged free of Hank's grasp, straightened himself, and swiped his hand over his hair to push it from his forehead. Hatred seethed from his eyes when he turned on Cat. His voice dripped with sarcasm. "I'm so sorry. Please forgive me, my love."

"Stay the hell away from her!" Hank barked.

"With pleasure," Justin rejoined. Before he strode away, he crushed the roses under his heel and sneered at Cat. "You'll look back on this one day and realize what a mistake you made."

"Is that a threat?" Hank stepped in front of Cat.

"No, it's just the truth. She's out of your league, and she'll realize it sooner or later. Then she'll be back at my door." Justin leaned to his left to catch Cat's eye. "Don't wait too long, love, or that door might not be open."

Cat's adrenaline spike ebbed as Justin stormed off, causing her body to shudder. Hank snatched her into his arms and held her until the tremors subsided. "Let's get inside," he said, then slid an arm around her waist and walked her to the apartment.

Her mind replayed the past several minutes, so she didn't speak.

As the elevator doors closed, Cat finally said, "I didn't expect you to still be here. You said you'd be gone . . ." her voice broke at the thought of wondering what she would've done had Hank not arrived.

Hank encircled her with his arms. "I'd just taken the last of my equipment to my truck. I came back to drop off your key and leave a note."

"I'm glad you did." Tears formed in her eyes. "I hope no one recognized me and snapped a photo. I want the focus to stay on our furniture, not my love life."

"Isn't any publicity good publicity?" When she didn't laugh, Hank used his key to unlock her door. Once inside, he asked, "Cat, where's your phone?"

"In my purse. Why?"

"You should call the cops, and call David about getting another restraining order."

"No cops." Cat searched for her phone. "I'll call David, though."

She pulled up her favorites list and selected David's cell phone number.

"Hey, Cat!" Vivi's voice chirped.

"Hey, V," she paused, surprised that Vivi had David's cell on a work day. "Is David around?"

"He's in the shower. Headed to the airport soon for a quick business trip. What's wrong? You sound funny."

"I need his help. Justin showed up today. He was the one sending those letters."

"I knew it. Oh, I *knew* it, Cat." Cat heard a jostling sound as if Vivi were in motion. "Did he hurt you? Are you okay?"

"I'm okay. But I need to talk to David."

Cat heard Vivi pulling her brother out of the shower and giving him the quick rundown.

"I'll be over in five minutes," came David's blunt response once he took his phone from Vivi.

"No need. Hank's here. Besides, Vivi said you've got to catch a flight. I only called so you could get the process started. Justin came by, admitted to sending me the anonymous notes I'd been receiving, and then ended up getting into a fight with Hank."

"What anonymous notes?" She heard David curse on the other end of the line.

"Please don't snap at me," Cat said in a tiny voice before explaining the notes to David. "Justin admitted to sending them."

"He broke the terms of the restraining order. It prohibited *any* contact."

"I know. That's why I'm telling you."

"What happened today?" he asked.

Her voice cracked as she recounted the skirmish with Justin. "But listen, David. I don't want him arrested, I just want him kept away. Another arrest will bring publicity I can't afford right now, and it could cause him to sue Hank for assault. If Hank ends up in jail, that will kill our business before it gets off the ground. Not to mention that we don't want Hank to be spending time and money on defense attorneys."

David fell silent for several seconds. "Okay. I think you can go through family court to get an order of protection without involving the cops. I'll pull the old file and ask someone to get things started. You probably have to appear, but maybe you and Hank can just provide an affidavit, given the past history with Justin. I can't promise no publicity, but we can avoid an arrest."

"Do whatever you can. Thanks."

"You're welcome. I'm glad you weren't hurt. Can I speak with Hank for a minute?"

Another shudder passed through her from thinking about the high wire she'd just walked with Justin. She'd felt trapped by fear of him, of being hurt, of bad publicity. Every choice could've been a misstep.

While Hank spoke with David, Cat stumbled into the kitchen to get a drink and calm herself. The cool water soothed her throat. After setting the empty glass in the sink, she bent over and drew several deep breaths.

Two years.

She'd wasted two years—two potentially fertile years—on that maniac. How many other foolish choices had brought her to this point . . . twenty-eight, damaged goods, lost, afraid?

"Are you okay?" Hank stepped behind her and rubbed her shoulders. He then embraced her from behind and kissed the side of her head. "I think I'll stay for a while, until you're settled."

She turned in his arms. Squeezing her eyes shut, she burrowed into his chest, clinging to him. Wonderful Hank, who rode to her rescue despite the way she held him at arm's length. "I'm sorry you got sucked into Justin's BS. I wish I'd been smarter when you and I first met. So many things would be different now."

"Don't apologize." He cupped her face.

"I know I frustrate you. I probably even hurt you sometimes, although that's the last thing I want. See! I'm a mess, Hank. You deserve so much better. God, you must regret the day Vivi tricked you into looking at my closets."

"Regret it? I treasure it." His warm gaze melted the anxiety from her body, easing the tightness in her muscles. "Don't you get it? When we're together, I see a future that isn't only about taking care of everyone else. It's exciting and irresistible, just like you. And seeing you smile is well worth whatever trouble you or Justin stir up."

Cat's heart welled up with the unspoken promise in Hank's words. Would he still be there once the luster wore off? Once he learned the truth?

She'd started with a good plan: casual lovers, maybe good friends, and a new career. The reasons for that plan hadn't changed, but now her heart begged for more. So much more. She'd been fighting its demands, for his sake and hers. Yet, in Hank's arms, her willpower fled.

She lifted her head and kissed him.

The brief appearance of his little dimple warmed her soul. He kissed the tip of her nose. "I've got something to show you."

"I'll bet you do." Cat tugged at the waistband of his shorts.

"I'm talking about your closets."

"All done?"

"Uh-huh." He grabbed her hand and tugged her down the hallway. "And I've got a surprise."

"I love surprises."

Although she'd been marking his progress for weeks, she gasped at the beautiful end product. Thin mirrors were inset within the polished bird's-eye maple doors. Crystal hardware provided a touch of elegance to the cabinetry.

"It's perfect, Hank." She noticed he'd tossed her decorative bed pillows in the window seat to make it look pretty. "I love everything about it except for the fact that I now have a lot of unpacking and organizing to do."

"Open them up and look inside." He stood back with his arms folded across his chest. "That's the surprise."

She opened one of the doors. "Oh my God!"

Her clothes hung in the closet. Within seconds, she'd opened the other doors and drawers, each time shrieking. He'd organized her wardrobe. She spun on her heel and ran to the old closet. When she flung open the bifold doors, she found all of her shoes and handbags neatly aligned on the various shelves. Clapping her hands, she twisted around. "You're amazing!"

Her smile was so wide her cheeks hurt. She charged at Hank and pushed him onto her bed. "Really, Hank. You're amazing."

His breathing escalated immediately. He weaved his fingers through her hair and pulled her on top of his body, kissing her with long, hungry sweeps of his tongue. Her own breath felt shallow as she hastily removed his shirt. His touch felt like home.

"Catalina," he whispered as his mouth lingered at the sensitive spot below her ear. "Tell me this means as much to you as the business."

"No talking. Just kiss me."

He paused, as if deciding whether to press for an answer. Then his dimple reappeared on that left cheek. "I loved unpacking your lingerie. Show me what you're wearing today." He nuzzled the spot beneath her ear and she felt the corners of his mouth curl in anticipation of her reply.

"My favorite color." She weaved her fingers through his hair.

His head popped up, and he eagerly shoved her shirt up to peek. Delight enveloped his features when he exposed a fire-engine-red bra with pink ribbon accents. "Red's my new favorite color." He slipped his finger inside the bra to push it out of the way before he began kissing his way down her chest.

"Mm," she murmured.

Slowly, Hank stripped her clothes away until they were both naked on her bed. She savored the scent of his skin, the feel of his hard muscles beneath her hands, the heaviness and heat of the friction created as they moved against each other.

He rolled on top of her and smiled. "I've been picturing us in this bed since the first time I saw this room." He kissed her again.

His damp, hot breath whispered against her ear as he nibbled on her earlobe. "I can never get enough of you." She felt his erection pressing against her thigh and reached for the thick shaft. He groaned as the muscles in his back rippled, making her feel sexy and powerful.

"Me on top." She rolled him over. "Hands above your head."

Hank's intense expression indicated he was restraining his impulse to take her quickly. He grabbed the top of her headboard as her tongue stroked the centerline from his chest to his navel.

Hank was huge and hard—intimidating—but she'd never backed down from anything, so she sucked him into her mouth as deeply as she could.

"Cat!" Hank swore. The muscles in his arms bulged. His knuckles whitened against the edge of the headboard. His head fell back and groans of pleasure tore through his chest.

She cupped him and pumped him with her mouth while his body writhed beneath her. Within a minute she felt his hands on her head.

"Catalina," he uttered while yanking her up the length of his torso. He growled something unintelligible before plundering her mouth with his tongue.

In two seconds, she was on her back with him buried inside her. He watched her face intently. With each thrust of his hips, he exclaimed her name in passionate, rasped whispers until they exploded together in a dizzying orgasm. Afterward, he cuddled her against his body and stroked her hair.

She felt lazy, happy—an unfamiliar contentedness unique to being with Hank. She closed her eyes, determined to enjoy it without analyzing it further.

Cat lay in the afterglow of lovemaking until a sprig of panic twisted through her mind, puncturing her short-lived sense of peace.

Justin had caused her to fear men. Her diagnosis had caused her to fear commitment. Now Hank was causing her to fear being alone.

He made it all but impossible to resist the pull in her heart—the thrilling sense of falling from a cliff with the security of landing gently in warm water. She owed Hank better than withholding her affection, than withholding the truth.

But keeping quiet allowed this little bit of happiness to go on. He liked her, might even be falling in love with her, but could she hold on to a man who so clearly valued family when she couldn't give him one? Wouldn't that only bring them both pain?

Hank lifted onto his elbows and kissed her eyelids. "I meant to take my time, but you knocked me off my game with your little power play." His expression suddenly shifted to one of concern. "What's wrong? You look upset. Is it Justin?"

"It's not Justin." She closed her eyes, unprepared to have a serious discussion.

"Is it us?"

She opened her eyes, and swallowed hard, but words wouldn't come.

"Stop running from me, Cat. I won't hurt you or let you down or lie or whatever the hell all the other men you've known have done to make you so wary."

His gaze never wavered, but hers did. "You think you know me, but I'm not the glamorous, confident woman in magazines."

"I don't want her, Cat. I like you best when you let your hair down, like the night we met, or the time I found you scrubbing my mom's mirror, or watching you joke around with your brother. That's the woman I love. Fancy clothes and pictures don't mean a thing to me."

A brief smile curled her lips. *The woman I love.* But then she remembered her huge secret. "Maybe, but there are other things you don't know. Things I can't change. Things that aren't so easy to accept."

"We all have flaws. Trust me, Cat. Let me in."

Hank deserved someone who wasn't afraid of commitment. Someone who could embrace her own emotions. Someone completely, unselfishly honest.

Even if Cat found the courage to become that better woman and even if he thought he loved her enough to give up biological children, would he regret or resent that choice later?

And if she really loved him, how could she even consider putting him in that position?

"You don't understand."

"Then explain it better." But he stopped pressing when a tear ran down her cheek. He wiped it away. "Sorry. Don't cry."

He kissed her. "I'll wait until you're ready to talk. Just remember, whatever it is you think I can't handle, you're probably wrong. Look at my life, look at what I've borne for the people I love."

"Exactly why you deserve an easy, uncomplicated relationship. You are such a good man. Whatever happens in the future, know that no one has ever meant as much, or given me as much peace and comfort, as you have. I can never repay that." When she saw his face twist with frustration, she brushed his jaw with her fingers. "It's been an emotional morning. Can we end this discussion for now? We've got the show in two days. Let's get through that first, okay?"

Relenting, he sighed. "Speaking of which, I should probably head back up to Connecticut. Lots to do before I pack up the truck and hit the road. You're getting off easy by flying."

"Sorry, but I need to be there early to meet with the exhibition installation group I hired. By the time you arrive, I'll have everything settled. We'll be able to get a decent night's sleep before the show."

"Sleep?" He kissed her neck. "I can think of better ways to pass the time in a nice hotel room."

"Actually, so can I."

He slipped his fingers through her hair while his eyes drank in every aspect of her face. She felt him trace her collarbone then his hand wrapped around her nape while he gently pulled her into a kiss. “It’s a date.”

He eased away, but Cat caught his arm. “Thank you for today . . . with Justin, and everything you just said. Your feelings matter to me more than you know. It may not seem like it, but I really am trying to protect both of us from getting hurt.”

“I don’t need protection, Cat. I need you.” He kissed her one last time. “I’m patient, but even I won’t wait forever.”

Mom,

The trade show is tomorrow. Are you proud of me? I haven't seen Dad, although he's called me a few times with lots of unsolicited advice about my plans. I know, I know . . . he means well.

So much on the line: my reputation, Hank's financial stability . . . my heart. Of course, that last part has nothing to do with the show. Hank's not the only one who's sick of the limbo. I've made a decision. I'm going to tell him everything once we return from Chicago.

Wish me luck.

Chapter Eighteen

Hank wrapped a towel around Cat as they stepped out of the hotel shower, pulling her against his body for another kiss. *Best. Damned. Morning.* Waking up wrapped around her body ranked as the number-one morning of his adult life, even if it was only five thirty a.m. and the sun hadn't risen.

An auspicious start to an important day.

"Too bad this morning has to end so soon," she murmured in his ear.

Since he'd arrived in Chicago, she'd been anxious—and intense. Physically, she'd barely let go of him—which he liked—but he'd also caught glimpses of sorrow or regret, maybe even fear, in her eyes. At first he'd assumed the show had her keyed up, but instinct told him otherwise.

Of course, there had been a tiny brouhaha when a picture of him holding Justin on the pavement showed up on Instagram later that day. Some people had made nasty comments suggesting she liked violent men, which hadn't been flattering to either her or him. But if anything, most people had seemed sympathetic.

Cat had issued one brief statement about putting it behind her and focusing on her new venture. Within twenty-four hours the frenzy had died down, so he doubted the incident would hurt Cat's and his business.

Her hands swept across his back and over his hips, making him get hard for the millionth time since he'd arrived last night. When she pinched his ass, he bit her earlobe. "We should get going."

"I know." Cat kissed his neck while her hand clamped around his hard-on. "Can't seem to help myself. Up for a quickie?"

The towel fell away and her nipples tightened against his chest, sending another surge of desire through him. In no time, he lifted her and carried her into the bedroom, teasing. "Probably a good idea for us to release a little tension before our big day."

He crawled on top of her and thrust inside her body in one swift motion, foreplay unnecessary in the heat of the moment. He buried himself completely, staying deep while kissing her and undulating his hips ever so slightly. Nothing was more beautiful than the sight of her heated face and swollen lips. *Mine.*

Had what he'd said the other day made a difference, made her consider opening up? He needed her to trust him . . . trust in them.

"Hank," she moaned, rocking her hips. Her eyelids drifted closed as she arched her back.

He took one breast into his mouth, and his pace steadily increased while he teased her with his tongue.

"Hank," she panted. "God, yes. Faster . . . faster, please."

He answered her siren call by slamming himself inside her until she cried out and her muscles clamped around him, milking every last drop of strength from his body.

Once his heart rate slowed, he propped up on his elbows and kissed her. *Heaven.* Funny he could be so optimistic about the future despite the fact he was broke, lived with his mother, and had no plan B. But for the first time in a long time, he didn't want to worry or plan or be cautious. He wanted to live in the moment.

He wished they could stay here in bed indefinitely, but the clock was ticking and the doors opened to the public in several hours. "Okay, now we really have to go."

"I know." She grimaced.

Hank traced his finger from her forehead to the tip of her nose then kissed her quickly. "Get dressed."

Then his phone buzzed. "Jenny, you're calling pretty early. Everything okay?"

"Helen had to cancel today and Meg is working. I guess I'm going to have to miss class today, unless you know someone else to call."

"There isn't anyone else." He'd never needed other backup because he'd always been there to take care of any problem. He could hear Jenny's anxiety, but at twenty, she should be more than capable of handling their mom for one day. Hell, he'd started taking on grown-up responsibilities at seventeen. "Keep her comfortable. Play music she likes, maybe read to her from one of those magazines. If you're nervous about her choking, feed her yogurt and Ensure. Will Helen be there tomorrow?"

"I don't know. She's sick."

Dammit. No one would accuse Hank of being superstitious, yet Helen's sudden illness seemed like a bad omen.

"I'll be home in two days. Hang in there."

"But Mom's really fussy again. And today her eyes look weird, like they're sunken in."

"I know she's been more irritable and sleepless lately, but I think it's just the disease progressing. If you're really worried, see if Meg can come over to check on her later."

"Okay." Jenny paused. "Good luck today, Hank."

Hank tossed his phone on the bed and rubbed his hand across the back of his neck. He couldn't afford to divide his focus. Schmoozing potential customers would require his full attention today.

"You look upset." Cat tied the belt of her wrap dress. Even in casual clothing, she was breathtakingly pretty.

"Jenny's on her own with my mom all day. She's nervous, but it should be okay as long as my mom doesn't fall or something."

"I'm sure it will be fine. Try to put it out of your mind because we need to concentrate on this show."

"About that." He hesitated, knowing his next words might freak her out. He should've brought this up before now, but it seemed like the world had conspired to keep him quiet. "What would you say to making a last-minute change?"

"Tell me you're joking." Cat's hands stilled. "Not joking?"

"Every time I meant to talk about this, we got sidetracked by other issues, most recently Justin. I wanted to keep you happy and decided I'd just do it your way and see how it went. But on my drive up I had a lot of quiet time to think, and now I'm convinced I need to say how I feel before we actually go out there today."

She flicked one hand out in question. "And?"

"The thing I love most about building furniture is the artistry. Approaching each piece and making it unique. Letting the wood grains inspire me and dictate the shape and form of the furniture. I want to be free to make any design that comes to me, not have to replicate a handful of pieces over and over." When her forehead creased, he added, "Besides, you said your friend's privately commissioned table sold for top dollar. Custom design, one-of-a-kind pieces will give us a bigger profit margin and make the brand more distinctive—make it synonymous with individuality."

"And limit our customer base." She chewed her lip. "No inns, offices, retailers."

Hank shrugged. "Let's establish ourselves as the 'Armani' of furniture first, and then you can figure out how to mass produce knockoffs and sell those to hotels and offices and whomever else you please."

Cat sighed, her expression pinched with concern. "This completely changes our business model. Now these pamphlets depicting the lines and prices aren't accurate, Hank. I don't think we can use them."

"I'm sorry, but better we begin as we mean to go on. We've got business cards. We'll spend the next two days touting the benefits of having a 'Mitchell/St. James original.' Sell it like artwork instead of furniture. The website is less than a week old, so we can make modifications there without much notice."

She nodded, although she didn't look convinced. "I wish you'd have spoken up sooner. You've blindsided me and now I'm going in unprepared. I'd kind of mastered the basics of what I *thought* was our plan. Now that's meaningless. So you'd better be prepared to do most of the talking today, because I don't know how to describe the nuts and bolts of what you do. And without brochures to hand visitors, are you up to the task? We can't appear unprofessional."

"Are you kidding? I'm excited to discuss my work . . . to discuss my 'vision,' as you say. Don't worry, people will remember us."

She folded her arms, looking out the window over the city. Finally she huffed a short breath and shrugged.

"It's not ideal, but you need to be happy with your work. We don't have time to debate the issue now, so there's nothing else to say." She worried her lip, brows drawn. "Promoting it like art instead of furniture is a good angle."

He grabbed her and kissed her. "I promise I'll never pull something like this again, okay?"

"Get dressed." She smoothed her hair. "We have to get to the Merchandise Mart and make sure everything *else* is perfect before the doors open to the public."

~

Cat's stomach burned. Foot traffic in the neighboring showrooms exceeded that in theirs. Of course, those other rooms housed established furniture lines like Baker and Marge Carson. Companies with more history, products, details, and thick brochures!

Although she'd never been uncomfortable strutting on any stage, today she felt like a poser. She *was* a poser. Her and Hank's lack of experience showed. She'd rushed ahead and gotten them in over their heads, just as David and Jackson predicted.

The sales pitch she'd practiced and promoted no longer applied, which left her a little tongue-tied and left designers empty-handed when they wandered off to the next installation.

Of course, Hank's sexy mix of laid-back charm and passion excited a few designers who spoke with him at length. Still, she couldn't tell whether or not anything would come of the money or effort she'd put into this show.

"You might want to smile if you hope to draw people in," Hank teased.

She must've been scowling when the only visitors in their exhibition room exited.

"I'm upset."

"Why? So far the people I've spoken with seem genuinely interested in my work. I feel great!"

"I can only hope you're making a big enough impression that they will remember you after visiting one hundred other showrooms, because we've got nothing to hand them when they leave. Those brochures cost twenty-four hundred dollars . . ." She rubbed the creases between her eyebrows with her thumb. "How are you estimating pricing on customized furniture? Granted, your things look beautiful and attract interest, but who knows if any of it will convert to a single sale?"

She'd poured so much of herself and her hopes into this little company, she didn't know what she'd do if they went home empty-handed. Worse, she'd be on the receiving end of told-you-so looks from her family, her agent, and Hank's sisters.

"I'll repay you for the brochures." Hank looked chastened, which wasn't what she'd intended. Crap, not even "the model" could wear anxiety well.

"It's not the money, Hank. It's the lack of professionalism that makes me uncomfortable. I never went to a shoot or a show unprepared.

Everything was perfect—at least, everything within my control. Winging it is extremely awkward."

"I know you're upset, and I know this show is important." Hank rubbed her upper arms. "But this is a *first* show. I doubt anyone expects us to be as polished as companies that have been around for years. Let's keep that perspective and try to have a *little* fun. Other people will be turned off if we're uptight. It's a win if we really impress a handful of people this weekend, so don't worry if we don't excite a thousand. Everything will be okay."

"It's easier for you to say that when you're relatively anonymous." She shrugged out of his grasp. "I've got a brand to protect. My name and reputation on the line."

"We've *both* got a lot at stake, Cat." Thankfully his phone buzzed, because Cat didn't like his perturbed tone, or the reminder that his family's finances were on the line. "Jenny?"

Silence.

"Aw, dammit." Hank grimaced before pressing his hand against his forehead. "Take a breath and slow down."

Cat could hear Jenny's wail from two feet away.

"Dehydrated? How'd that happen?"

Cat bit her lip and stared at his pained expression. It sounded like something happened to his mother—something dire. She reached for him, but he shrugged away, intent on calming Jenny. "In an ambulance?" Hank winced at whatever Jenny said next. "Please stop crying, Jenny. It's not your fault. I'll get home as soon as possible. I'll meet you at the hospital."

He'll what?

He slipped his phone in his breast pocket and scrubbed his hands over his face. "Cat, I've got to go. I thought my mom's disease was just getting worse recently, but in fact we were seeing the side effects of serious dehydration. Dammit, how could I have missed it?" He raked his fingers through his hair.

"I'm so sorry, Hank." When she hugged him, his tension vibrated throughout her body. "Is Meg with her? Does *she* think you need to come home?"

"I didn't talk to Meg. She was in the ambulance with the EMTs. Jenny was following in Meg's car."

"Well, there you go. That's perfect. Meg's a nurse. She'll make sure your mom gets all the right care from the best doctors. Take a breath and try to calm yourself."

"Calm down? This is my fault! I've been so busy with you, I neglected my own mother. *I* missed the signs." Hank started searching for new flights on his phone.

Cat counted to ten in her head and tried to think of some way to relieve his guilt. In a quiet voice, she said, "Jenny and Helen were also with your mom every day these past weeks and neither of them realized what was happening, so don't shoulder all the blame. You aren't responsible for every single thing that happens to your family. You always do your best. It isn't a crime to take some time for yourself after all these years. Please don't feel guilty about that, Hank."

He barely glanced up. "I know you're trying to help, but I just need to get home."

"What you need is to slow down for a second. What can you actually do to help if you return? As difficult as it may seem, I think you should stay and finish the show. Let your sisters care for your mom for two days."

"Cat, my family needs me."

"Actually, Jenny and your mom need this venture to succeed, so you'd be serving their needs better by staying." When he didn't appear persuaded, she pleaded, "*I* need you, too. *Our* business needs you. You changed the business model at the last minute, so now *you're* the only one of us who can engage in a meaningful discussion about the furniture. I don't know about construction, wood grains, time frames, or any of that, so please don't walk out in the middle of the show. Besides, you drove all your stuff here. If you take it, there won't even be anything to exhibit."

Hank paced for a few seconds, apparently overwhelmed and looking for solutions.

"I'll catch a flight home this afternoon, see my mom tonight, and then fly back tomorrow afternoon to get everything." He strode off and turned the "Be Back Soon" sign over before closing the glass doors to their exhibit room. "Let's take a fifteen-minute break so I can fill you in on some basics in terms of timing to build these kinds of pieces, and ballpark price ranges. Then I've got to grab a cab to the airport."

She scurried behind him, her thoughts unable to keep up with his feet. "Fifteen minutes? You're the craftsman, Hank. Not me! *Please* don't bail on me after everything I've done to pull this together. Give your sisters the chance to prove they can handle your mom without you."

His eyes widened. "Did you miss the part where I said my mom was being taken to the hospital?"

"No, Hank, I did not. Did *you* forget that your sister is the nurse, not you? If you're being honest, rushing to Connecticut is more about your guilt than your mom's needs."

He scowled, apparently more dismayed than angry. "I want to be there for my mother. I give her peace, even if it's only because she confuses me with my father. When she's in crisis, I *will* be there. That's what I do for the people I love . . . for my family."

"I thought I mattered to you, too. That all of this mattered?" Cat threw her hands upward. "Is all of this nothing more than a whim?"

"It's not a whim, and you know it. The timing sucks, but you can't plan for emergencies. People will understand if you explain what happened. The designs speak for themselves. Don't make this worse than it is. Can't you see I'm torn enough without additional guilt from you?"

He really was planning to leave. He was running on pure emotion despite the fact that every single one of her points made sense. Her father would be appalled by Hank's illogical response. "Hank, even if you leave this minute, you won't arrive until late tonight, after your mom's already been admitted and is hydrated and resting, so in reality there's much less to be gained by leaving than by staying."

"There might be complications! If I stay, I won't be focused on selling. Do you honestly think I give a damn about convincing someone to buy my tables right now? It's the last thing on my mind."

"Such a blasé attitude. Then again, it's mostly my time, money, and name on the line at this point. Never mind that I also walked away from that jewelry deal for us." She saw a small group of people peering in through the door and her blood pressure spiked. "All this time I've thought your family used you as a crutch, but maybe the truth is that you use them as an excuse not to take chances."

Hank's eyes flashed with hurt and anger. "Is that what you think of me?"

"If you walk out on us now, you leave me little choice."

He turned his back on her, hands on his hips, head bowed. After a few seconds, he faced her again. "Well, if I use my family to avoid professional failure, then you use business to avoid personal relationships." He dropped his voice. "When I'm forced to prioritize, I'll pick personal relationships over business every time, Cat. That's the way it should be."

"Irrationally, it seems." She crossed her arms, hating the snappish tone of her voice, but unable to control herself. The disenchantment had finally arrived; she could see it in his eyes. She'd known this day would come, so why did she feel like a horse just kicked her in the chest?

Maybe the timing of this disaster—before she'd confessed her feelings and diagnosis—was fate's way of telling her to keep quiet. Was this the sign she'd wanted from her mother?

"That's all you're going to say?" He closed his eyes and exhaled slowly.

Even with the high ceilings and abundant windows inside the exhibit room, Cat couldn't breathe. The situation had spiraled out of control, unraveling all the progress she'd made these past two months. Yesterday, she'd been on the cusp of finding her footing with Hank and giving over to her feelings, but the fault line beneath her feet had shifted, registering a 7.0 on the Richter scale.

When he opened his eyes, she met his brilliant green gaze, but couldn't speak.

"I'm not going to stand here arguing with you when it's clear you just don't get it." He sighed. "Guess we don't fit as well as I'd thought, in which case there's really no need for me to stay. And no reason we should be partners of *any* kind."

"If that's your position, I can't stop you." Her voice sounded surprisingly calm considering how her heart had shriveled like a hard raisin. "For two months you've been begging me to trust you, to count on you. You'd convinced me to let down my guard, Hank—to let myself care about you, about us. But if your mom and sisters will always come first—even when you can't truly do anything to help, and even when it ends up hurting me—then maybe you shouldn't have made those promises."

"All this time *you've* been keeping me at a distance, yet now you want me to put you first?" He shook his head. "I'm flying home today and will be back tomorrow afternoon to pack up the truck. You might as well take off, too, because this," he gestured around the space, "is over."

Then he strode away, leaving her behind.

She watched him go, frozen in place except for her trembling lips. Her stomach clenched. Finally, she swallowed the hard lump in her throat and collected herself. Time to cordon off her exhibit and close up shop.

Hank could accuse her of a lot of things, but she hadn't quit on him. He'd walked away, not her. Now she'd need to find a way to spin this and call Elise, maybe get back that jewelry company's offer.

Everything would be fine. *Better* than fine.

In five or ten minutes, her throat would open again so she could breathe. Until then, she'd paste on her best camera-ready smile.

Mom,

I'm so mad and confused and embarrassed. Remember when I thought I might impress Dad by going out for high school lacrosse but then ended up with a concussion on the first day of tryouts? This is worse. Hank left me alone, in public, at our first (and now only) show.

Shame on me for believing I could be something—someone—I'm not. From now on, I'll stick to what I know.

Chapter Nineteen

Hank sipped his fourth cup of coffee, so he couldn't tell whether the shakes were due to the caffeine, his mom's health, or his fight with Cat. The flight home had given him time to think about the accusations they'd hurled. The fact she'd been dead wrong didn't make the loss hurt less.

But at least he'd be here for his mom, who surely hated being hooked up to all this equipment.

"She'll be in the hospital for a couple of days, and then I think we need to move her to a facility." Meg sipped her soda before continuing to fill Hank in on the details he'd missed while in transit. "Given her overall weakened condition, it's pretty clear that the situation has finally exceeded your and Jenny's ability to care for her and live your lives."

"Meg, not now. We've got a couple of days to make decisions." Hank noticed another round of tears falling from Jenny's eyes, so he wrapped an arm around her shoulders and kissed her head. "Don't cry. This isn't your fault."

It's mine. How had he been foolish enough to think he could juggle so many obligations and sneak away for four days without causing problems? He'd always feared something like this could happen, and the internal "I told you so" sucked.

"You look like shit, Hank," Meg said, tossing her empty tin can in the trash.

"Been a long day," he muttered.

"You know, you didn't need to run back here. There's nothing you can do, and Mom won't even realize that you're here." Meg took a seat. "I assume Cat's not pleased to be stuck there alone trying to sell you and your work. Will she end up shipping everything back, now? That'll be expensive."

Hank shook his head, recalling the dance of emotion Cat's face had exhibited—empathy, shock, rage, defeat. "I'm flying back tomorrow to pick up all the furniture."

"Were things going well before you left? Did you have a little fun, make a sale or two?"

Hank shrugged. "Doesn't matter. We're dissolving the partnership."

"What? Why?" Jenny chirped, on the verge of another round of tears.

Hank met Meg's gaze and swallowed his pride. "Because you were right. The timing isn't good. I can't do what needs to be done to launch a new business *and* take care of Mom."

"But I thought you signed contracts, put down deposits, started advertising?"

Hank winced, shoving aside the fact he'd put Cat in a horrible position by storming off. Dammit, he'd done the right thing. The fact she'd walked away from a boatload of money because she'd believed in him—in them, really—was neither here nor there. She could've stuck it out and made the best of talking to people. It was just one show, and if she hadn't made such a big deal about him leaving, they could've continued with their plans when she returned.

Of course, she'd been right about one thing: she'd depended on him, and he'd let her down.

Ironic that the only two people in his life he'd ever failed happened to be siblings.

"She must be really angry." Jenny bit her nail.

Hank just nodded, keeping his eyes on the ground. The day had begun with so much promise, yet ended in disaster.

"Will you just keep working for Jackson now?" Meg asked.

Hank shook his head. "He's already hired my replacement. I've only got another three weeks on the job."

"But you two are such good friends. Maybe he'll try to work something out."

Hank cast her a tired glance. "Right or wrong, I just basically broke up with his sister—cost her money, hurt her pride, and damaged her reputation. I doubt Jackson's going to look too kindly on that once he finds out. I made my bed, I'll lie in it."

"Have you spoken with Cat since you left Chicago?" Jenny asked.

"No. We both said some things, need some time to cool off. I suspect for now we'll limit our discussion to settling things with the business." He sat back and crossed his ankles, as if stretching his body could untangle the knots in his stomach.

"You probably won't believe me, but I'm sorry things turned out this way." Meg squeezed his hand. "Once I got over my surprise, it was nice to see you excited about the future."

"Nice dream while it lasted." He forced a grin so his sisters didn't have to worry about him when they needed to save their energy for their mom.

"At least consider keeping Mom in some kind of facility for a few weeks." Meg patted his thigh. "You need to focus on finding a new job, and maybe take a little well-deserved time for yourself."

Another irony. With his mom in the hospital, he'd actually have the time he would've needed to work with Cat if he hadn't destroyed that opportunity.

Meg rubbed his shoulder. "Or maybe you could go back to Cat and make this thing work."

Hank bent over, elbows on his knees, head bowed. There was no making things work. She'd claimed he'd convinced her to lower her guard, but it seemed like too little, too late.

He felt sorry for her and her siblings, for the way they struggled to be open and trusting. But no matter how much he wanted her, he couldn't pretend he could have a healthy relationship with a woman who wouldn't let him inside her heart.

Love shouldn't be so hard.

"I can't think about that now, Meg. I'm worn out. Let's get Mom through the next twenty-four hours before we start discussing her future care. But it makes no sense to put Mom in a home as long as I'm able-bodied. I can't afford a decent one, especially if I'm unemployed. Besides, I don't want to wake Mom or frighten her with an argument. This," he gestured around the room at the monitors, "is going to be scary enough."

His muscles and joints ached from exhaustion. "I need another coffee. Be right back."

Seeking a few minutes of privacy, he took his coffee to a small, outdoor courtyard. Three gulps later, he set the cup aside and dialed Cat. He had to coordinate getting his furniture back, although in truth, he knew more drove him to call her. His heart sank, although not in surprise, when her voice mail picked up.

"Cat, it's me. My mom's doing okay and apparently there aren't urgent complications with her kidneys or anything. I'm calling to talk about how and where I should get all my stuff. Call me, please."

After he finished his message, he downed the rest of his coffee and speculated about how Cat had spent her day. If he could go back, the only part of his reaction he'd change would be refraining from the personal attack. He'd no right to stomp on her feelings, to pick at that sore. Whatever wounds she guarded so carefully must be big, because Cat wasn't a weak woman. And as angry and disappointed as he was by her reaction to his situation, he didn't want to cause her pain.

He watched a swath of gray clouds pass over the moon. Was Cat looking at the sky, too? She might be nine hundred miles away as the crow flies, but her heart was infinitely further away.

Hank started when his phone vibrated in his pocket. Apparently Cat planned to restrict their communication to texts.

> I'm glad your mother is recovering. I dismantled the exhibit. Your pieces are in the U-Haul, which I've parked at the hotel. I'll leave the key for you at the front desk. I doubt there is anything you need to do in terms of dissolving the LLC, but I'll be in touch if I need a signature.

His fingers hovered over the phone keyboard, mind blank. A thousand thoughts crossed his mind, but he had neither the energy nor time to sort through them then and there. Eventually he typed, "Can we talk," but then didn't hit Send.

Another minute passed before he deleted the text. Talk about what? It seemed there was nothing left to say.

~

Cat's stiff muscles ached thanks to a hellish, sleepless night. Hiding red-rimmed eyes behind her favorite Versace sunglasses, she lumbered toward the lengthy security line, like a snail in thick mud, caring very little if she made her flight on time.

Caring very little about much at all.

He's gone.

Those words replayed on a continuous loop, wrapping around her heart and yanking it from her chest, leaving behind an empty cavern as heavy as a black hole.

She stood in line, staring blankly over the throng. Amid the families, couples, and businessmen, her gaze landed on an attractive, single, forty-something woman in the next line. Glossy blond hair in a neat bob, linen slacks paired with a flowing silk-blend top, and wedge sandals. Despite the perfectly pressed pants, manicured fingernails, and flawless makeup, her ringless left hand and empty gaze screamed of loneliness. Experience informed Cat's opinion, and sent an unwanted shudder down her spine.

A few feet ahead stood another middle-aged woman—mousy brown hair, no makeup, Gap sweatpants—with a young son in tow. Unlike the blond, the mother's eyes glowed with contentment as she spoke with her son. Smile lines around her eyes and mouth made her animated face more interesting. A sense of purpose practically vibrated around her.

Not long ago, if asked which middle-aged woman she'd prefer to be like a dozen years from now, Cat would've undoubtedly picked the first. Now her stomach turned over with the understanding she was doomed to become that very woman.

He doesn't love you. It wasn't real.

Robotically, she removed her shoes and belt and placed her phone in the plastic bin. When the TSA agent took a special interest in patting her down, she barely mustered a grunt of displeasure.

What did it matter? What did anything matter now?

Hank left her, and Mitchell/St. James was closing its virtual doors. Deep down she'd known this could—*would*—happen. Known she could never live up to his expectations. Known she'd end up worse off for having trusted him, for having fallen in love.

Granted, she hadn't expected to flame out so abruptly. Not with him or their business. Her reputation would take a hit. All the work she'd done, the steps she'd taken to get it right, had been wrong. And now she'd need to call that *Town & Country* writer and pull the piece that would've run in October's issue.

Did Hank even care? Had he any regrets?

He never responded to her text.

Perhaps that second slight served her right, considering that she'd refused to answer his call.

At this point, she didn't know which one of them had been more wrong or more spiteful. What she did know was that her entire soul got bruised in the battle.

On her way to the gate, she stopped at Starbucks and grabbed a coffee. With caffeine in hand, she took a seat at a tall table and bit the bullet.

"Elise?"

"Cat, I didn't expect to hear from you until after you returned from Italy later this month."

"I know." Cat closed her eyes and grimaced as she swallowed her pride. "I'm actually sitting in Chicago wondering whether we can revive the deal with the jeweler?"

"I thought you weren't interested."

"Well, I still don't love an absolute exclusivity clause. However, I'm wondering if suggesting a lesser lump-sum payment but a slightly greater royalty—for example, two-fifty up front and seven percent for two years—might reduce her initial risk enough to make her willing to be a little flexible with the exclusivity? I'd agree not to rep other jewelry and accessory lines, and I'd even restrict myself to only one other license deal during the term of her contract, but I'd like to retain a little control over my future."

"My concern is that you'd be setting your price too low, and that could hurt you with other endorsement offers."

"Can't we make the terms confidential?"

"I don't think this is the wisest course of action, Cat."

"I hear you, and I respect your opinion, but ultimately isn't it my call? I'd like you to feel her out, at least in a general, hypothetical way. If you don't want me to undersell myself, then just suggest the idea and let her come back with revised numbers."

"Fine." Elise paused. "Let's hope she hasn't been following your other venture, otherwise she'll know you're in a weakened position."

Cat absorbed the hit like a pro—it only hurt on the inside. Like most of the disappointments in her life.

"Thanks, Elise. I'll speak with you soon." Cat hung up, feeling marginally better.

Although her heart wasn't in this new project, pragmatism forced her to face reality. Her modeling days were winding down and she needed to explore other options now that Mitchell/St. James appeared dead in the water.

She winced at the memory of the harsh things she and Hank had said yesterday. Why hadn't he even tried to see her point of view? Even for a second? He'd come at it purely from a knee-jerk emotional perspective.

Her dad had always said that emotions were the worst foundation for decision-making. He'd definitely had a point when it came to work, but maybe she should question his philosophy when it came to personal choices.

Hank had devastated her when he'd walked out on all their plans . . . on her. Even if his excuse had merit—and an elderly, sick mom rushed to the hospital certainly had merit—his stubbornness had enraged her. Obviously, she thought as she tossed her empty cup in a nearby garbage can and continued her journey.

She felt for his difficult position, but she still disagreed with his decision. In either case, she'd handled the situation poorly.

Even now, as she trod toward her gate, the rush of mixed feelings made her legs wobble like a foal taking its first steps. Thankfully she reached her destination without falling on her face.

Not ten minutes later, she nearly passed out in the boarding queue when she saw Hank deplaning at a gate across the walkway.

He didn't notice her as he adjusted the small duffel bag slung over his shoulder. The deep lines in his face were visible from where she stood and, for one moment, a barrel of empathy washed through her. She twitched, restraining herself from calling out or running to him. Instead, she watched him walk down the hall, just as he'd walked out of her life.

Whatever anger and embarrassment she harbored because of yesterday's blowup, she loved him, and because of that, she knew letting go was the best thing she could do for him.

~

The next morning, Cat finished stowing Esther's groceries before joining her in the living room for a cup of Darjeeling. For whatever reason, drinking from Esther's fine china made the tea taste better.

"I already miss seeing your Hank in the hallways now that he's finished with your project." Esther stirred an extra lump of sugar in her tea. "Are you pleased with his work?"

"It's beautiful." Of course, now those magnificent armoires were just another reminder of Hank—a bitterly painful reminder she'd wake up to every day of her life as long as she stayed in that condo. "Not only did he do a beautiful job, but he also organized my entire wardrobe."

"How thoughtful. I could tell he was kind straightaway." Esther's expression grew pensive. "So, now what? Will you keep seeing him?"

"No," Cat said, setting down her cup. "Our business plans unraveled in Chicago. Actually, everything unraveled. It's over for good this time."

"That's only true if you don't care for him, dear."

"I really care for him, which is why this is the right decision."

"Why do you say that?" Esther's eyes sharpened. Had Cat not been so emotionally depleted, she probably wouldn't have gone on to share her diagnosis with Esther.

After the normal consolations, Esther sipped her tea, eyes awash with memories. "My sister never had children. She and her husband had a grand, adventuresome life together, and were perfectly content in their roles as aunt and uncle."

"Believe me, Esther, I know infertility isn't the worst thing that could happen to me. Although it seems difficult to imagine, I hope eventually I'll end up in some kind of committed relationship. Obviously I just need more time to process all the changes in my life before I can bring a man into the equation. Before I can ask or expect someone else to accept that fate, too."

"Are you sure you're not rationalizing away your fear?"

"No. Hank and I are very different people, and while opposites attract, they probably aren't meant to last." Cat shifted uncomfortably because she didn't want to regret losing Hank. Dammit, she should never have let him so close. Never should've imagined they'd ride off into the sunset like some couple in a romantic movie. If she would've simply abided by her normal habits—stayed unattached, stuck to what she knew—she wouldn't be looking for ways to mend her career or her heart.

Then again, she also wouldn't have experienced the feel of him. She wouldn't have learned that perhaps some men would accept the unglamorous version of Cat St. James. For that, at least, she owed him thanks. "Hank's life has been a string of loss and difficulty. Complicated and filled with sacrifices. He deserves an uncomplicated love and future."

Esther chuckled and set down her cup. "Oh, dear. Certainly you're old enough to know that uncomplicated love only exists in Disneyland."

"There are complications, and there are *complications.* Hank deserves what David and Vivi share . . . exuberant joy and a hopeful future."

"What about you?" Esther's grin fell as her expression turned contemplative. "Don't you deserve those things, too?"

Cat shrugged. "Maybe not. I haven't been very brave in my life—not like Vivi or Hank. I've made easy choices, many of them bad. So much has been handed to me—just because people favor those of us lucky enough to be born with good bone structure. So no, I haven't really earned that happy future. Not yet, anyway."

"Maybe it's time to be brave, then. Time to earn your happiness."

"Don't play Yoda, Esther." Cat leaned forward and clasped her hands together. "If you have something to say, just spit it out."

Esther's teacup clinked against the saucer. "Tell Hank how you feel. Tell him the truth and then let the chips fall. He might surprise you."

Cat lowered her eyes to study the intricate patterns of the Aubusson carpet while forming a response. "Maybe he'd be willing to give things another try, but I don't see how we'd end up in a better place in three, six, or nine months. I don't know if I could live with wondering if he regretted the sacrifice, either. At this point in my life, I should make the most of what's left of my career. I leave for Italy this week. I'm considering a licensing deal with a jewelry designer. I'm really busy, so I don't need a relationship."

"You sound very busy, dear." Esther lifted her nearly empty cup. "But be careful not to squander your time chasing too many things at once. That's the quickest way to end up with nothing."

Mom,

I'm staring at the orange-and-lilac-tinted clouds through the airplane window on my flight to Italy, wishing to see you sitting on one. I'm so sad these days, I'd give anything to hear your voice, see your face.

And I can't shake Esther's warning, no matter how many glasses of merlot I drink.

Chapter Twenty

Hank tore through a section of drywall in the Hudson's kitchen, sending dust particles spewing through the air, which caused him to sneeze. Jackson had taken Hank's replacement, Jim Walker, to another site this morning, thank God. He didn't need the reminder of his impending unemployment staring him in the face every hour of his day.

"Hey, old man," Doug called from across the room while hefting an old kitchen cabinet out of its space and setting it on the floor near his step stool. "Get a face mask or you're gonna hurt your lungs."

Hank grunted, ignoring Doug's advice. He couldn't care less about his lungs at the moment. Ever since Chicago, he hadn't cared much about anything one way or the other.

Thankfully Meg's job enabled her to check in on their mom several times each day, which alleviated a bit of his burden. He'd visited his mother each evening, bringing her good soup or her favorite pudding. But the grim reality of her future couldn't be ignored, no matter how hard he fought the truth.

Meg always accused him of being as stubborn as their dad, and maybe she was right. Look at how he'd been unwilling to accept the truth about his and Cat's situation until it bit him in the ass.

Still, he missed her. For a short while his life had burned with intensity. Her thoughtful gestures and sexy attitude had roused all his senses, making everything more vivid. He tormented himself by remembering little moments and details—her scent, her playful smile, the look on her face when she was beneath him—until he couldn't bear the pain. Then he'd physically unleash the anguish at work with a sledgehammer or a saw.

If Jackson were angry with him about the mess with Cat, he hadn't said anything. Most likely, Cat hadn't filled her brother in on the details of the spectacular argument. So Jackson might never know the full reason behind the end of Mitchell/St. James.

Just as well. Perhaps Hank could salvage that friendship once all the dust had settled and he'd found a new job.

Yesterday Jackson had mentioned something about Cat's trip to Italy. Hank glanced at the time and calculated six hours ahead. Had she finished working for the day? Was she alone? Did she miss him? If he called, would she answer? And when the hell would he stop feeling like shit?

Whack. He struck another blow to widen the doorway between the kitchen and family room areas. The shrill whirr of Doug's drill pierced his ears. He looked at Doug, who was now unscrewing the old upper cabinets from the walls.

For the first time, Hank felt old on the job. The toll of years of heavy manual labor made his joints ache. He hated the taste of drywall dust in his mouth and the tickle when it lined his nostrils. Another reason to be remorseful about the death of their ill-fated furniture business.

"I thought Jackson was coming here today with the new guy," Doug barked over the din.

"They'll be here." Hank swung the sledgehammer a third time.

"Yeah, right," Doug yelled. "'Cause he's so reliable."

Hank lowered the sledgehammer. "He gets the job done."

"I know he's your buddy, but you ought to take off those blinders." Doug stopped his drill. "I took this job because I'd heard good things about him, but he's off the rails. I'm ready to start looking elsewhere, especially now that you're outta here soon."

Doug's observations weren't completely inaccurate, but Hank despised two-faced behavior. Unfortunately for Doug, Hank was in no mood to be politic.

"Jackson's a good guy, Doug. If you're not happy here, then go somewhere else, but don't poison the crew with your opinions." Hank smashed the sledgehammer into the wall again. "Shut it or I'm going to have to warn Jackson about your bad attitude."

Doug's smug expression seemed downright evil. He fired up his drill again and yelled, "If Jackson shows up at all this morning, he'll be too hungover to pay much attention to you, anyway. He's gonna end up losing his business and then it'll be easy pickings for some other builder to come in and take over."

"I told you to shut—"

"What the fuck, Doug?" Jackson barked from the doorway connecting the kitchen and mudroom. Hank snapped his head toward Jackson, whose disheveled clothing and hair only proved Doug's point. Dark circles underscored his eyes, standing out against the ever-reddening flush of his face. "What did you just say about me?"

Hank lowered the hammer and held his breath. Two hotheads readying for a cockfight. Jim looked shell-shocked.

Shit.

"Jackson," Hank began. Jackson threw his hand out to silence him, then strode over to Doug's step stool. Anger rippled off his broad shoulders in waves.

"You're fired, asshole." He picked up Doug's screwdrivers off the counter and tossed them on the floor. "Pick up your shit and get the fuck out. Now!"

Doug jumped off the stool and jabbed his finger in Jackson's face. "You're the asshole!"

"I'm done talking to you." Jackson bared his gritted teeth. "Get the fuck out before I knock you into the next room."

"Hey, guys, calm down." Hank crossed the kitchen. "Separate corners."

Too little, too late. Both men were jacked up and ready to rumble. Doug spit into the sink.

"Fine. I'm outta here, Jack*ass*." Doug squatted to pick up his tools. He looked up defiantly. "Don't get too comfy with all your power. As soon as word spreads about your drinking, we'll see how many new projects you land."

A quick glance at Jim told Hank he might already be regretting taking this job. Jackson didn't help matters when he kicked Doug's toolbox out of his reach and yanked the man up to his feet.

Gripping him by his shirt, Jackson bellowed, "You're threatening me? Open your mouth and I'll slap you with a slander suit and anything else I can think of. I've got a six-year string of successful projects and happy clients. What the hell have you got?"

Doug shoved at Jackson. When Hank noticed Jackson form a fist, he grabbed Doug from behind to get him out of harm's way and spare Jackson a lawsuit. Doug twisted and elbowed Hank, sending him stumbling backward. He tripped over the old cabinets Doug had left scattered across the floor.

Hank threw his hands out to break his fall, but his left hand took the full brunt of his weight, sending shattering pain through his wrist.

"Holy hell!" He sat up, clutching his forearm above the throbbing wrist, which began swelling up like a balloon. "Dammit, I can't move it."

Jackson and Doug turned, stunned. Ray ran into the room, having heard the shouting and crash from the master bathroom where he'd been working, and nearly knocked Jim over. "Everything okay in here?"

"Oh, shit!" Jackson hustled to Hank's side. "That's fucked up. We've got to get you to the hospital."

"I told you sticking with him would lead to no good," Doug said to Hank, standing apart from them, arms crossed. "Now you won't be able to work anywhere with your lame hand."

"Wipe the shit-eating grin off your face." Jackson's menacing tone caused Doug and Ray to back up. "You have two minutes to gather your shit before I personally toss you off the property." Jackson stood. "Clock's ticking." He looked at Ray. "You got something to say?"

Ray shook his head. "You need help, Hank?"

"*I'll* get Hank the help he needs. You can keep working today . . . please. Jim, can you finish the kitchen demolition while I get Hank to the doctor?" Jackson looked at Doug, who'd gathered his things and then flipped the bird before storming out of the house. "Ray, if he comes back, call the cops to report trespassing."

Ray winced, but nodded. Hank hobbled to his feet and started walking toward the door.

Doug was right about one thing. The injury would sideline him for weeks or longer. How would he find work without the use of his hand?

Could things get any worse?

Jackson opened his car door for Hank before walking around to the driver's seat and starting the engine. "Can you believe Doug?"

"Not now, Jackson." Hank's entire arm throbbed. His wrist was beginning to bruise.

Jackson frowned apologetically and nodded.

"I'm sorry you got hurt." He stared out the front window—forehead creased, mouth set in a grim line. "You shouldn't have jumped in the middle."

"Yeah? Well maybe you shouldn't have flown off the handle and acted like a steroidal idiot, Jackson. You just set yourself up for legal hassles and other problems. Doug's not the only crew member talking about your behavior."

Jackson turned to Hank, wide-eyed. "What the hell?"

"I've been telling you for months to slow down and get it together. You push the crew too hard, you're not making good decisions at work, and between you and me, you *have* been drinking too much. That's the damn truth. And now you're down by another finish carpenter, yet you have four open jobs. Not ideal." Hank shook his head in disgust. "I knew something would happen, dammit. Just didn't think I'd be the one to suffer."

At least Jackson had the grace to look ashamed. "I don't want to fight with you, and I'm real sorry about how this will affect you in the short term. I'll help out. Don't worry about money."

"Fuck that. Your family thinks everything can be fixed by throwing money around. What if I can't fully use this wrist and hand in the future? How will I work? I could be seriously fucked, you know. Unlike you, I didn't go to college. I don't have a lot of options."

"That's not gonna happen." Jackson's brows pinched together. "Not gonna happen, Hank."

Mom,

I'm treading water. That's all I'm doing. Going nowhere, aiming nowhere. Just treading. No shore in sight. Almost as adrift as I was in the weeks before you died.

Do you think Hank misses me as much as I miss him?

Chapter Twenty-One

Cat tugged at her robe while the final touches of eye shadow and liner were being applied.

"Stop fidgeting," Angela, the makeup artist, ordered, her thick Italian accent softening her English.

Cat's butt hurt from sitting in the chair for the past ninety minutes while hair stylists and makeup artists poked and prodded her from every direction. She wanted to move. To scratch the itch on her nose. Mostly, she wanted to be alone. Thank God this was the final day of the shoot.

"You'd look sexier without that dark shadow in your eyes, Catalina," Angela said. "I know that look. Man trouble. What did he do? Cheat? Use you?"

He loved me and I pushed him away. "No man troubles," Cat muttered. Not entirely untrue. After all, Hank was no longer her man.

Cat had never before made such a gut-wrenching sacrifice for someone else's benefit. Since she'd last seen him in the airport, she'd felt cold. Cold to her bones, as if she'd been walking naked through midwinter sleet.

They say sacrificing for others feels good.

They are wrong.

All it had done for her was leave her empty yet filled with yearning, doubts, and selfish regret. Not to mention totally preoccupied by an overwhelming urge to run to Hank and beg.

"All done," Angela announced. *"Bellissima!"*

Cat stared at herself in the large mirror. Dramatic gray, green, and plum eye makeup extended well beyond her eyelids. The contours of her cheekbones and jawline were enhanced as well. She barely recognized herself. Just another mask people would see—dark and ugly to match her frame of mind.

She slid off the chair and proceeded to the wardrobe area to retrieve the outfit she'd be photographed wearing next. A young woman handed her high-heeled black sandals, a straight black velvet skirt, and a sheer black silk top with velvet leaf-shaped appliqués that barely covered her nipples.

The woman helped her into the clothing, and then directed Cat to the lavish set. The walls were swathed in deep red wallpaper. Smoky mirrored squares, sprinkled in rose petals, covered the floor. Gold brocade drapes hung on the false walls, and a glass table sat in the middle of the floor.

How fitting that, like much of her life, this was all make-believe.

"Oh, gorgeous, Catalina," Neil, the photographer, cooed. "Let's start with you lying on the table looking at the ceiling. Jean-Paul will kneel by your head and then we'll take it from there."

Neil snapped his fingers and a dozen other people positioned themselves behind lights and diffusion panels.

Cat stretched out on the table. The hairstylist quickly teased and fanned out her hair while Jean-Paul stood receiving his last-minute touch-ups.

"All set?" Neil asked.

Cat arched her back slightly and manufactured her best lusty stare as she looked into the eyes of the stunning, yet gay, Jean-Paul, whose face loomed over her own.

Not long ago this environment charged her. Beautiful clothes, beautiful people, a world of make-believe. For years this had been a heady experience. Now she simply felt numb. Each camera click stole another piece of her soul.

Just a few more hours.

~

That evening, Cat flopped onto her hotel bed and scanned the room service menu. Maybe something decadent—something chocolate—would lift her spirits. While she eyed the desserts, her phone rang. Her heart squeezed, as it had each time her phone had rung this week.

Please be Hank. She held her breath. Elise. *Shoot.*

She blew out her breath and answered. “Hello, Elise. Checking in?”

“Shoot wrapped up?”

“Yes.” Cat sat up against the pillows and picked at the hem of her shirt. “No surprises.”

“Good. Your professionalism is always appreciated.” Elise paused. “Have you finished reviewing my notes to the jewelry contract, because we should respond sooner than later?”

“I have.” Cat retrieved it from the nightstand.

She couldn’t confess how any enthusiasm she might’ve had for this job was diminished by the loss of her relationship with Hank. Nothing filled the void he left behind, not even a shiny new contract.

It wouldn’t look at her with love. It wouldn’t race to her side at the first sign of distress. It wouldn’t hold her all night.

“It looks okay.” Cat thumbed through the pages. “I know you don’t necessarily agree with me, but thanks for negotiating an exception to the exclusion. Let’s keep our eyes out for another opportunity that doesn’t conflict with this one.”

“That won’t be easy,” Elise replied. “It’s a very limited exclusion.”

“I know. But you know me . . . never say never.”

"So the furniture business is kaput?"

"Practically speaking, yes. Technically I haven't dissolved it yet." Cat frowned, realizing she'd been procrastinating. In fact, she hadn't done anything since boxing up the exhibit. Not a tweet, not a website modification. For all intents and purposes, Mitchell/St. James still existed. Had Hank noticed? Did he wonder why she hadn't taken down the site or made any announcements? "I haven't had time to deal with the legal issues of unwinding everything."

"Well, at least you didn't invest too much time or money in it. No lasting harm."

No lasting harm, unless you counted the damage to her heart.

Now her entire life felt offtrack, like she was speeding in the wrong direction. She didn't want to be alone, but she was too afraid to risk what little she had left and fail. Her head ached from the mental ping-pong.

"Let's talk when I return." Cat sighed, rubbing her temples, unsure what to hope for anymore. "I'm worn out tonight."

"Okay. When will you be home?"

"Tomorrow afternoon. Perhaps we can meet on Monday?"

"I'm free for lunch."

"I'll come to your office first."

"See you then."

Cat tossed the phone on the bed and rubbed her face. Her appetite had fled. Not even panna cotta sounded appealing.

She fingered the gorgeous silk-and-cashmere blue, orange, and white Fendi scarf she'd bought Vivi as a birthday gift. Like the wedding earlier this summer, she'd be dateless for Saturday's birthday dinner. Whatever happened next, she didn't want her family peppering her with unwelcome questions about the business or Hank, or to treat her with kid gloves because of her infertility.

After Chicago, she'd let everyone believe that Hank's mother's crisis had been the reason they'd pulled out of the expo. Vanity wouldn't let her admit her failure to her brothers so soon, especially given their pessimism. She doubted Hank would've made things more awkward by disclosing the truth to Jackson, so she should be safe from too much scrutiny this weekend.

She laid back and closed her eyes. *Hank.* She missed his voice, his blush, and that dimple on his left cheek. More importantly, she missed the way he'd made her believe in herself, and the way she'd relaxed around him.

She slunk down into the pillows, closed her eyes, and hugged herself. Her skinny Kermit-the-Frog arms weren't nearly as comforting as his arms. The only moments worse than those she spent missing him were the ones when she imagined him moving on with a new woman—flashing his dimple at her, holding her hand while walking around town, or making love to her.

Her stomach burned from jealousy, yet the images kept coming.

She grabbed her purse from the edge of the bed and popped open the bottle of Ambien. How many refills would she need before she could fall asleep on her own?

~

Cat turned on her phone as her plane taxied to the gate at JFK airport. A message! Sadly, just a voice mail from David.

"Cat, please call me as soon as you land. There's a change in plans for Vivi's birthday dinner. Need to give you a quick heads-up."

Cat hit the Callback button, curious about whatever surprise David had cooked up for Vivi. Her brother's recent romantic streak had been quite astonishing, really. Since taking up with Vivi, he'd been acting more like Jackson, who'd been a wild romantic until Alison left him.

"Hello, Cat," David answered. "You got my message?"

Cat smirked to herself at his no-nonsense communication style.

"Yes, sir. I'm still on the plane, but I called you immediately, as instructed." Her light teasing didn't elicit any response. "So what's the big change in plans?"

"First, I thought you'd like to know that the restraining order against Justin is in place for another year. I wish you'd reconsider pressing charges. He needs to receive a strong message."

Part of her would love to see Justin face some jail time, but she had neither the energy nor time to push for it or deal with more fallout from that day. She just wanted it behind her. *All* of it. "No. If I push, it will just incite him further. Let's not enrage him. As long as he can't come near me, I'm fine. He'll move on by next year."

"I hope so." She heard David sigh.

"So, what else? Your message mentioned something about a change in plans for Vivi's birthday."

"I need your word you won't say anything to anyone."

"Oooh, I'm all ears now." Cat grinned for the first time in days. "This sounds big."

"It's about Jackson."

"Jackson?" Her eyes widened.

"Yes." David paused. "I guess you haven't spoken with Hank?"

"No," she replied. "You know we had to shut down the exhibit. With his mom being so sick, everything's on hold. We may even disband."

"Sorry." He sounded sincere, but abruptly returned to the point of his call. "Jackson's in trouble and it's past time we stage an intervention. Vivi agreed to use her birthday dinner as the time and place. I'm not including Dad and Janet because I don't want Janet involved, nor do I think Dad's nonstop comparisons between Jackson and me would help matters. But, Cat, if you warn Jackson, he won't show up. I know you two are pals, but you must trust me on this."

Her thoughts scattered in multiple directions like the threads of a spider's web. She'd admit Jackson should ease up on his drinking, but an ambush didn't feel like the best way to help him. "I don't want to gang up on Jackson just because he doesn't play by your rules, David."

"Surely you don't deny noticing him drinking excessively this past year? Hank shared some business concerns with me earlier this summer, but I dismissed them until this week, when Jackson's former employee filed a lawsuit for assault, harassment, wrongful termination, and other claims. Hank was hurt in the fray, by the way. Considering the mounting evidence of how Jackson's choices are affecting his life, I think we've got to intervene *before* things get worse."

The lawsuit stunned her, but her first concern was Hank's well-being.

"What happened to Hank?" She pressed her hand against her chest, preparing for bad news.

"He broke his wrist when he tried to break up an argument between Jackson and the employee. He needed surgery and is facing a lengthy recovery." David waited for her response, but she couldn't think.

Hank had needed surgery, but he hadn't called her. He was moving on without her, just as she'd assumed. Reality weighed on her like a lead blanket. Hank's sisters must hate her even more for the physical and emotional pain she and Jackson had inflicted.

"Cat, I need you to share your concerns when the time comes to speak up." David's sober tone cut through her thoughts. "He won't listen if I'm the only one talking."

"Won't this make him feel more isolated? He'll just become more defensive and be more at risk."

"Then come and say nothing, but don't defend him or make excuses."

"You really think this is necessary?" She squeezed her eyes closed while pressing her fingers to her temple.

"Yes. This lawsuit proves he's out of control. Jackson was never violent. He never let personal problems affect his business. That's no longer true. Plus he looks like hell. He's drinking all the time. Let's catch him before he hits absolute bottom and hurts himself or anyone else."

"Okay." Cat bit her lip. "Have you thought about including Hank in this lynch mob?"

"Hank's fairly pissed right now. He cares about Jackson, but he's got more pressing matters to address, like his recovery and his mother's health. Besides, he's not family. This is a family issue."

"You're right." Cat rubbed her temples to stave off another headache. Nothing in her life was easy these days. Then again, life was rarely easy for anyone, so why should she expect anything different.

"See you tomorrow evening," David said.

"Yippee."

Cat waited by the carousel for her luggage, contemplating her conversation with David. She recalled the mess at Jackson's home, Hank's comments, and her own intuition about Jackson's declining behavior. A sense of dread closed around her when she imagined his reaction to being deceived.

And Hank was probably feeling desperate about his future, and his mother. She stared at her phone, debating whether to call him. But he'd never been one to embrace help, and surely she'd be the last person he'd take it from now.

She'd drawn a line in the sand, and he'd raced across it.

Message received!

Besides, if she saw him, she'd probably throw herself at him and beg him for another chance, which would embarrass them both. Clearly he'd been moving on without thinking of her. Scowling, she shoved her phone into her purse. She'd deal with Jackson first and then think of some way to help Hank from a distance.

Mom,

Watch over us tonight. I doubt Jackson will think we're helping him, so I expect things to get ugly.

I can't afford to lose another person in my life, but if I don't stand with David, we could lose Jackson forever.

Chapter Twenty-Two

Cat knocked on David and Vivi's door, hoping she'd arrived before Jackson. She looked at the gift box in her hand and wished tonight were only about celebrating Vivi's birthday.

"Welcome home." Vivi hugged her. "Thanks for the gift. Do you mind if I open it later? I'm feeling a bit queasy now."

"Me, too." Cat glanced at her watch. "What time is Jackson coming?"

"Any minute."

David handed Cat an iced tea.

"I could use something stronger," Cat muttered.

"Under the circumstances, I thought it best not to serve alcohol tonight." When Cat grimaced, David placed his hand on her shoulder. "I know you aren't comfortable with my plan, but we've got to convince him to make some changes."

"I agree." She patted David's hand. At least Cat didn't have to worry about deflecting questions regarding her, Hank, or their business tonight.

A heavy knock at the door startled them all. When David opened the door, Jackson strode into the apartment smiling—a gift in one hand and a beer in the other. *Oh, perfect.*

"Happy birthday, V." He tossed the package on the coffee table and pulled Vivi into one of his infamous full-body hugs. "I have to wonder what you could possibly wish for anymore, now that you're finally married to David?"

"Oh, that's easy." Vivi forced a grin. "Happiness and love for everyone in this room."

"That's your wish?" He kissed her cheek then gulped a swig of his beer. "Once a sweetheart, always a sweetheart."

When no one said anything, he cocked his head. "Uh, so what's for dinner? I don't smell anything. Are we ordering Chinese or going out?"

"We can decide later." David gestured toward the living room. "First, let's talk."

Cat sat in a chair, avoiding Jackson's gaze. Her fingers clutched the armrests. David and Vivi sat together, holding hands on the sofa. Jackson remained standing, crossing his arms and narrowing his eyes.

"I've trusted my gut my whole life, and it's barking right now. What exactly is the topic of discussion?" Jackson glanced at David then pinned Cat with a hard stare that made her stomach clench. "Sis?"

Thankfully, David jumped in. "We're all concerned about you and your drinking. You've put me off every time I've tried talking to you, but had I pushed harder, perhaps this lawsuit might've been avoided. Let's face facts, Jackson. You're in trouble and we want to help."

Jackson smirked and then defiantly drained the contents of the beer bottle. "I don't need your help. And if I'd known you were going to pull this, I'd have hired another firm to defend me against Doug's bullshit allegations."

"Hank doesn't think they're bullshit." David, still and unemotional, kept his gaze locked on Jackson.

"That's because he's a rule follower just like you. He doesn't color outside the lines." Jackson looked at Cat and waved an arm toward David. "Tell him, Cat. I love the guy, but he's a mother hen."

"I'm not here to talk about Hank," Cat replied, feeling insulted on Hank's behalf. Not long ago she might've joined Jackson in teasing David and Hank about their conservative natures, but now she missed it. "But he wouldn't lie about something this important. He's voiced his concerns about you to me. I can't pretend I'm not worried, too."

Jackson's eyes widened. "Are you kidding me?" He practically snorted before shaking his head. "You're gonna lecture me about *my* behavior? How often do you go out? Why isn't anyone counting your wineglasses, or watching the clock to see when you come home from the clubs? I've never said a word to you about any of that, by the way."

"I'm not being sued! I'm not living in a pigsty with empty bottles of scotch everywhere." Cat's heart ached from the sense of betrayal crossing Jackson's face, but she didn't retreat. "I wouldn't have believed it if I hadn't seen it with my own eyes."

"Fucking unbelievable. That'll teach me to be your shoulder to cry on. First you steal my employee, now you go behind my back and call me an alcoholic?"

Cat felt her cheeks flush. She closed her eyes to shut out Jackson's wrath and the memories of that night when he'd held her in comfort and tried to answer her impossible questions about men and love and babies.

"Don't attack Cat for caring about you," David interjected. "Just sit down and hear us out. We're all worried. We don't want your hard work to go up in smoke, or to see you end up alone or in jail."

"I'm hardly alone. And just because you've found marital bliss doesn't mean there's anything wrong with me playing the field. I'm only thirty. I've got plenty of time to settle down." Jackson refused to sit, choosing instead to cross to David's refrigerator, pull out a half-empty bottle of wine, and pour himself a glass.

"If you drink that, I'm taking your keys. You were drinking beer when you arrived, and who knows what you had before you got in your car." David's sharp tone sliced through the room. "Is a DUI next on your agenda? Maybe you're past caring for your own welfare, but have some consideration for innocent people on the road."

Jackson chugged the wine and slammed the glass on the counter. "You're not my keeper, David. I'm an adult and I can make my own choices. Right now, I think I choose to leave this party. Sorry, Vivi, but I didn't come here to be judged. Happy birthday."

David sprang off the sofa and blocked the door. "We haven't finished this discussion. If you want to prove you're a big man by drinking in front of us, go ahead. But you're not leaving."

"Move," Jackson warned.

David shook his head.

Cat noticed Vivi's watery eyes fill with concern, so she begged, "Please, Jackson. Just give us thirty minutes."

"For what?" he exploded. "Have I hurt anybody? No. Have I broken any laws? No. Have I lost any clients? No. Dammit, my only mistake was hiring that asshole in the first place. He provoked me. He shoved me. I didn't hit him. I just grabbed his shirt and told him to go. I'm not a drunk. I'm not passing out in bars or sleeping until noon. I'm a single guy running a business. You guys have no idea how tough it is to run a small business, especially in my line of work. Sometimes I relax with a few drinks. Big fucking deal!"

"Hank's hurt because of your behavior," Cat said, pissed off by his cavalier attitude toward an injury that jeopardized Hank's future.

Jackson stared at Cat but didn't argue the point. David's sigh drew both their attention.

"Not all alcoholics are fall-down drunks," he began, still standing guard at the door. "According to the screening questionnaires I've reviewed, a person is considered to have a serious drinking problem if they drink more than fourteen drinks per week or binge drink. Based on Hank's remarks and the lawsuit, you meet that criteria, and it's been affecting your work. Several members of your crew have noticed you hungover and agitated, which, by the way, will all come out during depositions unless you settle Doug's suit quickly. I suspect you've experienced a blackout or two in the past year. So maybe you're not completely addicted, but you seem to be heading in that direction. Am I wrong?"

Jackson hung his head. His jaw clenched and he rolled his shoulders twice as if seeking release of pent-up rage. When he looked up at David, the resentment in his eyes stole Cat's breath. "Don't pretend to care so much about me after the way you betrayed my trust."

"Betrayed you?" David's brows shot straight up. "When did I ever betray you?"

"When Mom died." Jackson's voice ripped from his throat. "You should've been here, mourning with us." Jackson gestured to Cat then back to himself. "But you had your big career to manage and your stupid fight with Dad, so you took off for Hong Kong and barely talked to any of us for eighteen months. You still don't trust me enough to share whatever's going on between you and Dad, but I don't even give a shit anymore.

"I always looked up to you, counted on you, even tried to compete with you. I thought we shared a special bond. But you left when I needed you most. You completely shut me out, so don't pretend to be on my side now."

Cat glanced at Vivi, who'd smothered a gasp with her hand. David's mouth had fallen open. His eyes reflected deep shock and remorse. Cat held her breath, wondering if David would finally tell them about that disagreement.

"Jackson, I've apologized for how I handled that time in our lives. My reasons had nothing to do with you or my career." David glanced at Vivi and shook his head in warning, which meant she knew the truth. Who knew Vivi had been keeping so many secrets this past year? David's voice dragged Cat's attention back to the present. "It may not seem like it, but I was acting in everyone's best interest. I made a promise to keep that issue between Dad and me, and I won't break the promise. I'm sorry I can't explain better, and I'm very sorry you felt abandoned. It never occurred to me that you or Cat needed me. You both had Dad, you had each other, and you had Alison at the time."

"Alison? Ha!" Darkness flashed through Jackson's eyes at the mention of his ex. "Another traitor."

"What did *she* do?" Cat asked, surprised by Jackson's venomous tone.

"She . . ." He closed his eyes, shuddering at a memory, and snarled, "She stole something irreplaceable. I don't want to hear her name again. Not ever."

"I never liked her." Vivi's gentle voice entered the fray.

Jackson snapped his head toward Vivi.

"She was selfish." Vivi rose from the sofa and slowly approached Jackson. "I never said anything because I thought you loved her. Tell me what she stole."

Cat held her breath, unsure of what would happen next. Jackson stood still, shaking his head as if at war with himself, unable to resist the onslaught of Vivi's odd combination of empathy and vulnerability.

A fresh wave of tears filled Vivi's eyes as she reached out to hold his arm. "Jackson, please. I love you like the brother I lost when I was six. You watched me struggle through all these years with my dad's drinking. Don't make me suffer through losing you to the bottle, too. Stop being defensive. Be objective. Hank's hurt, your business is at risk, and we're all concerned. Something has to change."

Undaunted by the typical St. James reserve, Vivi wrapped her arms around Jackson's motionless body. Her face pinched as if she were debating with herself, then she closed her eyes and softly stated, "I'm pregnant, Jackson. I want this baby to know and love you like I do. Don't make me afraid to let you be part of our child's life. Please. Let us help."

Cat stopped breathing. She glanced at David and mouthed, "Pregnant?" He nodded, looking torn about how the news came out, then redirected his attention back to Jackson and Vivi.

Stunned, Cat swallowed a bitter mix of joy and jealousy, which burned going down, like too-hot coffee.

Obviously the announcement hadn't been planned. Vivi acted on emotion and instinct, and from the change in Jackson's posture, she'd been effective. But still, she'd totally blindsided Cat, whom Vivi had to know would be especially sensitive to pregnancy news.

Later. Cat shook her head and refocused on the scene unfolding in the kitchen.

Tears welled in Jackson's eyes. He pulled back and looked at her stomach, his voice choked. "You're pregnant, V?"

She nodded and sniffled. Jackson glanced at David. "How long have you known?"

"Just found out two days ago." David remained leaning against the door, watching Vivi worm her way beneath Jackson's defenses.

Jackson's face crumpled. He glanced at Cat.

The full weight of his empathy settled on her shoulders. But something else flickered in his eyes, too. Something painful.

When he finally spoke, his words were barely audible. "I'd already be a dad if Alison hadn't aborted our child. But she didn't love me. She didn't want to marry me. And she didn't want to be a mother."

Cat and David gasped, but Vivi cried, "Oh, Jackson," then hugged him tight.

"How come you never told me, especially after everything I recently shared with you?" Cat demanded, misdirecting her anger toward Alison at her brother. "Obviously this happened well over a year ago."

Like her, Jackson had parenthood snatched away, although he still had the ability to start a family. Still, how awful for him to have had Alison terminate the pregnancy on her own, as if his feelings meant nothing. It struck her as unfair that one potential parent had all the say over something so irreversible.

"It's why we broke up." His hand raced through his hair. "The baby would've been born last December. He or she would be crawling by now, maybe getting ready to walk." He shook his head. "That whole first year after Mom died sucked. I missed her," Jackson glanced at David, "and you. When Alison first told me about the pregnancy, I was happy for the first time in fifteen months. It seemed like a sign that things would be okay. It wouldn't have replaced Mom, but I'd have had a wife and baby. Then Alison decided to terminate the pregnancy. She wouldn't even consider having the baby and letting me raise it on my own, even though I begged." As if talking to himself, he whispered, "I would've been a good dad."

Cat watched Vivi stroking Jackson's hair and envied her fearlessness—her knowing what to do and say—in the face of emotional upheaval. Vivi forced Jackson to meet her gaze.

"Yes, you would have. You *will*, some day. In the meantime, I need you to be an uncle." Vivi squeezed him again. "I knew something was wrong last summer. I even questioned you on the deck at Block Island, remember?" When Jackson prepared to defend himself, Vivi covered his mouth with her hand. "There's no shame in hurting when people let you down. And there's no shame in admitting to mistakes.

"Look at me! My mom's and brother's deaths drove my dad to drink, and look at how long I blamed myself for that accident and all the consequences. I kept my mistake bottled up and let it affect most of my life. I know all about needing to escape, Jackson. But you've got to find a healthier way. Please, before you get hurt, or hurt someone else . . . even some jerk like Doug what's-his-face."

Whether in true accord or merely from emotional exhaustion, Jackson nodded. He glanced at Vivi's flat stomach again.

"I'm gonna be an uncle to a pip-squeak with a big appetite." He flashed a crooked grin. "That was a helluva way to make the announcement, Vivi. I never figured you one for emotional blackmail."

"Hormones." She smiled, easing the tension still vibrating in the room.

Jackson rubbed the back of his neck before glancing at David. "I'm not an alcoholic. Maybe I've fallen into some bad habits, but I don't *need* to drink. It just helps me relax."

Before David responded, Vivi jumped in again. "You should talk to someone about all the betrayal you've been feeling, and maybe take on fewer projects to reduce stress." Vivi turned toward David. "And you two need to sit down and build a bridge over the gap that still exists."

"If I promise to think about counseling, can we end the inquisition tonight?" Jackson turned back to David. "I'm talked out."

"Give us your word you'll seriously consider it?" David asked. "And you'll stop drinking until you sort things out."

"Fine."

David pushed off the door and hugged Jackson. "I love you, brother."

"Congratulations on the baby." Jackson slapped David on the back.

Cat rose from her chair somewhat dazed, as if she'd just watched the saddest movie. But this was real, and it affected all the people she most loved—including Hank. In that instant, she craved a connection to them, to anything.

Against her natural instincts, she crossed the room to join the group hug. Having the arms of those closest to her wrapped around her relieved a bit of the loneliness she'd felt all week. And to think this group would soon include a baby.

Cat would be an aunt. One who would spoil the child and then hand it over to the parents to discipline. She peered at Vivi. "I hope it's a girl so I can teach her everything I know."

"That'll be fun to watch," Jackson teased. "But I'm pulling for a boy who'll be a charming lady-killer like his uncle."

"Well, I'm just praying for a healthy baby," Vivi said, rubbing her tummy. "By the way, I'm starving. Can we order dinner now?"

Cat excused herself while the others debated the takeout order. She shut herself in the bathroom, needing a private moment to digest the news.

Like a storm-swollen river, life kept moving at a quick pace regardless of her setbacks. Lately she could barely keep her head above the water. A fresh wave of pain for her own losses, for the babies she'd never bear, and for the love she'd left behind, deluged her.

Unlike Jackson, she couldn't blame someone else for her situation. This intervention may have been intended for Jackson, but seeing how his denial had screwed up his life made her realize how she'd been destroying her own.

Maybe Vivi and Esther were right. Maybe the time had come to tap into the courage to be honest. And maybe, by doing so, she'd finally prove to herself she was worthy of love.

She was wiping a stray tear from her eye when she heard a quiet rap at the door.

"Cat?" Vivi asked.

Cat opened the door to find Vivi looking chagrined. "I'm so sorry about the way I blurted out my news. David and I had planned to talk to you first, but I just reacted to Jackson's belligerence. It popped out before I even thought about how it would affect you. The last thing I wanted, though, was to hurt you."

Cat swallowed the lump in her throat. "I know, Vivi. I understand. It may not look like it right now, but I really am thrilled for you and David. Don't let my issues steal one second of your joy. And you did get Jackson to calm down and listen. Honestly, I'm still reeling from *his* bombshell, too."

"All three of you take after your dad—closing up like you can shut off your feelings. But feelings always find their way out. You all make it so much harder by retreating." Vivi exhaled before she hugged Cat. "I won't press tonight, or even tomorrow. But soon you and I need to talk about whatever has happened with Hank."

"Talking won't help," Cat rubbed her forehead before continuing, "But maybe Jackson can. Do you think he'd come home with me before he returns to Connecticut tonight?"

"Why? Are you worried that Justin's lurking around?"

"No. I just need him to do me a favor." Cat sighed. "Make a delivery, actually."

Vivi cocked her head and narrowed her eyes. "If you think you're leaving this bathroom without letting me in on your plan, think again."

Mom,

I guess you know all about David and Vivi, and Jackson. Without you to confide in, we've all been walking around hiding our secrets and pain.

I know you wouldn't want that for us, so I'm taking the risk of exposing myself to rejection. The only thing more terrifying than losing every scrap of pride I've ever had is the thought of losing my last chance with Hank.

I hope this choice I've made is brave enough to earn a happy ending.

Chapter Twenty-Three

Hank was sitting at his kitchen table toying with a cold cup of coffee when Jenny entered the room.

"Going for a run." She pulled her hair into a high ponytail. "Need anything before I take off?"

Hank shook his head and waved her off. Staring at the dormant video monitor lying in its cradle, he let the eerie silence settle in his bones. Nothing stirred in the house now that he'd been sidelined and his mother spent her days and nights in the nursing facility where she'd remain until he regained full use of his hand. *If* he regained full use of it.

Besides, his mom's condition deteriorated a little more each week. Odds were pretty good she might never return home, despite his best intentions.

The freedom he'd dreamed of for years—the choice to stay inside, go for a walk, or do anything else he wanted, whenever he wanted—held no relief. He'd been gutted to a hollow shell, fumbling around, unable to move forward.

No Cat, no work, no mother to care for. Nothing.

He absentmindedly tapped the splint against the table a few times. The damn contraption made him think of his mother again. What a pair they'd make if she were here with him, sitting and staring into space together.

Of course, at least he understood the circumstances of his life and situation. He couldn't say the same for his mom. Every morning he wondered whether she awakened in terror, in an unfamiliar bedroom, surrounded by unfamiliar faces and sounds. Imagining her tears and confusion crushed him.

He stood up, placed the coffee cup in the sink, and leaned against the counter.

Through the window, he saw Jackson's truck pulling into his driveway. *Hell.* He'd been avoiding talking to him for the past few days, and didn't feel much like dealing with him now. But Hank learned long ago how to accept the inevitable.

He opened the door before Jackson knocked.

"Hey," Jackson said. Hank noticed Jackson's clean-shaven face. For the first time in months, he looked like himself. "Can I come in?"

Hank gestured with his head then closed the door behind Jackson. "Grab a seat."

"Where's Jenny?" Jackson glanced around for signs of life.

"Out for a run." Hank collapsed into the recliner. "We'll be visiting our mom later today."

"Hank, I'm sorry. I know how much you wanted to keep her here." Jackson squeezed the thick manila envelope he'd been carrying. "What's the doctor say about your wrist?"

"Meg got me in to see a big shot at Yale who used some new kind of pins set inside the bone. It's supposed to shorten the recuperation period and improve my chances for a full recovery. I really hope it works. In any case, I'm not to use it much for the next eight-to-ten weeks. Hurts like a son of a bitch, though."

"It's my fault." Jackson plopped onto the sofa and leaned forward, resting his elbows on his knees after setting the envelope on the table. "I'm sorry for how I acted, and for the way I've been treating you and the crew the past several months."

"I appreciate the apology, but I've got bigger things on my mind right now, like filing for disability, and praying therapy gives me back my hand."

"Shit, Hank. My fuckup really screwed you over, and I want to make it right." Jackson scrubbed his hand over his forehead. "I know you've spoken with David."

Hank nodded and frowned.

"So you know Doug's suing me for assault?"

"Yes," Hank replied. "I'm not surprised, given the way Doug felt about you. Man, I wish you'd have kept a lid on your temper."

"I know. He provoked me, though. It's not like I hit him. I just grabbed his shirt. He shoved me . . ." Jackson stopped and waved his hand. "Sorry, I know I still should've walked away. Now I'll be paying for it by racking up attorney's fees."

"I think your bigger problem will be keeping the projects on schedule with another man down."

"Well, that's part of the reason I'm here." Jackson inhaled through his nose and nervously tugged on his earlobe.

Stunned, Hank held up his lame arm. "You don't expect me to work now, do you?"

"Not as a carpenter, no. But I have a proposition for you."

The last St. James proposition I accepted broke my heart, Hank thought warily. "This oughta be interesting."

"I guess you haven't spoken with Cat about Vivi's birthday party." Jackson grimaced. "My family basically turned dinner into an intervention."

"No kidding?" Hank rubbed his good hand across his left cheek. "Sorry I missed it. Did anyone get through to you?"

"Vivi and her crocodile tears," Jackson said. "She's pregnant, by the way."

"Really?" A stab of envy punctured the happiness he felt for her and David. "So you'll be an uncle soon."

"Yes, which is one reason why I need to get my shit together." Jackson stood and started pacing. "I'm *not* an alcoholic, but I'll admit to drinking to reduce stress and tune out. Guess I can't honestly say it hasn't affected my judgment at times, and my relationships. So, I'm going to make some changes."

Hank didn't think Jackson fully comprehended the extent of his problem, but at least he was taking a step in the right direction.

"I'm glad, Jackson. I'm sorry it took all this to get your attention, but better late than never." He leaned forward. "Still, what's that have to do with me?"

"Well, I could really use your help."

"How so?" Hank frowned.

"I want to get out of town for six or eight weeks. Go someplace where I can get some help, clear my head, and work through the things that pushed me off balance. You know our projects and the business basics, and the crew respects and trusts you, so I thought you could take my place while we both recover. I'll pay you my salary, give you a bonus to help offset the cost of your mom's new accommodations, and I'll get the bookkeeper to come in more often to help with the paperwork."

Jackson stopped himself and glanced at Hank. "You're the only person I trust, and it would make me feel better if you'd let me compensate you somewhat for what's happened. I'd still be available by phone when needed. Maybe we could set up weekly conference calls or something. And, when I come back, you can keep working for me unless you find something else you'd rather do."

Hank sat back in the chair, dumbfounded. When Jackson had arrived earlier, he'd never anticipated this conversation. Run the business for a couple of months? Could he do it? He wouldn't mind the pay upgrade or help with his mom, and this wouldn't be charity, either. "You need to hire at least one new carpenter before you go."

Jackson smiled. "I know. I'll take care of that, but you should meet with the prospective candidates, too. I mean, if you're willing to help me out. I know I don't deserve it, considering how I ignored your warnings."

"I'm glad you're stepping back. I can probably get you through the existing projects, but don't count on me to actively seek out new ones. I don't know enough about bidding work to feel comfortable with that responsibility."

"Deal." Jackson stuck out his hand.

Hank stood to shake Jackson's hand, but Jackson yanked him into a man hug and slapped his back. "Thanks, man. I'd hoped you'd say yes."

"You're welcome."

Jackson tilted his head. "So, I've got one more task to complete, then I'll get out of your hair."

Hank raised a brow and held his breath.

Jackson nodded toward the envelope on the table. "Whatever is in there is from my sister. She asked me to give it to you, and for you to return it 'when you're done,' whatever that means." Jackson lifted the envelope off the table and handed it to Hank. "I know it's none of my business, but she seemed damned sad the other night. She's not as tough as she likes to act. I don't know what happened with you two, but if you think it can be fixed, try."

When Hank remained mute, Jackson held up his hands again. "Okay. Don't answer. Just thought I'd give it a shot. I'll call you tomorrow and we'll work out how to transition things before I take off. My goal is to be out of here by October first, if possible."

"Where are you going?" Hank asked. "Rehab?"

"I'm not sure." Jackson stopped and looked at the sky. "I'm thinking Vermont. Maybe private counseling, hiking, fishing, and kayaking will give me time to settle my mind and recharge."

"Good luck with that," Hank said before Jackson turned, waved, and went to his truck.

Hank leaned his body against the closed door, mulling over Jackson's remarks about Cat. He'd spent the past two weeks in agony, in large part from regret about the way he'd handled their situation, the things he'd said to her in Chicago.

Sitting back on the sofa, he tore open the envelope, half expecting it to be the legal documents necessary to dissolve their short-lived company. Instead her diary landed on his lap with a thud.

Stunned, he turned it over, remembering the first time he'd seen it in her room at Block Island earlier this summer, when she'd been so drunk all her defenses had fled and she'd asked him to stay.

His heart thumped hard in his chest. The most guarded woman he knew had just handed him her most private thoughts. He stared at it, rubbing the soft leather with one hand. The trust she'd just thrust into his lap humbled him beyond words. So much so, he almost didn't want to invade her privacy by reading it. *Almost.*

Before he opened the journal, he decided not to read any entries that preceded the wedding weekend. Whatever had happened before that had no relevance to everything that had occurred since.

Resolved, he opened the book and flipped to the weekend of June 11 and began reading.

~

Hank approached Cat's apartment door with a dry mouth and nervous stomach. Too late he remembered it was Sunday. She'd be going to Esther's this afternoon. Maybe she was already there.

He should've called before coming, but he didn't want to risk her shying away.

He blew out a breath and straightened his shoulders before knocking. He licked his lips and stared at the door. Nothing. He raised his hand to knock again but she suddenly opened the door.

"Hank." Her eyes widened. "What are you doing here?"

"Can I come in?" Her beauty had always kicked his knees out from under him, but today all he saw were shadows of sorrow dimming her face. When he held up her diary, her lips parted with a slight gasp.

"Of course." She took it from him and stepped back, granting him entry. Her gaze rested on his splint. "I'm sorry about your injury. How's your wrist?"

"I won't know for a few months." He extended the splinted arm. "I'll start therapy soon, then we'll see."

"What about your mom?" Her brows pinched together in concern. "How will you manage?"

"She's in a facility for now. Not sure when or if she'll ever return home."

Cat moved toward him but then stopped and linked her fingers together in front of her body. "I'm so sorry. I know it's the last thing you wanted to have happen. Is there anything I can do to help?"

Come back.

"Not really. Turns out you were right. There really wasn't anything I could do for her after all."

Cat shook her head. "I was wrong to force you to choose. I panicked, and I let it get the better of me. For what it's worth, I'm sorry for the way I behaved." Her mouth twitched into a grim smile. "I suppose it doesn't surprise you. Seems I'm always having to apologize for my bad behavior."

"Actually, I owe you an apology, too. I did make you promises I didn't live up to, and I'm sorry I didn't stop to consider what you needed that day." He hesitated, unsure of how to proceed. He decided to take a page from her playbook and change the subject . . . ease into the conversation. "Jackson told me about the intervention."

"It was unpleasant, but necessary." Cat wrapped her arms around her waist. She gently twisted her torso side to side as if she were rocking an infant in her arms. That thought saddened him because, after reading her diary, he knew she believed she'd never be anyone's mother. "I hope it works."

"I think it did." Hank waited to catch her eye. "He says he's making some changes. Even asked me to step in for him while he takes off to figure stuff out."

"What?" Cat's eyes widened again, this time with alarm. "Taking off to where? How do we know he's not running off just to get away from us and do whatever he wants?"

"I believe him. Between what happened with Doug, and Vivi and David's big news, he sees the need to change. Don't worry."

"So you know about David and Vivi." Cat straightened her spine and smiled, but he could see pain behind her eyes.

"Yes. It's wonderful for them" His voice dipped. "But after reading about your diagnosis, I have to ask, how are you feeling? No one would blame you if it hurt a little."

Her eyes met and held his for a few seconds. He kept his gaze steady and reassuring so she'd know he didn't pity her. So she'd realize he wasn't going anywhere, either.

"I'll probably experience mixed emotions throughout her pregnancy, but I won't let it interfere with their happiness." Cat's rueful smile tugged at his heart. "Don't worry about me. I'm tougher than I look. By the time the baby arrives, I'll be fully ready to be a loving aunt."

Hank ached to comfort her. To figure out how to lessen her sorrow. But first he needed to convince her that he didn't care about her diagnosis and that he wouldn't regret that decision—ever. "Can I sit?"

"Sure." She sat in a chair, fidgeting with her hands and the hem of her shirt. "Would you like something to drink?"

"No, thanks." Hank shook his head and cleared his throat. He tugged at his shirt collar because, despite the air-conditioning, his body temperature spiked about ten degrees. "Listen, I'm going to say what I came here to say, and I want you to hear me out. Really *hear* me."

Cat nodded and sat on her hands.

"First of all, thank you for trusting me with your journal. After the way things ended, I don't think I deserved it. I've chewed myself out many times since leaving Chicago, but didn't know what to do or say. After getting that text from you, I decided to give you the out you seemed to want.

"Second, I want you to know I didn't read everything in your diary. I only read the pages since Vivi's wedding. Now I understand why you looked so fragile that weekend, why you drank so much, and a big part of the reason why you've been pushing me away. I wish you'd have felt safe telling me the truth sooner. Maybe then I could've convinced you that you aren't any less of a woman in my eyes just because you can't have kids. If you believe nothing else I have to say, know that you're the most amazing woman I've ever had the privilege of knowing.

"I know you think you did me a favor by walking away. And one day I might've found and loved some other woman, but she'd never be you. She wouldn't dream big dreams for herself and everyone else she cared about. She wouldn't try to have it all, or push me to my limits. She wouldn't challenge me when I was wrongheaded, or tease me just to push my buttons, or teach me that the only way to have a life worth living is to create it myself instead of waiting for it to happen." He cocked his eyebrow and grinned. "And she sure wouldn't be a woman with your sexy lingerie."

Cat's eyes misted, but she remained stock-still. Hank leaned forward.

"If you don't love me—if you can't see yourself being happy with me and my simpler life—then I'll accept that and walk away. But don't push me out because you're afraid I can't be happy with you. 'Cause the truth is, I'm not happy without you, Cat."

His eyes stung from his own damned tears. "I'm not pretending the fact we probably won't ever create children together is insignificant, but it also doesn't mean we can't create a family. Somehow, some way, we can. It's too early to make lifelong promises, but let's at least be willing to take a chance. To figure out if what's between us is something that can last. You won't be the only one risking your heart, Cat, 'cause I'm already there."

Hank crossed the room and kneeled beside Cat the instant he noticed her lips trembling. He raised her hand toward his mouth and kissed her wrist. "Please trust me when I tell you I know my own heart."

"I want to believe you." She wiped beneath her eye and sniffled. "You have to know how much I want to believe you."

"Believe it. Roll the dice with me," he said before he pulled her into a kiss that carried two weeks' worth of emotion and longing. *Home.*

"I missed you, Hank. I missed you so much." Her wet cheeks brushed against his neck as he held her tight, thankful to God for giving him another shot.

"I missed you, too."

An urgent rush of desire caused him to push her deeper into the chair and claim her mouth with the hungry kisses of a starving man. Cat's hands slipped beneath his shirt and scorched his skin. He locked eyes with hers, reveling in her heated gaze and swollen lips.

He glanced down at her shirt. His voice turned husky. "What skimpy underwear are you hiding under there? More red?" Using his good hand, he tugged her open collar aside to expose a white floral-embroidered underwire bra. The contrast between the innocent appeal of the fabric and the sinfully sexy woman aroused him beyond measure. "I love your fancy bras."

He dragged his mouth across her cleavage and over the sheer material, sucking it hard. Cat arched her back and moaned.

"I missed this," Hank uttered against her skin. Goose bumps broke out along his back wherever her hands brushed his skin. "I love the way you taste."

"I love the way you make me feel," she murmured into his ear.

Hank held her close. "I love you, Catalina. Don't shut me out again, okay?" His thumb was caressing her cheeks when he felt a tear. "What's wrong?" She shivered, so he tried to hold her tighter despite his splint. "Tell me."

"I hope you don't ever regret me."

"Don't be afraid, Cat." Hank smiled and kissed her collarbone. "I'll never, ever regret you."

Epilogue

Mom,

This is the first Christmas I've looked forward to since you died. I put your lighted angel on the top of my tree and made a wish, although it seems like most of my wishes have already come true. One will never happen (your meeting Hank), but I finally believe some day, some way, I will be a mother.

When that happens, I hope I can be half the mother—half the woman—that you were.

Cat pulled into Hank's driveway and parked behind his truck. She swung open the front door and called out, "Hello?"

No answer. She crossed to the master bedroom, which he'd moved into recently. Although his mother never returned home, Hank had left her room untouched until she died the week following Halloween. Two weeks later, Cat had helped Jenny clear out the room and then convinced Hank to repaint and decorate it for himself. She popped her head inside the door, but it was empty.

Swiveling around, she walked through the house and into the backyard. A faint melody emanated from his shop, and she saw lights on through the garage windows.

Once his wrist had healed well enough to be optimistic about a full recovery, they'd revisited their plans for Mitchell/St. James and taken a private commission to build David and Vivi a dining room table.

Cat loved watching him work, so she sauntered over to the garage to peek inside.

Hank sat on the floor, wiping down the legs of a gorgeous burled-wood writing desk. When the door creaked, he swung around.

"Hey, I didn't expect to see you this evening. I thought you had a final today," he said. "Shouldn't you be studying?"

"Early morning test, which I'm sure I aced. I'm free until January now." She crossed her arms to fend off the cold. "What are you working on?"

"This isn't for a customer." He grinned. "It was going to be a surprise for you, but now you've busted me."

"For me?" She stepped closer, confused.

Hank stepped aside and gestured toward the desk. "I figured you could use a desk now that you're pursuing a marketing degree."

"I love it!" Cat ran her hand along the top, then frowned. "Did I just ruin my Christmas gift?"

He reached for her and pulled her in for a kiss. "Not entirely. You'll have to be patient for the rest, though."

"Not my strong suit," she admitted. She glanced over his shoulder at the desk again and noticed two shallow drawers. Easing out of his arms, she started to open one, but he batted her hand. "Oooh, now I'm really curious."

"Don't!" he said, too late.

Unfortunately, she'd already managed to duck beneath his arm and open the drawer. Inside sat a ring box. "Oh!"

Hank rested his hands on his hips and shook his head. "*Now* you've ruined your Christmas, and all my plans."

Cat should have felt sorry and apologized and maybe even been a little sad, but all she could do was smile and bounce on her toes. At least her response made Hank grin—a good thing under the circumstances.

"Guess there's no reason to make you wait another five days, is there?"

Cat shook her head, which elicited a chuckle from him.

Hank withdrew the little velvet box from the drawer, his grip so tight with anxiety his knuckles were white. "I had an elaborate, romantic scavenger hunt planned, but maybe it's better that I do this here in the dusty garage where you first opened up to me about who you really are and what you need.

"We've certainly had our ups and downs since we first met, but even in our worst moments, you captivated me. I can barely remember my life before you blew into it like some crazy monsoon, turning everything inside out and upside down—in the very best way. I can't imagine life without you, and I don't want to have to try. So I hope you'll agree to continue down this road we're on. Together I know we'll build an amazing business, family, and life if you'll agree to marry me."

He'd barely finished his sentence when she jumped into his arms and kissed him.

"Don't you even want to see the ring?" He laughed.

"Of course I do!"

He opened the box and withdrew an emerald-cut diamond set in a band of pavé diamonds. Classic, elegant, perfect. As he slid it on her finger, he whispered, "Merry Christmas, Catalina. I love you."

"I love you, too, and I can't wait to be your wife."

Hank ran his hands along her thighs, grabbed her butt, and kissed her. "Jenny's not home. Wanna go inside?"

"You know it." She kissed his neck.

He lifted her up and spun her around in his arms, sending a flurry of sawdust into the air around them, which caused Cat to sneeze.

"Bless you." Hank set her down. He regarded her with reverence as he trailed his finger along her jaw. "Bless you, Catalina," he said before kissing her.

She wrapped her arms around his neck. *Bless us.*

ACKNOWLEDGMENTS

Many thanks to my family and friends for their continued love, encouragement, and support.

And none of this would be possible without my agent, Jill Marsal, as well as Chris Werner, Krista Stroever, and the entire Montlake family believing in me, and working so hard on this story.

A special thanks to Tom Throop of Black Creek Designs, who patiently answered my questions about his background and his handcrafted fine-furniture business (and for making me the *most* gorgeous desk). For the sake of fiction, I took liberties with the information he provided, but I so appreciate all of his time and input.

A very special thank-you to my friend Ramona, who opened up her heart to me about her past experience so that I could portray elements of Cat's reaction to her infertility in a realistic way.

As always, my Beta Babes (Christie, Siri, Katherine, Suzanne, Tami, and Shelley) provided invaluable input on various drafts of this manuscript.

And I can't leave out the wonderful members of my CTRWA chapter (especially my MTBs), who provide endless hours of support, feedback, and guidance. I love and thank them for it as well.

Finally, thank you, readers (especially those who wrote to me asking for Cat and Jackson's stories), for making my work worthwhile. With so many available options, I'm honored by your choice to spend your time with me.

ABOUT THE AUTHOR

Photo © 2013 Lorah Haskins

Jamie Beck is a former attorney with a passion for inventing stories about love and redemption. In addition to writing novels, she also enjoys dancing around the kitchen while cooking, and hitting the slopes in Vermont and Utah. Above all, she is a grateful wife and mother to a very patient, supportive family.

Newsletter: oi.vresp.com/?fid=e24107dc99

Facebook: facebook.com/JamieBeckBooks